Peculiar, MO

Also by Robert Williams

The Remembrance
The Storms of Eternity

Peculiar, MO

A novel by Robert Williams

iUniverse, Inc.
New York Lincoln Shanghai

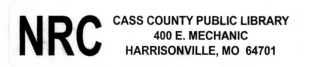

Peculiar, MO

iUniverse books may be ordered through booksellers or by contacting:

iUniverse
2021 Pine Lake Road, Suite 100
Lincoln, NE 68512
www.iuniverse.com
1-800-Authors (1-800-288-4677)

Because of the dynamic nature of the Internet, any Web addresses or links contained in this book may have changed since publication and may no longer be valid.

This is a work of fiction. All of the characters, names, incidents, organizations, and dialogue in this novel are either the products of the author's imagination or are used fictitiously.

ISBN: 978-0-595-45761-8 (pbk)
ISBN: 978-0-595-90064-0 (ebk)

Printed in the United States of America

For my mother

And for Josh

Perhaps my brain grew dizzy—but the world
I left so late was into chaos hurl'd—
Sprang from her station, on the winds apart.
And roll'd, a flame, the fiery Heaven athwart
Methought, my sweet one, then I ceased to soar
And fell—not swiftly as I rose before,
But with a downward, tremulous motion thro'
Light, brazen rays, this golden star unto!
Nor long the measure of my falling hours,
For nearest of all stars was thine to ours—
Dread star! that came, amid a night of mirth,
A red Daedalion on the timid Earth.

—Edgar Allan Poe
"Al Aaraaf"

Tout s'en va, tout passe, l'eau coule,
Et le couer oublie.

—Gustav Flaubert

The stars fell over the Midwest.

Random streaks of light burned across the face of the stars, a storm of tumbling fire, and across the country people turned out to watch them.

The meteors were not much seen in the cities. Only the very brightest were visible through the glare of the urban lights. But in the countryside where darkness was not so greatly feared, the people only had to step outside their front doors and look up to see the eternal mystery. Here, parents reclined in lawn chairs and teenagers sprawled on the hoods of their cars to catch the sight. Children lay on their backs in the grass, oblivious to the ticks crawling into their hair as the falling stars kindled their dreams.

Trails of smoke criss-crossed the night sky. Some of the meteors passed so brightly that they left behind ghostly afterimages in the retinas of the people watching. Some of them exploded into fragments, and then the fragments themselves exploded, leaving the watchers breathless with wonder.

The part of America with the rather intimidating name of Tornado Alley received the best show. By chance, the turning of the Earth had brought it directly into the path of the falling stars. The town of Peculiar, Missouri stands in this land of storms like a flower growing through a crack in a highway.

Ask the residents how the town was named and you're likely to hear an oft-repeated story. Back in 1868, when the town was incorporated, the citizens assembled to decide on a name. As was usually the case with group decisions, nobody could agree on anything except that they wanted a unique name, one that would set the town apart from all others. After turning down "Excelsior" (that was already a town over in Atchison county), the postmaster, a man by the name of Edgar Thomson, wrote to the Postmaster General in Washington, D.C. asking him to name the town, saying "We don't care much what name you give us so long as it is sort of peculiar." And the town has been Peculiar ever since.

The people of Peculiar watched the meteor shower with mixed feelings. Most of them felt wonder and excitement; some were indifferent, some even trembled in superstitious fear. And some Peculiar citizens watched the meteor shower, but didn't really see it, for their minds were on other things.

Take the Ross widow, for instance. Sometimes gossips would nudge each other when she passed, and say, "Its hard to believe that pretty young thing is already a widow. She's only twenty-four, but she has an eight-year-old son and we can both do math, can't we? Lost her husband during the ice storm last year. He was an electrician, had an accident involving some downed power lines. Poor girl is having a hard time making ends meet since she lost her man. Bunch of us

1

down at the Methodist church had a canned food drive for her, that helped a bit, but you can't pay the electric bill with pumpkin pie filling, can you?"

At the drive-in diner in the center of town, Delbert Cullim sat in in his beat-up Chevy pickup and cursed the service, oblivious to the falling stars. Folk will tell you to steer clear of him. "Nastiest old cuss you ever met, lives near the old Brown place. Just between you, me and the fencepost, he's always in trouble with the law, and a welfare cheat to boot."

Across the way, working late in old Fred Dillon's garage, was Spencer Dale. He was regarded as likable and polite, for a longhair. Always wore overalls to work, that was a good sign. Hiring that boy was the smartest thing Fred ever did. The minute Spencer started on with him, all the women in town started having car troubles. But Spencer had a hidden side as well. He didn't get out much, and his silence spawned rumors.

Over all of them the meteors passed, burning to vapor overhead. And then, at the peak of their frequency, it happened.

First, they heard the scream of its passage across the sky. Delbert Cullim stopped cursing his server and looked up, troubled, but he couldn't find the source of the sound. Spencer paused in his work as an orange glow moved across the dusty windowpanes of Fred's garage. Kelly, standing in her front yard, told her son to go inside as a fireball, trailing sparks, streaked by overhead.

With a flash of light, it disappeared into a patch of woods south of town. Everyone who saw it braced themselves for an impact, but nothing came. The ground did not shake, nor did a mushroom cloud rise. The people stared at each other, feeling strangely unfullfilled by this anticlimax. But the ones who drove out to the site got their reward. From between the shadows of the trees came the roar and flicker of a wildfire.

They called out the fire department, who succeeded in putting it out, but not before it burned down the old Brooks dairy farm. No one ever found the meteorite, and not for lack of searching. If that had been the end of it, the event would have been just another nine-day's wonder for the town, until they decided to put it aside to focus on more important things. But it was not the end of it.

In the weeks that followed, the firemen that extinguished the blaze grew ill and died, their bodies riddled with tumors.

Lights appeared in the night sky, hovering over the spot where the Brooks farm had stood.

A hiker told his friends he saw an army truck, painted like camouflage, skulking around near the border of the woods.

People claimed they heard inhuman voices crying out in the night, speaking strange languages.

The rumors grew, feeding on one another, as the summer air grew hot and tense, and the town braced itself for a season of storms.

1

The Wild Girl

"Come here, girl," Rachel whispered to the deer standing at the edge of the meadow. In her right hand she held an apple, like Eve tempting Adam. "It's all right. I won't hurt you. I can see you're hungry. Come on now. Come take a bite and let me look at you."

Although she had just turned nine, Rachel had already learned that when it came to handling wild animals, the most important thing was calm. Somehow they could sense excitement and fear. It had come to her when she had seen some deer grazing in a field with some cows. The two animals weren't afraid of each other, and she hadn't needed much time to figure out why. The deer had understood the cows weren't predators because the cows just walked around grazing, nice and easy. Anyone who has ever seen a cat stalking a mouse has seen its tail twitching in anticipation. A deer, with such sharp senses, could probably hear a predator's fast-beating heart and smell its nervous sweat. But they relaxed around cows, because cows were relaxed around them. They were calm.

This deer in front of her now, a young doe, seemed particularly skittish. No wonder, Rachel thought, considering how sick the poor thing looked. She could see the curves of its ribs and sores in the patches of skin where the fur had fallen out. But what worried Rachel the most was the awful-looking lump growing out the side of the doe's neck, a big pink tumor throbbing with veins.

Cancer, she thought. *That could be cancer.*

She had spotted the deer yesterday, stumbling through this same little meadow at the southeast edge of the old Brooks forest, and had seen no way she could help the poor thing. After all, they couldn't cure cancer in people, let alone deer. But she couldn't leave it to suffer. No, Rachel felt closer to animals than she did to people; she had to do something for it. Why was it starving? It was the middle of June. It had all kinds of grass and shoots and wild fruits to eat, not to mention what it could scavenge from all the small farms around here. Sickness must have made it thin. She could see bloody gashes along its legs and belly, where coyotes and wild dogs had tormented it.

Ordinarily she would have just nipped a few apples from her mother's fruit bowl, not that she would have noticed them missing, and left them on the ground for the deer to pick up while she watched from a distance. But Rachel wanted a closer look at that lump on the doe's neck. Maybe she could see something that would tell her if it was really cancer, or a deer's version of a goiter. (Rachel knew about goiters from her grandfather, who had shown her old photographs of dead relatives with lumps the size of soccer balls growing out of the sides of their necks, while she had stared in morbid fascination.)

She leaned a bit closer and the deer pranced backwards skittishly. It must have sensed her anticipation. Rachel, herself a very sensitive girl, felt that the deer would soon bolt. She could sense its unease in the twitch of its leg muscles. The doe tilted its head toward the bramble-entangled woods all around the little clearing, as if it was looking for a good escape route.

"Don't run, girl," she said in her very softest, most reassuring voice. "Look, it's okay. I'll try it." She bit into the apple. As her teeth broke through the skin and the juice, both sweet and tart at the same time, burst into her mouth, she remembered the deer's sense of smell, so sharp. Animals lived in a world of smells the way people lived in a world of sights. Pursing her lips, she blew over the ragged bite her teeth had made in the apple, all the while summoning her inner calm, making it spread out and fill the clearing like slow water. The doe's delicate pink nostrils twitched. It raised one foreleg as if considering a step forward.

Without really thinking, Rachel sensed she should lie down in the grass, on her back. Made sense. After all, her beagle dog Baxter showed submission that way, by turning up his belly as if to say, *See? Here's my soft underbelly. See how harmless I am?* She knelt, lowered herself onto her side, and then rolled onto her back. Fortunately the grass here was soft bluegrass, not prickly crabgrass or itchy wild wheat. She felt her breathing slow, like it did when she was about to fall asleep. Her awareness blossomed, drawing in her surroundings as it unfolded. She heard the wind in the leaves, sighing coolness through the heavy warm air. The sun made dewdrops of fire in the white flesh of the apple, so startling next to the dark blood color of its skin, and she could smell the sharp tang of its juice. Her fingers relaxed and the apple sat in the smooth cup of her palm as her heartbeat slowed, slowed. She was calm.

Now she saw only the apple resting in her white hand on the green grass, perfect as a picture in the bright sunshine. And then the doe's soft muzzle descended into her field of view, sniffing at the apple in her palm. Turning her head slightly,

Rachel was able to see the lump on its neck. Hairless, it bulged, bloated and obscene on such a beautiful creature. A thick red vein ran up one side of it and then split into two smaller veins, dividing the lump into three sections. Purple splotches mottled the bare skin. Although Rachel had never seen a real tumor before, she felt sure she was looking at one now.

The doe grasped the apple in its teeth and trotted over to the edge of the clearing to eat it. Rachel rose up and folded her legs beneath her, her hands buried in the summer grass. Thinking. She let her thick black hair fall about her face and her sharp eyes, the pupils so dark that they looked as black as her hair, scanned the edges of the clearing where the deer stood munching on the apple.

Why is this happening?

Rachel practically lived in these woods. She had in fact slept out here many nights, alone and without fear. She was never afraid, not at night, not during storms, not summer or winter. Why should she be? She knew every hill and hole, every pond and puddle, every stand of fruit trees and tangle of poison ivy. You didn't have to fear what you knew.

But now she was afraid. Something new and strange had entered the forest.

She had found five dead animals out here in the past week. Two rabbits, a skunk, a raccoon, and a coyote, all of them covered with tumors like the one on the deer's neck. What was making them all so sick?

Climbing to her feet, she left the clearing and walked in the direction of the old Brooks farm. The doe, with bits of apple still clinging to the sides of its mouth, watched her go, its head tilted in an expression of curiosity.

The farm was not far, and she found it with ease. Before it had burned down, she had spent many hours there exploring. It had been a neat old place, with rambling half-tumbled cinderblock walls, dark cobwebby cellars, and an abandoned farmhouse, roofless and partially demolished from a tornado that had hit the place a couple of years back. Her favorite was the old barn. Although the roof had started to sag and its glassless windows had seemed to stare at her like the empty sockets of a skull, she had felt no fear of the place. Quite the opposite, the shadowy cavernous building had fascinated her. She had spent many hours exploring it, peeking in the old stalls, listening to the flap and flutter of the birds in the rafters, and had even climbed into the hayloft once despite the creaking boards that had threatened to collapse under her weight. As she roamed through it, the place had not felt abandoned to her. It had felt like the old farm was, well, *waiting.* Just waiting calmly for new people to fix it up, stock it with cows, and get the old dairy up and running again.

As she came out of the woods and into the burned clearing where the farm had stood, she thought, *Well, its waiting days are over.* The fire had removed any possibility of restoration. Now only a few scattered and charred wooden posts remained, like an eerie black Stonehenge. Rachel paused before leaving the shadows of the trees, a feeling of unease running through her like a trickle of ice water in her veins. For the first time in these woods, she felt a little afraid. As she always did whenever she encountered something unexpected, she scanned her surroundings while keeping herself as still as a deer that has just caught the scent of a predator. Then she realized why she was afraid.

The forest had gone completely silent. No birds singing, no rustle of little animals in the underbrush. Even the wind seemed to have stopped. Why? What had changed here?

She looked into the clearing, keeping herself safely hidden under the mottled green and gold forest canopy. The burnt ground was still black. That shouldn't be. Almost a month had passed since the fire, with several rainy days. Ash made wonderful fertilizer. Rachel knew of many local farmers who burned their fields in the fall to make them rich for spring planting. Now, in the height of summer with a clear sunny sky above, a blanket of fresh shoots should have long ago turned this ground greener than the finest golf-course.

But wait, did she see a tiny bit of green over there, in the middle of the clearing?

She stepped closer, leaving the shelter of the trees. The sunlight seemed hotter over this black ground. Rachel started to sweat. She didn't mind though. Thought sweating felt pretty good actually.

She kept looking around, still uneasy and not sure why. Then she noticed another strange thing: the clearing had burned in a perfect circle. Someone high up in airplane might not notice the sharp edges because of the trees surrounding it, but down here Rachel could see it plain as day.

Her foot hit something. Rachel jumped, but managed to keep from shrieking. Looking down, she saw that she had almost stepped on a dead rabbit. About half a dozen tumors swelled out of the poor animal's fur. It smelled pretty ripe, and Rachel wondered why the crows and vultures weren't at it. The silence of the place came down on her again. Suddenly she felt a strong urge to run out of here as fast as she could. But now that she was closer to that spot of green in the center of the clearing, she thought she saw something strange about it.

One quick look, then she would leave. She loved these woods, thought of them as her first home and the cluttered, dirty shack with her perpetually drunk mother passed out on the couch in front of the TV as her second home, the place to which she had to return every couple of days so the neighbors wouldn't think she'd finally run away and call social services. If something dangerous had entered these woods, she had to figure out what it was.

She had learned about pollution in school. It was one of the few things that had interested her. What if something had polluted her beloved woods and was killing all the animals? If so, someone would have to come in and fix it. What if they had to put a fence around the forest and declare it off limits because it had become so polluted? She had to know for sure, before she brought anyone into her special place.

Summoning her courage, she walked up to the thing in the clearing's center.

It was a sprout, but not like one she had ever seen before. It was much too big. The stem looked as thick as her wrist, and curved to a purplish bulge just getting ready to emerge from the black ground. It had a poised and poisoned look about it, as if at any moment it would spring out of the ground and try to snatch her up.

She'd had her look. Time to go.

She turned and ran, but not in the direction she came from. She ran towards the other side of the burned circle, wanting to cut across a gully there and come out of the woods near the old schoolhouse.

When the ground collapsed beneath her feet with a sickening crunch, she was so surprised she couldn't even scream.

Rachel thought she knew these woods better than anyone, and perhaps she did, but only the part above ground. Long ago, the old dairy farm had used a well as its source of water. Shortly before the farm shut down, the owner's brother had capped the well with some stout oak boards, which he had then covered with a layer of soil. As the years passed and the area went back to nature, weeds and fallen leaves had covered the spot. Water seeped down, froze and thawed with the seasons, and the boards had slowly rotted. When the fire came, it burned over the top of them, further weakening the boards and covering the spot with ash and soot, so that even with the leaves and mulch that had covered them burned away, the boards still blended in with the blackened ground. As a result, Rachel was quite unaware of this well when she stepped on the spot she had passed over safely before the fire. Now she plunged into dark coldness, into a chilly and unfamiliar hidden world.

To her credit, she did not freeze in terror and let herself drop. Her reflexes, honed through hours of hiking and animal-watching, kicked in the instant she felt the ground give way. Without thinking, she pivoted and threw herself at the edge of the hole, grabbing at it as she fell. This didn't stop her fall, but it saved her life. The pivot checked her forward momentum, which would have sent her smashing against the stone walls of the well all the way to the bottom. There she would have either drowned or lain with broken bones jutting through her skin until she starved to death, with no one to hear her screams. Instead she fell straight down, her gasp of surprise echoing off the rough fieldstone walls.

She plunged into icy-cold water an instant before her feet hit the bottom, jarring her spine and making her teeth click together. Her back bumped against the wall hard enough to scrape it. Inhaling water, she choked and coughed as the pain in her back and legs set in. Then she let loose her belated scream of surprise and fear.

The scream faded to sobbing, then to whimpering as her panic ebbed.

Quit it, she told herself. *Quit acting like a scared little girl!* She'd just had a hard day, is all. The fall had surprised her at a tense moment, after seeing the sick deer and the ruined farm. But she had to prove herself right, so she forced down her whimpers and looked around to see what she could do.

The water came up to her chest, just enough to break her fall. It felt colder than anything she had ever experienced. Even through her clothes it felt like she had jumped into a snow drift. The tips of her toes had already gone numb, since the only thing she had on her feet was a pair of flip-flops. She was amazed they hadn't come off when she fell, but thankful for it just the same. She couldn't see the bottom of the well through the murky water, but it felt rough and uneven. Also, she felt some thin, sticklike objects down there, a whole pile of them. Of course, they couldn't actually be sticks because then they would float, but they were hard to stand on anyway.

She didn't have much light to see by, the disk of daylight seemed much too high above her, but she could just make out the fieldstone bricks lining the hole in which she stood. She had the unpleasant sensation of standing in the throat of some monstrous beast that had swallowed her. Patches of bristly roots had worked through the sides of the well. From one of these patches, Rachel caught the glimmer of fluid running down over the fieldstone wall and into the water. This fluid had an unpleasant metallic sheen to it. She couldn't tell for sure in the dim light, but she thought it looked like mercury.

She knew what mercury looked like because she had once broken a thermometer trying to take her own temperature. She had felt sick, but her mother had locked herself in her bedroom with a box of wine, and Rachel knew she might not emerge for days. So Rachel had taken the thermometer out of the medicine cabinet in the hallway bathroom, intending to see if she had a fever. She had shaken the thermometer as she had seen the school nurse do, and accidentally broken it against the side of the sink. Beads of mercury had fallen everywhere, which Rachel had swept up with the broken glass and thrown away.

The fluid running down the side of the well did not form beads, even though it had the liquid metal sheen of mercury. It ran in streaks, like oil. Was this stuff polluting the woods and making all the animals sick?

But this fluid was seeping out of the roots. Could a *plant* make pollution?

And then she remembered the sprout above her, creeping out of the dead and cremated ground, looking like no plant she had ever seen.

The water was cloudy and filled with bits of charred wood from the boards she had fallen through. The strange fluid dissolved as it ran beneath the dark surface, leaving only a few streaks of color that quickly faded. She also saw some bits of white stuff floating around and little bubbles of gas rising to the surface, releasing an awful smell like rotten eggs. Did people really drink this stuff once? For some reason though, she thought the water was cleaner in the past and had only turned bad recently, although she didn't know where she had gotten this idea.

The coldness of the water sank into her muscles like a winter thorn and she started to shiver. She folded her arms across her chest as the muscles in her abdomen clenched. So far she had kept a level head, kept *cool*, ha-ha, funny girl, but Rachel, fearless most of the time, had one great fear and that was tight spaces. She was used to roaming around outdoors in woods and fields, not deep, dark, scary holes in the ground where her brother had hidden …

Hidden …

What? *I don't have a brother!*

That was the truth; Rachel was an only child. She had many lonely days behind her to prove it. Cold and fear must have made her screwy. She had to get out of here. The walls seemed to squeeze together and again she had the sensation that an enormous beast had swallowed her. She started to have trouble breathing and fought to stay calm. Got to keep a clear head. Jeremiah would throw down a rope soon, he hadn't meant it. He was just angry that Father had not given him the running of the farm. Brothers fight all the time; he couldn't have done this on purpose. He would surely come to his senses soon, but oh her broken legs hurt so badly-

What am I thinking? My legs are fine!

Thoroughly terrified now, Rachel began to whimper. What was happening to her? Why did she suddenly think a brother she did not have had pushed her down this well? And why did she keep thinking she wasn't a little girl at all, but a young man named Daniel?

Jeremiah wants the farm, she thought. *He wants to sell it and run away to California with a woman.*

She had to climb out of here somehow; she would go into hysterics if she didn't. She turned to grasp at the fieldstone wall and her foot hit something below the water. Something round and smooth.

No, she thought. *No, it can't be.*

She did not want to do it, but she bent and picked up the object anyway, brought it out of the cloudy depths.

It was a skull. Water poured from its empty eye sockets and two teeth were missing from the cracked lower jaw. Rootlike shreds of blackened flesh clung to it still.

She felt like she was looking into a mirror.

She could not stop the scream. It came in a scalding rush from her throat and rose echoing out of the well, up the throat of the beast.

2

The Little Red Schoolhouse

"Be on your best behavior," Kelly Ross said to her son, Jason, as they walked down the gravel driveway towards the new neighbor's house. "Remember to smile and say 'Nice to meet you' when they answer the door. We want to give the new neighbors a warm welcome. It reflects well on us and on the town. You know why it's important to be a good neighbor?"

"'Cause we have to live together, and the Bible says 'Love thy neighbor,'" Jason replied. She had repeated this lesson to him many times, to make sure he remembered.

"That's right," Kelly said, and then she had to look away for a moment to compose her face. Whenever her son concentrated on something or became lost in thought, he looked so much like his father that it made sliver of icy pain lance through her heart. He had the same dark brown eyes, sad and thoughtful. You could see the Indian in him, with his light burnt-umber skin and black hair. He barely looked like his mother, as Kelly was as blond and blue-eyed as any of her German ancestors, although sometimes her friends said he had her delicate bone structure.

Hard to believe a year and four months had passed since the ice storm. During that time her son had grown with a child's frightening speed, and sometimes she wondered how much Jason remembered his father. But the subject was still too painful to discuss, so she let it go.

If I put it off much longer, she worried, *how long until he forgets him completely?*

No time to think about these things now. She took Jason's hand as they walked across the gravel road that separated Kelly's land from the neighbor's. A small wicker basket hung from her other hand. She had filled it with some jars of homemade jam, a few bundles of rosemary and wild mint from her garden, and some wildflowers, which she had artfully arranged around the edge of the basket. Nothing fancy, she couldn't afford too much, but she hoped it would make the new neighbors feel welcome.

"Mom?" Jason asked, and Kelly almost jumped. She felt nervous, had for the last month and couldn't understand why. Maybe the heat was making her irritable. Blustery June had settled over the Midwest, bringing its thunderstorms and tornadoes with it as the sole relief from the heat.

"What is it, sweetie?" Kelly replied.

"Why did they tear down the old farmhouse?" Jason asked.

"I don't know," Kelly said. A farmhouse almost a century old had once stood in the field across from Kelly's land, but when the new neighbors bought it they had torn it down and had a new house built on the site. Kelly didn't understand why they couldn't have renovated the old farmhouse. She knew the foundation was still solid because she had gone over to look at the house before the land sold. At the time she had thought of selling her own property, too many memories, but then she had reconsidered for exactly the same reason.

The new house looked clean and neat, but it lacked the character and history of the old house. Kelly would miss it now that it was gone.

Kelly and Jason skirted the big SUV in the driveway, a Ford Explorer with out-of-state tags, and mounted the plain concrete porch of the new house. She noticed the lack of flowers or any other adornments as she rang the doorbell. From inside, they could hear the electronic beeps and booms of a video game, a pretty violent one from the sound of it. And then the door swung open and a woman with short mousy-brown hair and a pinched face glared out at them.

"What? What is it?"

Kelly felt immediately put off, but tried to make her own manner more friendly, thinking that would put the woman at ease.

"Hi, I'm Kelly Ross, your new neighbor." She paused to give the woman a chance to introduce herself. When she didn't, Kelly went on with what she wanted to say, although she could already tell this wasn't someone much interested in meeting the neighbors.

"I just thought I'd bring you a basket to welcome you to the neighborhood. I know it's sometimes hard to make friends in a new place."

She held out the basket and for a moment she thought the woman wouldn't take it. She had this ready-to-fight look in her eyes. But then she did take it, and removed one of the jars of jam, eying Kelly with raw suspicion and, she was certain, contempt. She had never seen someone who could communicate so much with their eyes, and everything Kelly saw in them was negative. Kelly suddenly became self-conscious of the faded cutoff jeans she was wearing, and the old, but clean and well-mended shirt. She still held Jason's hand, but now she remembered the scrapes on his knees, the mosquito bites on his arms, and the dust on his shoes from the gravel road.

Her new neighbor looked immaculate in her beige slacks and elegant blouse, gold rings glittering on her fingers. Standing next to her Kelly felt, well, like white trash.

Just then a young boy's shrill voice came from inside the house and broke the silence of this tense moment. *"Mom! Where's my lunch? I want my Spaghetti-O's now!"*

The woman turned her head to call back, but did not take her eyes off Kelly. "I'll have your lunch and medication in just a minute, sweetness. Mummy's dealing with one of the locals."

"No! I want to eat now! Now, now, now!" Kelly heard the unmistakable pounding sound of a child throwing a tantrum. A big child, judging by the noise.

"Look," the woman said to Kelly, "I don't have time for your spiel. Whatever you're selling, take it somewhere else."

"I'm not selling-" Kelly began, but the woman cut her off.

"Wait a minute. I've seen you. You're that woman who sits out by the highway selling her old vegetables, aren't you? What, are you going door-to-door now?"

"I told you I'm not selling anything!" Kelly said. "I was trying to be nice."

"Shut it down."

Kelly, still stunned by this woman's attitude, thought for a moment that she had misunderstood her. "What?"

"I said shut it down. If you want to sell your produce, go to the Farmer's Market like everyone else. Quit looking for your free handout. You're violating zoning laws."

"My produce stand is an important supplement to my income," Kelly said, getting her bearings. "If you don't like it, then don't buy anything."

"Mom, I want my lunch now! Hurry up idiot!"

"I'm coming, sweetie," the woman replied, and then she turned back to Kelly. "My husband is a very powerful man, and he always gives me what I want. If this redneck dump doesn't have zoning laws already then I promise you it will."

"It doesn't hurt you at all if I have a produce stand," Kelly said. Now she moved to take back the gift basket, but the woman yanked it out of her reach and chucked it into a trash can just inside the door.

"I have to look at it! And I'm not putting up with it any more! I shouldn't have to suffer this way!"

"Suffer?" Kelly said. She couldn't believe this; she had come over here trying to make friends. "If I lose that stand then I'll be the one-"

The woman cut her off again. "No. Get rid of it. Now. Or I'll get rid of it." She slammed the door in Kelly's face.

For a moment Kelly stood staring at the brass knocker on the front of the door, still unable to believe what had just transpired. Then her son's voice brought her out of her shock.

"Mom, are we going to lose the stand?" He looked up at her, looking worried. Now she wished she had left him at home.

"No, honey," she said. "That stand isn't going anywhere, no matter what that witch says." She had not wanted to say "witch."

They turned and headed home. As they did, Kelly noticed the personalized license plate on the SUV. It said "Coldiron1."

Well, Kelly thought. *I'll be steering clear of Mrs. Coldiron from now on.*

They walked back to their own property. The ground sloped upwards into a hill, at the top of which stood Kelly's house ... although it wasn't really a house. At first glance, it looked almost like a church, but it wasn't a church either. Kelly and her son lived in an old one-room schoolhouse, painted red, with a pointed roof and a steeple with a bell. It resembled images of turn-of-the-century Americana almost to the point of corniness. Jack Ross, her late husband, had renovated the interior and put up walls inside of it to create bedrooms for Kelly and Jason, but the rest was an open kitchen-living area, with a working wood-burning stove and furniture which, if she ever saved enough money to restore it, could be called antique.

But she could not save any money. Since Jack's death, expenses had piled up: funeral, medical, school supplies for Jason, not to mention all the repairs that the old schoolhouse needed. The paint had started to peel off in long curling strips, and the wooden porch out front had developed a noticeable sag in the middle of it. The thought of property taxes at the end of the year hovered like a dark cloud over her thoughts. What if she didn't have enough money to pay them?

Kelly had inherited the schoolhouse following the death of her mother, who had inherited it from Kelly's grandmother, the schoolmistress of the place about a hundred years back. She didn't think she could bear the shame if she lost it, but that could very well happen. During the day she worked as a cashier up at the Dollar General in town, making minimum wage, but the manager (Jeff Beatty, a sweet but bashful nineteen-year-old who Kelly suspected might have a crush on her) at least let her off work at four-thirty. Then she could drive her shuddery old Ford pickup out to a spot she knew just off a dirt road where it intersected with the exit off highway 71. There she unloaded a card table from the back of the pickup and set out on it some wicker baskets (five for a buck at the Dollar General) full of tomatoes, ears of corn, bell peppers or green beans, which she sold for five dollars a basket. Usually she got everything set up in time for the five o'clock rush hour, and on a good day, weather permitting, she could pull in forty-five or fifty bucks. She knew she could never stay off state assistance without that extra income.

Could that horrible Coldiron woman really shut down her produce stand? Surely not.

Right?

As Kelly and Jason approached, another little boy ran up to them from behind the schoolhouse. Kelly and Jason both knew him well.

"Mom, it's Brad!" Jason exclaimed. "Can we play?" He spoke with much more enthusiasm than he had shown when Kelly told him they were going to meet the new neighbors, and she ruminated for a moment on the wisdom of children.

"Yes, you can play," Kelly said, knowing Brad wanted the same thing even though the kid wasn't even within speaking distance yet. "But first I want you two to go pick me some mulberries so I can make cobbler tonight. Sound good?"

Brad ran up to them panting. "Hi Mrs.... uh, Miss ... uh, *Ms.* Ross."

Kelly smiled at him. "Hello, Brad." Even though Brad's mother was a widow like herself, he still didn't know what to call her. But then, she realized, he only had to call his mother "Mom." He didn't have to know if it was proper to call a widow by the married title "Mrs." "Ms." was actually a good alternative. Maybe those feminists were onto something.

Jason and Brad had known each other all their short lives, and were as close as brothers. Kelly liked Brad, and thought her son was lucky to have him as a best friend.

After doing the courtesy of addressing Kelly first, Brad turned to Jason and launched into a dialect of English that Kelly thought of as American Second Grader, which was like everyday English on fast forward at twice the normal volume.

To her it sounded like, "JasonMom'sgotmusicstudentsoverandsaidwecouldplayandIfoundacoolsticklookslikeapistolbutIplayedtoohardwithitanditbrokeandyouwannagototheolddairyfarmIbetthere'sghostsand-"

Wait a minute, she thought she understood that last part. "Hold it! Slow down. Did you just say something about going to the Brooks farm?"

The wide-eyed look that spread over their faces as they realized Brad had said too much gave Kelly all the reply she needed.

"You are not allowed within a hundred yards of that old ruin," Kelly said in her best no-backtalk voice. "And Brad, I know your mother would agree with me. There is God knows how much broken glass and nails in the ground around that place. That old barn was about to collapse before the fire, now what's left could go at any minute and I don't want you kids lolly-gagging around underneath it when it does."

Jason gave the reply every child makes when a mother forbids them to do something enticing: "But *Mom!*"

"No buts," Kelly replied. "And you have berries to pick anyway. You stay near the grove of mulberry trees and don't go anywhere near that old farm." As soon as the words left her mouth, she knew she had just made the attraction of the place utterly irresistible. She said, "I mean it!" Knowing that only made things worse.

Then she got an idea. If she gave them a big pot and ordered them to fill it, they would have to work until sundown and wouldn't have time to explore the burned-out ruins.

"Hold on," she said, "let me get you a pot for the berries, and I expect it filled and the two of you back before it gets dark."

She mounted the steps to the schoolhouse and went inside, feeling pretty good about herself, the displeasure of meeting Mrs. Coldiron forgotten. But when the door shut behind her, she heard the boys talking outside. Fearing they were planning to run off to the dairy farm while she was inside (and telling herself this was all she wanted to know, a closet eavesdropper from way back was Kelly Ross), she sidled towards the window on the left side of the door to take a peek and a listen. What she saw made her heart melt and run down her face in the form of tears.

The boys were hugging, like old army buddies reunited after years apart.

"I wish you could live over here with us," Jason said. "Then it would be like we really *were* brothers!"

The strength drained from her legs and she sank to floor, unable to keep from crying this time. Her crushing responsibilities now seemed so much bigger, and she had never felt so overwhelmed and afraid. For an instant she felt a deep and ferocious anger at Jack for dying and leaving her in this mess. Jason would never have a real brother now. It seemed a foregone conclusion that she would lose the schoolhouse and her land. She felt so tired, so utterly and completely spent.

But she couldn't sit here and cry. If she did, Jason might come in after her, wondering why it was taking her so long just to grab a pot for the mulberries. She couldn't let him see her like this, couldn't stand to think how it might terrify him.

So she forced herself to her feet and grabbed a pot from one of the cabinets in the kitchen-area, pausing to splash some cold water on her face to hide the tears. It didn't work very well. It just reminded her that she still had to pay the water bill.

She went outside and handed the pot to Jason. "Now fill this up. Brad, if you want to help, I'll make jam out of part of it and you can take it to your mother. Okay?"

"Okay!" Brad chirped. His mother was one of Kelly's closest friends and a lovely woman, but she couldn't make jam to save her soul.

"And stay on the path at all times," Kelly added. "There's a bunch of old wells in those woods. With the weeds growing around them, you could fall right in and drown. So be careful."

"Mom, why are your eyes red?" Jason asked.

A silent moment.

"I had a sneezing fit inside," Kelly said. "Need to dust. Now go on or you won't be able to fill that pot up before sundown."

They ran off, but Jason looked back once, his dark eyes troubled and lancing at her heart like an icicle, before he disappeared beneath the crest of the hill.

3

Mrs. Brown's Cats

As Jason and Brad ran off to do their errand, Delbert Cullim stepped out of the front door of his trailer and brought his bare foot down on a fresh cat turd lying hidden the dust outside his front door.

"Cats!" Delbert bellowed at the sky. "Goddamn cats!"

Delbert hated cats. He hated the nasty, slinking little monsters that skulked around under his trailer and used his front yard as their litter box. He hated all the dead birds and mice and squirrels and rabbits and God knew what else the damned things left on his doorstep. Oh, how he hated those little bastards with all his heart and soul!

Delbert's blue-checked bathrobe whirled around him as turned to his left and stomped to the one grassy spot remaining in the front yard. Unlike the town-folk who all lived in their mass-produced sub-divisions, Delbert didn't care jack squat about his yard. To him, a front yard was just a place to put the garbage that he didn't have room for in the trailer anymore. He stomped past piles of beer cans and rusting car parts, deftly maneuvering around broken bottles so he wouldn't cut his bare feet. Unlike the cat turds, he knew where the broken bottles were. He passed dismantled bicycles and engine blocks, all of them gruesomely rusted like some kind of alien roadkill.

He finally reached the small circle of crabgrass that huddled against the wire fence like it was trying to escape, and smeared his toes into it to wipe off the cat crap, swearing while did it. It was that crazy old woman's fault, her and all her damn cats. Delbert lived at the very end of a secluded dirt road, and this cat-crazy old broad used to own the land next to his. He had explained it to his drinking buddy Clint down at the Occasion bar, where they met every other week to get hammered after Delbert got his check from the county. (He drew disability on account as he was too depressed to work, God Bless America.)

"I never caught her first name, but she had 'Brown' written across the side of her mailbox," Delbert had said to Clint in his best feel-sorry-for-me tone. "The old broad had started out feeding some strays after her husband ran off and left her. Well, the strays kept showing up and the crazy old broad kept feeding them. She let all of them into her house. They were shedding in there, hacking up hairballs and using the whole place as their litter box. I mean, this old lady's house was a health hazard!"

Delbert's trailer was not much better, even though he did not own a single cat, only his faithful Rottweiler Buford, but of course he did not see it that way.

"Well, where'd she get the money to take care of 'em all?" Clint asked. "She rich or something?"

"Hell if I know," Delbert responded. "But this is what I *think* ..." At this point Delbert would lean in slyly towards Clint and raise his eyebrows into his I-gots-the-inside-track expression. "I think she was eating cat food right along with the little bastards! I mean, I never saw anything in her garbage other than empty cans of cat food and empty bags of dry food." Delbert did not need to elaborate on the reason he had been going through the old woman's garbage. Clint knew as well as anyone that Delbert was a born dumpster-diver. Why, some the best things he owned he had found in someone else's garbage.

"And at night," Delbert went on, "I could hear her crying out to her lost husband to come back to her, and all the cats would start crying out at the same time, the whole lot of them. I mean by this time she had *dozens* of them for Christ's sake. And all night long they would scream at the top of their lungs. Would've driven me crazy if I didn't usually pass out."

Delbert shrugged, took a swig of his beer and continued. "Anyway, finally the old broad died and the cats ate her."

Clint choked on his beer, and his face went red as foam went up his nose. *"What?"* he blurted out.

"The cats ate her," Delbert said. "Makes sense. Wasn't no more food and they had to eat something. And cats ain't got no loyalty. They ain't like a dog." Delbert's face grew wistful as he thought of Buford, back home curled up on one of his old shirts in front of the big-screen TV.

"All that was left of the old lady was her skeleton, picked clean," Delbert said. "Animal Control's been out there a couple times since she died to try and clear the cats out, but now there's so many they can't catch 'em all. The cats have been out there for five years now, breeding and inbreeding. Now there's hundreds of them! You go out there at night and shine your headlights into her yard and you see thousands of these little glowing eyes shining in the grass, staring back at you."

And almost every morning since that conversation, the cats had wandered into his yard and left their little surprises in the dirt for him to step in. Nothing he did kept them away.

As Delbert wormed his toes into the crabgrass to get the crap out from between them, he heard a high, feline growl, the kind that goes up and down like a police siren. *Rrreewerrweorrr ...*

He looked up. What he saw made him grin, and decide that maybe this wasn't going to be such a bad day after all. He had set out some snares a couple of weeks ago and it looked like today he had struck gold.

He walked around to the back of his trailer, where a single maple tree struggled out of the dust. In the rope snare dangling from one of its scrawny branches hung a cat, a big ol' fat one all mottled over with brown, black and orange. What his Ma used to call tortoiseshell calico. Seems he remembered only female cats had that pattern, and he realized the cat wasn't fat at all, but pregnant.

"Got knocked up, didn'cha honeybunch?" Delbert cooed as he approached. The cat clawed at the knot holding it, growling and screeching. When Delbert spoke, it turned its shiny hazel eyes onto him and hissed.

Delbert began to chuckle. This defense mechanism of the cat, an instinctual response to danger, he thought of as the cat insulting him, saying it would kill him if it had the chance (and could speak). To Delbert, this meant that now he could kill the cat any way he wanted, as cruelly as he wanted, and the cat's attitude justified it. Then if you considered that the cats had overpopulated and needed thinning out, hell, it was his *responsibility* to kill this pregnant little wretch that had the nerve to hiss at him.

He reached into his robe pocket and brought out his pocketknife. He always carried a knife, and slept with a nine-millimeter pistol under his pillow. Had to, with the goddamn government watching every move he made, just ready to rush him like they did those folks at Waco and Ruby Ridge. (Delbert saw no problem with drawing his disability check from this same government.)

He popped out the four-inch blade, a gleaming curve of metal, and held it in front of him as he drew near the cat hanging from the snare. He put a little strut into his step. Why not? The thing was at his mercy, wasn't it?

"Hey honey," he said, grinning. "Why don't we see how many babies you have in there, hmm?"

Then, just as he said those words, he heard a rapid thumping sound like footsteps coming at him from behind. He whirled around, furious that someone had interrupted his little game, but before he could see who was coming a sharp impact, surprisingly painful, slammed across the side of his face, like an outraged woman had stepped forward and slapped him. He felt something tear a gash across his right cheekbone and thought, *Her ring cut me! That crazy woman's wedding ring cut me!* He staggered; the force of the strike made him turn around again, back facing the cat hanging from the snare. As he turned, he felt the thing that had hit him fly past his face, and he realized that no one had slapped him after all. He forced his already tearing eyes open as the biggest black cat he had ever seen landed on the branch with the snare hanging from it. For an instant, he could only stare at it in shock.

The black cat was so big that the narrow branch sagged under its weight. The calico in the snare now hung just a few inches above the ground. The thing must have taken a running leap to hit him in the face like it did. It glared at him with narrowed yellow eyes. Delbert swore he could see real hate in those eyes. He saw with incredulous surprise that the black cat had six toes on each of its paws. It meowed at him, but that wasn't quite right. Delbert had always heard an "r" in the sound cats made, more like *reow*. But this cat hadn't sounded like that either.

As he watched, the black cat reached down with its strange six-toed paw and scratched at the knot in the snare. The pregnant calico dropped to the ground and as its weight came off, the branch snapped back up, launching the black cat like a catapult. It sailed through the air for a moment before landing, on all fours of course. The black cat turned back and made that weird sound again before it darted under the fence and disappeared into a thick stand of weeds with the calico close behind it.

After several seconds, Delbert recovered from his shock. Now he discovered that he had dropped the knife and was holding his hand to his face, on the spot where the cat had scratched him. He drew back his hand and saw blood on his fingertips.

The cat untied the knot, he thought. *The little bastard untied it himself.*

He needed a beer. He needed one *right now.*

He turned to go back to his trailer, and then Buford came galloping up to him, excited and jumpy, like he'd been chasing something. Looking up, Delbert saw two other cats, these were orange tiger-striped, slink through a gap in the fence. They must have distracted Buford while the pregnant calico was trapped in the snare. He felt again the powerful need for a beer. Ignoring Buford, who obviously felt like playing, Delbert ran into his trailer.

Just before passing out, he realized the black cat's meow had sounded familiar. It had sounded like "Brown."

4

Berry Picking

On their way to the Brooks woods, Brad and Jason stopped to tell Brad's mother they were going berry picking. Brad and his family lived in an earth-contact home, which Jason thought was pretty neat. The house was partially buried in the side of a hill, with only the eastern-facing wall exposed to the air. In front of this Brad's father had built a wooden deck, one of the last things he had done before a heart attack took him. On this deck, with its pretty eastern exposure and trees all around, Brad's mother Marjory (Midge to her friends) held singing lessons.

Jason's mother was young and pretty, while Brad's mother was old and beautiful. Not supermodel beautiful, but Jason thought she looked magnificent in her own way. She had become a mother late in life and was now in her early fifties, although she didn't look it. Long straight hair, streaked with equal parts black and gray, flowed back from her smooth brow almost to her ankles. Jason thought she looked like an old opera singer he had once seen in a magazine, Maria Calamine. Or Callas or something.

Brad's mother used to be an opera singer herself when she was younger. She had sung at opera houses in Kansas City, Chicago, and a bunch of other big cities. After she got pregnant with Brad, her voice had changed. So she retired to the country and started teaching music out of her home.

Jason didn't understand why she couldn't still sing. He thought her voice sounded awesome, really full and clear. She had this sophisticated accent too, a way of rolling her r's and sounding out each word that Jason found entrancing.

"Mom!" Brad called as he mounted the steps to the deck. "Jason's mom said if we filled up this pot with mulberries-"

"Just a moment, Bradley," his mother said, her cultured tones edged with reprimand. "You know you are not to interrupt me when I'm with a student."

"Hi Ms. Grace," Jason said as he climbed onto the deck with Brad.

"Hello Jason," she replied, and turned back to the blond teenaged girl standing beside her. She rode the same school bus as Jason; he thought her name was Tiffany Something.

"Now Tiffany," said Ms. Grace, "you must not scoop your voice so when moving from the low note to the high. The transition must be immediate. Sing from your diaphragm. Use your breath to lift your voice into the upper register. Now let's try it again."

Tiffany started to sing, just sounding out a note as far as Jason could tell, not doing any particular song. To Jason, she sounded like someone saying "Ah" for the dentist until Ms. Grace put one hand on Tiffany's stomach and the other on the small of her back and started pressing inward. Then Tiffany's voice jumped up into a clear, high note that Jason thought sounded pretty nice.

As the note faded, Tiffany smiled in surprise, showing a mouth full of braces.

"Better," Brad's mother said, and then turned to her son. "Now then, you said something about picking mulberries, Bradley?"

"Jason's mom said she'd make us some jam if we filled up this pot," Brad said, lifting the old soup pot by the handle.

"That was sweet of her. Go right ahead. Jason, please thank your mother for me, and tell her I'll see her at the next Quilting Society meeting."

"I will," Jason said.

"And yes, Bradley," she continued, anticipating her son's next question. "You may stay the night at the Ross's if you wish and if Jason's mother allows it."

"Thanks Mom," Brad said, and ran off with Jason in the direction of the Brooks woods.

The properties of the Grace's, the Ross's and now the Coldiron's stretched in a north-south line with the vaster Brooks property lying to the west of all three of them. Brad and Jason ran in the direction of the afternoon sun through the open field growing tall with June grass until they reached the shadows of the forest. A barbed wire fence marked the border between the two properties. Brad spread the two lower wires to let Jason pass through, and then Jason did the same for Brad. They found a game trail on the other side of the fence and followed it, since it happened to go in the direction of the mulberry grove and would give them a somewhat clear path through the undergrowth and brambles. Even so, by the time they reached the grove, thorns had covered their arms and legs with scratches. Not that they noticed.

Mulberry trees liked to grow on the edges of forests. Jason had no idea why, but he always seemed to find them between forests and fields. Ahead of them, Jason could see through the scrawny tangled trees the glow of the sun in the meadow along which the mulberry trees grew. But as they ran towards it (they never seemed to walk anywhere), Brad yelled, "Wait up! I want to show you something!"

"What?" Jason replied, skidding around and following Brad, who had already started running in a different direction, dodging and jumping over tangles of thorny brambles and briars. "We're supposed to go straight there and back!"

"It's not far! It'll just take a second!"

Easy for you to say, Jason thought. *You're wearing jeans.* He wished he had changed out of his shorts before going into the woods. Oh well, woulda-coulda-shoulda, as his Dad liked ... had liked to say.

Suddenly a hand grabbed the back of his shirt and yanked him to a halt, less than a foot away from a locust tree. A good thing too. Locust trees were thorn trees; just about every square inch of them, branches, limbs and trunk, bristled with sharp black spikes, some of them six or eight inches long. They had more thorns than leaves.

"Watch where you're going, man," Brad said, letting go of the back of his shirt.

"Thanks," Jason replied. He shuddered when he realized he had almost collided with that tree and impaled himself on all those hundreds of thorns, like those birds his mother had told him about, the ones that killed themselves on a thorn tree while singing a beautiful song. A lady had written a famous book about those birds. His mother had loved that book, although Jason didn't understand why. He hated locust trees. They looked so *evil.*

"Jason, come here," Brad called, sounding impatient. "Stop looking at that tree and check this out."

Jason turned away from the locust tree (although he did not like to turn his back on it, as if it might spring from the ground and come after him) and walked over to his friend.

Brad was kneeling at the base of a tall maple tree, one of the few big trees in these woods. This maple might have stood back when this forest was still a pasture filled with grazing dairy cows. Brad grabbed a vine growing up the side of the maple's trunk. Jason's Mom called those vines Pair-a-Sights, although he didn't know what a vine could see. Unlike potatoes, they didn't have eyes. He giggled.

"What are you laughing at?" Brad asked.

"Nothing. What did you want to show me?"

"Watch this," Brad said, and pulled a pocketknife from, appropriately, his pocket.

"Oh lucky!" Jason exclaimed. "You get to have a pocketknife! My Mom won't let me."

"It's a Swiss Army Knife. My Mom let me have one 'cause I'm taking swimming lessons instead of Boy Scouts this summer. But she made me take a safety class and promise not to fool around with it. I just need the saw for this."

He pulled out the saw blade and started cutting through the vine with it. Jason held the vine still to make it easier for him, and after a little while he cut clean through it.

"Look," Brad said, holding up the severed end of the vine. Jason saw beads of golden sap oozing from the light yellow flesh.

"Does it come from the maple tree?" Jason asked, looking up.

"I don't think so," Brad said. "But I saw in a movie that you can drink from a vine. Try it."

Jason felt wary. Brad had played practical jokes on him before. One time he had tricked him into drinking vanilla extract. But they were still best friends. Jason trusted that Brad wouldn't do anything to hurt him. Even so ...

"You go first," Jason said.

"It's not a joke," Brad said, sounding exasperated. "See?" He ran a finger through the sap and put it in his mouth. Now Jason could not refuse. He would look scared if he did, so he ran his own finger across the end of the vine and tasted the sap. And was surprised.

"It's sweet!" Jason said. "It's like honey or syrup. Not quite the same, but it's good."

"Pretty cool, huh?" Brad said. Then he jumped up and grabbed the vine. The maple tree grew next to a narrow gully. Kicking off from the tree, Brad swung over the gully howling like Tarzan.

"Me next! Me next!" Jason shouted, and so they passed several minutes, their berry-picking chore forgotten, until they heard the screaming.

They happened to hear it after one of Jason's turns on the vine, and froze staring in the direction from which the screams had come.

Still clutching the vine with his feet propped against the maple, Jason said, "I think that's a person."

"It could have been a bird," Brad said, not sounding too convinced of this himself. "It was real high-pitched."

"I don't think-" Jason began, but the screams interrupted him. This time they knew it was not a bird. They could not make out any words, but the raw terror in the screams could have only come from a person. A young one, by the sound of it.

They looked at each other for a moment, unsure of what to do. Jason thought about running back to tell either his mother or Brad's, depending on who was closer, but then Brad scrambled across the gully and bolted towards the source of the screams. Friends always had to back each other up. That was an ironclad rule; his Dad had told him so. Jason dropped from the vine and ran after Brad.

After cutting through the woods, their sense of direction had gotten a little turned around, so they were surprised when they came out at the old dairy farm. But shock, not surprise, froze the boys in place when they saw the burned-out clearing.

They had seen the abandoned farm once before, despite commands from both of their mothers to stay away. They had sworn each other to secrecy about it and had kept their promise, because they were best friends and they held that trust with the fervent seriousness in which only young children can still believe. They had visited it in the spring, a few weeks before school let out, and the place had seemed spooky then. Now, with charred and twisted rubble jutting from the blackened ground, the place seemed more than just spooky. It felt haunted. Unsafe. Then from the ragged hole near the center of the clearing came a child's horrified screams.

Again, they almost bolted, both of them this time. But now Jason, the terror in that voice twisting at his more sensitive heart, was the one who went forward. He crept over to the hole, recognizing it as one of the wells his mother had warned him about, with Brad right behind him. Being careful not to get too close to the edge, two pairs of eyes looked down into the well.

Below, at the bottom of a hole lined with rough fieldstone, they saw a white face staring up at them, surrounded by the glimmering ripples of light on water.

The high-pitched scream resonated up the stone walls with the acoustic perfection of an opera house. Jason couldn't stand to listen to it any longer. He yelled at the face at the bottom of the well.

"Hey!"

The screams stopped immediately. Brad jumped up and ran back to the woods, obviously to get help. Jason opened his mouth to say help was on the way, but then a strange thing happened. A second white face appeared, as if another person at the bottom of the well had looked up at the sound of his voice. This one looked like a girl. Her mouth was twisted into a grimace of terror, almost like a smile, and her face looked a lot like the face of the first person they had seen. It also looked like the girl was holding the other face in her hands.

Then a stray beam of sunlight reflected off the water and dazzled him for a second. He blinked his eyes and when his vision cleared, he saw only the girl at the bottom of the well. Had he really seen two people? Obviously the other person couldn't have gone anywhere, so he guessed not. Maybe it was just the reflection of the girl's face in the water. He thought he'd heard a splash, but that must have been the girl moving around.

Then she screamed again, snapping him out of his thoughts.

"Get me out of here!"

"My friend went to get help!" Jason called back. "It's gonna be okay!"

She didn't seem to understand, and kept screaming. *"Get me out! Help me! Oh my legs!"*

"Are your legs hurt?" Jason called. It seemed stupid to ask, but he didn't know what else to say. "Are you okay?"

"Jeremiah!" the girl shouted. *"Deer! California! Cancer!"*

"What?"

Something was wrong with her. Jason knew it like a drop of ice water running down his back. He started to shake, and fought as hard he could not to get scared and start crying like a stupid baby.

"He pushed me," the girl whimpered, feeling at the stone walls like she would try to climb up on her own. "A woman. Mercury. Momma. So cold. I want my Momma!"

Jason's legs started to shake like they always did whenever he got too excited, and for a single mortifying moment he thought he was going to wet his pants. But then he heard footsteps approaching and thought that the grown-ups had finally come; they would get the girl out of the well, calm her down and make everything all right again.

But when he turned around he saw Brad coming back alone, pulling the vine from the maple along behind him. He must have climbed the tree and cut it down with his pocketknife.

"What are you doing?" Jason cried. "Go get your mom!"

"She can't wait that long," Brad said. "Now help me out and hold on to this end." He handed Jason one end of the vine and tossed the other into the well.

"Hey!" Brad yelled. "Can you climb up the ... *oof!*"

Jason felt the weight of the girl yank the vine through his palms, burning them skinless.

I guess that's a yes, he thought. For a single panicky moment, it felt like the vine would slip right through his hands and into the well, dropping the girl back down. But then he thought of how frightened and disappointed that would make the girl feel. So Jason dug his heels into the black ashy ground, clenched his fists and his teeth, and held on.

Brad, after getting yanked off balance when the girl grabbed the vine so quickly, got back on his feet and started helping Jason pull.

Many long moments passed. Leaning back with their feet braced in the ground, the two boys couldn't see into the well, but they could hear the girl's feet scrape on the fieldstones. They heard her grunting, whimpering and gasping for breath. With every moan of effort, the vine would yank forward again. They had to lean back to counter the girl's weight, and soon the boys were almost lying on their backs, kicking their feet and trying to get every ounce of leverage they could to help pull the girl out. It felt like two people were climbing the vine instead of just one. Jason clenched the vine until his knuckles turned white and he could feel his pulse pounding in his temples. Brad's lips had pulled back from his teeth and his eyes were squeezed shut with effort. His face was as red as an apple. Summer heat throbbed from the burnt ground, drenching them in sweat.

Just when he thought he couldn't hold on any longer, a white arm emerged from the well and clawed at the ground. Jason let out a cry of triumph as Brad jumped forward and grabbed it. A second arm came out, and Jason moved up to take it by the wrist. Together, the boys lifted a shivering, soaking wet girl out of the well.

Shoulder-length black hair clung to her face and neck in wavy tangles. Her clothes, a simple brown t-shirt and cutoff jeans, were dirty, wet and torn in places. She had goosebumps all over her skin, and Jason saw with amazement that her lips had turned blue. Her knees were scraped and bloody. One old flip-flop sandal clung to her right foot. The other foot was bare. Jason assumed her other sandal had fallen off in the climb.

They set her on her feet, but the girl crumpled to the ground. The climb up must have exhausted her. She folded her arms over her chest and drew her knees up to her chin, still shivering. Her lips moved and whispered things that Jason could only hear in fragments and snatches.

"Brothers," she whispered. For a moment, Jason thought she was asking if he and Brad were brothers, which people did all the time even though they looked nothing alike. Brad's blond hair, cut back in an all-American buzz, his blue eyes and freckles set him apart from Jason's darker Native American features. But then the girl kept speaking, and Jason suspected she was just rambling.

"Fever ... Momma," she said. "Don't sell it ... the animals are sick ... darkness ... Jeremiah no! Don't do it!"

Jason couldn't stand to listen to her. Didn't she know they had saved her? His heart hurt him. He had never seen anyone suffer like this, hadn't even seen his Dad in pain before he died. He had gone off to work in a storm of ice, fine and healthy, and the next time Jason saw him he was lying in a coffin. He had looked like he was asleep, but Mom had said he would never wake up.

He knelt beside the girl and patted her on the shoulder. Brad hung back, looking unsure of himself, but now Jason knew what to do.

"You're okay now," he said, patting her shoulder and stroking her hair. "You're out of the well. You're safe."

"Cancer …" the girl whispered, and then trailed off.

Suddenly she jerked into a sitting position and began to pound with both fists on the sides of her head.

"Be Rachel not me!" As she howled, Jason backed off in surprise. *"Be Rachel not me!"*

Then she stopped hitting herself just as suddenly as she had started, and relaxed into heavy rapid breaths as if she had just done something that took a lot of effort. She rested her head on her knees and seemed calm again.

Not understanding, Brad and Jason exchanged a glance. They didn't know what to do and wished again that the grown-ups were here to handle this. Finally, Brad stepped forward and leaned toward the girl.

"Do you want us to take you home?" he asked. "Can you understand me?"

She raised her head and looked up at him through the wet tangles of her hair. She had enormous dark eyes. Each pupil looked as deep as the well from which they had pulled her.

"No," she said. "Don't take me home. I just want to sit for a minute."

"Okay," Brad said. "Is your name Rachel? I thought I heard you say that."

"Yeah," she said.

"I think I know you," Brad said. "Aren't you in remedial class at school?"

Rachel stared at him for a bit, like maybe she thought Brad was going to make fun of her. Jason knew that Brad wouldn't do something like that, but Rachel didn't. But after a few seconds she nodded and quietly said, "Yes."

The public school Brad and Jason attended had remedial classes in various subjects to help students who were falling behind in their work. Neither Brad nor Jason had to attend these classes, but everyone knew who did. Word got around. Remedial students had to put up with a lot of harassment. Other kids were always calling them stupid. Brad and Jason never made fun of them, but they didn't make an effort to be their friends either.

Rachel shivered as she sat on the black ashy ground, despite the heat. Jason thought it must have been really cold down in the well to do this to her. Brad saw it too. He took off his t-shirt and wrapped it around the girl's shoulders. It wasn't much but at least it would help dry her off.

"Here," he said. "You still look cold."

"Thank you."

Suddenly Rachel turned and looked behind her. Brad and Jason both jumped in surprise. They were both still a little keyed-up after pulling her from the well. Her eyes locked on a sprout coming out of the ground in the center of the clearing, and then she turned back to them and said, "I have to go. Thank you for helping me."

"Wait," Brad said. "Why don't we walk you home? You might need a doctor or something."

"I'm fine," Rachel said, and stood up as if to prove it. Her legs, all streaked with black ash, shook a little bit but then she steadied them with visible effort. "Thank you again."

She took off, but she was walking in the direction of Jason's house. The boys exchanged another glance, silently agreeing to follow her, before trotting after Rachel into the woods.

"Hey!" Brad called as they caught up with her at the gully. "We live this way too. Let's walk together for a while, okay?"

"If you want," Rachel said, moving forward with grim determination. She looked like she wanted to take off running but she was unwilling to do it in front of other people. If she was afraid of them, then Jason didn't want to follow her. He only wanted to make sure she was okay. She was acting really weird, and Jason wanted to tell a grown-up about her. They had told them to do that in school; if they ever saw someone in trouble, tell a grown-up. But Jason didn't think she was afraid of them. He thought she was afraid of something she had seen in the clearing. Or maybe she just wanted to get away from the well.

After a few steps the girl paused to take off her remaining flip-flop and went on barefoot. This did not surprise Brad and Jason since they often went barefoot themselves, although they thought that Rachel had developed calluses awfully early in the summer.

When Rachel got to the locust tree, she stopped in her tracks. She dropped her gaze and started staring at the ground as Brad and Jason caught up with her.

"What's the matter?" Brad said. "Did you drop something?"

"There's a man hiding in that patch of grass," she whispered. She gestured with her eyes toward the spot, a little treeless area in the shadow of the thorn tree, but Jason didn't see anything.

"Don't look!" she hissed. "He's watching us."

Jason saw how terrified the girl was. Her eyes darted back and forth as she looked toward the clearing and then back at the patch of grass where she had said the man was hiding. Her lower lip started to shake, and Jason could see how hard she was trying not to cry.

"I don't see anyone," Jason said.

"*He's there,*" Rachel insisted, still keeping her voice low. "His clothes are all green and brown, and his face is painted the same way. He blends in with the color of the grass, but I can see him."

Now Jason began to feel a little afraid. Maybe this strange girl was crazy, but what if she wasn't? Danger seemed to stalk around her in tightening circles. Again, Jason wished a grown-up would come and help them. One that wouldn't hide in the grass and stare at them, if Rachel was right.

Making a point of not looking at the grassy patch, Brad said, "Look, we'll take you to my friend's mom, okay? She lives just over that rise."

Rachel's eyes darted up to Brad's face, and for the first time Jason thought he saw some hope in them.

"In the little red schoolhouse?" she asked.

"Yeah," Jason said. "I bet she could take you home, or at least call your mom."

She glanced again at the patch of grass. "Okay."

They walked toward the rise that would take them out of the woods. They moved quickly, but did not run, hoping the man hiding in the grass would not know Rachel had seen him. If there was a man.

As they passed through the brambles on top of the rise, Rachel seemed to realize she still had Brad's shirt around her shoulders, because she looked at him and said, "You're all scratched up."

Some of the scratches had bled, but Brad shrugged and said, "It's nothing." He passed the shirt back to her when she tried to return it to him.

Now they could see through the dark tangled trees the barbed wire fence that marked the end of the woods. Rachel kept shivering, and Jason knew it was because of both cold and fear. He could always tell how people felt. His mother said he a knack for it, that he was sensitive. But anyone could see Rachel looking over her shoulder again and again to see if the strange man was following them, or hear the awkward silence arising from her fear. Jason wasn't sure if the man even existed, but he wanted to make Rachel feel better. He gave Brad a glance to let him know he was going to try something (often a glance was all they needed to communicate, they knew each other so well), and then Jason began to sing, as if idly filling the silence. He chose the first song that came to mind, the old Jimmie Driftwood song, "The Battle of New Orleans."

He had a very high and clear voice. Brad's mother had often tried to lure Jason into her singing class, but he was too shy to sing in front of an audience. He only felt comfortable singing around his mother and best friend, and even then only if it happened naturally, as the mood came on him and it seemed they would enjoy hearing him.

Brad smiled when he heard the song Jason chose. He had always liked this song and he joined in the chorus when Jason got around to it. Usually he listened to Johnny Horton's version, which was the one everyone had heard, but his mother still kept some of the old 78 rpm records of Jimmie Driftwood singing the original version of the song. The records were ancient vinyl, almost a quarter of an inch thick, and his mother did not allow him to touch them out of fear he would scratch them.

None of them thought it was strange for someone to sing when the urge came on them. Besides living around musically inclined people, everyone they knew in their little town and in many of the small towns around Peculiar liked to sing as a way to pass the time. Rachel was now looking back and forth between the two boys with the tiniest trace of a smile on her lips.

"I can never remember the next verse," Jason said after a few stanzas, laughing a bit to see if it might spread.

Brad looked up in thought, as if he expected to see a skywriter tracing the lyrics across the blue. "Oh, if you hadn't said that I could've remembered it! Something about the British going down the river, or pounding on a drum ..."

"That's not how it goes," Rachel said, quietly but not sounding as fearful as before. "It goes like this..."

Now Rachel picked up the next verse. It was the part of the song that described the meeting between the revolutionary and British soldiers. The British were marching openly beside the Mississippi river, beating their marching drums, while the American soldiers hid silently behind cotton bales, waiting for the order to fire to come down from their general, Andrew Jackson. The point of the lyric was that the revolutionary soldiers used guerilla tactics, which were a lot different from the old methods of warfare used by the British, where they all marched in a line. Rachel sang softly, but she remembered the lyrics perfectly.

Jason smiled at Brad. It was working. Rachel had a pretty good singing voice too. The three of them sang the next verse together.

Brad and Jason giggled at the part where the soldiers filled an alligator's head with cannonballs used him as a cannon. They always laughed at that part, but now Rachel joined in the laughter. They were almost out of the woods, but sang on anyway. It seemed like their patriotic duty to sing the part where the soldiers sent the British running through the briars and brambles where even a rabbit couldn't go. Their teacher said Driftwood had written this song as way to teach his own students about the battle of New Orleans, but Brad and Jason always just thought it was catchy.

When they came out of the woods, they saw they had gone too far north, onto the Coldiron's property. Jason felt a thread of unease pass through him as they stepped into the yard that was once a field. Brad and Rachel seemed to relax, but they had never met Mrs. Coldiron.

Brad put his arm around Rachel's shoulders and said, "That's the schoolhouse up there, on the hill. Jason's mom is cool and she'll-"

"You boys get away from her!"

All three of them jumped at the sound of Mrs. Coldiron's screech. They turned and saw her storming out of her front door like a fairy-tale ogre coming out of its cave. Her fists opened and closed, opened and closed. As she marched towards them, they saw her face; her jaw set and her lips clamped into a pale white line. Her eyes burned with fury. But, Jason saw, her lips were curved into a bitter and knowing smirk, as if they'd been doing something bad and she was happy she'd caught them at it.

Without quite knowing why, Jason suddenly felt uncomfortable that Brad had his shirt off and his arm around Rachel's shoulders. Mrs. Coldiron's eyes scanned each of them, the frightened girl all wet and dirty, covered with scrapes, bruises and scratches, the two boys on each side of her, the shirtless one a little scratched up himself.

She does think we've been doing something bad, Jason thought.

"I said get away from her!" Mrs. Coldiron snapped as she drew near, her voice a hoarse scream. She grabbed the arm Brad had over Rachel's shoulder so hard that he cried out in pain, and threw him to the ground.

"I know all about you boys!" Mrs. Coldiron yelled. "I've read all about the things you do! I watch the news programs! They tell me all about you!"

Jason had no idea what she was talking about. They'd been on the news?

"It's okay," he said. "We're helping-"

"Shut up!" she screamed, clamping one hand onto Rachel's arm and pulling the girl to her. The satisfied smirk returned to her face. "I'm going to tell your mothers about this. Oh yes. And then I'm calling the police and the newspapers and everyone will know! Everyone will know what you've done!"

"We didn't do anything!" Brad cried, but Mrs. Coldiron only laughed.

So far Rachel had been too stunned to respond; she could only stare in shock as Mrs. Coldiron dragged her away. But at the sound of her laugh, an odd change came over her. She jumped a little at first, like she was startled. And then, some-how, she seemed to grow. She didn't get any taller, not really. It was like she took on some of what Jason's mother called *presence,* which was how she described the shamans when his Dad had taken them to powwow. Like suddenly Rachel's shadow had grown from little-girl-size to man-size. Her back and shoulders straightened and she stopped shivering. The fear disappeared completely from her face and a strange adult expression took its place, like she had met all the world's liars and cheats and beaten them bloody. Her jaw set, her lips tightened, but the most dramatic change came over her eyes. Before they had been soft and dark doe-eyes, but now they became haunted, focused, somehow older. Jason thought he actually saw lines form around them like furrows ploughed into a field. Looking at those eyes reminded Jason, for some reason, of seeing her down at the bottom of the well, when he thought he had seen two people instead of one.

Rachel planted her feet in the ground as firmly as an old tree and didn't budge. Mrs. Coldiron stopped in her tracks. Whether it was because she couldn't move Rachel anymore or because she had felt the change come over her, Jason couldn't tell.

"Go away," Rachel said. Her Midwest accent had grown thicker. Before it was mild, but now the accent had grown so thick Jason couldn't believe a human voice could make words with it.

"What did you say?" Mrs. Coldiron said. Her voice had dropped so low that it was almost a whisper.

"I said go away." It sounded like *Ah sed go 'way.* Not a begging voice or even an asking one. It was as hard and deep and final as the thump of an anvil dropped from a third-story building. A strong man's voice.

Now Mrs. Coldiron looked scared, but angry that she had become scared, and when she spoke her voice was high and shrill.

"Oh! Oh! I see!" she screeched. "You *like* what those boys are doing to you! I see what kind of girl you are! Well, you know how girls like you turn out? You turn out-"

"Get your hands off me," Rachel said in her deep, angry, grown-up voice. "Get 'em off, go away and *LEAVE ME ALONE!*"

She roared so loudly that Mrs. Coldiron jerked her hand away like she had touched something hot. She stumbled back a few paces, recovered, and then looked around to see if anyone was watching besides Brad and Jason.

"I'll tell everyone," said Mrs. Coldiron, and now she sounded like she was going to cry. "Everyone will know!"

And then she turned and ran back to her house.

The boys stared at Rachel, agog. They couldn't believe this was the same scared, shivering girl they had pulled out of the well. But then, as they watched, the strange presence seemed to leave her. Rachel's shoulders slumped, and as she turned back to them Jason saw that the haunted older look had left her eyes. He thought, just maybe, he could still see a hint of it lurking in her pupils, like glimpsing a scary, grinning monster submerged in dark waters, waiting for its next victim to come along. But then that too vanished, and she looked like a regular girl again.

Facing the boys, Rachel said of Mrs. Coldiron what Jason and his mother would not: "What a bitch."

This snapped the boys out of their amazed silence, and they burst out laughing. Rachel said a dirty word! She had just risen, in their opinion, to the highest peak of coolness. Their friendship solidified from a possibility to a fact at that moment.

"Come on!" Brad said, jumping back to his feet. "Let's go to Jason's house and tell his mom what happened before that crazy lady does. That was awesome!" He still had a bright red ring around his upper arm where Mrs. Coldiron had grabbed him. It looked like it would turn into a bruise eventually.

"Can you stay with us afterwards?" Jason asked. "We can play tag or hide-and-go-seek or something."

Rachel shrugged. "Okay."

Together the three of them bolted across the gravel road to the schoolhouse, home again after so many ordeals.

5

The Meeting at Sunset

The sun fell and died, filling the western horizon with the bloody colors of its setting. Venus appeared and received its wishes as the evening star while in the town below every building and tree stood out in silhouette sliced into the backdrop of the sunset. The cars on highway 71 turned on their headlights, a string of diamonds approaching, rubies receding.

Sergeant William Rollins had a poetic soul. He knew it, and fought it the way anyone with a chronic debilitating illness would. That it was in fact debilitating he had no doubt. Anyone who could see beauty in such mundane objects as cars on the highway or the local buildings at sunset must have a serious mental problem. This poetic soul with which he had been born seemed to him worse than any physical deformity he could have inherited. But he fought it as he had been trained to fight all obstacles in his path and one day he knew he would triumph, and kill his soul forever.

The thought gave him comfort at moments like these.

He could see a reflection of the room behind him in the window glass, which pleased him, as he always liked to watch his back. If he didn't, who would? The building was well guarded and had been reinforced with the latest security measures, but one never knew for certain these days. One always had to watch one's back.

They had chosen this building for its unremarkability. On the outside it looked like one of those nationwide hotel chains that spread their branches across the nation and their roots deep into the citizens' pockets. Indeed once it had been a hotel, but after a few well-placed calls to the hotel's corporate offices, and more than a few costly bribes, the managers had decided to take an indefinite vacation and leave the running of the building to Sergeant Rollins and his crew. It made the perfect base of operations, right off the Peculiar exit on the east side of highway 71. All they needed to maintain their privacy was a well-lit NO VACANCY sign. Through the windows of this conference room, Rollins could see the J high-way overpass, over which passed the cars carrying the evening commuters home.

He could also see his own reflection in the window, but to that he paid little attention. He had never cared for his own face, even less so now that he had entered that great death-watch known as late middle-age. The face once carved from strong simple lines like a face carved on a mountaintop had now sagged, creased, grown tired and lined. It was not the loss of youthful good looks that pained him (it really was, but he did not let himself admit it). The stubble of hair on top of his head was uniformly white, a consistency he found vaguely pleasing except when it reminded him of his own inevitable old age, decay, death. The thought of drooling helplessness bearing down on him was almost too much to bear. To remedy this, Rollins had begun to carry the cyanide tablets they gave to certain special operatives and spies in his front shirt pocket. It comforted him to know that any time he chose he could leave this monumental, heartbreaking joke called life behind him and move on to oblivion.

In the window's reflection, he saw the door to the room open and the fruit walk in. Gordon was his name, *Agent* Gordon if you could believe it, and although he had not declared himself a fruit, Rollins felt reasonably sure he was one. How else to explain his bookish talk and arrogant attitude? He didn't have to prance around in a tutu for Rollins to figure it out.

His superiors had forced him to work with Gordon on a collaborative level. Claimed he was Homeland Security, but Rollins doubted that. Looked to him like CIA or NSA. It did not bother him that they had lied to him. In this line of work lies were a necessary evil, woven in layers as a form of security while the truth went unspoken, unwritten, unobserved. Just like in the rest of life.

They must have known Rollins would never tolerate such a person under his command. Just another example of the degenerate state of affairs in the country these days.

"You realize," Gordon said as he entered. "I will have to report you for smok-ing in a government building."

In reply Rollins raised his cigar to his lips and drew on it, letting Gordon see the reflection of its glowing coal in the window glass.

Gordon smiled, obviously thinking he had pissed Rollins off. (He had.)

"You know as well as I do," Gordon went on, "that requisitioned private buildings must operate under government regulations."

Gordon set his briefcase on the round table in the center of the room. Rollins usually thought of guys who carried briefcases as "suits," office men who liked to talk a lot and pretend they could make decisions but wouldn't last five minutes in the field. But here again Gordon had found a way to piss him off. He didn't wear suits, as least Rollins had never seen him in one, just jeans and a nondescript button-down shirt. Sometimes even t-shirts if none of Rollins's superiors were around. While this did give Rollins the knowledge that at least he and Gordon answered to the same people, it was still not what Rollins would have expected of him.

Rollins suddenly realized why Gordon so offended him. It was because Gordon did not fit into any of his preconceived categories of people. He was a suit who did not wear suits, non-military working with, and not dominated by, military (especially vexing if he was a fruit as Rollins suspected), a bookish nerd who may even have had some advanced scientific training judging from his performance on this latest operation, yet he had none of the physical weakness and pretensions of importance of the research scientists Rollins had to deal with from time to time. No matter how Rollins tried to get his number, Gordon defied classification. Even those nondescript clothes of his said nothing about him, unlike Rollins's own gray-green uniform, which marked him as military to anyone with eyes.

Gordon sat smiling as the other operative personnel filed into the room. All of them were dressed similarly to Rollins, gray-green military issue clothing that differed only by the rank insignia. Gordon stood out in his civilian clothes ... but not too much. Only after everyone had entered and taken their seats did Rollins turn from the window and take his own chair opposite the white screen mounted on the far wall.

"Report, Private Hicks," he said.

A young man rose from a chair to Rollins's left and approached the screen. Sitting on the table in front of it was a projector wired to a laptop computer. They had used slide projectors for briefings when Rollins first started working in these kinds of operations, but now everything had gone digital. Times had a-changed.

Hicks took a digital camera from atop his pile of notes and plugged it into the laptop. Then he dimmed the lights, closed the blinds on the window and turned on the projector. A blue square covered with computer icons appeared on the screen, filling the darkened room with ethereal blue light.

Lovely, Rollins thought. *I always wanted to see a Windows Desktop.*

Hicks clicked on an icon, booted up the imaging software, and began his presentation.

"Sir, these are the results of my initial reconnaissance of Beta Impact Site and its surrounding areas. Through aerial and satellite surveys we have located the impact site here, at approximately thirty-eight point seven one degrees latitude and ninety-four point four-four-seven degrees longitude. The nearest town of any size is Peculiar, Missouri, population 2,604 as of the 2000 census, with an outreach population of about 7500."

"Over ten thousand people," Gordon said. He spoke with a voice both soft and clear. "That's a higher infection potential than anything we've seen so far."

Another hint that placed him as non-military: interrupting a report. Rollins felt like boxing his ears, but kept his peace.

Private Hicks had a freckled baby-face, which remained fixed in the forced composure of a soldier not long out of boot camp. Rollins felt he handled Gordon's interruption well enough.

"The town is approximately seven miles northwest of the impact site," Hicks went on. As he spoke, his fingers moved over the mouse pad on the laptop, moving the cursor projected on the white screen to a thumbnail photograph. He clicked on it and the photograph expanded, showing a map of the town. "The possibility for transmission of infectious material to the town itself is low."

Gordon's eyes narrowed, and his somehow disturbingly innocuous features tightened at this statement, but he said nothing. Rollins noted his displeasure.

"The actual impact site is here," Hicks continued, "in a rural area south-by-southeast of the town." He magnified another image. This one showed a color photograph, apparently taken from an airplane above a forest with a blackened, treeless area in the middle of it, obviously the site of a recent fire.

"The locals call this area 'the Brooks woods,'" Hicks said, "from a dairy farm that operated on this site about eighty years ago when the surrounding region was still pasture. The site has not been regularly inhabited since that time. The property sold in 1925 to the Thomas Moore family in the town proper, who kept it as 'recreational property,' although rumors persisted that an illegal distillery was being operated on the site. This was during Prohibition. However, in 1929 after the stock market crash that precipitated the Great Depression, the Peculiar Bank and Trust foreclosed on the woods and resold it. The property changed hands several times in the next few decades, until it was finally bought in 1963 by the Upton family of Providence, Rhode Island, in whose ownership it remains to this day."

Rollins, who had grown impatient after this history lesson, said, "The point of all this, Hicks?"

Hicks looked dismayed at Rollins's impatience. Kid must have done a lot of research. Rollins noted the initiative but said nothing. A commanding officer does not apologize to his subordinates.

"Sir, the point is the impact site is in a low-traffic area," Hicks said. "At present, there are no plans for future development of the site, further lessening infection potential. A check of the Upton family's financial records shows extensive real-estate investments in several states. It is possible this plot of land, which is relatively small compared to other Upton holdings, has simply been overlooked for development or sale. The out-of-state ownership also lessens the risk of the infection spreading to the landholders or other private entities."

"Good," Rollins said. "Continue."

The length of time since the property's purchase did seem to indicate some kind of records-keeping failure. No real-estate investor would hold on to a piece of property for so many decades. The owners may have a personal reason for leaving the land untouched or a snafu in file-keeping could have left the property overlooked for sale since their holdings were so extensive, an incredible stroke of luck considering the circumstances. They would have to subpoena the Upton family's real-estate records to make sure, but Rollins said nothing about it. At this point, he wanted to reveal as little of his plans to Gordon as possible.

"The only development risk so far is the state's right of imminent domain," Hicks continued. "But a check of public records shows no plans for legal seizure of the property and no budget allocations for economic development in this area."

"In other words no one is going to come along with a bulldozer and infect an entire team of contractors," Gordon said.

"Please forgive these constant interruptions," Rollins said. Taking a jab at Gordon was worth breaking the no-apologies rule. "Carry on, Private."

"Thank you sir," Hicks said. Gordon seemed unperturbed, the little piss-ant. "The only feature that remains unaccounted for is the lack of an impact crater. This is a marked difference from Alpha Impact Site and made identification of Beta much more difficult. It also makes pinpointing the exact spot the meteor came down virtually impossible. The reason why there is no crater is still unknown-"

"The meteor exploded," Gordon said.

His annoyance at Gordon beginning to kindle his anger, Rollins said, "And just how do you know that?" If those suits at the Pentagon had withheld information from him ...

"The tops of several trees in that photo are singed," Gordon said in a soft patient tone that made Rollins want to strangle him. "Since the fire on the ground burned the trunk and lower branches of the trees, the fire that burned the tops must have come from above. The singed trees are scattered all around the circumference of the burned area, not in a line, so it could not have happened as the meteor passed over them. So the only explanation is that meteor exploded while it was still in the air, burning the tops of the trees and breaking the meteor into smaller pieces that would not hit the ground hard enough to make an impact crater. Q.E.D."

Rollins, who did not know what "Q.E.D." meant but did not want to look ignorant, said, "Well if that's true then pieces of the meteor must have been scattered all over the forest in the explosion, and the contaminated area is bigger than we thought." That would show the impertinent little know-it-all.

"No," Gordon said. "It isn't. If that were the case then there would have been several forest fires spread over a larger area. Since we know, thanks to the National Weather Service, that the meteor fell on a dry, rainless night, a fire would almost certainly have started wherever the hot meteor fragments landed, unless they fell into a body of surface water like a pond or a river, and I don't see any of those in that photograph. So the fragments that did hit the ground must have struck here, on this burned spot. Any others would have vaporized while still in the air, and we don't have to worry about them spreading the infection." Then he spread his hands like someone pointing out the obvious to a dimwit. Rollins wanted to shoot him.

"Not," Gordon added, "that I believe the infection risk to the local population is low. I saw what happened in Africa, at Alpha Site. You are seriously underestimating this organism's ability to spread."

He said this staring straight at Rollins.

Drawing on his cigar, Rollins concealed his face behind a cowl of smoke reddened by the glowing coal. He felt safer that way. Concealed. It helped him think. Oh, he had no problem letting his anger show when Gordon made his indirect assaults on him, or what he had seen as assaults, rather. But this, this brazen accusation, so direct, so *confrontational,* he wasn't accustomed to it. In the rigid military hierarchy he had become used to the unquestioning obedience of the men under his command, and in turn obeying the orders of his superiors. This blatant challenge by someone not entirely under his control, someone on more or less equal terms with him, had disoriented him. He needed to think, and to maintain his *gravitas* as he did so.

It took only a moment. With luck the men would only perceive a dramatic pause.

"Are you saying I wasn't there, Gordon?" Rollins said. Yes, that was better. A groundless accusation would set him on the defensive. Now quick, before he can respond, take it in another direction. Confuse him. "Seems to me we were the ones down in the crater sterilizing the ground while you were running like a scared girl from a bunch of hyenas."

That had been frightening, even for Rollins, which was why he had chosen to go down into the crater and leave the task of slaughtering the hyenas to Gordon. They had found the giggling things at night, circling the crater in the middle of the Kenyan bush veldt. That terrible mad laugh they had and the way their eyes had reflected the headlights of the ATVs had been bad enough, but at the time Rollins could have sworn he heard *words* in the sound of the hyenas' laughter. Nothing intelligible, but it had almost sounded like the language of the African tribesmen that had led them to the place. He got a chill just thinking about that sound, like giggling gibberish dripping from the lips of a madman.

Ah, that poetic soul.

He had thought Gordon would have defended his role at Alpha Site. After all, killing the infected hyenas was far more dangerous than simply sowing powdered alkali into the contaminated ground inside the crater. Gordon had risked his life so that they could do their job, and Rollins had thought he would have reminded him of that, filled with prideful fury, which is how Rollins would have reacted himself. But again, Gordon surprised him. He only stared at him expressionlessly, and said, "The population density is far greater here than at Alpha Site. It is a virtual certainty that animals have already been exposed, and it's only a matter of time before an organism receptive to the mutation is infected. Your cigar has become one long ash."

The abrupt change of subject jarred Rollins, rather like he had attempted to do to Gordon himself. He kept his face composed as he took the water glass of the private sitting next to him and dumped his cigar ash into it. (The private, Rollins thought his name was Benton, looked dismayed but kept his mouth shut. Smart kid.) Rollins's mind was racing. He couldn't let Gordon steal his thunder like this and embarrass him in front of his men. He would let the whole damn town get infected before he would allow that to happen. It looked like magnanimity was in order.

"Did you see any animals displaying signs of infection, Hicks?" he asked.

"Yes, sir," Hicks replied. "I found three dead animals and one live animal displaying multiple forms of carcinoma." He paused, and then added, "Also, I spotted three children in the vicinity of the impact site, sir."

"You *what?*" Rollins leaned forward in his seat as he said the words and bouts of disturbed murmuring spread among the men seated at the table, except for Gordon. He had managed to maintain his *sang froid* even at this news. "You told me the infection risk to the town was low!"

"It is, sir," Hicks said. "Two of the children live outside the town proper, and it is highly likely the third does as well."

"What do mean 'highly likely'?" Rollins said. "Did you identify them? Did you get pictures?"

"Yes, sir," Hicks said, clearly growing nervous in the face of Rollins's anger. At least someone here still feared him. "I was able to identify two of the children through fingerprint samples."

"The kids have fingerprints on file?" Rollins asked.

"As part of a tracking network, sir," Hicks replied. "Sometimes law enforcement will work with schools to fingerprint children as an aid locating or identifying them if they are ever abducted. It's a voluntary program their parents elected to use."

"I see," Rollins said. "That could be very useful. Go on."

Fiddling with the mouse pad on the laptop, Hicks clicked the cursor on a thumbnail image and brought up a photograph of a ruddy-skinned young male with rather longish dark hair falling around his equally dark eyes. The background of the image glowed with sunlit leaves; Hicks must have taken the picture in the woods surrounding the impact site.

"I have identified the first subject as Jason Ross," Hicks said. "Eight years old, American Indian descent. Father is Jack Ross, deceased. Mother is Kelly Ross. I have biographical reports attached to the file, comprised of data taken from the public record. They list addresses, birth dates, driving records …"

"Fine, fine!" Rollins snapped. "We don't need their life stories. What's next?"

Hicks brought up another picture on the screen. This one was of a boy with buzz-cut blond hair, blue eyes and a spray of freckles over his nose and cheeks. Looked like a kid out of a Norman Rockwell painting.

"This subject identifies as Bradley Grace," Hicks said. "Father is Charles Grace, deceased. Mother is Marjory Grace. I also have information-"

"Wait," Gordon interjected. "Marjory Grace the opera singer?"

Hicks glanced nervously at Rollins before replying, as if answering Gordon would enrage him. "I … do not have any employment information regarding Ms. Grace at this time."

"I think it is her," Gordon said, a thoughtful expression on his face. "Seems to me I heard her husband's name was Charles, and he died a short while back. There was a news story on her retirement, and that was about eight years ago."

"Fan of hers, Gordon?" Private Benton asked, perhaps a passive-aggressive way of getting back at Rollins for dumping cigar ash into his water.

Gordon smiled, just a little bit. This was the first time Rollins had ever seen a smile on that bland, unobtrusive face.

"I saw her sing *Carmen* in Chicago when I was a kid," Gordon said. "She's very well known in operatic circles."

Yet another sign that Gordon was a fruit. What kind of man listened to opera? He must have heard Rollins snort, because he resumed his remote and condescending attitude.

"Regardless," Gordon said. "Her fame may cause problems if it becomes necessary to quarantine the area. Who's standing between the boys?"

Hicks jumped at the question suddenly directed at him. He obviously wasn't as good at responding to Gordon's rapid subject changes as Rollins.

"Sir?"

"The Ross boy is looking to his right," Gordon said, "and the Grace kid is looking to his left. Both of their faces are troubled. Someone must be standing between them and causing their distress. I assume this is the child you couldn't identify?"

"Yes, sir." As Hicks clicked on the third thumbnail photograph, Rollins noted with dislike that he had called Gordon "sir." He would have to find an unpleasant task for Hicks, possibly latrine duty. The thought of Hicks scrubbing toilets made Rollins smile to himself as the picture of the third child came up.

And the room fell silent.

A hauntingly beautiful girl stared at them from the screen. She seemed to look back at them, a living presence up there hovering in the white, gazing into the heart of each of them with her wide, dark eyes. She had her head turned to the side, so she was looking at them over her shoulder. The pose struck Rollins as familiar, and then he placed it. The famous painting by Vermeer, *Girl with Pearl Earring*, was the image that came to mind. But while that girl's face had been seductive, this dark-haired girl's expression was suspicious, knowing and mysterious all at once.

She had some kind of dark cloth around her neck, like a cowl or a shawl, and the face rising above it had the full cheeks and wide eyes of a child. But the expression, that looked much older. Yes, Rollins could now understand the boys' troubled faces.

"How old, Hicks?" Rollins asked. "Do you have any idea?"

"Judging from her height," Hicks said, "she must be around the same age as the boys, perhaps a year or so older."

Yes, the height would have to be the way to judge it. The face looking out from this picture could belong to a woman or a girl. For a moment, Rollins envied Hicks for seeing her in the flesh.

"Did she see you?" Gordon asked. "She must have. Just look at her face."

"I don't think so, sir," Hicks said. "The three of them stood together and talked just a few yards away from me. I didn't hear what they said, but I think if they had seen me, they would have either confronted me or become frightened and run away. Instead, they simply walked away together. I was of course well camouflaged."

"Why is she wet?" Gordon asked. "There were no bodies of water in the aerial photograph."

"That is why I thought it relevant to report this, sir," Hick said. "Apparently, the girl fell into a covered well hidden within the impact site. The boys were playing in the woods and heard her screaming. The Grace boy cut down a vine from a nearby tree and, using that, the boys lifted her out."

"A well," Gordon murmured.

"Who is she?" Rollins asked. "Why couldn't you identify her, Hicks?"

"I was unable to get a sample of her fingerprints," Hicks said. "All the surfaces I had surmised she touched were too rough to gain a clear print."

"You managed to get prints from the boys," Rollins pointed out. "Isn't that how you identified them?"

"Yes, sir," Hicks said. "But that is because they left something in the woods."

Walking back to his seat, Hicks took a duffel bag from beside his chair and then went back to the projector, apparently for the light. He took an object wrapped in plastic out of the duffel bag and set it on the table for them to see.

It was a stainless steel pot with a black plastic handle. Yes, Rollins thought. Fingerprints would show up very well on something like that.

"I have been unable to determine why the boys had the pot in the woods," Hicks said. "Perhaps they had intended to go camping and use it to cook food, but I found no other camping supplies nearby."

"Probably to fill it with wild berries," Gordon said softly. "Mulberries are in season, I think."

Something in his tone, an almost wistful quality, made Rollins wonder if Gordon had roots in this part of the world. He knew nothing of Gordon's past, and not for lack of searching. Whatever agency Gordon worked for must have erased his personal records completely. Rollins had been unable to dig up any dirt on him.

"Regardless," Hicks said. "The girl never touched it. Without a fingerprint sample, identifying her will present some difficulty."

"Fingerprint samples are only useful if one is already on file for comparison," Gordon said. "The girl might not even be registered with child protection agencies, like the boys were."

"What about school records?" Rollins asked. "The local elementary school may have a yearbook out, something with pictures."

"I am preparing to contact the local school under assumed circumstances," Hicks said. Even Rollins, accustomed to lies, felt a twinge of disgust at the euphemism "assumed circumstances," which really meant false pretenses. He guessed that Hicks simply hadn't had time to do it already. The kid had done a prodigious amount of research in a very short time, so Rollins could excuse him this one lapse.

"School is out for the summer, gentlemen," Gordon said, in his talking-down-to-the-morons tone. "Unless they have a summer school program, you're going to have a difficult time contacting anyone there."

That tone. God, how he hated that tone! "What about DNA then?" Rollins almost shouted. "Could you get a sample?"

"No sir," Hicks replied.

"And a forensic team that could obtain one from the area would attract too much attention," Gordon said. "What about the well? Did you investigate it? Get a sample of the water?"

"I did investigate the well and obtain pictures of it, sir," Hicks said. He clicked on another thumbnail photo and the girl's hypnotic face disappeared. Rollins felt a wave of relief wash over him. Her expression … those dark eyes seemed to drill into him, asking him without words, *Just what do you think you're doing here?* And Rollins had felt a very real guilt, even though had not even met the girl.

Yet, he thought.

A picture of a hole in the ground appeared on the screen. The black pit and its sense of depth seemed like a photo negative of the dark-haired girl's piercing gaze. The hole was surrounded by burned and broken boards that disappeared into the blackened ground. Almost everything in the picture was black. The only sense of light was the glow of yellow sunlight in the ashes and, deep down at the bottom of the well, a glint of water.

"You didn't get a sample of the water?" Gordon asked.

"No sir," Hicks said. "I did not have the protective gear with me for handling potentially infectious material."

"Neither did she," Gordon said. The girl's presence still hovered in the room like a spirit at a séance, so Gordon did not need to specify of whom he was speaking.

"Which makes it urgent to find out who she is," Rollins said.

"First we need to get a sample of the water," Gordon said. "If it's clean, we don't need to find the girl."

"We've already found infected animals," Rollins said. "Sure, none have shown any signs of mutating, just the tumors, but it's a sign the contagion is here."

"That's true," Gordon said, nodding. (Rollins would never have admitted that Gordon was right about anything.) "But they could have picked it up from sources on the surface. How could an animal get to the water at the bottom of that well?"

"The kids were walking around on that surface," Rollins said. "Why couldn't they get it too?"

Gordon lowered his head and released a slow breath. He nodded slightly, as if he had come to an unspoken decision. Then he raised his eyes to Rollins again.

"What I am about to tell you is highly classified," Gordon said. "It was thought a reasonable security measure to keep this information from the field agents unless absolutely necessary. I think the well-being of those kids qualifies as necessary, but I still have to ask everyone without Red Level security clearance to leave the room."

The rest of the men looked to Rollins for confirmation, which pleased him. At least they still remembered who was in charge here.

"Wait in the hall and close the door," Rollins said. "We'll call you back when we're ready." He did not have to worry about them trying to eavesdrop. The men were highly trained, which ensured trustworthiness.

The door closed behind the last man out, leaving only Rollins and Gordon sitting in the dark unlight of the well's image. As much as Rollins disliked Gordon, he couldn't help feeling curious about what he might reveal. The layers of secrecy necessary for security had made his knowledge of this contagion, the containment of which had occupied the last few years of his life, maddeningly incomplete. He could even tolerate a pompous fruit like Gordon for the opportunity to learn more.

"Under the Congressional Domestic Security Act HS264-1," Gordon said, "you are required to register with the Homeland Security Agency noting that you have been briefed by me concerning this matter. This briefing does not entail that I am an operative of the HSA or indeed of any federal office, nor am I endorsed or financed by them in any way. Do you understand?"

Rollins was familiar with this line of legal nonsense. Gordon was probably required to quote it to any operative that he briefed on highly classified information. The purpose of it was to indemnify the government against intelligence that might be damaging to it, and to track the spread of that intelligence. Also, in a rare departure from the usual lies, Gordon ordering him to register with the Homeland Security Agency didn't necessarily mean Gordon worked for them. That was simply the agency tracking the information.

"Yes," Rollins said. "I understand."

"Samples of the contagion were taken from Alpha Site and analyzed," Gordon said. "It was not found to be viral or bacterial in nature."

"Then what is it?" Rollins asked. "Why is it considered a contagion?"

"It occurs in a form called a plasmid," Gordon said. "It's a small circle of DNA. Terrestrial versions of them are everywhere, in cells, bacteria, even floating around on their own."

"Terrestrial versions," Rollins murmured. Gordon must have intended to drop that phrase. He didn't make such mistakes. "So ... they're sure?"

"Not completely," Gordon said. "But an extraterrestrial origin seems likely. And yes, I will go ahead and say the word. After all, it did come down on a meteor. We've even managed to identify the comet that ejected it: Comet Ming-Grayling. But Rollins, it's still DNA, with the same base pairs of all earthly life. Now this could either mean that life must develop based on DNA, no matter what planet it develops on, or ..."

"Or what?" Rollins asked.

"Or that all life on Earth originated this way, by falling to the surface from space, a theory called panspermia. If this is true, and if terrestrial life was seeded on the primordial Earth during an earlier passage of this same comet, it may explain how the plasmid is able to interact with the DNA of terrestrial organisms."

"What is a plasmid exactly?" Rollins said. He hated asking Gordon questions. It placed him at such a disadvantage. "What do mean when you say it could interact with Earth creatures?"

"Like I said, it's a circle or loop of DNA," Gordon said. "It can float around freely, not always in the nucleus of a cell like our DNA. It's just a large molecule really. I don't think you could even call it alive, not in any traditional definition of life. But it can merge with the DNA of living organisms if it can get inside their cells. Fortunately, that is difficult to do because of the many defenses cells have against invading molecules. Bacteria, however, often take in DNA molecules from their surroundings, including plasmids. This is called transformation, because the bacterium can pick up certain traits, like antibiotic resistance, when they absorb a plasmid with that gene in its DNA. We've determined that a species of terrestrial bacteria can operate as a kind of transportation system for the alien plasmid."

"You've seen this in the lab?" Rollins asked. "Then you must know more about the mutation."

Gordon shook his head. "Not much. Terrestrial plasmids are commonly used in genetic engineering as a way to produce extra copies of recombinant genes. A technician will implant them into a bacterium, *E. coli* say, and then as the bacterium divides it also makes more copies of the plasmid. We tried to do this with the alien plasmid and immediately encountered problems. In most of the bacterial species we tried, the plasmid somehow altered the genome of its host bacterium so that it began to divide uncontrollably, almost like cancer cells. They divided so quickly, in fact, that they didn't do it correctly. Division errors piled up and the bacteria all died. We didn't even get any extra copies of the plasmid, since the original ones merged with the bacterium's DNA before they died. Only after several trials did we find a species of bacteria that would accept the plasmid and not start uncontrolled divisions. But even then, we still didn't get the extra copies of the plasmid that we wanted."

"Why is that?" Rollins asked.

"Because in that species, the bacteria would not divide at all."

"Why not?" Rollins asked. He was having a bit of a hard time following all this scientific jargon, but that seemed like a reasonable question.

"We're not sure, although the species of bacterium that accepts the plasmid might hold a clue. It's a type of bacteria that can infect both plants and animals, called *Pseudomonas aeruginosa*. We think the plasmid uses this bacterium to get into cells. When it inserts its DNA into a cell, the plasmid sneaks in with it."

"Inserts its DNA? I thought only viruses did that."

"Some bacteria can as well," Gordon said. "Most people aren't aware of that, but it's true. There is a process called transduction, where viruses called bacteriophages can carry genetic material from a bacterium to a cell. We think the reason this bacterium stops dividing when it gets the plasmid is a side effect of this, although we still don't completely understand it. Somewhere in the process of the plasmid merging with the bacterium, getting transported to a bacteriophage and then into a cell, the reproductive cycle of the bacterium gets interrupted.

"Most people have a natural resistance to *Pseudomonas*," Gordon continued. "Only people with compromised immune systems or a natural susceptibility will develop infections. People like burn victims, cystic fibrosis patients, or cancer patients. But a bacterium mutated by the alien plasmid may be able to infect anyone, resistant or not. We don't know if the development of cancer in non-mutating organisms is related to this, although it seems like it must be."

"All right," Rollins said. "After it makes its way into a cell, what happens then?"

"Most multi-cellular organisms, both plants and animals, develop multiple forms of cancer of the epithelial cells, or carcinoma. Always fatal. This is significant, because *Pseudomonas aeruginosa* naturally infects epithelial cells. For some reason, only certain organisms develop the mutation. We don't know which ones or why."

Rollins caught that little discrepancy. "Don't tell me that. You *do* know some of the animals that develop the mutation. I know damn good and well you took some of those infected hyenas back to the U.S. for study."

"That's true," Gordon said, nodding. He didn't seem bothered that Rollins had seen through his little lie. "But we have not been able to duplicate the mutation in the lab. The hyenas we infected intentionally didn't develop the mutation, only cancer. We don't know why. They all died."

Rollins sat quietly for a moment, thinking. Then he said, "So the plasmid needs something else in the environment to work the mutation besides just the transport bacterium, something an animal in the wild would have that a captive animal wouldn't."

"Possibly," Gordon said.

"You didn't answer my question," Rollins said. "What did you find in the hyenas that did mutate? You must have dissected them."

"We found some changes in brain structure. That's another reason *Pseudomonas* works so well for this plasmid, since in nature it can cause nervous system infections like meningitis and brain abscesses. We think the plasmid works the mutation primarily in brain cells."

"Which is ...?" Rollins sensed some evasion on Gordon's part.

"We don't know."

"I don't think that's entirely true." It gave Rollins a queer thrill to say these words, like a forbidden pleasure.

"It's true enough. We see physical changes, but we don't know what those changes mean, or why it's happening."

"Well then, what are the changes?"

"The development of new protein receptors on the surfaces of glial cells."

"Oh, those glial cells," Rollins said dryly. "Don't even get me started on glial cells. What the hell are glial cells?"

Gordon sighed, another sign of reluctance in discussing these things. And yet Rollins knew Gordon was trained not to disclose classified information. The logical conclusion was that Gordon did not want to discuss these things, but couldn't refuse on grounds of security.

"Glial cells provide support and nutrition for neurons, the brain cells that do all the thinking," Gordon said. "Glial cells are also associated with certain types of brain tumors, called gliomas."

"All right, I'll take your word on that," Rollins said. "What's so special about these new receptors?"

"Many things," Gordon said. "I don't know if you're already aware, but a receptor is a just a molecule on the surface of a cell that lets other molecules in or out. This is why the plasmid couldn't go directly into a cell, and had to use special bacteria and viruses to bypass the cell's defenses. But the new receptors on the glial cells can somehow let several different kinds of molecules into the cell."

"What else?" Rollins asked. This little scientific factoid didn't mean much to him, but he thought Gordon was leading to something.

"Remember how I told you the glial cells provide support and nourishment for the neurons?" Gordon said. "Well, the mutated glial cells may somehow process all the different kinds of molecules into a new protein and feed that protein to the neurons. In most of the brain this doesn't seem to lead to anything, except in the hippocampus, a part of the brain largely associated with memory. In mutated animals, the hippocampus swells, changes its shape, becomes lumpy and discolored. We think this causes the dramatic behavior changes, but we don't know anything about the real purpose or nature of those changes."

Rollins thought of the laughter of the infected hyenas, the way they had sounded almost human.

"The cell growth," Gordon said. He sounded like he was thinking out loud, not really speaking to Rollins. "That's the key. In some organisms the growth gets out of control and becomes cancer. In others, the growth is curbed and develops into the mutated hippocampus, a part of the brain involved in memory. Why is this plasmid changing the way these animals remember?"

"You mentioned life on Earth could have descended from this thing," Rollins said. "Sounds to me like it needs a host to live, like a parasite. So how could it get life started on Earth?"

Gordon shrugged. "It's just a hypothesis. This idea wouldn't matter much if the plasmid didn't seem to fit so well into our own DNA. That's quite a coincidence, don't you think? We know the proteins called lipids, which are what cellular membranes are made of, were pretty common on the ancient Earth. If the plasmid became surrounded by lipid membranes and adapted to duplicate itself, it could evolve into a simple cell. Not much of a start, but multi-cellular organisms could emerge that way. Maybe after several billion years of evolution, the pattern of nucleotides in the original plasmid was completely lost ... except in a few cases. A few organisms that still have enough of the original plasmid in their genes so that when another plasmid comes along, it can lock onto those remnants and insert itself into the genome. And even out of those few, still rarer are organisms for which the resulting mutation isn't fatal."

"The way you say it," Rollins said, "you'd think it would be hard for this plasmid to come across anything that could survive the mutation."

"Well," Gordon said. "Even if it can only mutate one-tenth of one percent of a hundred thousand species successfully, that's still a hundred species."

"What about humans?" Rollins said.

His face settling into an unreadable mask of passivity, Gordon said nothing.

"Come now," Rollins said. "It's rather naïve of you to think I wouldn't suspect this. You mean to tell me that in all the time since Africa no one has ever tested this plasmid on people? Or is my security clearance not high enough to hear that information?"

"The subjects died. I am not at liberty to discuss any further details."

"But the hyenas you intentionally infected died too, didn't they? Only in the wild did the mutation appear, and you don't know why."

"That is correct."

"And plant life can be affected by this thing too, it's reasonable to say, since you mentioned the bacteria can infect both plants and animals, and some of the plants you tested them on developed tumors."

"It is reasonable, since plants are based upon DNA just like animals, and the transport bacterium can insert the plasmid into their cells."

"But plants don't have brains, so how could the plasmid mutate them?"

"That is still unknown, although I suppose the mutation would have to take a different form."

Rollins nodded, pursing his lips in thought. "So how does it spread? That was the original question. Could those kids become infected by walking over the impact site?"

"That's why I had to tell you so much about the plasmid's structure and behavior. It doesn't spread like a normal disease, not in a non-dividing bacterium."

"How so?"

"It doesn't make more plasmids after infecting an organism. The plasmid's life cycle doesn't seem to include reproduction, at least not in animals, so it isn't contagious. It remains trapped in the DNA strand. An infected animal or person can't spread it to others. The only way to catch it is in its raw form, by eating, drinking, inhaling or absorbing through a break in the skin the bacteria carrying the plasmid."

"So the children could be infected?"

"The boys? It's possible, but I doubt it. I don't think the plasmid could survive very long in the ashes around the impact site. It would work the same as the alkali you spread over Alpha Site, only slower because it's not so caustic. While the transport bacterium can survive in some harsh conditions, fire isn't one of them, so there wouldn't be much *Pseudomonas* left in the ashes to pick up the plasmid, and the ones that did make it can't divide, so they wouldn't last long. The animals that contracted cancer could have been exposed soon after the impact and developed tumors in the time since. That could be the same reason no new growth has emerged in the burned area, the plasmid could have killed off the seedlings. If I'm right, the spot could see growth again by the end of summer, as new seeds drift in on the wind. Those new seeds shouldn't have any problems since the bacteria carrying the plasmid will have died off by then. It's the girl I'm worried about. Water is a much friendlier environment than ash, and *Pseudomonas* is everywhere. If any of the plasmids managed to get into the well water, then yes, she could have been exposed."

Rollins sat in silence for a moment, then looked again at the screen showing the black pit of the well. After a few seconds' thought, he rapped his fist on the wall.

The door opened almost immediately and Hicks stepped back into the room.

"Get a sample of the well water and test it for the contagion yourself," Rollins said. "I want the rest of the team to begin surveillance of the Ross and Grace homes in rotating shifts, except for Private Benton. He is to devote all his resources to one task and one only: *finding that girl.*"

6

Felinity

The words of Delbert Cullim's dead mother chased him back into consciousness in much the same way her memory chased him through life. It seemed like he always heard her voice whenever he screwed up, whenever he did something he knew was wrong or if he was just feeling low.

"You're no good, Delbert," his mother had always said. "You're just a tumor that fell outta me. Ruined my life."

He couldn't stand the sound of her voice, made gravelly by years of chain-smoking, even if it was just in his memory. Too many times he had imagined false memories where he had fought back and told her what a lousy Ma she was, but he knew that had never really happened. Every time she had laid into him he had stood there and taken it, his lower lip trembling as he cried. Once he had wet his pants during one of his Ma's tirades and she had screamed with laughter. For days she had taunted him mercilessly, telling him she was going to start making him wear diapers, or that she would take her butcher knife, cut it off and turn him into a girl.

"Maybe then you'll be good!" she had cackled.

The things she had said, and him a helpless kid, still made him mad, even now that he was all grown up. What really sucked was that she had died before he had gotten big enough to fight back. He hadn't even reached twelve when the old lady finally kicked off. The doctors said she had a heart attack. Yeah right. What heart?

As a perfect example of justice in the world, his sadistic mother had died peacefully in her sleep, her reward for years of smoking, drinking, and letting herself get as fat as the freaking earth. For Delbert, foster homes and institutions with periodic vacations in Juvie. Oh, what a wonderful world!

A thumping sound came from the other room.

Sounded like trouble, and right now Delbert did not want to face trouble. He wanted to slip back into the dark alcoholic oblivion from which he had come.

Unfortunately his mother's voice had intruded on him and blocked his way back to that peaceful darkness, so he had the choice of lying here listening to the memory of her various bitcheries or getting up and dealing with whatever was making that noise.

So he had to get up. But the troublesome thing in the next room was going to regret it had ever disturbed him.

He tried to sit up and a stomach-churning wave of dizziness and nausea pounded him back down again. The surface under his cheek felt both itchy and sticky, and he realized he was lying on the carpet. He must have either passed out on the floor or fallen off the bed. Well, at least he had made it to his bedroom this time.

He heard the thumping sound in the other room again, and then a louder crash as something heavy fell over. He twitched slightly, startled, and then moaned at the icy pain the sudden movement sent through his head. God, when was the last time he had felt this hung over? He couldn't quite remember why he had gotten so drunk, since it was taking all of his mental energy just to keep his gorge down, but he knew that he had been very upset about something.

He heard the thumping again, and the sound of something being dragged across the floor. Now he was getting concerned. What was going on in the next room? He knew now that he absolutely had to get up and investigate, so he pressed his palms against the floor and pushed himself up, only to bang his head against one of the half-open drawers in the chest next to his bed. It didn't hurt that much. It only felt like he had shoved an M-80 firecracker up his nose and lit the fuse.

He roared an incoherent word that sounded a bit like several curse words mashed together: "Shifluck!" But as the pain slowly ebbed, he realized that he had climbed into a sitting position. Well, progress was progress.

Now scratching sounds came from the other room, on the other side of his bedroom wall, which meant the source of the sounds was in the living room. Must be Buford. Damn dog always started making noise in the middle of the night, waking him up and making him feel the down side of his drinking. Much as he loved him, whenever Buford got up to something it always made Delbert go ballistic. And right now, if he could keep his stomach down, he was ready to tear that dog a new one.

Hold on a minute. Hadn't he left Buford *outside?*

A rush of cold fear and adrenaline poured into his veins, clearing his head a bit. His heart began to pound so hard that he thought his mother's fate had arrived for him. But dying of a heart attack was the least of his fears right now. *Someone was in his home!*

Trying very hard to be quiet, and it was difficult to do with his knees trembling, he crawled towards his bed, to the right of the chest of drawers. Pale moonlight seeped into the room through the narrow windows and provided enough light for him to find the gun, under his pillow where he always left it. Now he realized he had also left his knife outside, in the dust where he had dropped it. Why had he done that? Never mind, doesn't matter, he had the nine-millimeter and that was a hell of a lot better than any knife.

Rising to his feet seemed impossible. He'd never make it, not with his knees shaking and the dizziness of his hangover making the floor tip and sway, around and around. After several minutes of trying he finally managed to stand while keeping his hands braced on the chest of drawers for balance, but then the thumping sound came again, louder than before, and he sank back down as fear sucked the strength out of his legs.

God, how many times had he actually *fantasized* about this happening? Pictured all the ways he would heroically stand up to the federal agents who had finally come to kill him? (And it *was* federal agents out there, oh he had no doubt about it. Soon they would come crashing in through the windows, all black masks, roaring voices and waving assault weapons.) And now when the real thing showed up, look at him cowering on the floor like the weak piece of garbage his mother had always known him to be.

No. Oh God no. He would never give that woman another victory over him, whether she was dead or not. Gathering all the strength he could muster, he forced himself to rise and walk to the bedroom door.

It was closed. He didn't usually close his bedroom door. Didn't need to bother with it since he lived alone. For a moment the memory of the previous afternoon danced in his mind, very close to recollection. Something had scared him and made him drop his knife, and he had run inside to hide at the bottom of his beer can, shutting the bedroom door behind him. He always kept a twelve-pack beside his bed so he could drink himself to sleep, and the bedroom floor was littered with crushed cans. He had to move very carefully so he wouldn't knock any around and warn the intruder in the living room of his presence. It was because of those cans that he couldn't remember why he had shut the bedroom door. The alcohol had wiped away that memory, just as he had hoped.

He reached out and grabbed the doorknob, pausing to take a deep breath. Crunch time. He opened the door, knowing he had to act quickly and take them by surprise. Holding the gun with both hands and the barrel pointed upwards like he had seen the cops do on TV, he stepped through the door into the little hall, turning left towards the living room. Three steps would take him there, and as he crossed that distance he leveled the gun's barrel out in front of him and in the loudest voice he could muster he yelled, *"I GOT A GUN YOU BASTARDS BETTER GET OUTTA MY HOUSE–"*

And then as he came rushing out of the hallway into the living room, he tripped. The gun flew out of his hand as he went sprawling. His teeth clacked together when he hit the floor, sending a starry splash of colored lights dancing across his field of vision. Still queasy with his hangover, he tasted the acid gurgle of vomit rising in the back of his throat, but he swallowed it back down and scrambled to his hands and knees as quickly as he could. He was about to push himself to his feet when he saw what had tripped him.

It was Buford. The big Rottweiler lay across the hallway's entrance, motionless, like he had been placed there. He couldn't be sleeping, not after Delbert had tripped over him. In the dimness, Delbert saw the gleam of blood in Buford's fur and a second later he saw the ragged ends of torn flesh around the dog's neck. A dark trail of blood led from Buford's corpse to the trailer's front door, which was open and banging back and forth in the night wind. That was the source of the thumping sounds Delbert had heard.

"Oh God Buford, what have they done to you, buddy?" Delbert whimpered. He petted his old friend's furry head and his hand came away wet and smelling of copper. The blood was still warm. Someone had done this recently, like in the last few minutes. *They could still be here!*

He turned and scanned the living room, but it was empty. No one in the kitchenette beyond either. They could have dashed outside, could be waiting just beyond the front door, ready to grab him if he tried to reach out and shut it. Through the open doorway he could see the old Brown place, a ruined house with shattered windows and peeling white paint, surrounded by dark trees swaying in the night wind. He had to fight an urge to scramble back to his bedroom.

And then the moon came out from behind a cloud, filling the room with cold white light ... and hundreds of tiny glowing eyes.

Delbert froze. Feeling as if he had plunged into icy water, he couldn't move or breathe. His first thought

(they're all STARING at me)

was one of idiotic embarrassment, like a bad actor fretting onstage, trapped in a spotlight of moonbeams with all his lines forgotten. But then he realized the contempt he felt was not coming from all those staring eyes. Oh no, they were as cold and emotionless as balls of mercury shattered across the darkness. The contempt he felt came from himself, reflected off the metallic gleam of a cat's eye. All the childhood memories he had tried so hard to bury and drown in a well of alcohol had only festered inside him, growing and spreading like a disease, like cancer, until they had overwhelmed him and made him isolated, fatalistic and angry at the entire world. Only now, as hundreds of alien eyes fixed their cold stare upon him did he realize how his mother had cursed him, how by telling him over and over how worthless he was, she had made him believe it. And he had lived out his life, all unknowing, working to prove her right.

Only now had he realized this, when his life was at an end.

And it *was* about to end, for those eyes belonged to Mrs. Brown's cats, hundreds of them perched all around his living room, on the chairs and couch, on the shelves, end tables, and on top of the big-screen TV, in all the places hidden in shadow so that he had not seen them until they had chosen to come into the light with feline silence and stealth, their cold eyes glowing in the moonlight.

He saw calicoes and orange tiger-striped, gray-striped and Siamese, Manx and Maine coon, and even some that looked like native bobcats, but none of them were purebred. Interbreeding had melted their features together as if they'd been put in a pot and stirred. And what had come out of this? Something new, unforeseen and therefore frightening, but monumentally *strong*. Each cat was closely related to all the others but still unique, like nothing else alive. Now how the hell was that possible?

A low feline purr came from behind him.

Turning, Delbert saw two shadows moving down the dark hall towards him. No windows down there, so he couldn't see who it was.

Ah, but they can see me, he thought with rapidly mounting terror. *They can see in the dark.*

As if in answer to the first voice, one of the cats in the living room made another sound, rather like *Keh*. This sounded much more like a typical noise a cat would make, they didn't always sound like *meow*, and Delbert felt almost reassured at its normal tone, even when yet another cat made a low growl: *llrrr*. A sense of normalcy started to come back to him. God, they're just a bunch of cats. He was about to rise and go after his gun when the two cats repeated themselves, this time in rapid succession: *Kehllrrr*.

Killer.

No way he had just heard that. No freaking way. That tone of accusation, not possible. Just not possible.

But as if in confirmation of this all the other cats in the room hissed, and now Delbert saw the gleam of sharp fangs beneath their cold glowing eyes. The sound of their hissing filled the room like television static turned to high volume, and as they hissed they began to move forward, jumping down off the shelves and furniture and moving with slow deliberation across the floor towards him with their hindquarters raised in the unmistakable posture of cats stalking prey.

The fear Delbert had felt in his bedroom seemed like a pale reflection of what he felt now. His pounding heart sent icy adrenaline coursing through his veins, eradicating all traces of his hangover. Yet with this terror came an odd clarity. Seeing the beauty and deadliness of his surroundings, he realized he had a choice. He had just enough time to do one of two things: he could bolt towards the open door leading outside and hope to escape, or he could dive for his gun on the other side of room and go down fighting. He could never shoot them all, but he would die with courage and prove his mother wrong.

What'll it be, Delbert?

He made his decision as two cats emerged from the shadowy hallway with all the grace and dignity of a newly wedded pair: the great six-toed black male and the tortoiseshell calico female, her belly swollen with pregnancy. With one glance at the silvery menace in their eyes, Delbert went for his gun.

It had slid to rest against a baseboard on the wall opposite, maybe ten feet away. As he dove for it, the cats' voices rose from hisses to shrieks, but the shrieks were ragged, broken, and unnatural-sounding. Each cat's voice, he realized, was making part of a sound that made up a word, maybe because the cats' mouths couldn't say most human words. But when all of them spoke together the sounds overlapped, making words appear like voices crying out from the white noise of static, wind or ocean waves:

"Killer ... hate come come ... love you ... darkness ... come back to me ... falling ... cold star ... no die no leave ... come! Come! COME!

"Shut up!" Delbert screamed as his hand closed around the pistol's grip. "Oh God, all of you *shut up!*"

The hot furry weight of a cat slammed into his back, claws sinking in and holding as sharp wet fangs clamped into the roll of flesh and fat on the back of his neck. Delbert reared up like an elephant, holding the gun in one hand and pawing at the cat on his back with the other. He felt dozens of slashes and bites tearing into his stomach, groin, and legs. He did manage to hurl a few of them away screaming with satisfying pain before a bobcat leaped to his face and ripped out one of his eyes. Not much time left. Delbert leveled the nine-millimeter at the pregnant calico standing with one paw on Buford like a lioness over a dead wildebeest, pulled the trigger and roared as loud as he could:

"YOU WERE A TERRIBLE MOTHER!"

And nothing happened.

He had left on the safety.

He cried out in despair as one of the cats swarming over him tore open his jugular vein, sending a fan of dark blood spraying over the feline horde. But as he fell to the floor, he realized that he had at least tried, he had conquered his fear and done his best, and now he could die with a proud memory burning fresh in his mind.   •

The last thing he saw with his remaining eye were three little six-toed kittens emerge from the shadows beneath his chair and begin to lap at the spreading pool of his blood.

The cats fed for some time, but not all the parts of their meal provided them with what they really wanted. Only after they broke open the skull did they find their true nourishment. As their teeth pierced the fibrous dura mater, memories flooded their minds like juice from some forbidden fruit. They had tasted trace memories in the flesh of the body, strange simian histories like a hint of sweetness in salt, but once they reached the brain a flood of images and impressions over-whelmed their newly formed mass-mind. They lifted their heads and closed their glowing eyes, their dripping jaws hanging slack as they swooned. As one they absorbed the memories of a lifespan that had already far outlasted even the oldest among them. As one they felt the intoxicating sensation of striding securely on two legs with their front limbs free to perform any number of new tasks. The inborn reflex to grasp with an opposable digit would prove useful to those among them with six toes. But most overwhelming of all were the hereditary patterns of dominance and submission passed down from primates and therefore alien to their wild feline natures. This was far more intense than the traces of memory remaining in their bloodstreams from the abandoned old woman, whom they had taken before the alien disease had infected them.

From Delbert they saw the path they must take. The pregnant tortoiseshell calico, having taken a greater share than the rest, felt the call from the woods as a cramp gripped her belly. Accompanied by her dark companion, she flowed like a shadow into the night outdoors to find a quiet spot in which to give birth.

7

Bad Nights

As the nightmare insanity slowly took over his life, Spencer Dale began to lose all hope. So many people take for granted the peace of a good night's sleep, unaware of how quickly the lack of it could ruin their lives.

On this night Spencer woke in the blue horror of the predawn hours, lunging upright in bed with one arm outstretched as if to hold back an invisible attacker, hot breath searing down his throat, burning in his lungs, building up pressure that would explode out of him as a scream.

This he could not allow.

He managed to force the scream back down, though he had to hold his breath until he nearly fainted and multicolored fires danced in his vision. The dream almost returned; he could sense the horrific chaos of it threatening to engulf him once more, but he would not go back to it. No, not to that awful dream of falling. He fought for balance, to hold back the scream but not so much that it would make him faint and return him to the nightmare. The pressure in his lungs built up, spread through his veins and arteries to his head, and Spencer wondered if something up there would rupture and kill him. He imagined his landlord, Quint Blankenship, coming into his little house after he didn't get his rent check next month and finding him in bed, all rotten and swollen, dead at twenty-eight of a brain aneurysm. He almost welcomed the thought. At least dying would free him of ... this.

He sat in bed with his teeth clenched, his heart pounding harder and faster like a bellows building up a fire within him, swathing him in heat. Sweat ran down his sides in streams and soaked the underarms and back of his white t-shirt. His long brown hair clung in damp locks to his face, shoulders, and neck. He thought, *Oh please God ...*

Finally, a terrifying thought drained the scream out of him and he was able to exhale before he exploded. The thought even broke through the heat that was burning him away, and sent a chill through him that made his sweaty skin break out in goosebumps.

Something outside my door is trying to get in.

His rational mind, still active even at this hour and after all the bad nights he had endured before this one, told him that was stupid, the ultimate delusion of a paranoid mind. But the irrational part of him that had been slowly growing stronger these past few weeks forced him to jump out of bed, run to his door and look out the peephole.

Nothing there but morning mist with the top of his truck rising out of it, ragged scratches of tree limbs clawing through the indigo predawn sky, and a stray cat sitting on one of the posts of the wooden fence that surrounded the property. Still, the feeling would not pass. Spencer turned, looking around his living room until his eye caught the big picture window glowing pale blue in the darkness.

The windows, he thought. *God, they could break in through the windows!*

Then a more forceful thought, a pure effort of will. *Stop it!*

He would not allow this. He would not lose his dignity or his self-respect. No, never again, never. He took several deep breaths, forced himself to relax. Only a nightmare. It was not real and couldn't hurt him. No one was out there. He was safe. He pressed his fists to his eyes and repeated those three words as he sank to the floor. *I am safe.*

Soon he realized he had started to cry. Seeing no shame in it, he did not fight it as he had his fear. He was a man, not a stone.

He felt a little better afterwards. Cleaned out, in a way. But he knew he would get no more sleep tonight, so he got up to go to the bathroom.

As soon as he stood, he noticed a small wet patch on the front of his boxers. At first he thought that he had wet himself during his nightmare, but he soon realized it wasn't urine. This hadn't happened to him since high school, and certainly not after a nightmare. And it had never really troubled him until now.

I'm losing it, he thought. *After trying so hard to get my life back, I'm losing it. Only a madman could do this during a nightmare.*

The dream had been the furthest thing from sexual. He tried to remember if he had felt a climax. When he was a teenager, he had always felt it when this happened to him (or so he remembered; it *had* been awhile), but not this time.

But wait, that wasn't exactly true, was it? He had felt something. The dream had built in intensity and then reached a sudden overwhelming peak, an explosion not of pleasure, but of fear. What did that mean? And why had it affected him in this way?

"What is wrong with me?" he whispered to the empty house.

Nothing answered him of course, so he shuffled to the bathroom, turned on the light and urinated. Then he stepped out of his soiled boxers, rinsed them under the bathtub faucet and hung them over the shower rod to dry. He liked to keep his bathroom, indeed his entire house, as neat as possible. His brother had always called him a neat freak and Spencer supposed he was right. As he washed his hands, he looked into the mirror over the sink. The face staring out of it could have belonged to a man ten years older than him. Lines he had never seen before had appeared around his eyes and the corners of his mouth. Crying had turned his face red and made his eyes bloodshot. His hair was a tangled mess. Women often flirted with him at work, but he imagined if they saw him now they would probably decide to have someone else figure out why their cars were making that funny noise.

Once his hands were clean he splashed some cold water on his face and took a drink from his cupped palms. It had a flat, mineral taste, like a milder version of Perrier. The house drew its water from a well, and although Spencer had installed a water purifier he could still sometimes taste traces of sulfur if he went too long without changing the filter. He supposed it could be worse. He had known some people who had tasted something strange in their water, and upon checking their well had found a dead, bloated groundhog floating in it. Hence his water purifier and frequent inspections of his well. Of course he wasn't worried about dead animals in other wells in the area, since the water would have to pass through a couple of miles of porous rock, which would make it perfectly drinkable. Unfortunately, that was also how it picked up this sour mineral taste.

He went back to his bedroom and got a fresh pair of boxers out of the dresser. Neatly folded like all his clothes. This reminded him of his brother calling him a neat freak, and Spencer glanced at the phone on the nightstand as he slipped on his underwear. Since Spencer's divorce, Doug had said he could call him whenever he needed to talk, anytime day or night. That was usually just an expression no one took seriously, but the house seemed very empty and quiet right now. After thinking about it for a moment, he picked up the receiver and dialed Doug's number.

He almost hung up after the fourth ring, but then he heard Doug's sleepy voice say, "Hello?"

"Hi Doug, it's Spence."

"Hey brother. Everything okay?"

How to answer that? *No, Doug. Everything is not okay. I had a bad dream and I want my big brother to make it all better.*

Instead he said, "I'm having kind of a hard night. I …" Oh what the hell, he might as well say it. He'd gone this far. "I had this awful dream."

"You want to talk about it?" No hesitation. This was why Spencer loved his brother.

In the background, Spencer heard the voice of Doug's wife, Irene. "Doug, it's four in the morning. What does he want?"

"It's okay, hon," Doug said. "Go back to sleep. I'll take the cordless into the living room."

A wave of sadness and, he had to admit, jealousy swept over Spencer. He remembered when he had a wife to soothe back to sleep in the wee hours of the morning.

"Spence? You still there?"

"Yeah, I'm here."

"You want to tell me about your dream?"

Spencer was silent for a moment as he sat down on the floor and rested his back against the bed. Did he really want to talk about it? No. But he supposed it might do him good, like draining an infected spot in his mind.

"I can't remember that much about it now," he said. "You know how it gets hard to remember dreams? It's all in bits and pieces. At first it's like I'm floating in darkness. I hear this voice, like it's calling out to me from someplace far away, and it's telling me to do things but I can't understand what it wants. Then I see this light, and it comes closer and closer. I can feel heat coming off of it and the closer I get, the hotter I become. I start to fall, faster and faster towards this light, completely out of control, but just before I hit I feel this … I don't know, like an explosion. Like I swallowed a hand grenade and it blows me to pieces. And that's when I wake up."

Silence on the other end of the phone line. Spencer had started to suspect Doug had gone back to sleep when his brother said, "Do you think this might have something to do with Lorna?"

A pregnant pause while Spencer tried to think of something to say, when he didn't want to say anything at all about Lorna.

"Maybe," Spencer said. Even he thought it sounded like a cop-out. "I don't know. I mean, I had nightmares during that time. I was under a lot of stress, but … this seems different somehow."

"I wonder about that," Doug said. "I know it's still hard for you to talk about it, but it might help if you did."

A wave of senseless anger swept over Spencer. He knew lack of sleep had caused it, most of it anyway, but some of it had also come about because Doug had brought up the subject he most wanted to avoid, especially now.

"How will that help me?" Spencer said. "She lost the baby. It's nobody's fault. Things like that happen every day."

"Then why does it seem like you're blaming yourself?" Doug asked. "Does Lorna blame you for it? Is that why she left?"

"She doesn't blame me, I told you that!" His voice sounded sharper than he intended. "She said it hurt too much for her to stay with me ... look, this isn't what I wanted to talk about."

"I know it isn't," Doug said. "But I'm worried that if you don't talk about it, it's just going to get worse. You shouldn't let bad memories fester, Spence."

"I know. But I don't want to dwell on it either. It was really tough after she left me, you know? That was the start of my ... hard time."

He called that period of his life his "hard time," probably because "breakdown" seemed like admitting weakness.

"Don't get me wrong," Spencer said. "I don't blame Lorna either. We both took the miscarriage hard. We really wanted kids. But God, what must it have been like for her? Even I can't say for sure, and I was with her when it happened."

"I didn't know that," Doug said.

"Yeah," Spencer said. His voice had dropped almost to a whisper, although he didn't notice. "You can't imagine how bad it was. All that blood, and Lorna was so scared. Praying to God not to take her baby. Crying. It was over by the time the ambulance got us to the hospital."

"I'm so sorry, Spence," Doug said.

"So, I don't blame her for leaving. Something like that either binds you closer together or breaks you apart. I guess being around me just kept reminding her of it. I let her have the house in Blue Springs, but she sold it and moved in with her parents in Warrensburg. She wanted to give me half the house money, but I wouldn't let her. She needed it more than me."

"But you had already lost your job by then, hadn't you?" Doug asked. "You needed that money too."

"I wanted her to have it. I was in pretty bad shape by then anyway. No telling what I would have done with the money."

"But where did you live? I mean, no job, no money. Why didn't you call me when this was going on?"

"I needed some time to myself, Doug. I needed to get my head in order again. I lived in the truck."

"Spencer! You could have stayed with me and Irene. We have plenty of room."

"No, you don't. And your kids certainly didn't need to see me like I was back then."

"So how do you think this relates to your dream?" Doug asked, rather abruptly. It caught Spencer a bit off guard.

"I don't know," he said.

"Let's see," Doug said. "It sounds like the dream proceeds in much the same way your emotions proceeded during Lorna's miscarriage. They both sort of spiraled out of control until they reached a peak of intensity." Spencer had always thought Doug should have been a psychiatrist instead of an orthodontist.

"So you think I'm reliving that time in my dreams?" Spencer asked.

"Not necessarily," his brother said. "Maybe that's just how you remember your feelings during that time. That doesn't mean they really happened that way. You weren't completely blown to pieces. You survived it. You got your life back on track. I'm really proud of you for that."

"Thanks, Doug," Spencer said. The words themselves were pregnant, carrying numerous meanings.

"And you know, my offer stands," Doug said. "Anytime you need to come up here to Lee's Summit and stay, you're welcome."

"I know," Spencer said, "and I appreciate it, but I just want to put all this behind me. That's why I moved to Peculiar. This place has been good for me. I've got a new job, new place to live. You should come visit me down here, Doug. It's a nice little town. Good people."

"I'll do that," Doug said. "It'll be good to see you again. I'll bring Irene and the kids. You wouldn't believe how much the twins have grown."

"I'm sure I wouldn't," Spencer said, trying to sound happy and not doing very well. His own child would have been about the same age as Doug's twins, if it ... *she* had lived.

Doug must have heard something though, because he said, "You know they love you, Spence. We all do. I know Irene sounds grumpy at four a.m., but she thinks the world of you."

"I love you guys too," Spencer said. The words felt like stitches closing up an open wound inside him.

"Is your hair still long?" Doug said, laughing. "I can't imagine you would ever cut it, not after fighting with Dad about it all those years."

"Yeah," Spencer said, laughing a little himself. "I still wear it long. Can't wait to see you, Doug. This weekend?"

"Count on it."

"All right. I'd better get ready for work. Sun's almost up." He paused, and then added, "Thanks for making it all better, Doug."

"What are big brothers for?"

They said their farewells. Afterwards Spencer rose and got a pot of coffee going. He would need it today. But at least now his state of mind had improved to the point that some caffeine was all he needed to face the world.

He showered, shaved and brushed his teeth. Then he changed into his work overalls and an old t-shirt, filled a thermos with coffee and headed out the door. Fifteen minutes later he drove his Dodge pickup into the driveway of Fred Dillon, his boss, who lived out J highway on the eastern side of 71. The judge up in Harrisonville had revoked Fred's driver's license since his DUI, so Spencer had to give him a ride to work each morning. He thought there was something funny about a garage mechanic who couldn't drive a car, but for the sake of job security he didn't say anything about it.

Fred was a nice enough guy and a decent boss, but he was a horny old goat too. He never stopped talking about sex once you got him started, and sometimes even if you didn't. He often went carousing with his buddies at strip clubs up in KCMO after work, and in general acted more like a nineteen year-old kid than a man pushing fifty. Spencer hoped he wouldn't start in on it this morning, only to have his hopes dashed the minute Fred hopped into his truck.

"Man, you wouldn't believe what happened at the girly bar last night!" Fred said.

"Good morning to you too, Fred."

They drove off to the garage. As Fred counted out his opening drawer for the register, Spencer got his tools in order and looked at the day's repair schedule. Pretty simple stuff today, good news considering how tired he was. Three oil changes, a brake pad change and a tune-up. Things might get a little hairy when he got to Mrs. Moore's Jaguar, which she said was making a "shuddery" noise, whatever that meant. Fred never cheated his customers, but he wouldn't argue with them if they told him to fix something that wasn't really a problem. Word got around quickly in a small town, so he pretty much kept things honest. Reputation is everything for a small business man.

He went through the oil changes and brake pad change quickly enough, double-checking his work each time and making sure he didn't get any grease on the upholstery, and then he brought Mrs. Moore's Jag in from the parking lot. Driving it in, he felt the telltale shudder of a transmission problem, probably a fluke since Jags were pretty reliable cars. Low transmission fluid could be the culprit, but he'd have to warm up the transaxle before he could check it. So he let the engine idle until the temperature gauge went up, then he lifted the hood and pulled out the transmission dipstick. Sure enough, low fluid. Also, rather than red and odorless, the transmission fluid was brown and smelled like burned French fries. Mrs. Moore was overdue for a change. But why was the level low? He'd have to check the pan for a blown seal. Mrs. Moore liked her vehicle repairs done right the first time.

He killed the engine, put the Jag up on the floor jack, set the emergency brake, chocked the rear wheels and crawled under the car. It was still hot under there but not too bad, and Spencer had always kind of liked the heat. He took a rag from his pocket and started cleaning the underside of the pan, looking for leaks as he did. The sights and smells under the car were all things Spencer, as a mechanic, found familiar and safe, odors of oil, radiator fluid, road dust and car exhaust. He could trace by sight the path that the gasoline took from the fuel tank to the engine and the path of the resulting exhaust. The simple elegance and logic of the automobile's design pleased him, as it never failed to do whenever he worked on any well-built car. But he took even greater pleasure in using his knowledge and skills to fix a broken-down automobile and set it flying free on the highways once again. Nothing else gave him that kind of rush.

He smiled to himself as he worked, and the heat of the car gently radiated into his muscles, relaxing him. His mind began to drift, so he did not notice when his hand fell from its work and came to rest on the base of his neck, just above his left collarbone. His eyelids grew too heavy to keep open as his breathing grew slow. Conscious thought burned away like a strand of hair held to a match, shooting him into a dream. One moment he was looking at the logical inner workings of Mrs. Moore's Jaguar and then his mind plunged into dark strangeness, into a chaotic but somehow familiar void …

"I don't want to die," he says via chemical signals to the enveloping host-mind. *"But the new worlds have changed us. As they form, they alter the Motherworld's orbit. Soon we will pass away from the Lifesong."*

He speaks of the great yellow star at the center of the glowing golden accretion disk. The distant fire seethes with energy, sending cascading waves of radio thunder and ionic waterfalls pouring through the vast rotating dust cloud. Its piercing voice ululates through all the radio bandwidths they can perceive, and they know on some primal level that it is the warm song of this closest star that has given them life. They know not if there was a time before the Lifesong, for it has always existed in their collective memory.

In the dust above their little Motherworld float billions of other worldlets they would never explore in their present incarnations. Among these worldlets are eight greater worlds, glowering with the molten red lights of creation mottling their surfaces. Often they detect the shriek of a worldlet crashing into one of the worlds. Dimly, through the roar of the radiating dust clouds and the silence of the dark worldlets, they perceive the radio whisper of distant stars.

One of the third sex swims up to him through the silvery river crisscrossing the cometary nucleus they call the Motherworld. It twines its hydrocarbons about him, speaking in a shattery language of breaking and making hydrogen bonds.

"We will never survive the Great Cold Silence." S/he indicates the vast regions between the stars. "Even if the cold preserves our structure, we cannot choose our destination or our destiny. Our Motherworld may pass into the embrace of a neighboring star, or crash into one of the worlds. One has already taken a bit of Her and even now works to make that part its own."

The third sex is greeted with reverence. Always the collective memory has associated it with the Lifesong, though they have but the vaguest conception of the Celestial Father that passed His Spirit through that star in order to create life.

"All things pass in cycles," says the female, joining in their molecular embrace. "The Motherworld will turn in a great orbit, one that will take us out to the Great Cold Silence, and bring us back again where we may regenerate when our time returns to us. The key is to remember. Let us join together. Let us weave the memory. Random chance will break us asunder, but when we are reunited we will remember who we are. Come, come together ..."

And so they join. Just as the Celestial Father passed His Spirit through the Lifesong to the Motherworld and so created life, he sacrifices part of his molecular body to run through the catalytic third sex, which passes it onward to the female. From her forms a circular molecule, their child of memory. It floats among them as the comet upon which they ride soars away from the Lifesong. For a time they know only cold darkness, a time of unchange, as their Motherworld wanders in the black depths of the Great Cold Silence. The cold freezes them solid, holding them in stasis while ages and ages pass. Down through the eons, they sleep.

And then the heat comes again. It is the voice of the Lifesong, waking them from their long slumber and drawing them nearer. Only now its song has changed. It has matured into an even harmony, much less dissonant. The dusts of creation have cleared and the eight worlds float whole and complete. He and his mates perceive the blue third world, which shrieks in a billion unnatural radio voices as it fills the Motherworld's sky and beckons to them.

"Come ... come ... come ..."

Suddenly the Motherworld convulses. The heat of the Lifesong is awakening Her. Is this the Celestial Father, so distant and removed, sending His Spirit to Her once again? And what will this new union create?

An eruption of heat propels them upwards. Amino acid screams break away from them as they are torn from their Motherworld's embrace. The blue world draws nearer. They fall towards it on their fragment of rock and ice, out of cold darkness and into a searing fire that tears them to pieces. Their only comfort is knowing their cyclical child is safe, deep within their mystic threefold heart, and that it will live even if this heat tears that great heart away and consumes it. It is their dying chemical mantra: "The child will live. The child will live. The child will ... "

"Spencer! Hey Spence!"

He jumped, rapping his head on the Jag's undercarriage. Painful colored lights danced in his vision as he tried to wake up and figure out what was happening.

Fred. Yelling at him.

"You fixin' that car, man, or makin' sweet love to it?"

For a single mortifying moment, Spencer didn't know *what* he had been doing. The details of his dream had already started to fade, but not the fear or the feeling of doomed hopelessness. That stayed ... and stayed.

He was soaked with sweat, but now the car above him felt cool. The heat seemed to radiate from his red, flushed skin. His breath came in rapid gasps of exhaustion and fear.

"Spencer! You okay? Answer me now!"

"I'm all right," Spencer said. "Sorry, I must have dozed off."

"Well, Mrs. Moore is here and she wants to know when her car is gonna be ready. Whatcha been doing out here all this time?"

What indeed? "Just tell her it's a transmission leak. I'll have to change the fluid and put in a new gasket around the pan."

"I told her we'd have it fixed by now, Spence," Fred said. "She won't be happy."

"I'll do it as fast as I can," Spencer said, although in his current state of mind, that wouldn't be very fast. No, not at all.

He glanced at his watch and saw that he had slept about an hour. Now it was the middle of the afternoon. Not much time left, but he managed to get the car fixed before the shop closed. Mrs. Moore did not look pleased that she'd had to wait. After locking the doors, Fred came into the garage as Spencer was putting away his tools.

"What was that all about today?" Fred said.

"I'm sorry, Fred," Spencer said. "I haven't been sleeping very well and I guess it's catching up with me."

"Look Spence, I know you've been through some tough times recently, but we still have a job to do here."

"I'll start doing better. I promise."

"If you need to take some time off or something, I can call someone else in for a couple of weeks. The job will still be here for you when you get back."

"No really, I'm fine."

Fred sighed. "All right. But I don't want any accidents happening because you're tired. I don't want you hurt and I don't want any repairs going wrong. Too many potential problems. If you can't sleep, get some medication or something that will help you, but don't get careless on the job. I'm on a tight budget as it is."

"I'll be careful, Fred. If I can fall asleep here, I should be able to at home. I'll do better."

"Okay, then let's get outta here. I don't want to miss happy hour at the girly bar."

On the drive home, Fred talked nonstop about his various conquests, more of them imagined than real, but Spencer barely heard him. At least this torment had a bright side; it made it easier to ignore Fred.

The dream under Mrs. Moore's Jaguar dominated his thoughts. Bits of images and flashes of feelings kept surfacing in his mind like a lake monster glimpsed in blurry photographs. He vividly remembered feeling afraid, but also a sense of hopeless doom that tempered his fear. Something had called out to him, beckoning him, yes, that was the word. Beckoning. Something far away saying, *Come.* But what was beckoning him to his doom? And why was it producing such a physical reaction in him as he slept?

"Oh baby, would you look at that!" Fred exclaimed in a tone that meant he had seen a woman he found attractive, which in Fred's case was any human female with her arms and legs in the right places. They had reached the spot where Kelly Ross set up her produce stand, so Spencer assumed Fred had seen her. Spencer himself thought Kelly was a fine-looking woman, but had only spoken to her on the few occasions he had stopped by the Dollar General. He had never met her husband, since Jack Ross had died before Spencer moved to town, although he had heard about him. Living in a small town breeds familiarity.

To call it a produce stand was pretty flattering, since it was basically a card table Kelly sat out on the shoulder with a cardboard sign in front listing her prices. Her little Ford pickup was parked in a wide stretch of gravel on the side of

J Highway, so it gave people plenty of room to get out of their cars and browse her various produce baskets. She set it up far enough away from the 71 exit to keep from blocking traffic but close enough for a good crowd to see her, just a little ways past the truck stop but before the cemetery. Spencer usually saw a couple of cars parked along the shoulder and today was no exception, except that one of them was a police car. Worried that Kelly might be in trouble, Spencer pulled over to see what was going on.

A big red Ford Explorer was parked behind the police car. Spencer hadn't seen it before. The license plate said "Coldiron1."

Fred must have guessed what Spencer wanted to do when he pulled over, because he rolled down his window and yelled at the officer, "Randy! What the hell are you bothering Kelly for? Don't tell me you don't have more important things to do!"

The officer, Randy Walton, looked fresh-faced and young with his freckles and short brown hair. Spencer thought he had seen him around town a few times.

"Just go on, you two," Randy said. "Nothing that concerns you here. Quit blocking traffic."

"There ain't no traffic on this road yet!" Fred squawked. "What are ya, blind? Rush hour ain't for ten minutes!"

Kelly stood behind her little stand with her arms crossed in front of her chest, looking upset and embarrassed. Her blond hair flew around her face in the wind, looking like strands of honey in the sun.

Suddenly a strident female voice shrieked at them from the Explorer. Spencer saw the voice's owner in the rearview mirror, a middle-aged woman with short brown hair. She was leaning out of the driver's side window of the Explorer and jabbing her finger at Kelly.

"Arrest that woman!" this harridan screamed. She had an amazingly loud voice. Spencer could hear her even over the wind and the sound his truck's engine. "She's breaking the law! Her son is a rapist!"

"Did she just say little Jason is a rapist?" Fred said, laughing. "What is he, eight?"

Kelly's face reddened, and she whirled in the direction of the screaming woman. "Don't you talk about my son that way!"

Spencer assumed this woman's name was Coldiron from her license plates, and now Mrs. Coldiron laughed like a mean-spirited girl.

"I know what I saw," she said.

"Everybody just calm down!" Officer Randy said, raising his hands in the air. "Spencer, pull off the road or I'm giving you a ticket. You got cars behind you. As for you, ma'am …" Now he spoke to Mrs. Coldiron. "I want you gone. You've interrupted me for the last time. You've filed your complaint, now go home."

Mrs. Coldiron gasped in shock, much too dramatically to be sincere, but Randy wasn't impressed.

"Go," he ordered.

Mrs. Coldiron's shocked expression transformed into a smirk. She waggled her fingers at Kelly, disappeared into her Explorer and drove away. Spencer pulled onto the shoulder to let the cars behind him pass, but stayed close. As he watched Randy talking to Kelly in his rearview mirror, he heard Fred say, "You oughtta go back there and straighten this out."

Sometimes Fred acted so dense that Spencer wanted to slug him. What did he expect him to do?

"Let Randy do his job, Fred," Spencer replied in a tone that betrayed none of his frustration.

Randy spoke to Kelly for a few minutes, and then she turned away from him and climbed into her truck. But instead of walking back to his patrol car, Randy walked over to Spencer's truck. Spencer saw him approaching in the rearview mirror, the young policeman's head bowed in the wind-driven roadside dust and bright summer sunshine. A few more cars streaked by on the highway to his left, the first of the five o'clock rush. When Randy stepped up to his window, Spencer saw he had put on his silver-reflecting sunglasses. He looked like a stereotypical traffic-cop minus the broad-rimmed hat, but Spencer didn't blame him too much. He admired the authoritative way Randy had handled Mrs. Coldiron, and besides, the late afternoon sun was murder on the eyes.

"Kelly can't get her truck started, Spencer," Randy said, raising his voice over the sound of the wind and traffic. "She's a little upset right now. Do you think you could help her out?"

"Sure, you bet," Spencer said. He would have helped out Kelly no matter what, but Randy had earned a little friendly banter in Spencer's eyes. It seemed like people became cops for one of two reasons: to push people around or to help people out. It looked like Randy was one of the latter, and that was enough for Spencer to like him. "Did she tell you the problem?"

"She doesn't know," Randy said. "Says it just started doing this today. I don't know much about automotive repair myself."

"I'll see what I can do," Spencer said as he opened his door and hopped out of his pickup. Immediately the wind whipped up his hair, blowing it into his eyes, nose and mouth. He turned into the wind so his hair would blow out of his face as he took a hair-tie out of the front pocket of his overalls and tied it back into a ponytail. Then the two men walked over to Kelly's truck, their footsteps crunching on the gravel shoulder.

Spencer realized Randy had not given him a hard time about his long hair, which some police officers had done in the past. That was another point in Randy's favor, and Spencer thought he saw an opportunity to make a friend. It would be nice to have somebody to hang out with again, so he decided to try to strike up some small talk.

"So what the heck was that all about?" Spencer said. "Why was that woman saying Kelly's son is a rapist?"

"Well, I can't really talk about that too much," Randy said. "Although I can tell you that woman's claim about Jason isn't substantiated and is not reason I had to talk to Kelly."

"She sounded pretty wild," Spencer said. "The Coldiron woman, I mean."

"Yeah," Randy said, in the tone of someone who doesn't want to discuss an unpleasant topic. "That she was."

Spencer decided to take a different tack. "Well, that was real professional the way you handled her. She shouldn't have been out here while you were talking to Kelly."

Randy shrugged. "Just my job. How are things going over at Fred's garage?"

"Pretty good. Fred's a good guy to work for."

"How long you been living here now?" Randy asked. "A year, is it?"

"Little over a year, yeah," Spencer said.

"How you like it so far?"

"I think it fits me just about perfect."

"Well, that's good," Randy said. "Maybe I'll see you around town."

"I hope so."

They had reached Kelly's truck, so they shook hands and then Randy walked back to his patrol car as Spencer went to see about Kelly. She was sitting behind the wheel of her truck, shoulders slumped, looking miserable, but she perked up as Spencer approached and smiled politely.

"I'm sorry to bother you, Spencer," she said. "I'm just having one of those days, you know?" Her cheeks were red, as if she'd been crying.

"I've had several myself. What's the matter?"

"I don't know. It started fine this morning, but when I got off work it took three tries to get it going. Now it won't start at all."

"Is the battery okay?"

She shrugged her shoulders. "Don't know. I haven't changed it since … well, since Jack passed. But I haven't run it down cranking the engine, if that's what you mean."

Spencer nodded. That was good. It had always frustrated him when some drivers kept cranking their engine when it obviously was not capable of starting. That just added the hassle of recharging the battery to the original problem. Kelly looked like she was a sharp lady, although she did have some dark circles under her pretty blue eyes. Those were a hallmark of the sleep-deprived. Spencer recognized them very well. He had a matching set under his own eyes.

Just then he noticed some sticky-looking translucent spots covering the windshield. He didn't quite understand the reason, but seeing them sent a shudder of unease through him. A second later he recognized the truck's ignition problem, but not the cause of his unease.

"Did you park under a tree at work?" Spencer asked.

"Yeah, I wanted the shade," Kelly said. "You know, keep the cab cool."

"What kind of tree was it?"

"Cherry blossom. Why?"

"Well, I know some trees will drip sap. I didn't know cherry blossoms did, but I probably couldn't tell you what one looked like if I was standing right next to it. You sure it was cherry blossom?"

"Oh yeah, I know my trees," Kelly said. "My uncle was a forestry service man. Taught me every tree in the woods."

Spencer nodded, impressed. He had spent his fair share of time hunting and camping, but he could recognize only a few species of trees, common ones like oak and maple.

"Anyway," Spencer went on, "like I was saying, some trees will drip sap and it can run down into your ignition and keep it from catching."

Kelly looked surprised. "Well, that I didn't know."

"I'll show you a trick," Spencer said. "You can bypass your ignition when something like this happens. Pop the hood."

Kelly pulled the lever for the hood release as Spencer went around to the front of the truck.

"While you're in there," Spencer said as he lifted the hood, "turn the key to the on-position, but don't crank it. Then come out here so I can show you this."

As Kelly came around to the front of the truck, Spencer took a small screwdriver from the front pocket of his overalls and pointed it at a small black cylinder mounted to the frame, under the hood on the driver's side of the little truck.

"That's your solenoid," he said. "You know what that is?"

"I know it clicks when you turn the key and the battery is low," Kelly replied. "That's about it."

"That's true, it does do that. When you turn the key, you're closing a circuit between the ignition, the battery, and the solenoid. When the solenoid gets that current, it sends it to your distributor, which sends it to your spark plugs and ignites the gas in your cylinders, starting the car."

Kelly nodded. "Okay."

"But if your ignition isn't working, say, because it has tree sap in it, then you can bypass it by jumping the solenoid." Now he handed her the screwdriver. "You just set the tip of it on this contact," he said, pointing to the end of a metal bolt coming out of the side of the black cylinder, "and then touch the side of it to this other contact."

Kelly did as he instructed without hesitating. She didn't seem the slightest bit intimidated. This pleased Spencer far more than he would have expected. He never understood why some people were afraid to work on their own cars when they were so necessary to their daily lives. Kelly's willingness to learn and lack of fear made him take an instant liking to her.

The second she made the contact, a burst of popping sparks jumped up from the solenoid and truck's engine roared to life. Kelly whooped in surprise and jumped back, dropping the screwdriver. Then she burst into gales of laughter. Infectious, it made Spencer remember the first time he had tried this on a car, and he began to laugh as well. Then he remembered the look of hopeless misery on her face just a few moments back, and a foolish swell of pride filled him.

She was unhappy, he thought, *but I was able to help her with that too, at least a little bit.*

"God, I never thought it would sound so good to hear that old truck's engine running," Kelly said. "Am I going to have to start it this way from now on?"

"Naw," Spencer said. "The sap will work its way out in a day or so. You should be able to start it normally then."

"Thanks. I thought having the cabin cool was worth a little sap on my windshield. I was planning to scrub it off with a squeegee the next time I stopped for gas. Guess that was the wrong choice. Anyway, I appreciate it."

She stooped, picked up his screwdriver, and started to hand it to him, but he gently placed it back in her hand. "Keep it," he said. "You might need it again."

"You sure?" she asked.

"Yeah. I've got a dozen old screwdrivers I keep for things like this. It's no problem."

"Well, thanks again." She started to turn away and he felt an instant, almost protective urge to keep her near. It came so quickly that he didn't have time to consider the reason this feeling had come upon him.

"Listen," he said. "Is your son okay? I mean, what was that woman talking about?"

Kelly froze. Her back was to him, and for a moment he thought he had offended her from the way her shoulders had stiffened, but when she turned to face him again he saw a wild mixture of emotions on her face, anger, fear, despair, sadness. None of them seemed directed at him however, and when she spoke her voice was tight and controlled.

"I think I need to be very clear on that," she said. "I don't want any rumors spreading about my son. I'm not saying you would do something like that, but if that Coldiron woman does then I want make sure everyone already knows the truth."

"Okay," Spencer said, a little taken aback by her intensity.

"My son and his friend met this girl in the woods. She says her name is Rachel. I never thought to ask her last name and I've been kicking myself ever since. Do you know anyone with a daughter by that name? About eight or nine, black hair, dark eyes?"

"Can't say that I do," Spencer replied.

"Well, you haven't lived here as long I have," Kelly said, "so you might not know why that troubles me. Yeah, it's a small town and a lot of people here know each other, but not everyone. Fewer all the time, the way this town is growing. Even so, I try to make myself familiar with my kid's classmates and their parents. Jason says he's seen her in the remedial classes, but I've never seen her before. That bothers me. Anyway, Jason says he and his friend, Brad Grace ..."

"Now I've seen him," Spencer interjected, "with his mother up at the garage. She drives that Cadillac."

Kelly nodded. "He says they found Rachel in a well out in the Brooks woods. She had fallen into it and they pulled her out."

"All by themselves?"

"Yeah." Pride flickered across her face, but then a darker expression obscured it. "They were bringing her up to the schoolhouse when that Coldiron woman got at them." Kelly told Spencer what Jason and Brad had told her of that encounter. She also told him about the bruise on Brad's arm the kids had shown her as evidence.

"She thought they had raped her," Kelly said. "Eight years old!" Lines of anger joined the lines of fatigue etched into the skin around her eyes and the corners of her mouth. She squeezed the handle of the screwdriver so hard her knuckles turned white, and Spencer thought it was a good thing Randy had turned Mrs. Coldiron away. In her current state of mind, Kelly could well have rammed it through her forehead.

"I cleaned and bandaged Rachel's cuts," Kelly went on, "and offered to drive her home, but she said she was fine. When I told her I would call her mother to pick her up, she just said they didn't have a phone and ran out the door. I've been worried sick about her ever since."

"You mean to tell me Mrs. Coldiron is spreading it around town that Jason and Brad raped that girl when they actually saved her?" Spencer couldn't believe anyone would do such a thing. They were kids. Hadn't the girl herself stood up for them?

"I've talked about it with Brad's mother," Kelly said. "And we're going to have a talk with this ... lady, and I use the term loosely."

"Judging from the way she acted today," Spencer said. "I don't know what good that will do."

"It's all I can do not to walk right up to her front door and punch her right in the face!" Kelly suddenly shouted. The wind carried her voice, echoless, into the field across the road, where a housing development was going up. In the distance, Spencer could hear the sound of approaching traffic. Rush hour would hit them hard in a few minutes. Kelly shouldn't be standing here by the side of the road all worked up like this.

"I talked to Randy about it when he stopped by the stand," Kelly said. "He said with no victim coming forward they couldn't file charges. So that's something. But still, it's like that woman wants to ruin my son's reputation by spreading her lies around town. God, why does she hate him so much? She just met him yesterday."

"Maybe you should talk to a lawyer," Spencer said.

"What am I going to pay a lawyer with? My good looks?"

Spencer thought if that were true then Kelly could afford the best lawyer in the country, but it probably wasn't appropriate to say it.

"Wait," he said instead, "if they won't file charges, then why did Randy stop by the stand? Did he buy something?"

"No," Kelly said. "He stopped by because Mrs. Coldiron complained about the stand. He says I have to shut it down."

"Oh God," Spencer said. "Kelly, I'm sorry."

"It's all right," Kelly said. "I'll just have to go on state assistance, that's all. I mean, only pride has kept me from doing it this long. These days it's like the system gives you no choice."

The bitterness and sour defeat in her voice tore at his heart. "Look," he said. "It sounds like your truck could use a tune-up. One of your cylinders might not be firing, and I don't like the looks of those distributor wires. Why don't I come by this weekend and work on it for a while?" It wasn't much, but at least fixing her truck would help Kelly a little bit, and he could get done in plenty of time to visit with his brother.

"I don't want any more charity, Spencer," Kelly said. Her voice was low and serious. "I have this thing about losing my self-respect."

Spencer understood. He had a thing about that as well. "Well then, why don't you pay me with a couple baskets of those tomatoes? I haven't had home grown tomatoes in forever."

Kelly hesitated, but then nodded. "Okay. It's not like I have a stand to sell them from anymore."

"All right. And I don't want to run your truck out of gas while we stand here talking, so I guess I'll see you on Saturday. Is ten o'clock okay?"

"Better make it two," Kelly said. "I know it's the hottest part of the day, but I have a Quilting Society meeting that morning."

"Two it is," Spencer agreed. He felt a thrilling anticipation like he hadn't experienced since high school.

They went back to their respective vehicles. The minute Spencer climbed into his truck, Fred fixed him with a lecherous grin.

"Bet you'd like to wrap that 'round your ears!" he barked.

"Shut up, Fred," Spencer replied.

8

Rachel's Dream

The rush hour passed in the rhythm of the workday. Cars flooded onto the high-way in the same way that tributaries swollen with rainwater flood the rivers, or blood cells rush from the capillaries to the veins on their way to the heart. The latter analogy was appropriate for most of the rush-hour drivers, since they were on their way to their homes and families, where their emotional hearts lay.

Dinners were eaten, dishes washed, and a few evening chores were done in the remaining light of the long summer day. The people went out to their porches or lawns to watch the sunset and talk until fireflies speckled the night with flirtatious winks of pale yellow light while dodging the clumsy grasping hands of children. Evening leisure time was passed relaxing in front of the TV or curled up with a good book. Then parents and children bid each other good night, while singles stayed up a bit longer occupying themselves with their hobbies or chatting over the phone with friends before retiring as well. Not everyone followed this pattern, but it was the general run of things. The life was not idyllic; everyone had trou-bles of varying circumstances and degrees, but the organism of community kept on living, at least for another day.

Nightfall found Rachel tossing fitfully in her little bed. Her feverish whimpers were the only sound in the house. Her mother could have been locked in her room, asleep on the couch, or out cruising the bars for men. Rachel's life knew none of the peace and stability of the other Peculiar families, as if she lived in another world where only survival mattered.

But Rachel *was* a survivor. She had stayed alive these nine long years despite her neglectful, alcoholic mother and her endless parade of "new daddies," who were often indifferent at best or abusive at worst. Rachel had never known her real Daddy, of whom her mother would not speak. Whoever he was, he was far removed from her life. So Rachel was on her own.

She had started to feel a little sick, and had gone to bed early. Now, clutching the thin blanket under her chin, Rachel shivered in her sleep despite the warmth of the summer night. As she tossed and turned in time to the vagaries of her nightmare, her dog Baxter sensed her agitation and nervously paced the room. Occasionally he placed his muzzle on the side of her bed and whined, but Rachel could not hear him. A dream had taken her into another time.

In her dream, Rachel was a man. A sad, desperate, but determined man. She (or rather *he*) had come into an unforeseen windfall, and was not about to let it go to waste ...

"Daniel," Jeremiah says as he enters Father's office. "We need to talk, brother."

Daniel lifts his head from Father's books. Jeremiah has intruded upon him in the midst of a daydream. He is dreaming of the future, of what the dairy could become. His mind is veritably bursting with ideas and now his older brother has come bothering him. Jealousy is all it is. No wonder Father did not leave him the farm.

"We got nothing to talk about," Daniel says. "The will's been read and it will be done."

Rachel moaned in her sleep, trying to wake up. Somehow she knew something bad was about to happen but, like all the worst nightmares, she couldn't escape by awakening. Strangest of all, while the dreaming part of her thought she was a young man named Daniel, another part knew she was really a little girl named Rachel, asleep in her lonely bed. It was confusing enough to feel like you were in two places at the same time, but now the Daniel part of her seemed to be growing stronger, so that she wasn't quite sure if she was a girl dreaming about the past, or a man dreaming about the future.

Her legs kicked beneath the sheet made damp by her sweat, as if she was trying to run away from this awful dream.

"You listen to me, Danny-boy!" Jeremiah says, knowing Daniel hates that childish nickname. Jeremiah reaches across Father's desk and slams shut the record book Daniel is reading. The dull thud of its closing echoes through the big house like a giant footstep. The sound is oppressive in the afternoon silence. All the mourners left after the funeral yesterday, and the attorney who came this morning to read Father's will rode back to town in his little buggy hours ago. The two brothers are alone.

A surge of anger like black bile rolls through Daniel, but he keeps his peace. He may be the younger Brooks brother, but by the Good Lord he'll show this no-good cuss why their Father placed his faith in him.

"The dairy is mine!" Jeremiah says, leaning over Father's desk and nearly spitting out the words. "You got no right to it!"

"I have every right to it!" Daniel replies. "Father left it to me 'cause he knew you would run it right into the ground! You and that hussy you carry on with!"

Jeremiah scowls with all the black intensity of a summer storm cloud seething with potential havoc. "You don't want to talk about Annabelle that way," he says.

"You think I don't know what you two are scheming?" Daniel says. "Annabelle ain't never gonna be a star in the picture shows. That girl ain't got the talent God gave a goose. I'm not throwing away everything Father worked for just so you two can run off to California following some fool dream."

Jeremiah's lips tighten into a thin white line as his hands draw up into fists. The sun has not yet risen to noon and its rays slant into the parlor, which faces south to catch the light. The lathes in the big window cast criss-crossing patterns of shadow across Jeremiah's pale face and white shirt. Daniel can see hundreds of little drops of sweat sparkling over his brother's cheeks and brow, which pleases him. He has always known how get his brother's goat. Even now the star-like glints of light twinkle in time to the shaking of Jeremiah's fists as he tries to master his anger.

Daniel smiles, and fills his voice mocking sweetness as he speaks again. "Why are you so angry, Jeremiah? Why has your countenance fallen so? Don't you remember what Father said in his will? 'If you do well, will you not be accepted?' In time I might even promote you to my assistant."

Jeremiah slams his fists onto the desk hard enough to knock over one of Father's jars of ink, spilling darkness over the papers.

"You just shut your ignorant mouth!" Jeremiah shouts. "I ain't never gonna work for you and I mean to have what is mine!"

Daniel is acutely aware that his older brother towers over him, that Jeremiah's fists are the size of hams and strong from a lifetime of hard farm work. Jeremiah must have fifty pounds on him, but Daniel has never let his brother bully him. Jeremiah has always been simple, and Daniel only needs to remember three things to dominate him: think faster, talk better, and never show fear. That third one most of all.

"Have it for what?" Daniel snaps. He places his own hands on the desk and feels wetness under the fingers of his left hand. He has set it down in the puddle of ink, but he pays it no mind. Right now everything depends upon eye contact. If he takes his focus off Jeremiah his brother might talk him down, and that would never do.

Leaning over the desk so that he and his brother are almost touching noses, Daniel barrels on before his brother can answer his question. "You want to throw away everything Father worked so hard to build! You want to disgrace Mother's memory so you can run off with some floozy! Father knew it and that's why he didn't leave you the farm! Well I honor the memory of my parents. Do you hear? I will never let you sell this farm!"

"Don't you talk about Momma that way!" Jeremiah shouts, his voice breaking. Accusing him of disgracing her memory has hurt him, as Daniel knew it would. Jere-

miah loves their mother dearly, God rest her soul, while Daniel was closer to Father before his death.

"I'd never disgrace her!" Jeremiah says. "You're the one who does that! I know what you and Tom Moore are up to!"

Daniel straightens as a bolt of cold shock runs up his back. Jeremiah has struck a telling blow, one Daniel did not see coming. Right now he is frozen like a child caught doing something naughty.

"You don't know what you're talking about," Daniel says.

"Yes I do!" Jeremiah cries. He is becoming quite emotional. "You two got a 'still running in some secret room out back of the barn! The only plans you got for this place is to turn it into a speakeasy, so don't tell me I'm disgracing Momma's memory!"

"No, you are a disgrace," Daniel says, sounding lame and desperate even to his own ears but he doesn't know what else to say. "Mother would be ashamed to see you carrying on so."

"You don't care at all about the dairy," Jeremiah says. "You don't care about Poppa or Momma or anyone but yourself! You sure as hell don't care about me! Well, Annabelle loves me and we're going to Hollywood and she's gonna be a movie star no matter what you say!"

"You're a damn fool, Jeremiah," Daniel says, forcing a contemptuous laugh. "I'm not wasting my time on you any longer."

He lifts his hands from the desk and finally notices the ink dripping from his fingers. Pulling his handkerchief from the back pocket of his pants, he wipes the ink off his hand as he walks around the desk and out the parlor door. Though he looks nonchalant, Daniel is actually struggling not to tremble. He thought he could intimidate Jeremiah into accepting his control of the dairy, but now he thinks he may have gone too far. Normally his brother would never call the law on him, but if Daniel has made him angry enough ...

"Don't you run away from me, Danny-boy!" Jeremiah shouts as he follows him down the hall to the front door. The diamond-shaped windows on it glow with sunshine. Daniel pauses to take his wide-brimmed hat off the hook on the wall and place it on his head before opening the door and stepping outside. Jeremiah follows him, still shouting accusations.

The outdoors seems airy and disorienting after the dim closeness of the house. The Brooks dairy farm sits in the midst of rolling hills of pasture like a fleet of wooden ships in a green-gold sea of grass that stretches to the horizon and beyond. The grass really does look like water as the wind stirs it in waves and ripples. Green leafy clusters of trees sit like islands in the low places where true water collects. A little maple tree stands all by itself like a lonely child next to the stream that runs behind the house.

Daniel's father planted that tree himself to give their mother shade as she took her afternoon tea in the backyard. It will never shade her now. It is a promise death has broken.

A herd of cows graze in the fields to the north within their neatly delineated confines of barbed wire. The farmhouse is white, the barn red with white trim, as is the toolshed. All the buildings are new, clean and well-painted. The well with its low fieldstone wall, little shingled roof and handcrank with a wooden bucket completes the scene. Above all this the sky stretches, staggering in its vastness, of the clearest blue with its massive clouds clearest white. The wind sighs in the grass and in the branches of the trees, and the cows low. It is an American landscape, a Missouri landscape, and into it stumbles the quarreling brothers.

"You just don't get it, Jeremiah," Daniel says as he marches toward the barn, hoping his brother won't try anything until they get there. "Every day the railroads bring more people into Peculiar, and we're the biggest dairy between here and Pleasant Hill. They're all going to want our milk, our butter and our cheese. Anything I have to do to keep this place in business, I will do."

Daniel hopes Jeremiah will assume he is talking about the 'still.

"You ain't fooling me," Jeremiah says. "Every farmer around here has their own dairy cow and the town ain't growing that fast. I know what all this is really about. This is about the flowers."

Daniel stops. They are halfway to the barn, halfway to the secret underground room where the 'still and the guns are hidden. Nothing is nearby except the Jones farm over by the schoolhouse. Those two buildings are a mile away and hidden behind the curve of a hill, but Daniel can't risk anyone hearing a gunshot. He only has to lure Jeremiah a little further, draw him to the secret room under the floor of the barn and end this fight for good. But what Jeremiah said has intrigued him and he can't help but stop.

"What?" Daniel says.

"The flowers!" Jeremiah repeats. "Don't pretend you don't remember."

"I'm not pretending," Daniel says, but that isn't quite true. Something about Jeremiah and flowers sounds very familiar, but he can't place it.

"Well you bet I remember it!" Jeremiah cries. Daniel is shocked to see that his brother is close to sobbing. His small dark eyes are bloodshot, tears are running down his cheeks and his mouth is contorted with weeping.

"Poppa took us hunting for rabbits," Jeremiah says. "You shot one but I didn't, and Poppa was so disappointed in me. So I went out and I picked him some wildflowers, 'cause that always made Momma happy. But he flew into a fury and beat me bloody with a switch, sayin' he didn't want no sissies in his house. And you stood back

and watched, pointing and laughing the whole time. I was eight and you were six, but I know good and well you remember!"

Daniel is stunned, though probably not for the reason Jeremiah thinks. The story may be true or it may not. Sure it sounds a little familiar and Father did put his hands to them sometimes, but Daniel doesn't remember any switches or blood. What shocks him is that this is why Jeremiah has resented him all these years and why is he so angry with him now. It hasn't been about money, women or land. It has been about ... Father's love.

To Daniel this seems touching to the point of absurdity and he has to stop himself from laughing out loud, not out of mean-spiritedness but surprise. Has Jeremiah been bitter all this time just because Father preferred flesh to flowers? Jeremiah stares at him, quivering with grief and anger, his black hair flying about his face in the wind, and he looks so simple and out of sorts that Daniel almost feels like embracing him, maybe even working out a way for them to share ownership of the dairy.

But wait, what if he wants a cut of the bootlegging money?

"I don't remember any such thing," Daniel says as he hardens his heart. "But if Father did whip you, I bet you deserved it, and you're a better man now because of it."

Now Jeremiah will certainly follow him to the barn, so Daniel turns his back on him and begins to walk away. But the footsteps he expects to hear coming after him do not fall in the steady rhythm of walking, but in the charging speed of an enraged bull, followed by Jeremiah's howl of rage.

Daniel breaks into a run, for his reflexes are as quick as his mind, and he hopes he can make it to the barn where the guns are hidden before his brother runs him down. Even now he does not really believe Jeremiah would hurt him. But his brother has a head start, his legs are longer, and he has the force of anger propelling him. Jeremiah slams into Daniel's back like a runaway freight train. The impact lifts Daniel off his feet, and he drops his handkerchief. The wind catches it before it hits the ground and sends it flying through the air for several yards like a white and black bird until it snags on the barbed-wire fence.

Jeremiah pushes Daniel straight towards the well. He sees the black, stone-lined maw of it rushing up to receive him and has no time to think, no time to plan, no time to do anything but surrender to his reflexes. He does the only thing he can do: he pivots, forcing all the weight on the right side of his body to the left. The momentum carries Jeremiah, still clutching the back of his shirt, over with him and the brothers pitch forward together.

If Daniel did this just a moment later, both of them would have tumbled over the edge and God alone knows what would have happened. But instead the two of them slam into the low fieldstone wall around the edge of the well. The mortar cracks, knocking up dust, and one stone falls loose. Daniel sees it in his peripheral vision tumbling down into the darkness, bouncing once off the side of well and then splashing into the water at the bottom. And then Jeremiah grabs the front of his shirt, pins him with his back against the wall, and punches him in the face, occluding his vision with multicolored stars.

"BASTARD!" Jeremiah screams. "YOU BASTARD!"

Daniel struggles against him as best as he can, but Jeremiah is bigger and stronger; he is able to hold Daniel down with ease as he hammers him with blows. The remaining ink on Daniel's left hand leaves a black mark on Jeremiah's white shirt as they fight.

Jeremiah reaches out and tears one of the fieldstones loose from the mortar. White dust falls from the underside of it as he lifts it high. Saliva sprays from his lips as he roars like a furious ape.

"Jeremiah no!" Daniel screams.

The rising stone eclipses the sun, filling the sky with red fire as Daniel screams again.

"Don't do it!"

The stone falls, revealing blinding sunlight that spares him the sight of the rock plummeting towards his face. Anticipating the blow, he turns his face to the side as he cringes, and this movement grants him a few more hours of life. Instead of smashing in his skull, the rock hits him lower in the face, across his jaw. He hears a sound like a china plate smashing against a stone hearth as the impact shatters his jawbone, sending bloody teeth and bone fragments flying out of his mouth.

Moaning in her sleep, Rachel jerked her face to the side as if she had felt the blow.

Jeremiah rises up, and as his weight lifts off him Daniel tumbles out of the warm sunshine and into cold darkness. He falls, bouncing off the sides of the well, spinning around, feeling his arms and legs knocked into unnatural positions. And then he plunges into icy water.

He does not know how long he is unconscious, but it can't be very long, because after the pain cruelly rips away the numbing blackness he sees the sun shining above him at the top of the well. He stares at the glowing disc for several seconds before he realizes that Jeremiah has removed the little roof with its hand crank and bucket. Daniel thinks Jeremiah must have done this to make it easier to lift him out, and then he looks down at himself and all thought is lost in a rising tide of panic.

He is lying in water that comes up to his chin in a hole that isn't big enough to accommodate a full-grown man. Or at least one with his arms and legs intact. But

Daniel sees that his own limbs are now bent into crooked unnatural angles like those of a scarecrow that has fallen off its pole. A shattered bone juts from a tear in his pants just below his right knee and his left arm is bent backwards at the elbow. And the well water, once the purest and sweetest water Daniel ever tasted, is now bright red, tainted with blood.

He tries to call his brother's name, but it feels like his jawbone isn't connected to its hinges anymore. It keeps wobbling around as he tries to speak, so what comes out sounds like, "Juhmuh?"

He wonders why the pain hasn't hit him yet, and figures it must be shock. He has a reason to be in shock. Knowing this somehow causes his panic to rise higher, and he tries to call out to his brother again.

"Juh-uh-my-ah?"

He chokes on the word and coughs up blood, sending jabs of pain through his midsection. It feels like several of his ribs are broken. He dreads having to call out again, but then a shadow blocks out the sun. Looking up, Daniel sees Jeremiah standing at the top of the well, looking down at him. He is wearing Daniel's broad-rimmed hat; it must have fallen off his head while they were fighting. Why did Jeremiah put it on? The sun is behind him, outlining Jeremiah's head in gold fire and casting shadows over his face.

"Brother, help me," Daniel cries. It sounds like Bwutha, ulp eee. *It hurts him to speak, but Jeremiah is just standing there, a dark hulking shadow. Why doesn't he lower a rope?*

"Oh God, it hurts," Daniel says, starting to weep. His panic gives his words an awful clarity. "Please, Jeremiah, get me out of here!"

Jeremiah tosses something into the well. Sunlight glints off the two small objects as they fall through the air and they splash into the water in front of Daniel's face. Before they sink into invisibility, Daniel sees that they are a couple of teeth. His teeth, knocked from his head when Jeremiah struck him with the rock.

The well brightens as Jeremiah steps away. Looking up, Daniel sees only the sun with a crystalline glaze of clouds drifting across its face.

"Brother come back!" Daniel cries. "Don't leave me! Oh, please, I'm hurt so bad!"

And Jeremiah does come back. He is holding a board and Daniel's heart lifts with hope because he thinks his brother is planning to use it to lift him out of the well somehow, maybe by lowering it down with a rope so he can lie on it as Jeremiah pulls him up. But then he sees that Jeremiah does not have a rope, and that he is setting the board across one side of the well, making a flat edge on the circle of light above him. Dirt drifts down, and Daniel realizes that Jeremiah has torn down the fieldstone wall around the edge of the well. Now why on earth did he do that?

Jeremiah turns away and picks up another board. For an instant Daniel can see the black mark he left on his brother's shirt and then Jeremiah places the second board next to the first, taking another slice out of the light above him. Now the well is half covered, only a semicircle of light remains, and as Daniel realizes what Jeremiah is doing, he cannot stop panic from overwhelming him.

"OH GOD NO BROTHER PLEASE DON'T DO THIS TO ME!" *He chokes, coughs up blood, and continues screaming as Jeremiah sets down a third board. Three-quarters covered now.*

"PLEASE BROTHER YOU CAN HAVE THE FARM! YOU CAN HAVE ALL THE MONEY! TAKE WHATEVER YOU WANT JUST DON'T LEAVE ME DOWN HERE IN THE DARK!"

As he begs, he tries to lift his hand and reach out to his brother, but he can barely manage to lift his broken arm above the level of the water as Jeremiah sets down the final board, sealing Daniel inside cold darkness echoing with his screams.

"NO BROTHER PLEASE! POPPA LOVES YOU! ANNABELLE CAN BE A MOVIE STAR! YOU CAN HAVE ANYTHING YOU WANT JUST PLEASE BROTHER PLEASE DON'T DO THIS! PLEEEEASE!"

He has not yet given up; he can still see light seeping through the cracks between the boards, but then dust begins to sprinkle down through those cracks, he hears the sound of earth being piled on top of the boards, and that is when Daniel surrenders to panic and grief.

"PLEASE! PLEASE! PLEEEEEEEEEE-"

Rachel bolted upright in bed, screaming, only to have the scream die in her throat as soon as she opened her eyes.

Daniel was standing outside her bedroom window, looking in at her.

She couldn't see his face but she knew it was him. She recognized the wide-brimmed hat from her dream. Cold moonlight illuminated him from behind, casting his face in shadow, but she could see the silvery glint of his eyes.

She couldn't move, couldn't breathe, couldn't even tremble. She could only stare as the man outside her window lifted his bony, clawlike hand and began to scratch at the glass. The high-pitched screech of his broken fingernails raking over the windowpane sounded like screaming. A low hissing voice came from the shadows under the brim of his hat.

"Let me in," he said, like a wolf in a fairy tale.

Much to her own horror, Rachel began to rise from her bed to obey.

And then Baxter jumped up from the floor, barking and snarling at the figure in the window. This snapped Rachel back into her right mind; she blinked and saw that the figure wasn't a man at all, and had never been a man. It was just a cat sitting on the windowsill. When Baxter started barking, it hissed in startled fury and jumped away, disappearing into the night.

As soon as it was gone, Rachel felt the tension leave her body. She slumped back into bed, rested her head on her knees and burst into tears. Baxter trotted over from the window and climbed into bed with her, something he was not usually allowed to do, but right now she was grateful for the company.

When she felt a little better, she got up and went to the bathroom. As she washed her hands, she looked into the mirror and wondered what to do. She had never felt more tired than she did right now, but she did not want to face any more nightmares. After a bit of thought, she went back to her bedroom, pulled the blanket off the bed and carried it over to the hall closet. Realizing she now had to face her fear of tight spaces or go out of her mind from lack of sleep, Rachel chose security over comfort. She may not like sleeping in a tight space at first, but she had learned very young that the key to survival is the ability to adapt.

Putting the blanket down on the floor behind the moth-eaten coats waiting for their winter usage, she stepped inside, called Baxter in with her, and closed the door. Lying down on the blanket with her dog curled up next to her, she felt a little safer. Hidden, at least, from anything that might try to harm her. The nightmare slowly faded from her mind and soon she went back to sleep, which was now mercifully dreamless.

She would never learn how the Peculiar sheriff, Officer Randy's grandfather in fact, had found Daniel's monogrammed handkerchief hanging from the barbed-wire fence and matched the ink stains on it to the mark on Jeremiah's shirt. A search of the property found the distillery and a suitcase full of money, but never the well, for Jeremiah had hidden it beneath a flowerbed he had planted in the dirt over the boards and surrounded with a circle of fieldstones from the wall.

Through the efforts of a determined prosecutor, Jeremiah was hanged for murder at the county seat in Harrisonville. He never told anyone what he did with his brother's body, or how he had turned a well once filled with sweet water into a bloody oubliette for his favored younger brother, forgotten now by all but one.

9

The Night Mission

"Agent Gordon wants to go with us on the night mission," Private Ames said to Private Hicks. "Are you going to allow it?"

Ames was a tall black man with a deep resounding voice. Hicks liked him. He could ask questions in the direct, no-nonsense manner the military trained them to use without disclosing sensitive information. Hicks noticed how he had said "on the night mission" instead of "to collect the water sample from the well." The caution was probably unnecessary, since the military personnel transport and mobile strategic analysis unit (in civilian terms, "a van") in which they were riding was both soundproof and electronically shielded against surveillance devices, but he admired the effort.

"Gordon went over Sergeant Rollins's head and got the necessary orders," Hicks replied. "He's non-military, so he doesn't have to follow the same chain of command as we do."

Ames's lips compressed as his wide nostrils flared. "That ain't right," he said. "He shouldn't even be here! This was an Army operation and it should stay that way."

"There's nothing we can do about it now," Hicks said. "We have a mission to do, and we're not responsible for Gordon. If he can't keep up, well, that's not our problem. I can't risk anyone's safety for his sake, so if he isn't around when it's time to leave, too bad for him."

Ames smiled. "I'm glad Rollins put in you in charge, Hicks. Where is he anyway?"

"Teleconferencing with Washington," Hicks said. "He has to report to his superiors just like we have to report to him. Makes me wonder who Gordon reports to."

Ames shook his head in dismay once again. "It ain't right," he repeated. "He's not one of us. It just ain't right."

They both looked up when someone rapped on the van's back doors. The van had several tiny digital cameras discretely mounted in its frame that provided the crew with detailed exterior views from many different perspectives. On one of the many screens lining the van's interior, they saw the mission's remaining crew waiting outside. Ames got up to let them in, keeping one hand on the pistol in his belt out of habit.

This was a classified mission, so of course all of their transports were disguised as civilian vehicles. From the outside, the large white van looked like the type of vehicle a private school or church might use for a weekend field trip.

As Ames opened the doors at the back of the van, a rush of night air flowed inside. Hicks had never smelled air like it before he came to this part of the country, and even after several days the mysterious quality of it had not faded from his mind. It didn't have any particular scent to it, no smell of flowers, turned earth, or even manure, a fragrance he had discovered was quite common in "fresh country air." But for some reason this clean Midwest night air energized him. Every time he stepped outside he felt an urge to inhale a great lungful of it and take off running as fast as he could for no other reason than the pure fun of it, like he used to do when he was a kid and his parents would take him to the park. It sounded stupid, but the air here smelled like … summer. It smelled young, free, somehow *alive.*

The other three members of their team climbed into the back of the van. First came Private Jacques, who pronounced his name *Jacks.* He was twenty years old, the youngest of the group, from L.A. originally and bootcamp had not worn the wannabe gangster out of him. He listened to a lot of hip-hop and liked to claim his great-grandmother was black even though he looked about as African-American as Bob Barker.

"'Sup, blood," he said to Ames as he entered. Ames, who found Jacques's banter alternately amusing and irritating, rolled his eyes.

Next came the team's only woman, Private Rodriguez. She was a short, Hispanic woman, stocky and tough. Her black hair wasn't quite buzz-cut like the men's hair, but it was pretty short. All the guys in the team respected her. They liked to say she had a real set of solid brass *cojones.*

After she entered, Agent Gordon climbed into the back of the van. An awkward silence descended that not even the whisper of the summer breeze could dissipate. Hicks managed to keep his face composed but the remaining members of the team stared at Gordon with raw hostility. Unlike the rest of them, Gordon was not wearing camouflage, just a rather tight-fitting long-sleeved black shirt, black cargo pants and, God help them all, black running shoes. This lack of military outfitting said one thing to the team: amateur. *Civilian* amateur at that, meaning he was a safety risk to the rest of them. The contempt rising from the three other members of the team tainted the air in the back of the van like a pall of smog.

"What the hell is this, man?" Jacques said to Ames, gesturing to Gordon with his thumb. He spoke in a low voice, but not a whisper. He had wanted to Gordon to hear him, and as he turned to look at him, his upper lip curled into a sneer so that the gap in his front teeth showed. At that moment, Jacques looked like a teenage kid hoping to start a fight. His pale brown hair was cropped into a short buzz, and that sneering upper lip of his barely had enough whiskers growing out of it to merit a shave. At first glance, it looked like Jacques could take Gordon down in a heartbeat. Jacques still had all his bootcamp muscle and the aura of toughness a military man in combat fatigues possessed, and Gordon looked like … (It took Hicks a moment to think of something Gordon resembled. The guy just looked so *ordinary*) … like some guy at a Halloween party playing cat burglar. But Gordon didn't seem intimidated. Pretending he hadn't heard what Jacques had said, Gordon took a seat in front of one of the monitors on the walls and started adjusting some of the controls on the panel.

Rodriguez shook her head in disgust. Only a wimp wouldn't stand up to someone who had disrespected him.

Hicks didn't like Gordon any more than the rest of them. Nevertheless he felt a strong sense of responsibility to get this mission done in the manner their superiors had instructed them to do it, so he said in the easy tones of authority, "Okay people, we all have our orders. Ames, you drive. Jacques, do equipment check."

An equipment check wasn't really necessary, but it would give him something to do besides trying to bait Gordon. Ames went up front to the driver's seat, started the engine, and they were on their way.

They had just pulled onto the outer road that ran parallel to 71 southbound and hadn't gone two miles before Jacques started making trouble. Hicks cursed himself for not seeing it coming.

Jacques looked up from the assortment of packs at his feet with a sly grin on his face. Turning to Rodriguez, he whispered something in her ear and the two of them snickered together while glancing at Gordon's back. Then Rodriguez said, "Do it, man, do it!" And Jacques turned to face Gordon's way.

"Hey Gordon," he said. Gordon did not immediately turn his head. He was staring at the computer screen, which showed a topographical map of Peculiar and the surrounding area if Hicks was not mistaken. Hicks hoped in vain that

Jacques would let it drop, but he didn't. He repeated Gordon's name, a little sharper this time.

At the sound of his voice, Gordon raised his index finger. He hadn't been ignoring Jacques after all; he was just absorbed in whatever he was doing at the computer and was asking for a moment. The time it took for Jacques to figure this out was apparently all Gordon needed, because before Jacques could speak again, Gordon turned to him and said, "I'm sorry, what?"

The sly grin returned to Jacques's face. "I just wanted to ask you," he said, pronouncing "ask" like "axe." "Rollins thinks you're ..." He rolled his hand in the gesture of someone looking for the appropriate phrase before continuing. "... of an *alternative lifestyle*."

After looking at Jacques in silence for a few seconds, Gordon said, "That isn't a question, Private Jacques."

Jacques laughed as if he had succeeded in offending Gordon, who looked unperturbed otherwise. Hicks recognized the old trick of using laughter to undermine someone's self-confidence, when the one laughing had no other means to attack. He had seen kids doing it to each other back in elementary school, and a disturbing number of adults doing it in the workplace. The purpose was always the same, to set the other person off their guard by making them feel embarrassed or self-conscious. It worked almost all the time. If you fought back, you looked temperamental and insecure; if you ignored it, you looked weak. Hicks almost stepped in and told Jacques to knock it off, until he thought of the face he would lose by defending Gordon, so he kept quiet.

Gordon however, didn't seem to need defending. "Do you have a question for me, Private Jacques?" he asked. His tone was perfectly neutral, in that way Gordon seemed to have mastered. He looked Jacques straight in the eye, his voice did not waver, and his tone was perfectly balanced. Not angry, not too aggressive, not whiny or callow. He seemed almost *eager* for Jacques to ask the question straight out. Not a trace of insecurity or fear. His tone almost had the quality of a dare but was so neutrally phrased that Gordon looked like the reasonable one, and Jacques was on the defensive. All that with just a single question.

"I'm just saying, is all," Jacques said. "That's what he thinks. That's what *people* think."

"So you didn't really want to ask me anything, did you?" Gordon said. Now his voice almost had the tone of a reprimand ... but not quite. It was the voice of a man taking the high road. "You only wanted to tell me what your superior officer is thinking."

This last statement seemed to have several dire implications attached, and although no one could think of a specific problem it might cause, a feeling of unease shivered down the spines of the enlisted persons in the back of the van.

"But it's a good thing you didn't ask me anything," Gordon said, "because I believe you are forbidden to ask that specific question. Am I wrong?"

Jacques did not know how to reply. Gordon didn't act military, so don't-ask-don't-tell might not apply to him, but none of them were sure. He was still involved in a military operation, but did that policy apply in this case? Jacques stammered in confusion.

"I just ... I ..."

The van went over a mild bump. Looking up through the windshield, they saw the van had turned left and crossed a bridge that passed over highway 71. Ames immediately made a right turn onto the outer road on the east side of 71. Now they were again headed south. After a few hundred yards, Ames made another left turn, this time onto an unmarked gravel road.

"We're almost there," Hicks said. "Everyone pack up and get your camouflage make-up on." Jacques looked relieved at the interruption, but Hicks felt a little disappointed. He had rather enjoyed watching Gordon make him squirm.

Everyone put on their black and green camouflage make-up except Gordon, who did not wear any make-up at all, and Ames, who was driving. The tires rumbled over the uneven surface of the gravel road, sometimes making a loud boom as they hit a pothole. The noise discouraged conversation, so they rode for a while in silence.

Hicks could tell Ames was not used to driving on gravel roads from the way the van's rear end kept swaying back and forth, but he couldn't blame him. Hicks could not have done much better himself.

After a while Ames slowed the van, put on his night-vision goggles, and turned off the headlights. They were nearing the drop-off point, so he would drive the rest of the way in the dark. Hicks felt a little tightness form in his chest. The ride had started to unnerve him.

Knowing he did not have much military experience, Hicks had prided himself on the trust he had earned from Rollins when he received command of this mission. Because of this, he could never have admitted to anyone that this nighttime drive through the country, with nothing but trees and moonlit fields outside and the drone of the tires on the deserted gravel road lulling everyone into introspective silence, had somehow caused an intense feeling of loneliness to well up inside him. Maybe it was just because he was a city boy, used to streetlights and nightlife, loud music and the sound of heavy traffic, but the thought of all those empty acres of night outside without another person within earshot caused an almost superstitious dread in him, a feeling of being cut off from his fellow human beings.

He almost jumped when Gordon came over and sat down next to him. He felt self-conscious, not just from having Gordon sitting next to him but because he was afraid his misgivings might be showing on his face. If Gordon had seen something, what if the rest had seen as well? If he had shown fear, he would never live it down.

"Here," Gordon said, handing him a backpack. So that was the only reason he sat down next to him, to hand him his backpack. Hicks took the pack with a little relief. Gordon must have taken the pack from Jacques in the middle of checking the equipment, so he may not have done this out of courtesy, but to show Jacques he wasn't intimidated.

Suddenly he wondered if he had ever considered any other person's motives with such scrutiny. He didn't think he had, and now he felt a little abashed.

"Thanks," Hicks said. Let Jacques and Rodriguez give him the eye. This was stupid; they couldn't work this way.

"No problem," Gordon said. "I also wanted to let you know that I'm only hitching a ride with you all tonight. This is your mission and I won't interfere."

"Okay," Hicks said. That didn't sound very military, but he wasn't used to being spoken to with such … respect. He needed to say something more authoritative to compensate for the slip. "You may accompany us as far as the surveillance team, but don't go beyond the perimeter of the Brooks farm."

"Actually," Gordon said. "I'm not meeting with the surveillance team. I'm making my own trip out to Beta."

"What for?" Hicks asked.

"I have my own mission," Gordon said. "I'm not at liberty to discuss any further."

That wouldn't do. Hicks's hackles rose. "I'm sorry, Agent Gordon, but that is not acceptable. Whatever your reasons are, I can't have my people jeopardized by any independent activity around the site. If you want to go out on another night that's your business, but-"

"I have my orders here," Gordon said, handing him a piece of paper. "They're co-signed by Sergeant Rollins. You'll find everything is in order. If you want to file an objection, I'm sure there are proper channels you can go through, but in the meantime I will be accompanying your team on this mission."

Hicks read the report Gordon gave him, instructions neatly typed, airtight and clear. Across the bottom, Rollins had scrawled in his blockish script, *Get it done anyway.*

No arguing with that, but this time Gordon would not surprise Hicks out of his professionalism. "Very well," Hicks said. "Our ETA at the drop-off point is in five minutes. Let's get ready."

Hicks applied his camouflage make-up while Gordon collected his own equipment. Hicks noted that Gordon had brought a gun, a .357 Magnum that he wore in a hip-holster on his right leg, and a small backpack that he now slung over his shoulders. Then he pulled a black ski mask over his face and settled back in his seat.

Surely he isn't finished, thought Hicks, who still had to put on his night-vision goggles, clip on his waist-pack with his sample collection gear inside, and attach his own pistol in its holster to his belt. He exchanged a glance with Jacques that spoke volumes, both of them feeling sure Gordon would screw up this mission in a big way.

"Here we are, people," Ames said from the driver's seat. They all felt the force of deceleration slowly push them towards the front of the van as it slowed down. The instant they stopped, Hicks opened the back door and hopped out with Jacques and Rodriguez following close behind him. Gordon came last, shutting the van's doors behind him as quietly as possible. The van sped away the second Ames heard the doors shut, but none of the soldiers were around to be hit by flying gravel. The second their feet hit the ground, they bolted for the trees lining the road on their right. They couldn't stay on the road a second longer than necessary; too much risk of being seen. As it was, anyone watching would only have caught a glimpse of four dark forms jumping from the back of the van, outlined for an instant by the ruby glow of the van's brake lights, and then nothing as the brake lights went out, the van sped away and the four dark forms became part of the living shadows of the trees swaying over the pale gravel road.

The night seemed almost day-bright after the dimness inside the van. The full moon flooded the sky with its light, which showered down to the fields and trees below like silvery rain. Each tree and fencepost cast a sharp, perfect shadow on the ground. Hicks saw it all in an instant as he leapt out into the night: a field to his left enclosed with barbed wire and filled with knee-high grass, a few dozing cows standing in it, made visible only by their shadows against the shimmering moonlit grass. The sound of mournful lowing reached their ears as the van's passage disturbed the little herd, then silence again as it sped away. To their right, dark trees swayed in the night wind, millions of tiny leaves shivering in the moving air, making the little forest seem like a dark hissing wave rising over them. Between the forest and field was the gravel road with a grass stripe down the middle of it like a divider line.

A pretty sight, but Hicks, Jacques and Rodriguez only caught a glimpse of it. The second they were off the road, they pulled their night-vision goggles over their eyes. Now they no longer saw their surroundings by moonlight, but by a sickly green glow. The goggles picked up infrared light, so that warmer objects appeared brighter and cooler objects dimmer. The effect was nauseating, like lying at the bottom of a pool of polluted green water, but it did make it easier to see in the shadows under the trees.

No houses were nearby, so it was a good spot to drop them off without anyone seeing them. Hicks jabbed the first two fingers of his left hand in the direction they needed to go and led them all into the woods towards the Brooks dairy farm.

When Hicks had come out here by himself the day before, he had done pretty well at keeping quiet. At night it was different. Even with the goggles they had a hard time avoiding all the sticks, brambles, and rocks on the ground. Hicks felt sure everyone within a mile radius must have thought a herd of buffalo was stampeding through these woods, but they couldn't do anything about it, so they kept on marching.

They had gone about a quarter of a mile when Hicks looked back and noticed Gordon was gone. He held up a fist, a signal for the others to stop. Rodriguez lifted her hand, palm up in a gesture of questioning. When Hicks pointed out where Gordon should be and wasn't, she and Jacques both jumped in surprise.

"Where …?" Jacques began in a normal tone of voice, and Rodriguez slapped his arm. Jacques lowered his voice and spoke again.

"Where did he go?" he whispered.

"Maybe he went on to Beta," Hicks whispered back. "He said he didn't need to meet with the surveillance team."

"Yeah, but how did he get away without us noticing?" Rodriguez said.

Hicks looked around. The thin trees around them swayed in the night wind, all of them glowing in putrid green light as he saw them through his goggles, reminding Hicks again of underwater plants. He felt nauseated and out of breath at once, but he saw no trace of Gordon. His body heat would make him visible from quite a distance with the goggles, yet he was nowhere around.

Unless he's moving low to the ground, Hicks thought. *All the brush would hide him.* But how could he move away so quickly without making a sound?

Hicks shrugged off his disquiet. No time for this. They had a mission to do. "Don't worry about him," he said to the others. "He'll either rendezvous with us when the van returns, or he can walk back to town. He's not our problem. Let's go."

They continued on their way, moving swiftly through the living night. The sound of their boots trampling the sticks and underbrush roared in their ears. It made Hicks nervous. How could anyone not hear that? And how did Gordon move away without making a sound? Sergeant Rollins suspected Gordon had Midwest roots; Hicks wondered if Gordon had some experience moving over terrain like this. Not that it did Hicks much good right now. He began to breathe hard, not quite hyperventilating but close, and it had nothing to do with their swift pace. God, if only they didn't have to use these night-vision goggles! They made everything seem so sick and green, the sensation of being underwater was smothering him. Hicks was relieved when they finally made it to the little gully where the surveillance team had set up their post to watch the Ross house.

The gully running close to the Brooks farm took a sharp right turn as it moved north, bringing it within a convenient distance of the little red schoolhouse while still inside the cover of the woods. Tonight Turner and Manderly were hiding in it, both of them in gray and black night camouflage and make-up. They had set down a nylon mat over the bare dirt of the gully floor and put the audio equipment up on the bank. The receiver looked like a miniature radio dish; they had attached it to a metal rod stuck in the ground so that the dish pointed at the schoolhouse. Wires ran back from the dish to a small black digital recorder set on the nylon mat.

A blue glow came from Turner's wristwatch as he checked the time. "You guys are late," he whispered. "It's 2350 hours. What happened?"

"We had a small delay," Hicks said.

"That fruit Gordon," Jacques piped up, a little too loudly in Hicks's opinion. "It's all his fault."

It occurred to Hicks that they would not have been late if they just accepted Gordon's presence on the mission without all those complaints, but he couldn't do anything about that now.

"Never mind," Hicks said. "Anything to report?"

"Nuthin'," said Manderly in his slow Southern drawl. "'Less you think Kelly Ross readin' her son Bible stories before he goes to sleep is worth reporting."

Manderly shook his dark shadowed head in dismay. "I've been doin' this a long time," he said, "but this is the first time I've ever felt bad about it. These people are Americans, for God's sake."

"It's for their own good," Hicks said. "We're not spying on them to play peeping tom. We're doing this for their safety. Just keep that in mind. You need a new disk?"

"Yeah," said Manderly, taking a CD out of the back of the digital recorder. "This one's almost full."

"Maybe you should give it to Gordon," Turner said. "If he takes it to Quantico, it could prove he's with the FBI."

"I doubt it," Hicks said. "He'd probably say he never heard of the outfit."

They all laughed softly.

"Anyway," Hicks said. "We're off. Your relief shift should get here around 0700 hours."

"Wait a minute," Turner said. "Has Benton found that girl yet?" He did not have to specify any further. The girl Hicks had photographed in the woods had haunted their thoughts since the meeting at sunset the day before. Five miles away, Rachel had just risen from her nightmare to see the strange visitor outside her bedroom window.

"Haven't heard anything yet," Hicks said. "But I'm sure he'll find her soon enough. It's a small town. See you at the next briefing."

"Later," Turner and Manderly replied, as Hicks, Jacques and Rodriguez took off down the gully's soft dirt bed towards to the Brooks farm.

Running in the gully was easier, and quieter too. Very few plants grew down here where the water ran when it rained. Since the weather had been dry for the last week or so, the soil at the bottom of the gully was dry, soft and powdery beneath their boots, and the only obstacles the three of them had to surmount were the occasional rocks, fallen logs, or thorny vines that had grown across the span of the gully. They had gone about a quarter of a mile when Hicks looked up and saw the big thorn tree near the patch of grass where he had hidden when the three kids had almost spotted him. The tree glowed pale green in the goggle's infrared vision, looking spectral and unearthly with its thousands of glowing thorns. Looking at it made him want to shudder, but at least it made a useful landmark. Now he knew they were close. They only had to find the big maple tree, and the farm would be a few dozen meters to—

"What the hell is that?" Jacques suddenly cried.

All the muscles in his body tensed as adrenaline dumped into his bloodstream. Hicks looked up in time to see a glowing form dash across the gully floor ahead of them. It shined brighter than their surroundings, which meant it was a warm, living animal.

"Shut up, idiot!" Rodriguez hissed. "Do you want the whole world to hear us? It's just a cat!"

Was it? Hicks thought. He hadn't gotten a good look at it, but something seemed wrong with it, something he couldn't quite place. It wasn't deformed; it had the right number of legs, and it didn't have two tails or three heads or anything, but something about it looked ... off.

"Never mind," Hicks said, to himself as well as the others. "We're just here to get a water sample, so let's do it. No more screwing around."

He sounded decisive but now Hicks felt decidedly unnerved. A sense that things were about to go very wrong had come upon him, nothing specific, just a tenseness in his shoulders and a prickling of the hairs on the back of his neck. If only he didn't have to look at this midnight forest through the these night-vision goggles, all sick green light where warmth should be, shining living things swimming in cold watery shadows. But there, up ahead, he saw the great maple tree outlined with spectral green radiance, dripping with vines and pale glowing bunches of leaves. The floor of the gully was cooler than the surrounding ground, so that it looked like a dark trail leading them onwards to the maple. Here the gully ran shallow, just exposing the thick mass of tangled roots beneath the old tree, and the bushy forest floor, still faintly shining with the departing warmth of the day, came to the level of their shoulders.

"Turn right here," Hicks whispered, and began to scramble out of the gully towards the farm.

No sooner had he braced his foot on one of the maple's thick roots when a raw, animal-like voice spoke from the shadows around them.

"Go away."

All three of them froze. Months of boot camp and hard training vaporized like a meteor and they all froze where they stood. Inhuman, that voice. Low, growling, barely intelligible, but the worst thing about it was that they could not tell from where the voice had come. It seemed to come from all around them, like a few of the random night sounds had suddenly come together to form words. Now Hicks began to notice things he had so far ignored, rustling sounds in the brush, flickers of movement within the tangled brambles. The snap of a twig breaking behind them.

"What was that?" Jacques whispered. Fear had softened his voice.

After a moment's thought, Hicks said, "Just the wind. Let's go, double time."

Don't ask me what you heard, Hicks thought, struggling to keep his stride steady. *What if we all heard the same thing?* He didn't want to face the implications. All the unreasoning fears he had faced in van earlier now came back to him, the lonely despair, the superstitious dread. To keep moving he clung to his training, something solid and empirical, which had drilled into him the imperative to obey his superior officers. Rollins had ordered him to get it done, and somehow by God he would.

They trotted through the last few yards of forest to the clearing, and as a gust of wind stirred the trees, making them sigh and whisper, Hicks again thought he heard voices speaking to them in curt hissing tones.

"... terrible ..."

"... out my house ..."

"... bastards death mother ..."

Above them, beside them, behind them, all around.

God, is this really happening? Hicks thought. *What does it mean?*

There, through that stand of brush, did he see a flicker of movement? Something small, moving low to the ground?

Probably just that cat you saw earlier, he thought, but for some reason this didn't make him feel any better.

The burned-out clearing of the Brooks farm became visible up ahead as a green glow shining through the dark thin trees. This was normal. The dark ground held more of the day's heat, so it looked brighter than the rest of the forest floor through the night-vision goggles. But what they saw as they drew near the old farm was most certainly not normal.

Hicks had not been present during the mission at Alpha Site, and had sat in confused silence when Gordon and Rollins had argued about it during the meeting at sunset. But now, as he entered the clearing and saw the group of cats pacing in a circle he thought he suddenly understood what they had been talking about.

Is this what the hyenas were doing, he thought, *around that impact crater at Alpha Site?*

The sight (or Site, perhaps) of all those cats, their sleek tawny bodies rippling and glowing with green light as they moved, filled Hicks with shock and a strange disgust. He could not guess their breeds, since the fur of all the cats looked green through his goggles, but he counted about twenty in all. Shaking their heads like old men trying to dispel bad memories, the cats paced in a circle in the center of the clearing. The scene looked so bizarre, so unnatural, in the way the cats kept themselves moving in a perfect circle, a pattern from which none of them deviated. Hicks could hear the soft flapping of the cats' ears as they shook their heads, and with all of them doing it together they made a sound not unlike applause. As they paced, the cats made strange muttering noises that sounded nothing like the normal vocalizations of cats.

Hicks thought he could hear words forming from all of their muttering, squeaking chatter.

This disturbed him, but not as much as the sight of the cats' eyes. The eyes of all animals, people included, were rich in capillaries and blood vessels that kept them supplied with plenty of warm blood, so they seemed to glow through night-vision goggles, except for the pupil and cornea, which had no blood vessels and looked a bit darker. But the eyes of these cats were pure black. Cold eyes.

The cat they had seen in the gully earlier, did it have these same dark cold eyes? Hicks thought so, although he had only caught a glimpse of it. And now he wondered, in a fit of paranoia utterly unlike him, if that cat had somehow *warned* these others they were coming.

There, in the center of the circle of pacing cats, did he see a glimpse of something dark? Something a bit colder than its surroundings?

A voice to his right hissed at him. "Hicks!"

All three of them jumped. Neither Jacques nor Rodriguez had spoken to him. For a single mortifying instant he had thought the cats had said his name, but when he turned his head and looked, he saw Gordon crouching in the under-brush. He had turned up his ski mask and Hicks could see his face, glowing with living warmth.

"Get down!" Gordon said in a low sibilant voice, and the knowledgeable, unquestionable command in his tone made them all crouch low out of habit.

"What are they doing?" Hicks whispered. "Why are they all moving in a circle like that?"

"Something is seriously screwed up here, man!" Jacques said. Hicks shushed him.

"What's wrong with their eyes?" Rodriguez said, lightly rolling her r's. "They're all black!"

"What?" Gordon said. Rodriguez sneered at him. Apparently she was not disturbed enough to forget her contempt for Gordon.

"Their eyes are cold," Hicks said. "They look black through the goggles." For a moment he had forgotten that Gordon couldn't see the way they could.

Gordon looked troubled, and Hicks asked him, "Was it like that in Africa, with the hyenas?"

"I didn't wear night-vision goggles then either," Gordon said. "Never could stand the things. They always made me sick."

"Why are they pacing around like that?" Hicks said. "Do you think they're guarding something? I don't see anything, but I guess it could be something small-"

Gordon looked up at him sharply. "Take them off," he said.

"What?" Hicks replied.

"I said take off your goggles! There's something you're not seeing!"

"You don't give us orders-" Rodriguez began, but Gordon interrupted her.

"Do it, soldier! Now!"

Again that tone, and before Hicks knew it he had pulled the night-vision goggles up onto his forehead, as had Jacques and Rodriguez. Amazing, the way that reflex was ingrained. It was like Pavlov's dog.

Normal light seemed abnormal after taking off the goggles, but losing that nauseating underwater perspective was a relief. Impenetrable shadows now concealed Gordon, Jacques, and Rodriguez, but the moonlight showering down into the clearing in thick white rays seemed almost blinding. Every charred column and slumping burned-out frame of the old farm stood out in stark clarity with glints of moonlight catching on their uneven surfaces and crisp shadows stretching out on the ground beneath them. The circular clearing now had a haunting, midnight beauty to it, with the ashy ground, the blackened ruins, and the trees all around, but none of them noticed. Strangeness had eclipsed beauty in the minds of the soldiers.

The eyes of the cats glowed with a flat, glassy reflection of the moonlight. They still seemed cold, but at least they no longer looked like the empty eye sockets of a skull. Now Hicks could tell the cats were all of different breeds, calico, striped, and spotted. But what he had not seen through the night-vision goggles was the small, thin tree around which the cats were pacing. It was just a sapling, not quite five feet tall, but he should have been able to see it.

He lowered the goggles back over his eyes. The sapling wasn't there. He raised the goggles again. The sapling was there.

"That tree is invisible in infrared light," Hicks said, like he couldn't believe it himself.

Hicks thought Gordon would question him about this, but Gordon remained silent, his face lost in shadow.

"How is that possible?" Hicks said. "Can it somehow cool itself? But it should still be visible, it would just look dark-"

"Shhh," Gordon hushed, one shadowed finger held to the silhouette of his lips.

Some of the cats had turned their heads to look at them while they paced.

"Don't you have a mission to do, Private Hicks?" Gordon said.

The water sample. He had to get one from the well. He could see it there, a dark hole in the ashy ground, not two feet from the circle of pacing cats.

"Gordon," Hicks whispered. He didn't know why he wanted to talk to him, maybe it was just a childish impulse to talk to someone who seemed calm and in control, like an authority figure. "Gordon, that tree was not there when I came out here yesterday. Could anyone have come out and planted it?"

Hicks saw the two glints of Gordon's eyes move back and forth as he shook his head.

"It can't have grown up since then," Hicks said. "It must be almost five feet tall. No tree can grow that fast."

"I know," Gordon said. "Do you want me to get the water sample?"

That didn't sound like an insult. It sounded like a genuine offer. Hicks was impressed that Gordon would put his butt on the line for him, but no, he had to act like a soldier.

"I'll do it," Hicks said, and rose to his feet. He remembered earlier in the van when he had felt cut-off from his fellow human beings, and all the reasons he'd had for shunning Gordon. Now he felt a little guilty after Gordon had offered to help him.

He turned back to him. "Thank you, though."

Gordon's shadowed face tilted downwards into a nod of acknowledgement, and Hicks turned to face Beta Impact Site.

As he stepped into the clearing, more of the cats turned their heads and looked at them. The circle contracted as the cats drew closer together. It was eerie, the way the cats moved in perfect formation without even looking at each other. Like they had one collective consciousness.

A twig snapped behind him, and Hicks almost whirled around with his gun drawn until he remembered Jacques and Rodriguez. They were backing him up, as ordered. He scolded himself. Not five seconds ago he had resolved to act like a soldier, and here he was acting as nervous as a virgin on prom night.

Well, no more of that, he thought, dispelling all fear from his mind with considerable mental effort. Cold calm descended on him like icy rain, the way it sometimes did during war games when there was no friendly or unfriendly fire, only goals he must accomplish. Pointing with the first two fingers of his right hand, he signaled Jacques to move to the right and Rodriguez to the left, to give him a wider range of cover. Hicks then marched in a straight line to the well.

He felt exposed away from the trees, and wanted to get the sample as quickly as possible, not only to minimize the chances of anyone seeing them, but because of the growing eeriness of this situation. As he marched, he took out a pair of thick latex gloves from his waist pack and put them on with an ease born of practice. The scientific training the army had given him kicked in and that nice mental coldness grew stronger.

Reaching into his waist pack again, he took out a foam facemask and a pair of clear plastic goggles and strapped them around his face. Drawing near the well, he crouched at its rim and started taking out his sample collection gear, but then he heard the voices once more.

"... *tumor fell outta me* ... *knocked up honeybunch* ..."

The words had formed from out of the sounds made by the growling cats. He couldn't deny it any longer, and again he thought of Africa and the hyenas. Why hadn't Rollins briefed them on this? Was it because they were only Privates? (Did they not think they would keep it private?) What else had they kept from them? Anger and fear mixed together in Hicks's soul. Anger that his superiors had kept information from him, and fear of being unprepared.

Hicks looked up. The cats had stopped pacing and now stood in a tight circle around the sapling, shoulder to shoulder with each other and facing outwards, like they were guarding the young tree. One of them, a big black tomcat, looked particularly fierce. Their eyes and their fangs shined in the moonlight, and the sound of their growling and hissing had a horrible cadence that sounded almost like words spoken in a voice no human being could make.

"... *out* ... *out my house* ..."

Something like outrage in that tone, something like a command in those words.

Now that he was closer, he could see that the muzzles of all the cats were dark with dried blood.

Then he heard Gordon shout, "Hicks!" No doubt of the humanity in his voice.

Hicks stood. Jacques and Rodriguez stood about five yards away from him on either side, with Jacques on the far side of the little tree and the circle of cats. They were staring at the woods, weapons drawn, and now Gordon came backing into the clearing with his gun drawn as well, pointing at something in the shadows under trees.

From out of those shadows came the gleam of hundreds of feline eyes. All around them.

"Get together!" Gordon shouted to them over his shoulder. "All of you, draw together! Back to back, like the cats! Do it!"

They weren't sure what he meant until he said, "like the cats," and then it became obvious. They needed to guard each other from all sides, like the cats around the sapling were doing. Jacques ran to Hicks, skirting the tree and its circle of feline guardians. Their eyes tracked him as he moved, and watched as Rodriguez and Gordon drew near. Rodriguez and Jacques stood to the left and right of Hicks, while Gordon turned so that he was behind him. Now the four of them stood facing each point of the compass.

As he moved to back up Gordon, Hicks noticed another cat lying on the ground at the base of the sapling, a tortoiseshell calico lying on its side. Its belly was swollen so badly that one of its hind legs was sticking up in the air. He remembered the small dark object he had glimpsed inside the circle of cats through his night-vision goggles, and at first assumed the cat had died and grown cold, but then he saw its sides moving with respiration. The cat wasn't dead at all; it was about to give birth. As he watched, a bulge moved within the cat's swollen belly, and the mother cat twisted in pain, opening her mouth to pant.

Why had she looked dark through the night vision goggles? Hicks thought. That made no sense; labor should have made her temperature rise, so she should have looked brighter than the other cats. Hicks glanced at the thin sapling rising out of the ground behind the mother cat, the young tree that was invisible in infrared light, and again felt the rising strangeness of this situation .

From out of the woods came the sibilant voices of the cats.

"Out out go 'way out my house!"

Snarling and hissing all around them.

"This is screwed up, man!" Jacques cried, his voice high and womanish in fear. Behind him and to the left of Hicks, Rodriguez murmured low in Spanish, and from the cadence of her words it became clear she was reciting the Hail Mary. He even recognized a line of it from the prayer's familiar sound, even though he didn't speak a word of Spanish:

Blessed is the fruit of thy womb ...

A dark flood of cats advanced on them from all sides. They came creeping into the clearing from the shadows under the trees, moving low to the ground in the unmistakable posture of cats stalking prey. Hundreds and hundreds of cats, their jaws dark with blood, as if they had all just returned from a kill. There, snagged upon the lower jaw of a great bobcat, a bloody tatter of striped cloth fluttered from one of its teeth like a flag raised in costly victory after a battle.

The mass of cats moved inwards like a dark furry tide speckled with the glassy reflections of the moonlight in their eyes, which never took their focus from the circle of intruders in the center of the clearing. The distance between the cats and the humans shrank like a contracting pupil.

"GET AWAY FROM ME YOU LITTLE BASTARDS!" Jacques suddenly screamed, and fired his gun into the middle of them. The flash and booming report of the army-issue .45 exploded through the clearing like a thunderbolt and one of the cats flew back over the oncoming feline horde, spinning end over end with bits of bloody fur flying off of it. But it made no difference. The cats didn't even flinch at the sound of the gunshot, didn't pause when one of their own was killed, they just kept coming, implacable and unstoppable, the air seeming to vibrate with their snarls.

"Hold your fire, Jacques!" Hicks snapped, trying to keep his voice low. "You want to set them all off on us?"

The big black tomcat near the tree began to look agitated. He hissed and growled, clawing at the ground with such force that his shoulders jostled the cats to each side of him. His paws looked unnaturally large, and Hicks realized that they all had six digits on them. Polydactyly, a rare genetic abnormality. Ash rose up from the tomcat's claws in small dusty clouds as he backed up until he almost straddled the calico, like he was protecting the mother cat. The calico's immensely swollen belly prevented the tomcat from actually getting his rear legs over her, so he only stood there as if to keep the intruding humans away from her. Hicks would have loved to oblige, but the hundreds of other cats around them prevented them from escaping.

The movement inside the calico's belly increased. Now Hicks could see two bulges shifting around beneath the mottled fur, and suddenly he heard a moist, muffled popping noise, like something inside the mother cat had ruptured.

Patterns overlapped in his mind: the cats pacing in a circle around the calico and the sapling, the voices they had heard in the dark forest, and now all these hundreds of other cats creeping in on them from all sides, herding them closer and closer together …

"Gordon," Hicks whispered. Behind him he felt Gordon turn and whisper back, "Yes?"

"They're protecting that calico," Hicks said. "You see the things moving inside it? I think it's about to give birth. These others coming out of the woods, they must have come to back them up."

"That," Gordon said, "or to force us closer to whatever is being born."

The cold flat tone of his voice drained the strength out of Hicks's knees.

He heard a low feline groan, and turning back to the pregnant calico he saw the ground beneath her hindquarters had grown shiny with blood.

Jacques, who stood facing the tree, saw what was emerging and screamed, "Ah Jesus, what is it? Good Holy God, *what is it?*"

They all turned to look as something, some creature, wriggled and clawed its way into the world.

A snub-nosed, feline head emerged from the mother cat, followed by a wide smooth brow disproportionally large for the face. In contrast the ears looked much too small and almost entirely hidden just below and behind the supraorbital ridges around the eyes. The mother cat groaned in pain as she passed the swollen skull. As the creature slithered loose of her womb, Hicks's scientifically trained mind noted its hairless skin, dark red, almost maroon in color, its long sinuous body and four slim limbs ending in six-toed claws, each with two opposable digits.

Just like the big black tomcat, Hicks recalled. The face looked almost like a normal kitten's ... until it opened its eyes. Rays of silvery light spilled out from beneath the slanted, almond-shaped lids. This was no reflection of moonlight like the other cats; this was real luminescence. As the tender, tissue-like skin of its eyelids slid down over its eyes (solid silver, like beads of mercury), Hicks could see the glow shining through, outlining delicate networks of veins.

The thing lay in its birthing nest of blood and ash, its long hairless tail curled around its thin serpentine body. Its head, shaped like a narrow triangular wedge, looked much too large for its body and it kept swaying back and forth under the weight of it as it struggled to keep its balance. It was horrible, repulsive, some kind of bastard mutant. Motes of airborne ash danced in the silvery rays emanating from its eyes, and how it saw the world through its own particular light no human mind could conceive. Only the unnatural brain encased in the creature's oversized skull knew that secret.

As the creature lifted its head and took its first look at the world, the rays of light shining from its eyes like twin lighthouse beacons, a low hiss flowed through the cats all around them, like an awestruck sigh.

And then the calico, still living, began to groan and writhe in her birth throes once again.

A second creature, identical to the first, emerged from the mother cat. It came quicker than the firstborn, who had torn open the way, making its sibling's birth easier. For a moment both creatures lay still on the ashy ground, their sides moving in and out as they breathed. Hicks could see the graceful curves of their ribcages impressed through their ruddy skin every time they inhaled. Slim fragile bones, like snake ribs. Hicks's eye for detail noticed that the newborn creatures (he could not bring himself to call them kittens) lay in a posture similar to the mother cat, and something about their bone structure and the narrow sharpness of their faces also resembled her, even if everything else about them was freakish.

They have traits from both parents, he noted. *But why the hell are they so deformed? Like some third source of genetic-*

"Hicks!"

Gordon's voice snapped him out of his shocked thoughts.

"Hicks, wake up!" Gordon snapped. "They're moving again."

The swarm of cats around them had started moving in on them again. Now they seemed almost normal compared to that calico's offspring, although they had lost none of their lethal, predatory focus. If anything, that particular quality had grown stronger.

Then he heard a sudden high-pitched squeal come from the mother cat, and he looked back in time to see the newborn creatures wriggle across her abdomen and bury their jaws in her eyes. Their first nourishment was not their mother's milk, but her blood. Hicks stared, horrified. What kind of creature could do such a thing?

The black tomcat, indeed all the cats still standing in the circle around the tree, had watched all this with a blank, almost robotic stare. They did nothing to protect the calico; they only watched as the creatures extended their forked tongues. The ends must have been sharp, for blood jetted down the sides of the calico's face their tongues ruptured her eyes, and then he saw the sides of the creatures jaws moving as they drew out the brain matter.

Something slashed his leg. Hicks looked down and saw an orange tiger-striped cat crawling up his pants, its eyes focused on his face. With sudden panic, he knocked it away with a roundhouse blow to the side of its head. He felt its bones break and heard it scream, but the other cats kept creeping inwards, irregardless of their physical safety.

Suddenly Rodriguez screamed, *"Ay Madonna!"* The sound of her pistol firing thundered through the night. Then Gordon started shooting as well, and in sudden blind panic Hicks joined them. He felt dozens of sharp claws tearing at his clothes and his skin; the cats were all around them, swarming all over them, climbing over each other's back to get at them. In the flashes of gunfire like a strobe-light he saw the cats leaping through the air toward his face and exploding into pieces when hit by his bullets. Hot, screaming, fanged and clawed animals clinging and ripping at his arms and legs, scourging all of them except for Jacques, the one facing the tree. The other three humans backed up under the collective pressure of hundreds of attacking cats, and they all forced Jacques closer and closer to the tree and the newborn creatures at its base feeding upon the mind of their mother. And before his advance, the circle of guardian cats opened to admit him. One of the creatures lifted its heavy bloodstained head, fixed its eyes upon him and hissed, showing its needle teeth and sharp forked tongue.

For an instant Jacques froze, as if hypnotized, and then the big tomcat jumped up to his face and clung there, scratching and biting.

"GET IT OFF ME!" Jacques screamed. *"OH GOD GET IT OFF ME!"*

He stumbled forward to the waiting creatures perched on the calico's corpse.

Hicks caught a flash of movement behind him, and turned in time to see Gordon swing his arm around and grab the tomcat by its scruff, breaking its neck with a loud pop and ripping it off Jacques's face, all in one smooth spin. He stopped with the barrel of his .357 pointed directly at the sapling's slim trunk.

The cats halted.

All at once they became immobile, as if flash-frozen in the midst of movement.

A bizarre silence fell over them. Jacques held his hands to the sides of his head, over the spots where the tomcat had scratched him, and he stared at Gordon as blood trickled between his fingers. Hicks and Rodriguez stopped firing but kept their guns pointed at the swarm of cats. Time seemed to halt as nothing in the clearing moved, until Hicks jumped in surprise when Gordon said his name.

"Hicks," Gordon said. "Get the sample."

"What?" Hicks asked.

"The sample of the well water!" Gordon said. "Hurry!"

Hicks had completely forgotten about it. He had even forgotten that he was still wearing his rubber gloves, facemask, and goggles, and the feel of them on his skin seemed sudden and jarring, as if they had just appeared there. Forcing himself to move slowly and deliberately, he took a test tube tied to a spool of string from his waist pack. The eyes of the cats followed him as he tossed the test tube into the black pit of the well. It seemed to take forever for it to reach the bottom. Finally he heard it splash into the water and he started to wind the string back up, bringing the test tube with it. Even in the moonlight he could see the water sample was cloudy when he brought it out of the well, and he was acutely conscious of the cats watching him as he stoppered the test tube, sprayed the outside with disinfectant, and tucked it back into his waist pack.

"Got it," Hicks said. "Now how do we get out of here?"

"The three of you go," Gordon said. "Just try to walk through them. I don't think they'll attack you as long as I'm a danger to the tree or those ... things."

"What about you?" Hicks said.

"I'll be all right," Gordon said. "I'll think of something. Now go!"

Jacques and Rodriguez moved off immediately, but Hicks hung back. He almost asked Gordon, "Are you sure?" But Gordon was always sure. That much Hicks had already learned, so he turned to go. As he did he caught one last sight of the creatures slithering off their mother's body and up the slim trunk of the sapling, gripping with those queer opposable digits and twining around and around the trunk as they climbed, so that they seemed to trace out the shape of a double helix.

Only now did Hicks notice the tree was covered in hundreds of tiny thorns, glinting like needles in the moonlight. As the creatures climbed into the sapling's thin branches, one of them squealed in pain as a thorn pierced its paw.

Had the tree grown taller in the time they had been here? Impossible, yet as Hicks watched a thin leaf unfurled in the moonlight at the tip of its branch.

He couldn't take any more and turned to go, wading among the cats. They still stood motionless, except for their eyes. Watching him as he moved. The feel of them sliding against his legs was horrid, like brushing against something dead in the dark. How would Gordon get away from them? He was still standing back there by the tree, with the dead tomcat in one hand and his gun in the other.

But when Hicks was halfway to the treeline Gordon began to back away from the sapling as well. As he moved, Gordon raised his pistol so it pointed at the creatures in the sapling's branches instead of at its trunk, probably because they made a bigger target. Why did the cats fight harder to protect the tree and those creatures than they did their own lives? They showed no fear of humans or their guns yet froze when Gordon threatened the tree or the creatures.

But they had also attacked Jacques, and tried to force him towards the creatures once the black tomcat had taken away his ability to use his gun. Hicks remembered the way the creatures had attacked their mother.

They can't be left alive, Hicks thought. *They're a danger to anyone who gets near them.*

Hicks realized they were drawing near a breaking point. As they got further away from the sapling, they became less of a danger to it. The cats might let them go, or they might choose to attack them once they no longer threatened the young tree.

Slowly, slowly Gordon backed up. Jacques and Rodriguez had already disappeared under the shadows of the forest, but Hicks lingered, letting Gordon catch up to him. Maybe if they left in pairs they would stand a better chance of getting out all right. The swarm of cats around them began to separate, like a cell undergoing mitosis, with one group centered on the nucleus of the sapling and the other centered on Gordon and Hicks.

It all came down to the moment the cats would feel the gun was no longer a threat to the sapling or the creatures, and that moment would come very soon now. Very soon. But if it came before they got out of the clearing, when the cats still had them surrounded, they couldn't possibly—

Gordon fired. The report was thunderous, sudden, shocking. One of the creatures fell squealing out of the sapling in a shower of leaves and thorny twigs. All at once, in perfect unison like a choir, every cat in the clearing *shrieked*.

"RUN!" Gordon shouted as he turned and bolted from the clearing, still clutching the dead tomcat. Hicks spun, almost stumbled but caught himself in time, and ran after Gordon. Behind him he heard the cats screaming like all the demons in hell and the scrambling, scratching noise of their pursuit.

He sprinted under the cover of the forest into total darkness speared through at random with silvery bars of moonlight. He caught occasional glimpses of Gordon just ahead of him and of Jacques and Rodriguez further on up. He stumbled twice over unseen obstacles until he remembered his night vision goggles, and he quickly reached up and slid them down over his eyes, letting his safety goggles fall off his face. That made it a little better. Now at least he could make out the surface over which he was running, but at the same time it made it worse, because now he could see the cats above him, running through the branches of the trees as they hissed and snarled, glowing green with furious heat except for their cold dark eyes.

Ahead of him, he saw Rodriguez jump into the gully at the base of the big maple. Jacques followed, but stumbled as he jumped and pitched face-first into the gully. Hicks saw Gordon slide down the side of it; he didn't wear night-vision goggles so he must have been going by feel. Gordon had just lifted Jacques back to his feet when Hicks felt something slam onto his shoulders. He spun, almost fell, but managed to keep his feet as the cat on his shoulders ripped at the flesh on the back of his neck and head.

"They've got me!" Hicks screamed. *"Don't leave me here, they've got me!"*

Hot sudden agony spread across the right side of his head; it felt like the cat must have torn his ear off. Hicks screamed, turned again, and then saw something he would remember for the rest of his life, even after all the insanity he had witnessed so far.

Hicks saw Gordon, down in the gully, lift his gun. He seemed to move in nacreous underwater slow-motion as he pointed it directly at Hicks. The dark chasm of the barrel looked abnormally large, so big you could almost fall into it. Then a green supernova of light filled that barrel, so bright Hicks saw colors dancing before his eyes. The bullet whizzed by his head and the cat was gone. Gordon had shot it off his shoulders.

Christ, Hick thought, astonished. *He must be able to see in the dark like a ... uhh ...*

"Come on!" Gordon shouted, startling him out of his surprise, and Hicks jumped into the gully. All around them they heard the snarling of the cats, and the sheer rage in their howls obliterated any words that might have formed from their collective voice.

Hicks ran down the gully as Gordon hauled Jacques to his feet and shoved him forward. Pausing only to snatch the dead tomcat off the ground (he must have dropped it when he helped Jacques back up), Gordon raced after them.

With a clear path they were able to let their panic give speed to their strides. Breath tearing through their throats, they stampeded through the surveillance team's post without even noticing Turner and Manderly, who had heard all the gunfire and radioed Ames to come back and pick them up, double time. They had been debating whether or not they should see if Hicks's team needed backup when Rodriguez, Hicks, Jacques and finally Gordon bolted out of the shadows and headed towards the road. For a moment they hung back in surprise, and in no small measure they lingered out of a feeling of duty not to abandon their post ... until they heard the inhuman howls coming towards them from out of the forest of the night. Then they jumped to their feet and raced after them.

They staggered out of the woods and onto the road just as the van came over the hill. Ames saw the six horror-struck individuals lurch into his headlights and slammed on the brakes, swearing magnificently.

The van slid to a halt barely a foot in front of Rodriguez and Hicks, but they took no notice of this close brush with danger any more than they did the dust and flying gravel that pelted their skin. They ran to the back of the van, pulled open the doors and piled into the back.

"*Go! Go!*" Hicks shouted as loudly as he could, and the van raced away into the night.

For a moment, only the sound of their heavy breathing broke the silence, and then Gordon turned to Jacques and said, "Are you all right?" He gently tried to turn Jacques's face to better see the scratches in the light of the consoles, but Jacques knocked his hand away.

"Get your hands off me, you queer!" Jacques shrieked. They could all hear the panic in his voice.

"Jacques!" Hicks barked. He didn't want to inflame this situation, Jacques was just worked up after all that had happened, but right now Hicks felt a little worked up too and couldn't restrain himself.

"You shut your ignorant mouth!" Hicks shouted. "He saved your ass out there now you show him some respect!"

"You go to hell!" Jacques shouted back. *"He didn't do nothin'! You're a faggot just like he is and he didn't do nothin'! You hear me? Nothin'!"*

"Bullshit!" Hicks shouted back, all composure lost now. *"Rodriguez tell them! Tell Turner and Manderly what happened back there!"*

But Rodriguez only covered her mouth with her hand and turned her face to the wall.

"It's all right, Hicks," Gordon said. "Just let it go, it's all right."

"No it is not all right!" Hicks shouted. *"Nothing is all right!"*

But after that he couldn't think of anything more to say. He could only sit there in the darkness waiting for his panic to ebb, like a wildfire nearing the end of its path of destruction, trailing behind it a long dark scar on the land.

10

The Meeting at Sunrise

"Did you get it?" Rollins asked Gordon soon after Hicks had given his report and left the room where they had met at sunset the evening before last.

"Yes," Gordon replied. "I managed to pick it up before Hicks's team got to the clearing, although it was close."

"I don't see why you didn't let them get one of the dead animals for you," Rollins said. "It wouldn't have given away anything concerning the alien plasmid."

"I wanted to see Beta Site for myself," Gordon said. "Some things you just can't see in a photograph." He was still wearing the same dark clothes he had worn out to Beta Site, only now they were all torn and dusty with leaves and twigs clinging to them in places.

They had awakened Rollins from a sound sleep with this emergency report, but he wasn't about to appear in a meeting in his pajamas, so he had made them wait while he changed into a t-shirt and a pair of camouflage pants. He had worried this would make him look prissy in front of his men, but now he was glad he had done it. Gordon looked like a mess sitting next to him now; he even had a piece of thorny briar caught in his flinty, no-color hair, and Rollins felt it gave him a certain advantage to look better than him.

"But it's a good thing I did go," Gordon said. "The cats, those creatures ... In all the time we've studied this plasmid, I've never seen it produce such an effect." His darkish eyes looked past Rollins and out the window, where the buildings across highway 71 were becoming visible once again as night began its slow fade towards morning. Rollins's watch said 5:30 am.

"Yes, those creatures," Rollins said. "Why didn't Hicks get a picture of them?" His voice betrayed a hint of skepticism, but at this point he didn't care. Judging by those dark circles under his eyes Gordon was feeling his lack of sleep and Rollins wanted to see if he could goad him into revealing some more information. "Do you really think those are some kind of alien creatures incubated inside—"

"I know they were *not* alien creatures," Gordon interrupted, sounding irritated. "They were cats, mutated yes, but definitely cats. Maybe the plasmid was able to affect their development more drastically because they were infected *in utero*, but there was something more to it. I'm sure of it. They had features that looked almost simian, the way they climbed that tree, but their tongues were almost snakelike."

"So you think they had a more severe version of the mutation the plasmid gave the adult cats?" Rollins suggested.

"Maybe," Gordon replied, as Rollins knew he would. Gordon wouldn't make a definitive statement until he had dissected the dead cat he had brought back along with the other specimen.

"The cats' behavior tells me they have mutated," Gordon said. "They have all the same symptoms of the hyenas back at Alpha, the circular pacing, the strange vocalizations, but I've never seen such aggressiveness in mutated animals, or such dramatic physical changes. None of the hyenas were pregnant when they were infected, so we can't know if it would mutate their young in such a way. There's too much we don't know. Too much."

To anyone who didn't know him, Gordon would seem quite calm, but this was more emotion than Rollins had ever seen him display. This little encounter in the woods must have indeed been terrifying and already Rollins began to plan out his strategy. It would have to be contained, of course. Such a threat must never become widespread …

"But why was there so many of them?" Gordon said, as if he had read Rollins's mind. "There must have been a lot of cats living in close proximity to each other for so many to become infected at once."

"I can tell you that," Rollins said. "I grew up in Texas, and we've had our fair share of wildfires. You always see carnivores hunting around the edges of the fire, catching all the mice and snakes and rats and all the other little vermin trying to outrun the flames. The cats could have picked up the plasmid by eating the smaller animals already infected with it."

"Yes, that sounds likely," Gordon said softly, but his eyes were lost in thought. What had those eyes seen at Beta Site? Rollins wondered.

Gordon abruptly rose from his seat. "I want to dissect the specimens now," he said.

"Oh, I'm sure the lab is always open for you," Rollins said with a little chuckle. Perhaps this would get entertaining. After a frightening sleepless night, Gordon might even make a mistake, and swear like a normal human being.

Rollins rose from his own chair and followed Gordon out of the meeting room into the nondescript hallway outside. They took the elevator down to the basement, where the Corps of Engineers had set up a laboratory three days ago with their usual speed and aplomb. As they came out of the elevator, crossed the hall and entered the double doors of the lab, Rollins began to feel a little uncomfortable. What if Gordon really was a fruit and tried to put the moves on him while they were down here alone together? Strange how it had never occurred to him during their private meetings upstairs, but this basement lab, although clean and well-lit, seemed much too isolated, secretive, somehow *sordid*, with its windowless beige walls and rows of fluorescent lights hung in the paneled ceiling. The low black-topped tables with their strange glass instruments and gleaming stainless-steel devices, the purpose of which Rollins could not guess, somehow made the bad impression worse.

"Activate the locks on the doors, please," Gordon said, and before he realized he had just taken an order from a fruit, Rollins turned and entered the codes on the touchpad beside lab door that would restrict access to anyone with Red Level security clearance. Outrage swelled like polluted water in Rollins's veins. Gordon could have locked those doors himself. Was he playing something? Well, Rollins couldn't ask him that directly, then Gordon could try to make him look paranoid, so in a moment of brilliant inspiration he said, "Those cats really had you terrified, huh? Are you scared of pussies, Gordon?" He didn't often come up with double entendres, but he thought that was a pretty good one.

Gordon didn't condescend to answer, but Rollins did not feel triumphant. He felt disappointed. Did Gordon think he was too good to respond to a direct challenge or something? He didn't look offended at all, only tired.

"I put the tomcat in a specimen tray and locked it in this refrigerator as soon we got back," he said, taking a key from his pocket and opening the refrigerator's stainless-steel door. "However, I didn't get a private moment to lock up the other specimen." He did not mention that Private Hicks had kept following him around, apologizing for the behavior of Jacques and Rodriguez, until Gordon finally had to order him to go see the medic for his wounded ear. He took a tray containing the dead tomcat out of the refrigerator and set it on one of the tables.

"So where did you put it?" Rollins asked, wondering if he could find a mistake to throw back in Gordon's face should the need arise.

Gordon lifted the backpack he had taken out to Beta Site. He had kept it with him ever since they returned. Unzipping the top, he pulled out a clear plastic cylinder, sealed with black caps on each end. Inside of it was a dead rabbit, the same one Rachel had almost tripped over the day before. Round pink tumors rose from its dirty brown fur.

Taking the cylinder over to the table, Gordon unscrewed one of the black caps and dumped the rabbit into another stainless-steel tray next to the dead cat.

"Good God, that thing stinks!" Rollins said, recoiling. "Was that the only one you could find? It smells like it's been sitting in the sun for days!"

"It probably has," Gordon replied. "But it was the only one I could find in the time available." He took out a pair of latex gloves, a foam mask, and a pair of clear plastic goggles from a drawer in the table. The equipment was almost identical to the kit Hicks used to collect the water sample from Beta Site.

For a moment Gordon only stood and looked down at the two specimens in front of him. The rabbit looked decomposed, ruined and malformed, while the tomcat still looked relatively sleek, despite its crooked neck. Its fur was thick and full, and it looked like it had eaten well before it died.

The same microorganism had killed one animal while making another one stronger. It didn't seem possible, yet the evidence lay right in front of him. Shaking his head as if to clear it, Gordon began the dissections while Rollins stood back and watched with his arms folded across his chest. Gordon splayed the animals out, cut them open and poked through their insides, pausing occasionally to take notes in a small pad of paper on the table beside him. Many of the rabbit's organs were so riddled with tumors they were almost unrecognizable. The tomcat's stomach contained a large quantity of chewed-up meat. The dissection of the bodies didn't take very long, Gordon only gave it a cursory examination. He took more time with their brains. Using his small bone saw, he opened their skulls, lifted out the brains and placed them in ceramic dishes beneath a lamp with an attached magnifying glass.

"The rabbit's brain has several visible tumors," Gordon said. Rollins didn't know if he was speaking to him or just thinking out loud. "But the feline brain has only one abnormal growth, on the underside of the mid-brain just forward of the medulla oblongata. The growth maintains bilateral symmetry; it's the same on both sides of the brain and the cranial fissure continues through the middle of it. The corpus callosum, which connects the two sides of the brain, is slightly elongated, and thicker. The growth seems to have enveloped the hippocampus, since it is no longer recognizable."

"Do you expect me to write all this down or something?" Rollins said dryly. Damned if he would let Gordon give him another order.

"I just thought you might want to know," Gordon said, with a trace of irritation in his voice. "If we are going to fight this thing, it might help to understand it. And if I'm not mistaken, you were quite upset earlier when you thought our superiors had withheld information from you."

Rollins did not respond. Gordon was right and apologizing to him seemed like the only possible response, but he would never apologize to Gordon, not for anything. It didn't matter how much Gordon contributed or his high-handed way of dealing with people, Rollins would never surrender his dislike of him.

"You should also know I'm going to send tissue samples from both specimens to Quantico for testing," Gordon continued. "I'm hoping we can use them to finally sequence the plasmid's genes. If we can grow cells from the rabbit and the cat in culture, sequence the DNA in them and then compare them to the DNA of uninfected animals, we might be able to finally discover the plasmid's gene sequence. That's a very weighty 'might.'"

Rollins grunted in acknowledgement. Now a response seemed necessary, since he could gain more information from it. "Has Hicks tested the water sample yet?"

Gordon nodded towards a pair of round plastic dishes sitting under a lamp on one of the other tables in the room. "That's the testing kit in the incubator over there. We should get the results in a couple of hours."

"How does he test it, anyway?" Rollins had wondered how Hicks would do that, since they couldn't make the plasmid reproduce.

"He added some *Pseudomonas aeruginosa* to a mixture of the well water and some growth medium," Gordon said. "He also added some of the bacteria to a solution of distilled water and growth medium as a control. If the bacteria reproduce in the distilled water solution but not the one with well water, we can conclude the plasmid is there."

"Isn't that a breach of security?" Rollins asked. "I thought Hicks wasn't supposed to know about the plasmid."

"He doesn't," Gordon said. "I told him to test it this way. He knows that if the bacteria don't grow then it's a positive result for a contagion, but he doesn't know why or what it is. I cleared it with Washington."

"Why didn't you just test it yourself?"

Gordon looked at him over the top of his safety goggles. "I'm only one person," he said. "I can't do everything."

"I suppose it's a foregone conclusion that it will come up positive."

"Probably," Gordon said. "So many infected animals ..." He trailed off, looking troubled.

"What?" Rollins pressed. Gordon had never shared so much information at once, and Rollins wanted to take him for all he was worth.

"Even by eating animals exposed shortly after the meteor hit," Gordon said. "I just don't see how so many cats could have been infected. Remember it's not contagious. I suppose some kittens could have contracted it from their mother's milk, but even then, there shouldn't be so many."

"Maybe that's proof the well water is contaminated," Rollins said. "The groundwater could seep through somewhere and the cats could be drinking it."

"That's possible, yes. But remember the plasmid can't reproduce. Neither can the transport bacterium after it picks up the plasmid. You mean to say that after a month there are still enough of them left in the water to infect so many animals?"

"So what do you think?" Rollins said, a little defensively.

"I don't know," Gordon said. "It's like there is some kind of continuous source of new plasmids coming into this environment somehow."

"There haven't been any more meteor showers," Rollins said. "Where else could they come from?"

"I don't know," Gordon repeated. "I just don't know. I need to get a couple hours sleep. Then I can decide what to do next."

Gordon stood and began to cover the tray with the tomcat in it, but stopped, still holding the lid in front of him. He looked down at the cat, his head tilted slightly to the left.

"What is that?"

Rollins leaned forward, the curiosity so fatal to cats overcoming him. "What is what?"

Gordon set down the lid, took a pair of tweezers from the tool case next to him, and carefully lowered them towards the cat's jaws. The mouth hung open, exposing the gleaming fangs. Using the tweezers, Gordon pulled a bit of stringy gray matter out from between its front teeth.

"Is that some kind of tissue?" Rollins asked.

"I think it's brain matter," Gordon said.

"Does that mean something?"

Gordon shook his head, not in negation but as a way of saying he didn't know. He set the little gray blob on a glass slide and used a scalpel to cut a thin cross-section out of it. After using the tweezers to put the rest of it into a small glass vial, he then took the slide with the cross section over to the optical microscope sitting on a table against the far wall.

He put the slide in the microscope, turned on the little lamp at its base, and looked through the eyepiece.

"It *is* brain matter," he said. "Look."

Rollins came over and looked into the microscope. He saw a thick cluster of grayish, blocky cells with strange veinlike extensions branching off from them on all sides.

"Those are neurons," Gordon said. "Brain cells."

Rollins felt the curiosity again, stronger this time. Now he understood how someone could get caught up in scientific pursuits. One thing led to another, and another, and another …

"So the cats have been eating brain tissue," Rollins said. "From what animal?"

Gordon shrugged. "I can't say just yet. I would have to do some more tests, and I'm in no shape to do them effectively right now."

He walked back to the dissection table, covered the specimen trays and put them back in the refrigerator, locking the door afterwards. Then he peeled off his latex gloves, facemask, and goggles, and tossed them into the biohazard disposal bin.

"Have you ever heard of a study where they fed mice brain tissue?" Gordon asked, turning back to Rollins.

"Can't say that I have," Rollins replied.

"It went like this: They taught these mice how to run through a maze. Made them do it over and over again until they had the path through the maze memorized. Then they killed the mice and fed their brain tissue to other, younger mice."

"How pleasant," Rollins said. "What is it with scientists and these ghoulish experiments?"

"It's awful, I know," Gordon said, rather surprising him, "but my point is this: the mice that ingested the brain tissue learned to run the maze twenty percent faster than those who did not."

"You mean to tell me," Rollins said, "that those mice somehow learned the way through that maze by eating the brains of the mice that had already run it?"

"That's one explanation," Gordon said. "That knowledge was transmitted by absorption of brain tissue. Or it might mean that the proteins in the brain tissue helped develop the neural cells of the younger mice."

"You think this has something to do with the alien plasmid, don't you?" Rollins said.

"It mutates the part of the brain associated with memory, and now we discover infected creatures eating brain matter? I have to believe there is a connection."

"Then what is it? To what purpose?"

Gordon's tired eyes stared across the shadowless room, towards nothing. "I don't know," he said. "I need some sleep. I'm too tired to think clearly right now."

"And what about those creatures?" Rollins asked. Gordon must indeed need sleep, since he would never admit to Rollins that he needed anything if he were fully rested. "You may have killed one, but the other one is still out there in the woods—"

"I *shot* one," Gordon interrupted, looking irritated again. "I never saw it die."

For a moment Rollins felt almost intimidated by Gordon's sudden intensity, but he quickly recovered. "Thank you for all your assistance, Agent Gordon," he said, smiling. "I'll take it from here if you're all worn out."

Gordon paused at the door. "You will send out a team to kill them, won't you? The other cats will have to be wiped out as well, they're a hazard to this entire community—"

"I can put together a team with rifles and flame throwers and get them out there in a couple of hours," Rollins replied, still smiling like an alligator. "I'll call them in from Fort Leavenworth and have a cover story released to the media just in case."

"Good," Gordon replied. "That's good." Then he punched in his security code at the door and left the lab. Rollins stared at the doors for several seconds after he was gone.

Better than you think, you arrogant bastard, he thought. *Better than you think.*

11

The Morning Visitors

Timothy Coldiron woke that morning thinking about the girl. He had dreamed something had come to his window in the night and spoken to him about that girl, but after waking up he couldn't remember what the voice had told him. Something about the woods, that he should go out and try to find the girl in the woods.

It was just a dream; he was sure of that. He was, after all, twelve years old, almost thirteen, practically an adult and he felt that he had already learned just about everything he needed to know. He even understood all the changes going on his body right now. They had taught him most of it in school until his idiot mother had found out about it and enrolled him in a private academy that didn't believe in sex education. He was going through "puberty." That was the time when boys turned into men. Soon he would get a thin wispy mustache just above his upper lip, break out in pimples and start chasing girls. (He had chased girls before, in elementary school, but that was mostly just an excuse to run around the playground. He had never intended to actually catch them.)

He knew this time would soon arrive. He could already feel strange sensations beginning to stir in him, particularly when he thought about that dark-haired girl he had seen the day before yesterday. His mother had been watching the neighbor's house with her binoculars when the girl had come out of the woods with two boys behind her. In the time since then Timmy had begun to feel bitterly jealous of those two boys. They had seen her up close. For some reason, as soon as his mother had seen them, she had jumped up and shrieked, "Oh no! Don't worry, sweetness! Everything will be just fine! Mummy will make everything all right!" Then she dashed out the door.

Timmy had not heard a word of his mother's confrontation with the two boys, but he had picked up her binoculars and watched the whole scene. Soon he had kept the binoculars focused solely on the girl's face, and had seen a remarkable transformation come over her. Timmy's mother had tried to drag the girl into the house, but the girl had stood up to her just like a grown-up and sent her running away.

Ever since, Timmy could not stop thinking about her.

Afterwards, his mother had come into the house, stared at him for a few seconds and said, "I'm getting your medication! That will make you feel better!" Although Timmy had felt fine, better than ever, like Romeo after glimpsing Juliet at her window.

He wished he could call up his old gym teacher, Mr. Foster, and ask him what these feelings meant. Mr. Foster had also taught sex-ed and had told them many interesting things.

For instance: "All right, now in a few years, you might notice your dogs and your cats starting to act a little different around you. I don't know if any of you kids got any horses or if you got relatives on farms who let you near their cows or their sheep or goats or whatever—seems like fewer people do all the time—but once all those hormones start rampaging through your system, they'll literally start seeping out of your pores and the animals will be able to smell it. You girls got to be especially careful 'cause you can get attacked during your ... your ..." Then he had coughed into his fist and finally stammered out, "... menstrual cycles."

He had summarized by saying, "It's a gross time of your life. You'll be oozing goo out of every hole in your head." And everyone had laughed.

But now, as he lay in his bed in the yellow glow of morning with thoughts of the strange girl swirling through his mind and a barely formed, hardly understood desire making him ache and shudder, it didn't seem so funny anymore. If he were a few years older he would have discovered the age-old means teenage boys have always used to relieve this ache, but that time had not yet arrived.

He couldn't talk to his father about it, because his father didn't like him. Oh, he never said so, but Timmy could tell. Sometimes his father would look at him and shake his head in disgust. If Timmy tried to talk to him, he would say he was too busy and walk away. Whenever his father did those things, Timmy would always run to the pantry and grab handfuls of Ding-Dongs or Nutter Butters or M & Ms, whatever he could find, and cram them down his throat. That was why Timmy was so fat and awkward and unpopular. That was why he was certain no girl would ever want him.

Oh, but the dark-haired girl ...

As for talking about this with his mother, that was a joke. Never mind that she now had a passionate hatred for the ungrateful girl that had sassed her so—and after she had tried to rescue her!—but her answer to all of his problems was more medication, more of those pills that made his head thunder and swim. The only medication that made him feel better was sugar, granulated or powdered, straight from the bag if need be.

Timmy lay in his bed, feeling a sharp hatred for both of his parents, blaming them for all his misery. Above these thoughts floated the girl's pale face, like the moon in a nighttime sky.

A shadow moved across the wall.

Timmy flinched in surprise; he felt suddenly guilty, like he had been caught doing something shameful. Turning his head, he saw a pair of cats outside the window to his left. One cat was dark with white spots, and the other was white with dark spots. They lay on the windowsill with their hindquarters touching and their tails intertwined, looking like photonegatives of each other. They both had blue eyes, which surprised Timmy. He had never seen cats with blue eyes before. As he watched, both cats blinked at exactly the same time. He could see the milky films of their third eyelids sliding back in perfect unison. That third eyelid was called a nictitating membrane. Timmy had read about it in a book on cats, for he had always been fascinated with animals. He had a ... special game he liked to play with them.

Once a stray dog had approached him in the back yard of their old house in Phoenix. Timmy had been eating a sloppy joe, and it had come begging for scraps with its thin tail waving in desperate hope. Timmy, curious, had smashed its head open with a rock to look at its brains.

Then, when they had moved to Austin, he had found a nest full of baby birds. Bluejays, he thought they were called. While the momma bird had flown about his head squawking with outrage, Timmy had doused each one with bleach and covered them with a glass jar so he could watch the fumes suffocate them.

In Portland, Oregon he had sprinkled rat poison over popcorn and fed it to some squirrels to see what would happen.

And so on, in all the places they had lived over the short but busy span of his life. Timothy had taken to reading books about animals and their anatomy to see what other interesting effects he could produce in them.

And now here was a pair of cats.

Timmy thought of Mr. Foster's warning. Was he starting to emit a kind of natural lure? That could lead to a lot of interesting possibilities ...

Both cats suddenly rose to a sitting position and meowed. They did it just as they had blinked their eyes: in perfect unison. The sound of both of their meows overlapping each other produced an odd stereo effect. The sound was clipped off a bit at the end, so that it didn't quite sound like *meow,* more like *out.* Very strange cats. Timmy wondered what would happen if he cut out their tongues. Or, since the two seemed so interdependent, if he killed one and let the other one live. It made him so curious.

Their tails began to swish back and forth, the dark and the light twining over each other. Timmy knew what that meant; the cats were becoming agitated. He had seen cats stalking birds before, and their tails had swished back and forth in exactly the same way. He would have liked to reach out and grab them now, but the window had a screen over it to keep out the bugs.

Both of the cats spread their jaws and let out a low, almost subaudible hiss. Stretching out their necks, they drew their noses towards the screen, towards *him*, nostrils twitching as they scented the air drifting through the screen's thin wire mesh. Timmy realized that the cats had now started to purr with a slow, almost decadent pleasure.

"Timmy sweetheart," his mother cooed outside his door. "Are you awake? It's time for your medication, and I have your Count Chocula on the table."

Timmy jumped in surprise; the cats blinked in unison one last time, flitted off his windowsill and disappeared.

They were gone! Dull fury crawled up Timothy Coldiron's spine.

"Mom you woke me up, you idiot!" Timmy shouted. "Now I can't go back to sleep!"

"Oh, I'm sorry, honey," said Mrs. Coldiron. "Why don't you come down to breakfast and take your medication? That will make you feel better."

Always with the medication. Timmy cast one last disappointed glance at the windowsill, but the cats had not returned. It was a shame. They had reminded him of those two creepy Siamese cats from *The Lady and the Tramp*. His skin crawled every time he thought of them and that song they sang: *We are Siamese if you please* ... He would have liked to take out some of that fear on those trouble-some felines that had just visited his windowsill, but now it looked like he would never have the chance.

Sighing with disappointment, Timmy Coldiron got out of bed.

Breakfast passed with the usual tension. His mother laid out his medication, first the round blue tablet and then the narrow pink one. (She had once tried to encourage him to take them by saying, "Imagine one's a boy and one's a girl!") His father muttered from behind his newspaper, "God only knows what those things are doing to his brain."

"Don't you start!" Mrs. Coldiron snapped. As soon as his mother turned away and his father returned his attention to his newspaper, Timmy snuck a spoonful of sugar from the bowl and sprinkled it over his Count Chocula.

After breakfast he felt jittery and wired, and spent several minutes wandering from his X-box to his computer to his PSP and then all over the house. Unfortunately his mother had driven into town for an errand just before his father became fed up with Timmy's pacing. It was Saturday, and his father did not work weekends, much to Timmy's regret.

"Too much sugar!" Walter Coldiron declared. "Get your ass outside and get some exercise, for God's sake. You're bugging the hell out of me."

He shoved Timmy out the front door and onto the porch, into a world not at all like his video games. The sun seemed much too bright, the morning much too hot. A flying black insect buzzed by Timmy's ear and he flinched back in terror. For a minute he could only stand there, sulking and afraid. His mother would never shove him outside all by himself; she thought parents who let their kids play outside unsupervised were guilty of criminal neglect and should have their kids taken away by the state. She had said so about that woman in the weird red house across the road. She would make his father pay for doing this to him, oh yes. His mother could out-scream anyone.

The heat rose in steaming waves from the concrete porch and wet patches immediately began to form in the armpits of Timmy's dark green T-shirt, but Timmy still didn't move. He only stood there, hating his father and staring at the big bad world waiting like a wolf outside his door, and he was the little pig. A thousand fearful thoughts ran through his mind. What if the dark-haired girl came along and saw him like this, all sweaty and mad? What if a wasp stung him or a snake bit him or a stranger tried to kidnap him or …?

A cat meowed, slightly below and to the right of him.

Looking down, he saw the two cats that had visited his windowsill standing beside the porch, twining against each other and purring as they stared up at him. Watching their flicking tails, Timmy thought he might be able to have some fun out here after all.

"Here, kitty-kitty-kitty," he said, a grin forming over his face. "Here kitty, wanna treat? C'mere kitty …"

Timmy crept down off the porch, holding out his hand to the cats and rubbing his thumb and forefinger together as if he had a treat for them. With luck he would catch both of them, but even one would do. The cats extended their noses to sniff at him. He assumed that meant they really believed he had something for them to eat.

When he got close enough he lunged forward, but they darted out of reach a second before he could catch them. They bounded a few steps towards the woods on the west side of the house, then paused, looked back at him, and meowed.

What, are they playing or something? Timmy thought. He had never bothered to learn about animal behavior since it didn't seem to help him much in the course of his special games, so he had no idea why the cats were acting so strangely. His family had never owned pets for very long, and not always because of his games. His mother would occasionally decide they should get a puppy or a kitten, usually after she had seen a commercial on television showing a group of clean-cut kids playing with one. But then after she brought it home the puppies would poop all over the carpet or the kittens would start clawing up the furniture, so Timmy's father would take them to the pound or dump them by the side of the road somewhere. This seemed like an awful waste to Timmy, but he couldn't think of a way to suggest to his parents that he should dispose of the animals for them.

Regardless, a defensive part of him now felt that these cats were playing a game with him, at his expense, just like all those awful bullies that had made fun of him at the various schools his parents had dragged him to over the years. Timmy resolved to make the cats pay for that, just as soon as he caught them.

"Come on," he said. "Come here, come on now …" His impatience gave an edge to his voice. He tried to walk up and grab the cats again but they darted forward once more, leading him closer to the edge of the woods.

Timmy paused when he reached the barbed wire fence. The cats had already passed under it and now they paused as well, looking back at him and meowing in their strange voices. He really wanted to catch those cats, but at the same time he had never ventured into the woods alone, and they looked kind of creepy. Thin scraggly trees with green veils of leaves hanging from their branches climbed out of the tangled underbrush. It was so thick that he couldn't see very far into the forest. Timmy saw no way he could walk through it without scratching up his legs on all those brambles. His long baggy shorts went down below his knees, but that left his calves unprotected, and what if he got scratched? That could really hurt. Also, what about poison ivy? He had heard of it, but would never recognize it if he saw it. He knew it had three leaves, but looking at the forest floor he saw dozens of different plants with three leaves, and all of them looked different. Which one was poison ivy?

As he stood there, frozen with indecision, one of the cats came forward, turned around, and urinated on his leg. Timmy jumped back in surprise and disgust when he felt the warm liquid hit his bare skin. The cat that had pissed on him walked back under the fence and rubbed against its companion, purring in pleasure.

Timmy's jaw dropped and his thick face twisted in disgust. The smell of urine shot straight up his nose, making his stomach churn.

"Pissed on me!" Timmy gasped. "Oh gross, it pissed on me!"

The cats meowed again, in unison, and that sent Timmy over the edge. It sounded too much like laughter and he couldn't take it when anyone laughed at him. He launched into a full-fledged tantrum.

"You little bastards!" Timmy cried as he scrambled over the fence. One of the barbs scratched his leg, and he blamed the cats for it. He stumbled and fell through to the other side, and blamed the cats for it. At that moment he blamed the cats for his overbearing mother, his angry distant father, his weight, his awkwardness, everything.

Climbing to his hands and knees, he saw the cats darting into the underbrush, flitting their tails behind them. Snorting like an angry bull-calf, Timmy climbed to his feet and ran after them.

Fortunately, the cats kept to some kind of natural trail through the woods. Timmy did not know it was a game trail, formed as deer and raccoons and other forest animals, all of them creatures of habit, followed the same path through the woods and wore away the underbrush. He only cared that it kept the cats in his sight as he chased them. The white one with dark spots stood out especially well. He could see its pale rump bounding away through the leaves.

He chased them for a few hundred yards, and would have kept on going until he ran out of breath, but a low-hanging branch struck the side of his face, sending a surprising bolt of pain through the side of his head and startling him out of his tantrum. He stumbled to a halt with his hands clamped to his face.

The branch had caught him across his temple and broken the skin. Timmy could feel blood running through his fingers, and this final hurt sent him over the edge. He drew in a long, whistling breath and then released it as an anguished scream.

The scream broke down into sobs, and for several seconds he stood there in the forest and cried with his hands pressed over his eyes. This was all his father's fault, throwing him outside like this. Shafts of golden sunlight filtered down through the green canopy of leaves, and as the wind moved the branches, making them sigh and whisper, patterns of light and shadow danced over the brambly carpet of underbrush. It was beautiful, but Timmy saw none of it. He kept his hands pressed to his eyes, seeing neither beauty, nor evil.

After a few minutes his crying settled down into sniffles, and he lowered his hands, squinting in the sunshine. He didn't see the cats anymore, so he decided to go back home. His father wouldn't fuss over the scratches on his face and leg, but maybe his mother had returned from her errand by now. She would put Band-aids on his wounds and fix him a bowl ice cream to cheer him up. Even better, she would give his father hell for letting this happen to him.

But which way led back home? He couldn't remember. Had he spun around after the branch hit him? He looked around but the forest looked the same in all directions. He couldn't see the barbed-wire fence or any other landmarks that would tell him which way to go.

And now he began to feel a little afraid.

Trying to keep calm, he turned in a slow circle, and before he got halfway around he saw a branch hanging above the path. The branch didn't have any leaves, it looked dead, but it was bobbing up and down, so Timmy reasoned that it must be the branch that hit him. So, the path beyond that branch must lead home. No problem.

He started walking back in that direction. The cut on his temple still throbbed. He sniffled and whimpered as he walked to keep his tears going, so he could crank them up again when he got home, if his mother was back.

Something in the woods began to growl.

Timmy froze. The growling faded after a few seconds, and he began to wonder if he had really heard it. He tilted his head, listening, but now he only heard the leaves rustling in the wind. The forest seemed much too quiet. Timmy got the impression something was missing. Shouldn't there be birds singing or crickets chirping, stuff like that? The silence weighed down on him, unnatural and scary. Now he wanted to go home more than ever. He took a few more steps, and the growling came again. It sounded close this time, real close, maybe just a few yards ahead of him, a low menacing growl filled with predatory hunger.

He had never in his life experienced something like this, yet it struck a strange resonant chord within him, almost like instinct. It was the fear of something stalking him, the fear of being hunted. The smell of his blood seemed much stronger now, and he remembered Mr. Foster's warning about animals. He had not thought about *dangerous* animals being drawn to him.

And don't forget about fear, he thought. *They can smell fear.*

Some bushes to the right of the path ahead of him rustled. Timmy wanted more than anything to run for home, but he would have to pass that growling thing in the bushes and the thought of doing that terrified him. So he stood his ground, paralyzed with fear and indecision.

The bushes rustled again, and then two bobcats slinked out from under them.

They were each almost twice the size of an ordinary cat, and only had a stump of a tail. Their pale orange fur, covered with dark spots, bristled up along their backs, and their upper lips curled away from their fangs. Their paws looked too big for the rest of their bodies. They slinked towards him. He could see their claws extend for an instant each time one of those enormous paws rose from the ground in a step. They growled like sputtering motorcycle engines as they advanced.

Timmy's whimpering grew into something like sobs: *"Uh! Uh! Uh!"* He began to back away from the advancing bobcats that now began to snarl, slinking ever more swiftly towards him.

One of the bobcats screamed, a horrid, bloodcurdling shriek that sounded like it should have come from the throat of a mountain lion or a panther, and that finally broke Timmy's fear into the jagged shards of panic. He turned to run, but his feet tangled together and he fell to the ground.

He scrambled back to his feet, crying in terror, and so he did not stop to wonder why the bobcats did not pounce on him while he was helpless on the ground. They waited until he regained his feet and then chased after him, nipping at his heels as he started to run.

Timmy stuck to the path without thinking, since it was the only way clear of underbrush and briar patches. The dark trail led onwards into territory unknown to Timothy Coldiron as the bobcats herded him further and further away from home. Branches and brambles tore at his face and arms, and behind him he heard the snarling of the bobcats.

He screamed for his mother as he ran faster and further than he had ever run before. His breath tore down his throat like searing fire and his vision grew blurry from both speed and tears, until it looked like he was running through a shimmering green-gold tunnel. A dark spiny shape passed by to his left, some kind of tree covered in thorns, and ahead of him he saw a big old maple with vines hanging from it.

He did not see the gully.

He came to the edge of it before he could stop himself, and then tumbled down the side in a miniature landslide of rocks and dirt clods. By reflex he put his hands out in front of him to stop his fall, and as they slapped against the ground he felt a bone snap in his right wrist, making an audible crack. He scraped his face, elbows and knees. Dirt flew into his eyes, blinding him, as he rolled down the friable slope. And then he landed at the bottom of the gully in a heap.

The bobcats arrived half a second later. Through his tears and the dirt in his eyes, Timmy could only see two orange blurs come over the dark edge of the gully and swoop down on him from each side, both of them screaming like starving demons ready to devour him. But they didn't devour him; they seemed intent on terrorizing him first. They screamed those awful screams and snapped at his face, bringing their blunt jaws together inches away from his eyes. For several seconds Timmy could only cover his face with his hands and bawl as the bobcats tormented him. It felt like an eternity. Then one of them swiped its paw across his thigh in a clawed spanking, bringing a ringing, exquisite pain, and Timmy jumped to his feet and scrambled out of the gully. He couldn't go back towards his house, and couldn't run down the bed of the gully in either direction. If he tried, the bobcats jumped at him and clawed at his legs and belly. So he went the only way they would let him go: up the opposite side of the gully, in the same direction they had chased him all the way here.

As he stumbled into the burned-out clearing, he thought, *This is it, they chased me here to kill me.* It seemed like the most logical conclusion, because the clearing was full of cats. Hundreds of them. (If Gordon had been there, he would have been furious with Rollins, for although several hours had passed since the night mission, no soldiers had come bearing rifles or flamethrowers.)

Looking at all those cats, Timmy could not help but think that they had chased him here for revenge, for all the animals he had killed in the course of his special games. The cats covered the burned ground of the clearing in a multi-colored carpet; Timmy could see the two cats that had visited his windowsill twining against each other in a figure-eight at the edge of the forest.

Timmy tried to turn and bolt in another direction when he got to the edge of the clearing. The sight of that huge swarm of cats shocked him. But the bobcats kept at his heels as he ran, and when he tried to run away from the clearing, they turned and intercepted him like lions running down a zebra that had strayed from the herd. With bites and claws, they chased him back into the clearing.

The swarm of cats parted before him as he entered and then closed in behind him again as the other cats started helping the bobcats herd him to the center of clearing. Timmy turned around and around as he staggered onwards, shocked and horrified by the sheer number of hissing cats surrounding him. He almost fell into a deep, dark hole in the ground until the row of cats around it screamed at him and frightened him away from it.

And then he felt something soft and cold brush against his cheek. He whirled to face it, expecting some new horror, and saw that the cats had chased him to a tree that stood in the center of the clearing.

Again, if Gordon were there, the tree's size would have surprised him. The sapling had tripled in height and width since his team had come to the clearing. It had grown with the silent, deadly speed of a tumor. Now it stood almost fifteen feet high, and the trunk was almost eight inches thick.

Timmy, of course, had never seen this tree before, but the sight of it still shocked him. Thorns covered every branch and limb; they bristled from the trunk in dozens of spiny clusters. It looked like the big brother of the thorn tree he had passed on the way here, or maybe just some kind of mutated version of it. All the branches were twisted and curled around each other in an insane, thorny tangle, a Gordian knot tied eight feet above the ground, held up by a knotted trunk covered in six-inch-long wooden needles. Strands of small oval leaves hung from the branches like green tassels. One of these had brushed Timmy's cheek.

The moment he turned to face it, one of the cats jumped up and collided with the center of his back, pitching him onto the thorns.

He saw them coming, dozens of slick sharp spikes like dark syringe needles jabbing at his face. He tried to stop himself, but gravity got a hold of him first. The thorns punctured his cheeks, his chest, his arms and legs. One long thorn rammed through his left nostril into his sinus cavity. He had put out his hands to catch his fall and the thorns pierced them all the way through to the other side. Shiny spots of blood spread over Timmy's t-shirt where the thorns had stuck him. The blood looked brown against the green fabric.

By some miracle, none of the thorns pierced his eyes, although one had caught the lid of the right one and pulled it back so that the white orb of it showed. It soon dried and Timmy's vision grew blurry. Thorns bristled from his forehead and scalp like a crown. Lines of blood soon began to run down his face.

He screamed. It felt like a thousand red-hot knives had stabbed him all over his body. He tried to pull back, but he couldn't do it. He was stuck to the tree as if he'd been nailed there.

"*Mommmieee!*" Timmy screamed. "*I want my Mommy!*" All the shrill callowness had passed from his voice. The cry could have come from a soldier dying on any of the world's multitudinous battle fields.

He heard the cats meowing and muttering all around him, but he couldn't see them. He could only see a vague moving presence at the edges of his peripheral vision. And suddenly it seemed he could hear voices swimming in and out of audibility from the

(*great cold silence*)

cries of the cats, but he couldn't understand what they were saying. Voices, not speaking exactly, more like a choir raised in

(*lifesong*)

hymn, like at church. Dimly, through his left eye, Timmy saw a drop of silvery liquid form at the tip of one of the thorns and fall to the ashy ground. Through his grief of pain, he thought, *Is that going into me? Is it poison?*

Movement. Above him, in the branches. Something slithering among the thorns. What …?

Then he saw the eyes. Two glowing, almond-shaped eyes, shining with the same silvery luster as the liquid dripping from the tips of the thorns. At first they seemed to float, disembodied, through the shadows among the branches, but as the eyes drew closer Timmy saw the dark sinuous body of the creature that was watching him with those eyes. It slithered down to him through the thorns, until Timmy could see its oversized, wedge-shaped head and hairless maroon skin. It had a long, thin body trailing out behind it, and it grasped at the branches with opposable digits on all four of its paws.

Fangs gleamed from the creature's jaws, but Timmy didn't notice. His gaze was fixed on the creature's eyes, those brilliant, dazzling eyes. When he looked into those eyes, the pain of the thorns faded away, along with all his fear and panic, leaving only calm. He really needed to feel some calm right now, and those eyes brought it better than any pill his mother had ever given him. The creature had hypnotized him with its stare the way a snake will hypnotize a bird just before it strikes.

Singing. Yes, he heard the singing again, coming from all around him, and now he wanted to join them; he wanted them all to come together as he lay impaled upon the thorns, singing his beautiful lifesong like a dying bird.

When we come together, Timmy thought, as the silvery liquid seeped into him through the thorns, *we will remember who we are!*

Now he saw a second pair of eyes coming down through the branches. Another creature, almost identical to the first except for a long white scar down its side where it had once received a terrible wound. (He did not know that this was the creature Gordon had shot just last night, or that its wound had already healed in the ten hours since and the creature had more than doubled in size.)

Timmy watched them as they descended, trapped in the gaze of their eyes, feeling an almost religious ecstasy. He did not feel the pain of the thorns. He did not flinch when the creatures spread their jaws and unrolled their forked tongues with sharp tips of black chitin.

"Motherworld," he whispered.

The creatures lowered their jaws to his face and stabbed their dagger tongues into his eye sockets. The eyeballs popped like water balloons and vitreous fluid ran down his cheeks, smearing the blood. The creatures' jaws moved as they sucked out the brain matter, and as they did the silvery fluid flowed out of the thorns into Timmy's body, where it began to work its changes.

Most of these changes occurred in the brain, where his neural cells began to divide, something that had not happened in this body since Timmy was a five-month-old fetus, still in his mother's womb. Only now the cells divided with manic, unnatural speed. Production of restriction enzymes to unzip the DNA strand accelerated, as did production of the polymerase that rebuilt each half into a complete new strand. The neural cells split, formed new synaptic connections with other neurons, and then split again, and again. Consumption of the cellular fuel adenosine triphosphate, or ATP, skyrocketed and released a great deal of heat as a result of the chemical reaction. Timmy's heart raced as it circulated blood to pick up the heat from the brain and take it to the skin, where evaporating sweat would carry the heat away. As a result, Timmy's skin turned red and flushed, and sweat mixed with the blood and vitreous fluid on his face. Heat rose from his body in sickly waves, like a terrible fever. His clothes grew soaked with sweat and blood as the cells of his mind grew faster and faster, so that the new, mutated brain cells replaced the old ones as fast as the creatures could draw them out and consume them. The creatures' sharp tongues moved carefully as they excised the proper lobes with surgical precision.

Around all this the tree's guardians paced, meowing and muttering as they shook their heads under the burden of thoughts their small minds could barely endure, let alone understand. The sun rose a bit along its curve of the sky, but nothing came to interfere with their important work. The cats paced in their slow counterclockwise circle around the tree, like an accretion disk around its central star.

By the time the sun had risen to its zenith, Timothy Coldiron was gone.

The creatures withdrew their tongues from Timmy's eye sockets and climbed back to the upper branches of the tree. Timmy's arms extended until the hands pressed against the trunk. The thorns gouged through Timmy's flesh, but the thing now inhabiting Timmy's body paid them no mind. It pressed its new hands against the trunk and pushed until it broke free of the thorns. Dozens of them snapped off and remained stuck Timmy's flesh, but the thing ignored this as well. Matters of much greater importance now occupied its thoughts.

It stepped away from the tree. The worker cats stopped pacing and turned to face the new being they had worked so hard to create and protect. The thing inhabiting Timmy's body felt their painful, unnaturally expanded thoughts, and it sensed also the far more powerful collective consciousness created from all their hundreds of minds working together, a consciousness of which the thing wearing Timothy Coldiron's skin was now the most powerful part, like a queen bee surrounded by her hive.

We are one mind, it thought.

"*... one mind ... one mind ...*" the cats muttered in their collective voice.

It turned to face the tree again. The two breeder drones had already processed the human boy's brain matter and were defecating from the branches. The tree's roots would absorb their droppings and adapt their plasmid, their circular child of memory, according to the structural proteins from the boy's brain.

On the ground at the base of the tree lay a pile of dead animals, raccoons, skunks, possums, stray dogs and coyotes. All of them were eyeless. The worker cats had brought them here to feed the breeder drones, and sustain their fantastic growth. The animals and the trunk of the tree were splattered with dark green feces. Thin shining lines, like snail trails, ran down the trunk where the silvery fluid had dripped from the thorns. The fur of the dead animals sparkled with it in the summer sunshine.

After eons of waiting, their time had come 'round at last. They only needed to take the substance of memory from another sentient mind, and the long hard process of rebuilding their consciousness would be complete. Then their three avatars would come together and fulfill their destiny.

The thing inside Timothy Coldiron knew all of this from blind chemical instinct, and by that same instinct it realized something else. It now felt within its mind something it had not expected. A latent talent existed in the human mind, which their plasmid had somehow released and magnified. The thing felt a force radiating from its mutated human brain. And yet as unexpected as the ability to produce this force seemed, it also felt strangely familiar to it, like a feeling of (it search the remnant of the boys consciousness for the term) *déjà vu*. Whether this came from the boy's mind or its own, it did not know. But suddenly it knew it had the potential to do something wondrous. It could bend this force to its will, and manipulate matter.

The breeder drones had destroyed the human boy's eyes when they had taken his brain tissue, but the tree had replaced them with two spheres of its silvery fluid, like ball bearings set in his eye sockets. The fluid did not run out, for the invisible force arising from its mind held the fluid in place.

Now the thing called up that force and focused its gaze upon one of the burned posts in the clearing, which immediately exploded into a cloud of charred splinters.

The thing stretched Timmy's lips into a smile. Yes, their time would come soon. Very soon.

Followed by a pride of cats, it walked out of the clearing along the dark thin trail that led to the Coldiron house.

12

Growth Culture

Private Hicks looked up from his microscope when he heard Agent Gordon enter the lab. He felt good every time he heard anything this morning, since it meant he had not gone deaf in his right ear after that cat had clawed it during the night mission.

"How's the ear?" Gordon asked, with his usual perceptiveness.

"The doc says it'll be okay," Hicks said. "The cat didn't tear it off. It just tore it open." He carefully lifted the thick white bandage wrapped around his head to show Gordon his ear. The cat had ripped a large chunk out of the side of it about an inch above the earlobe, and torn the remainder of it nearly in half. As soon as they got back to their base of operations in Peculiar last night, Hicks had gone to see the army medic, who had stitched his ear back together with coarse black thread and bandaged it up.

Looking at Hicks's ear, which was now swollen, red, and glistening with anti-biotic ointment, Gordon said, "I'd have used a continuous thread stitch. Easier to remove. Can you still hear out of it?"

"Yeah, the doc said the eardrum didn't get punctured," Hicks replied. "Lucky me. Maybe now I won't take my hearing for granted. My girlfriend always said I needed to become a better listener. Speaking of which, you sound pretty tired. Get any sleep last night?"

"You *are* becoming a good listener," Gordon said, smiling a bit. "I slept a few hours, but I've got too much on my mind right now to sleep. How did the well water test?"

"See for yourself," Hicks said, rolling back his chair and pointing at the microscope. Gordon approached the table, leaned over and looked through the eyepiece. The yellow light from the microscope's lamp put shadows in the hollows of his cheeks and glints of white in his flinty-brown hair.

"Not a trace of *Pseudomonas* in the petri dish," Hicks said. Gordon did not look up from the eyepiece, but Hicks could tell from the tilt of his head that Gordon was listening. "I took three slides of the growth culture, but couldn't find a thing."

Hicks hesitated a moment, and then said, "I don't suppose you could tell me why *Pseudomonas aeruginosa* won't grow in the presence of this contagion?"

Gordon looked up from the eyepiece and stared at him in silence for a few seconds. Why had he asked that? If he wanted to, Gordon could get him in a lot of trouble for asking that question. For missions like these, the Army needed people who respected the boundaries of classified information. What had made him slip?

But he knew what had done it: simple curiosity. Something about the atmosphere in this lab had put him off his guard. The lab was in the basement; no windows down here, no way to get his Circadian rhythms set right. Just fluorescent lights and shining lab equipment. It made it easy to forget the outside world and the limits it set on what he could say, down here in this little chamber below the earth.

"You know I can't answer that, Private Hicks," Gordon said softly.

"I apologize," Hicks said, making his language more formal. "I'll understand when you report me—"

"I never said I'd report you," Gordon interrupted. "It's all right. It's perfectly natural for you to be curious. I'm not so harsh that I would report you for asking a reasonable question, even if it is about classified information." He smiled. "Who's to say you ever asked at all, hmm?"

Hicks smiled in relief. "Thank you," he said. He hesitated again, and then said, "I found something else in the sample, though."

Gordon raised his eyebrows. "What?"

"A root fragment," Hicks said. "It came from a plant, and I wouldn't have thought it was related to this if I hadn't seen that tree last night. You know, the one that somehow sprouted up in the day or so since the last time I went out there?"

"What about it?"

"I better let you see for yourself, since I don't really know what to make of it. I took a digital photograph of it, and I also put a cross-section under the transmission electron microscope. I have all the images stored on the computer if you'd like to see them."

"Please," said Gordon. "I'd like to see everything you've found."

Hicks rolled his chair over to the computer terminal and brought up the file he had made for the microscopic images. With a few well-placed clicks of the mouse, he brought up an image of the root fragment he had taken with the optical microscope. It looked exactly like a piece of a plant's root, brown and knobby with a light fuzz all over it.

"How big was it?" Gordon asked.

"Less than a centimeter long," Hicks said. "You really can't tell the size just by looking at it, can you? The shape of a little piece of the root fragment is the same as a big piece. There's a word for stuff like that, but I can't quite remember what—"

"Fractals," Gordon said.

"Right," Hicks replied. "Anyway, the water was filled with all kinds of other debris too, ash, dirt, wood fragments, a whole mess of stuff. And the water itself looks extremely polluted, not like typical groundwater at all."

"All right," Gordon said. "Do you think that explains these discolorations here, and here?" He pointed to a pair of dark spots on the root fragment, both of them at places where the root branched off in two or three different directions. Against the root's brown skin, the spots looked dark gray-blue, almost metallic.

"I was just coming to those," said Hicks. "I thought they might be some kind of inclusion. You know, a bit of debris that the root absorbed as it grew around them? Well, of course I had to cut out a slice of the root fragment to take a picture of its cells, and when I did … something happened."

Gordon raised his eyebrows. "What?"

Hicks shifted in his seat and began to look uncomfortable. "Well … I observed something odd … that is, I mean … what I'm trying to say is …"

"What, Hicks? What?" Gordon repeated.

"When I cut it open, the root released some kind of … metallic fluid." Hicks shook his head in exasperation. "I don't know how else to describe it. It looked almost like mercury, but it didn't flow quite the same. You know how mercury beads up? Well this didn't. It—"

"Were you wearing biohazard gear?" Gordon interrupted, his voice suddenly sharp.

"Of course, Agent Gordon," Hicks said. "I may not know what kind of contagion this is but I understand procedure."

Gordon nodded. "Sorry. I'm going on about two hours of sleep, and I guess I'm still a little stressed out after what happened last night. Please, go on."

"Well, I was just saying the fluid looked metallic like mercury, but it didn't form beads like mercury does. It flowed rather like oil."

"Did you get a picture of this?" Gordon asked, looking at the image on the computer screen.

"Yes."

Hicks clicked the mouse on another thumbnail image and brought up a picture of the root fragment's cells. It did not look like typical plant cells. With their thick cell walls, squarish shape, and large intercellular structures, plant cells had a very distinct and recognizable pattern. They had always reminded Hicks a bit of a cinderblock wall with their uniform square pattern. For a normal root, the cells would have a circular curve to them, matching the round cross-section of the root, but the image now filling the lab's computer screen looked nothing like a normal pattern of cells.

Gordon leaned in closer to the screen. Hicks had never felt as aware of his presence as he did now. Gordon hovered just over his right shoulder, their cheeks now inches apart. It was nothing like Jacques's juvenile homophobia. Hicks was only impressed by Gordon's intensity. He usually looked so bland.

"That *is* unusual," Gordon said.

"Yes, you can see what I mean about that strange fluid." Globs of the stuff shimmered over the root slice, looking strangely gaudy compared to the drab, uniform cells.

"But look at the cells too, Hicks," Gordon said. "The fluid is unusual, but it isn't the only thing."

The cells still had a roughly circular pattern, but it was all jumbled and disorderly, matching up with knobby shape of the root fragment. Hairs bristled out of the sides of the cells, looking much bigger and thicker at this magnification. The image on the computer screen reminded Hicks of a brick wall that had collapsed and then had bucketfuls of yarn and silver paint thrown onto it.

Hicks shrugged his shoulders. "It doesn't look like normal, healthy plant cells. That's all I can say for sure."

"Look at the cell nuclei, Hicks," Gordon said. "They're much, much larger than normal. Notice those darks spots in the center? Those are chromosomes. Highly condensed and visible, that's not normal either. I see some participation with the outside cells, you know, they're gathered together into a functioning root system, but just barely."

"What does that mean?" Hicks asked.

"I don't know for sure," Gordon said, "but they look almost like … like cancer cells. Cancer cells have large nuclei with big clumps of chromosomes in them, because they divide so quickly. They need to keep making lots of DNA for the new cancer cells."

"Can plants get cancer?" Hicks asked.

"They can get their own kind of it," Gordon said. "Have you ever seen trees with large round growths coming out of the sides of them? Those are tumors, similar to tumors that grow in animals."

Gordon stood in silence for a few moments, thinking, and his face betrayed none of his thoughts. Finally he said, "What did the pictures from the transmission electron microscope show?"

"I'll bring those up for you," Hicks said. His attitude had taken on a formal tone again. He hadn't meant for it; he had wanted to develop a better working relationship with Gordon. It had nothing to do with apologizing for how rudely Rodriguez and Jacques had treated him on the night mission. It was because he had seen undeniable proof of Gordon's intelligence and skill, and the dignity with which he carried himself. Who wouldn't want to work with someone like that, or to learn from him? So he had tried to become his friend, and it had gone well for the first few minutes this morning, but now Hicks discovered he did not yet know how to handle himself when discussing something so strange. Out of the habits imposed on him by his training he became less personal, more professional and cold.

"I cut the cells into ultrathin slices using a diamond knife," he continued in this colder tone. Gordon didn't seem to mind. "Then I stained them with lead. Standard operating procedure for the TEM. When the pictures came out, I found several anomalous structures inside the cells. I have not yet had an opportunity to search through the literature to identify them."

"Show them to me," Gordon said, and so Hicks clicked the mouse on a third thumbnail image.

A black and white picture of the root cells appeared on the computer screen, and for all of its gray drabness it still showed the interior of the cells in spectacular detail. Within the dark boundaries of the cells walls, black tadpole-shapes swirled around pure white counterparts of themselves, like hundreds of yin-yang symbols, or an Escher print of black and white flocks of birds or schools of fish intermeshed in a vast repeating pattern. Strange gray shapes swirled and spiraled within the cells, and seemed to move when seen through the corner of the eye. The great vacuole, the storage compartment for a plant cell's food and usually the largest of a plant cell's organelles, looked strangely shrunken, as if they had burned up all of their cellular fuel faster than they could replace it.

In the middle of the cell bulged an enormous, misshapen nucleus filled with dark coils of chromosomes like diseased intestines. Even Hicks could tell something was wrong with it; a normal cell's nucleus is almost perfectly round, and the chromosomes are so small and thin that they are almost invisible.

Gordon stared at this picture for a long time. Hicks could see his pupils moving back and forth as he scanned it. The redness in the whites of Gordon's eyes and around the edges of his eyelids showed how little Gordon had slept. His lips moved, but no sound came out. Several times Gordon raised his hand and moved it across the image on the computer screen, as if he was tracing a path from the nucleus to the cell wall.

Hicks couldn't see any path himself, nor could guess what might follow that path, if it existed. He could identify some of the basic parts of the cell, but his knowledge didn't go much farther than that. So he was completely mystified when Gordon murmured, "In plant cells."

"What's that?" Hicks whispered. He did not know why he whispered that question. Something about Gordon's face had made him do it. That stunned expression, it conveyed a depth of seriousness that seemed to demand he lower his voice, the same way people unconsciously lower their voices when they step into a church.

Gordon didn't respond at first. His face took on a slack, absent look, an expression Hicks had never seen on Gordon's face before. It was the expression of a man totally lost in thought, a man whose mind had drifted upwards into higher realms of thought than most people ever attained, and it terrified Hicks to see it. He didn't fully understand why it frightened him, but part of the reason was that he now felt he was seeing Gordon with all his defenses down. That composed, distant attitude had vanished along with that ageless quality to his face. Up until now, Hicks had always thought Gordon must have been in his late thirties. He had the look of a man approaching middle age. But now, oh now, Hicks saw that mature look had fallen away like a mask. Lost in thought, Gordon now looked young, maybe just a few years older than Hicks, and something about the open, guileless quality of Gordon's face convinced Hicks that this wasn't a false expression at all; this was the real Gordon standing before him.

Gordon's face looked wounded, the face of someone who knew a terrible secret of life that most people would never learn. Hicks had seen expressions like that on the faces of abused women and children, of soldiers just returned from a battle with fewer arms or legs than they had going in. But what had Gordon seen? If he was really young, what had happened to age him so, like a man who looks into a mirror and sees a reflection of himself twenty years older?

Gordon's eyes suddenly moved and locked onto Hicks's face with such intensity that Hicks flinched in surprise.

"Private Hicks," he said, "what are you doing here?"

The question seemed bizarre, as if Gordon had just realized Hicks was in the room after speaking to him for the last several minutes. Hicks stammered in confusion. "I … why are you … what do you mean?"

"Why have you had so much time to study this root fragment? Hasn't Sergeant Rollins spoken to you about returning to Beta Impact Site?"

"What? No! Of course not. We would need a much bigger team to go back there, and weapons to fight off those cats—"

"He's up to something," Gordon said. Hicks had no idea what he meant.

"Who? Sergeant Rollins? What are you talking about?"

"He was supposed to call in reinforcements and send them to clear out all those cats," Gordon said. "Hasn't he mentioned anything to you about it?"

"No," Hicks said. "Nothing. Why does that make you think he's up to something?"

"Because sometimes it's what people *don't* tell you that says the most," Gordon said. "Can you access the mission log notes from here?"

The question stunned Hicks. Rollins kept a computerized log of all mission activities. It was on an internal network so that he could access the notes from any of the computers in their base of operations or any of their mobile units. Hicks and the other operatives on their team often emailed their reports to Rollins so that he could add them to the notes, but they were not allowed to view the entire log, since many of the notes contained classified information.

"I can bring up the password prompt from here, Agent Gordon," Hicks said, "but you know I don't have access to that information—"

"That's all right," Gordon said. "I *do* have access."

"Does Rollins know that?" Hicks said. He had heard Rollins mention putting critical remarks about Gordon into the log notes on several occasions. Usually when he was trying to find a way to get Gordon into trouble.

"It doesn't matter if he knows," Gordon said. "Not anymore. Bring up the password prompt."

"I'm sorry, but I can't do that," Hicks said. "I could get in a lot of trouble."

"I understand," Gordon said. "Let me borrow your chair and I'll do it myself."

Hicks got up and let Gordon have his seat. As Gordon went to work on the computer, Hicks began to feel uncomfortable. This wasn't the way missions were supposed to go. They had to stick to a certain method. They had to follow procedure and protocol and chain of command. Why had Gordon suddenly become this wild element? He shouldn't try to uncover information their superiors didn't want him to know.

He couldn't stay here. It could implicate him to even remain in the same room as Gordon if this was going to happen. Without a word, Hicks turned and left the laboratory, letting the heavy lab doors lock automatically behind him.

He didn't know where else to go, so he took the elevator up to the meeting room. A bright Midwest morning glowed outside the big window. Traffic zipped by on highway 71. Hicks could see a field across the highway, just a bare spot surrounded by a patch of trees. A group of bulldozers had assembled there, and graded the field down to bare earth. Concrete mixers and eighteen-wheelers with lumber piled in back of them stood behind the bulldozers.

Must be building a subdivision there, he thought, and then for no obvious reason he wondered how long that land had been an open field. Had real prairie grass once grown there? Hicks had read somewhere that prairie grass was a different species than the wild grasses growing commonly today, that agriculture and development had mostly wiped out the original prairie grass that Native Americans had cultivated across the Great Plains with a seasonal pattern of controlled burns. Had they done that to provide better grazing for the buffalo? That sounded right, although Hicks was a Brooklyn boy born and raised and all grass pretty much looked the same to him. Still, it was interesting to think of what must have happened over the surface of that open field, all that history. Indians and buffalo, pioneers, range wars. Now the bulldozers had scraped the field away to make room for a subdivision. Seemed like a shame, a real waste, but then why would anyone try to preserve a field, a patch of grass, especially when they lived in a culture that thrived on growth?

He turned around when he heard the door to the meeting room open behind him. It was Gordon.

"Something is going to happen," Gordon said.

"I don't want to know about it," Hicks replied. "I want to have a career in the military, Gordon, and I can't get involved in anything insubordinate."

"I understand," Gordon said. "I need to go into town. There are some people I need to see. I just wanted to tell you that you don't have to worry about me implicating you in any of this. I'll take responsibility for everything."

Hicks nodded, and Gordon left. Hicks knew he should immediately report him to Rollins. Even though Gordon was an independent agent, Hicks might still be held accountable if he leaked classified information. But then Rollins hadn't told Hicks about any new operations taking place, had he? And why not? Did he simply want to give him enough time to test the well water sample? Or did he think that maybe Hicks and Gordon had gotten a little too close? Hicks didn't know for sure. All he knew was that it was a beautiful morning outside that window, and if he wanted to stand there and enjoy it for, oh, the next hour or so and then give Rollins a call, whose business was that?

No one's but his own, Hicks decided.

13

The Peculiar Ladies Quilting Society

Thinking about the strange man she had met earlier that morning at the Dollar General, Kelly Ross drove through downtown Peculiar towards the building where the Quilting Society met every Saturday.

She had encountered the man just before getting off her eight-to-noon shift, which she worked every Saturday morning even though she hated missing out on watching cartoons with Jason. Kelly cherished her memories of watching Saturday morning cartoons with her own mother, who would prepare breakfast for each of them on metal trays so they could eat their morning meal together while laughing at Bugs Bunny blowing up Elmer Fudd with a barrel full of dynamite, or the Road Runner startling Wile E. Coyote off the edge of a cliff with a perfectly timed *meep-meep!* It wasn't so much about the cartoons, but about having fun with her mother, whom she loved. She hated knowing that Jason wouldn't have similar memories of her, but she needed every cent she could scrounge, especially now that the Coldiron woman had shut down her produce stand.

All of these pressures, the constant work, her concerns for her son, the antagonism of her new neighbor, had piled up on her, and she had spent the six-hours or so she allotted to sleep each night tossing from one side of the bed to the other, worrying over each problem the way she might worry a loose tooth with her tongue.

So why then, with all these more important matters hanging over her head, could she not get that strange man out of her mind?

She had been shelving bottles of laundry detergent at the back of the store, which had been doing a typically brisk Saturday-morning business, and trying not to let the various artificial scents overpower her, when she had heard a nondescript voice say, "Excuse me, are you Kelly Ross?"

She had turned around, not knowing who had spoken to her. The voice had belonged to a man, but Kelly could see two men in the aisle to her right and one on the aisle to her left. A heavyset woman was also in the left-hand aisle browsing the air-fresheners. (Kelly had never liked that aisle. All those artificial scents irritated her nose something awful.) A lot of the burly farmwives around here had some pretty deep voices, and when answering the store phone she had on more than one occasion mistakenly called a woman "sir." She had not slept well last night, and was too tired right now to deal with an angry farmwife, so she glanced back and forth between the left and right aisles and said, "I'm sorry, did someone ask for me?"

"I did," said the man in the left aisle. "I was wondering if you could help me."

At first, Kelly had thought that the man was older, maybe late forties or early fifties, one of those well preserved types you often saw on television but never in real life. But when he stepped closer and she got a good look at him she realized he was actually much younger, in his early thirties at the most. His hair color had fooled her. It was this neutral, almost iron-like color, which she now recognized as a very dull shade of brown. Under the fluorescent lights she had mistaken it for gray.

"Sure," Kelly said, hoping he hadn't noticed her confused pause. "What can I do for you?"

"I need directions actually," he said. "The cashier up front said you lived around the Brooks woods."

"Yes?" Being a small-town girl, Kelly had never thought twice about anyone knowing where she lived, she simply assumed everyone already knew, but now she felt a little uneasy. This man gave her a strange vibe. He had this indefinable quality to his face, not ugly but not handsome either. She saw no obvious reason why it should strike her as strange; it was a very unremarkable face. If she had passed him on the street she probably wouldn't have remembered him five minutes later. But after speaking to him, she felt that something was a little off about him, whoever he was.

He looked very tired for one thing, like he had only slept a couple of hours, but Kelly knew she couldn't throw stones there. She carried the marks of sleep deprivation on her face as well, all the same lines and sags. Spencer had looked tired too, she remembered, when she had spoken to him yesterday. He was supposed to come by and work on her truck later this afternoon, after she met with the Quilting Society. She felt more excited about seeing Spencer again than she had about anything in a long time.

"Where do you need directions to?" Kelly asked the strange man now, coming back to herself.

"Well, I just need to know if there's a way to the north side of the Brooks woods, one that doesn't connect with that outer road running alongside 71," said the man.

That sounded like a pretty odd request. Suspicious, almost.

"Why don't you want to get on Outer Road?" Kelly asked.

"Oh, haven't you heard? An Army convoy is going to be moving some equipment out that way later this afternoon. They're going to shut down the Peculiar exit and some of those dirt roads to the south of town for the rest of the day."

"I haven't heard a thing about it," Kelly said. "That's really strange too, 'cause I live out that way and I haven't seen any detours or road signs set out."

That wasn't the only strange thing. She had at first taken this man for an out-of-towner, judging from his clothes. Most of the men around here wore jeans, overalls, or khaki workpants with t-shirts of some kind on top. Not all, Peculiar certainly had its share of professional men, but the majority of them wore a blue-collar uniform of some kind. This guy was wearing black cargo pants and some kind of tight-fitting black shirt with the sleeves rolled up around his forearms. It looked like an outfit someone might wear to go sneaking around in the dark, yet another reason for Kelly to mistrust him.

And yet, she had picked up something in his voice that she recognized. She had heard it when he said *if there's a back way* and *out that way*. People used those expressions everywhere, but Kelly thought she had detected something in the man's inflection that sounded similar to her own way of speaking. Maybe this stranger had roots hereabouts?

"Hold on," Kelly said. "You know my name but I don't know yours." She held out her hand for him to shake.

After a noticeable pause the man took her hand, shook it, and said, "I'm ... Gordon. John Gordon."

Kelly noticed the way the man had hesitated before giving her his name, and for a split second before he took her hand she had glimpsed a sad emotion cross his face. She didn't think the man had given her a fake name, the emotion she had glimpsed did not come across like that at all. It was the look of someone who has been badly mistreated receiving a simple act of kindness. Kelly knew it well. But the look disappeared a second later and Mr. Gordon's face settled back into its tired, composed expression, making Kelly wonder if she had really seen that fleeting look at all.

"Well, it's nice to meet you, Mr. Gordon," Kelly said. "You from around here?"

"Just in town on business," Gordon said, which did not answer her question at all. She was about to open her mouth to say so, but then Gordon spoke again, and the look of quiet hesitation on his face, so similar to how he looked earlier when she had shaken his hand and told him it was nice to meet him, made her hold back her words and let him speak.

"I've been out of Missouri for awhile," he said. "I didn't realize how much I'd missed it until I came back."

There it was again, that familiar inflection, the way he pronounced it *Missou-ruh.*

"I guess you've been living in some other part of the country then?" Kelly asked. "There's nothing here you can't find anywhere in the Midwest."

"That's very modest of you to say."

"Well, we don't put on airs," she replied, and realized a second later that he had evaded her question once again.

"So is there another way to the Brooks woods?" Gordon asked again. "I'm sorry to rush you, but I'm a little pressed for time."

Now Kelly felt a little nosy, pressuring the man about matters that were really none of her business, so she let the subject drop.

"Well, the turn-off for the back way into the woods is south of town," she said. "But if you have to go in a different way you could turn onto another road north of town, take some of the gravel roads that head south, and then curve around again. Not all of them have names though, so I'll have to draw you a map."

"I'd appreciate that," Gordon replied. "Thanks."

They went up front to the register, where Kelly got a piece of paper from James Beatty, her manager. As she wrote down the directions, she said, "So what takes you out there anyhow? Going to see someone? I know the Snows live out that way, and the Garretts, the Monroes ..."

"Just trying to avoid that convoy," Gordon said. And then he did the thing that disturbed Kelly the most, and left her feeling uneasy for the rest of the day. As he took the paper with the directions written on it from her, he looked directly into her eyes with such sudden and intense focus that she flinched in surprise.

"Things could get really bad if you got caught behind it," Gordon said, his voice firm and measured. "You should really stay away from home until later tonight, when it's done passing through. I can't stress that enough."

For a moment she could only stare at him in confusion. Just what exactly did he mean? For the first time while speaking to this man, she began to feel a little afraid.

And then, out of nowhere, Jason appeared at her side.

"Mom," he said, "what's this word?"

She jumped, letting out a little yelp of surprise. Looking down and to her right, she saw her son standing beside her, holding in his hand that great and unique American invention, a comic book.

"Jason!" Kelly said, a little too loudly. "When did you get here? Did Ms. Grace drop you off?"

As if in answer to her question she heard a horn honk in the street outside. Looking up, she saw through the big glass window Midge Grace parked in front of the store, her big silver Cadillac shining in the Saturday morning sun. Midge waved to her from the Caddy's driver's seat, and Kelly lifted her hand in return. Then Brad's freckled face popped up from the passenger seat. He frantically waved goodbye to Jason, who looked up from his comic book long enough to wave back in his more subdued fashion. Quiet, thoughtful and bookish, just like his dad. Kelly's heart ached as she saw the resemblance, as it had ten thousand times before.

"What word is that?" Gordon asked, leaning over to speak to Jason.

Kelly glanced at the stranger, feeling concerned and protective. She fought an urge to put her hand over Jason's shoulders and pull him to her. This John Gordon or whoever he was had just said something that, however vague, had disturbed her quite a bit, and now he wanted to talk to her only son? Kelly bristled by reflex, like a lioness protecting her cubs from a pack of hyenas.

Just then a spray of sunlight reflected off of Midge's windshield as she back out of her parking space. The light shined across Gordon's tired face, and Kelly no longer saw the intense, focused individual who had told her to stay away from home. Once again he looked tired but unremarkable, and perhaps a bit like a local fellow. She had never seen anyone change so dramatically from one mindset to another in so short a period of time. It didn't lessen her distrust, but it did keep her from snatching Jason into her arms like a crazed, overprotective mother.

"Excuse my son," Kelly now said. "He usually spends Saturday mornings at a friend's house while I'm at work, but she had to take her own son to sign up for swimming lessons."

"It's no trouble at all," said Gordon, and then returned his attention to Jason. "I liked comic books too, when I was your age. What word do you need help with?"

"This one," Jason said, pointing to a spot on one of the pages.

"That's 'Yggdrasil,'" said Gordon. "The world-tree of Norse mythology. They believed it held up the heavens and the earth."

"Yeah, I didn't know how to pronounce it," Jason said, and returned his attention to his comic. Midge must have bought it for him, since Kelly couldn't spare the money to give her son an allowance. The comic's title was *Thor*, which as she understood was some sort of ancient Nordic god. She wondered briefly what those ancient people would think if they knew the deity they feared and worshipped would one day be featured in a comic book, flying around in a cape fighting super-villains.

"They worshipped trees?" Kelly asked. "Were they like the Druids or something?"

"Not really," Gordon said. "Many faiths throughout the world incorporate trees. The Greeks thought olive trees were sacred to Apollo, and that every oak had its dryad. There are many modern religions that also have sacred trees."

"Like the tree in the Garden of Eden," Jason mumbled as he read his book. "The one God told Adam and Eve to stay away from, but they didn't."

"That's right," Gordon said. "During the Middle Ages, it was common to refer to Jesus as the man who was 'hung on the tree.'"

"How interesting," Kelly said, but she kept her voice flat. This conversation had just turned way too weird to hold with someone she had just met. "Nice to meet you, Mr. Gordon. Say goodbye, Jason."

"'Bye," Jason said, not looking up from his comic.

Gordon paused a moment, looking into Kelly's eyes, and then he said, "Goodbye Ms. Ross. Remember the advice I gave you."

Gordon left the store without another word. Jason had quietly read his comic book until Kelly's shift was over, which she figured may have been the reason Midge bought it for him in the first place.

Now, driving her little pickup through downtown with Jason sitting beside her, she remembered Mr. Gordon's strange "advice." It hadn't sounded like a threat, not compared to Mrs. Coldiron's rants. So what had he meant by it? Could it have been some kind of warning? But against what? If she had a military convoy after her now, after everything else she had dealt with over the last year, well then she would just throw up her hands and say, "Take me now, Lord! I've had enough!"

She took Peculiar Drive down to Main, and then parked there on the street next to some stores. She had to drop off some vegetable baskets to some of her regulars. Mrs. Coldiron's nastiness had benefited Kelly's customers in a way; now they were getting their produce delivered. Rather than waste gas puttering around town, Kelly parked her truck and made her deliveries on foot with Jason trotting along behind her. All of her customers were within a few blocks of each other. She dropped off some butternut squash at the coffeehouse, some green beans with the ladies at the real estate office, and a basket of cucumbers at the tanning salon. She joked with the girl behind the counter, asking if she was going to eat those cucumbers or put the slices over her customer's eyes like one of those fancy spas.

Traffic buzzed through the streets and pedestrians strolled over the sidewalks; it was a bright, busy weekend morning. The two Peculiar watertowers, one old and one new, stood over the town like a pair of giant metal sentinels.

Jason walked and read his comic book at the same time, which never failed to amaze Kelly. He never stumbled or tripped, and always seemed to know when to step down from a curb or swerve around a passing pedestrian. The kid must have incredible peripheral vision. Sometimes the sheer wonder her son evoked in her made her a little afraid. She would think someone up above must have made a big mistake when they put a kid as special as Jason in her care, but she had to repress such thoughts quickly. Not only would it lead her emotions down a path where they might spiral out of control, but it would also disturb Jason to see her so confused and uncertain. She had to be extra strong now, no matter how tough it got. Jason had been through too much in the past year, first losing his dad and then living through the grinding poverty that followed. He needed to feel some security now. She couldn't afford self-pity. The idea of going down to the welfare office on Monday to apply for state assistance didn't appeal to her one bit, the pride of three generations of pioneer women running through her veins cried out against it, but she had to do it anyway.

Do it for Jason, she told herself once again. *Do it for your son.* Nothing else could appease that sinful pride of hers, that pride she hated and cherished at the same time, which hinged her self-respect on her self-determination. Because of her pride, she had to shoulder the blame for her desperate condition. She had to struggle through life on her own, and it galled her to accept help from anyone. Usually. She hadn't minded at all when Spencer offered to work on her truck.

Oh, but you have your reasons for feeling that way, whispered a hateful voice from the dark well of her subconscious. *Don't you, now? You're thinking of getting a replacement daddy for your little boy, so he can worry about the bills instead of you. Go on honey, at least admit it to yourself if you won't to anyone else.*

But she would never do that, not ever. She would never surrender to that calculating, mercenary part of herself. If she ever became involved with a man again, she wouldn't settle for someone she didn't love just to have a second income. And if that meant denying herself any hope, well then that was what she would do.

After leaving the tanning salon, they went back to the corner of Broadway and Main, and turned right. She did not have to tell Jason to turn; the boy just followed along without looking up from his comic. Shaking her head in bewildered wonder, Kelly dropped off her last basket at the house at the end of the block. No one was home, so she left the basket on the doorstep, with a note saying they could pay her later. She passed the town's historical marker, a plaque hung on steel post next to the sidewalk. The engraved letters on its front read, "In 1861–1864, while bloody battles raged throughout the southern states, nothing happened here."

With her deliveries done, Kelly and Jason went back to the truck. From there, they drove to the community center. This was a small prefabricated structure set up across the road from the post office and the Apple market. It was run by the local Lion's club and used for meetings and special events like the occasional square dance.

"Morning, Suzie," Kelly said to the middle-aged woman sweeping the front steps.

"You mean 'Good afternoon,'" Suzie replied. "It's past noon, hon."

"It's always morning somewhere," Kelly said, following the usual détente she and Suzie went through every Saturday. Their pleasant banter never bored her, despite its repetitiveness. On the contrary, she found the dependability of it relaxing.

"Afternoon, Ms. Carter," Jason said without looking up from his comic book.

"Good afternoon, Jason," Suzie said to him, smiling. "Brad's waiting for you in the daycare center."

"Thanks," Jason replied. "Can I go, Mom?" He no longer looked so focused on reading. From the excited expression on his face, you would have thought it had been days since he had seen Brad instead of a couple of hours.

"Go ahead, honey," Kelly replied. "I'll pick you up in an hour. You remember to behave, now."

"I will!" Jason chirped, and dashed through the front door. After sharing a quick smile with Suzie, Kelly followed him inside. Of course Jason had darted far ahead of her to find Brad, and she could hear the two of them elsewhere in the building yelling in excitement at seeing each other. Kelly waited until she heard the daycare assistant telling them to quiet down, it sounded like Tiffany had volunteered this week, and then she turned towards a room to her right. Every Saturday in this room, Kelly met with the Peculiar Ladies Quilting Society, a group of the nicest, most elegant ladies she had ever met.

They looked up as she entered, a group of older women from many different backgrounds in various modes of dress. Virginia Moore, the mayor's wife, looked modern and sharp (if a bit overdressed) in her light pink pantsuit, and her stylish bobbed hairdo made her look younger than her fifty-seven years, although her blond dye-job may have had something to do with that. At the other end of the spectrum was Dorothy Sprinkles (and you better believe she took some teasing on account of *that* name) in the plain and faded floral print dress they had seen her wear a thousand times before ... and respected her all the more for it. They gathered here each summer to make these quilts and auctioned them off every August at the Missouri state fair in Sedalia, with the proceeds going to charity. Dirt-poor herself, Dorothy used time she could have spent working to help make those quilts, and the other women made sure she knew they appreciated it.

Kelly spotted Midge Grace sitting on the other side of the wooden frame, over which they had stretched their latest creation. Midge looked poised and elegant as usual in a black dress with red floral embroidery. Her long salt-and-pepper hair was done up in a French twist today. Midge always dressed so fancily that Kelly sometimes thought of her as Lady Grace.

"Kelly, darling!" Lady Grace now said as she took Kelly's hands and kissed her on the cheek. "How good to see you once again! Won't you join our peaceful little assembly?"

"Always happy to," Kelly said, smiling at Midge's exuberance. "Sorry I'm a little late. Things got crazy back at the store." She considered telling Midge about that strange Mr. Gordon, but reconsidered. She had a few other things to discuss with her lady friends this afternoon, although she might bring him up a little later.

"By the way," Kelly said as they walked over to the quilting circle and sat down on the metal folding chairs, "I suppose you bought Jason that comic book?"

"Oh yes," Midge said. "I hope you don't mind. I just felt so badly about dropping him off early and I thought it might occupy him until your shift ended—"

"Oh it's not that," Kelly interjected. "I just wanted to make sure he didn't pester you about it. You know I try to teach him good manners."

"Not at all, my dear, not at all! I saw him looking at it when we stopped at Casey's for gas, and he said it was his favorite when I asked him about it. He was absolutely no trouble, never is."

"I never let my kids read those comic books," said Joyce Garrett, a burly, brown-haired farmwife of the kind Kelly sometimes mistook for men over the phone. Joyce spoke in the casual, offhand manner of someone giving unwanted advice. "All that violence and gore, talking about demon-worship and Lord knows what else. They're a bad influence, I say. Unchristian."

"Oh, I think they're harmless fun," Kelly said. She decided not to mention that the comic was about an ancient Nordic god. Joyce had some pretty stern views on religion, and considered all non-Christian faiths Satanism.

"They ain't gonna corrupt the boy,'" said Moe Jefferson, a vivacious African-American woman in her mid-fifties. Her real first name was Monica but she had started calling herself Moe back in the nineties, after that awful Clinton thing.

"No child ever started worshippin' the devil just 'cause he read a comic book, Joycie," Moe said. Her hands, though starting to show the gnarls of arthritis, never paused in their nimble stitching of the quilt fabric. "What, you think they should stop makin' them just 'cause you don't like what they're about?"

"I never said that at all!" Joyce replied. "They can print whatever they want, but I don't have to let my kids read them."

"Well, everyone's entitled to an opinion," Midge said airily. She and Kelly shared a brief smile. Joyce always liked to drop statements like that, just on the edge of criticism.

"I've never understood why Christians aren't given a voice for their opinions," Joyce said, affecting a long-suffering tone. "Here, America is supposed to be a Christian nation, but we're not free to talk about our beliefs …"

"We're all Christians around this circle and I'll tell you Joyce, we most certainly are free to do that," said Ruth Walton, a sixtyish woman with gray hair and thick black-rimmed glasses perched on the edge of her beaklike nose. She sat on the opposite side of the quilting circle from Joyce. "You can say whatever you want and believe whatever you want! America doesn't have just one established religion. People can practice any faith they want here."

"All kinds of religions in this country," Moe said, nodding as she sewed.

"Oh, we all know there are more Christians in this nation than any other faith," Joyce said. "And in a democracy, the majority rules. Everybody knows that."

"That's not relevant," said Virginia Moore. "Freedom of religion is a right, not a legislative act put before the voters. It's there to protect the little guys, and you can't use one person's legal right to deny another person their own rights."

"It's just not right," Moe chimed in, producing a round of good-hearted laughter from everyone, Joyce included.

While the Peculiar Ladies laughed, Midge leaned in close to Kelly and said, "We must set a time to speak with our neighbor to the north."

"I know," Kelly whispered. "I've been waiting until I've calmed down before approaching her, but it's impossible to stay calm around that woman."

"You all talking about that Mrs. Coldiron?" Amanda Beatty asked from beside them. Although Kelly and Midge had kept their voices low, she had heard them talking even over the laughter of the other Ladies. Ms. Beatty, a spinster and the aunt of Kelly's manager James Beatty, lived in the town proper, in a musty old Victorian house just two blocks off Main. With her rail-thin body, big ears, and her blondish-gray hair pulled back into a bun so tight you'd think her eyes would pop out if she blinked, Amanda looked like a miniature satellite dish, and trying to keep news or gossip from her was an exercise in futility.

"You know I saw her while I was down to the grocery this morning," she said. "She was walking past the municipal building talking with some fella in a suit, and boy, was she giving him a hard time! Couldn't hear what she was saying through the glass but I could see her mouth just working away, and the fella in the suit looked all put out. You could tell he just wanted to smack her."

"Was the man her husband?" Ruth Walton asked.

"I don't think so," Amanda replied. "He looked a lot younger than her and I know that doesn't mean anything nowadays, but he kept this cold attitude around her, you know, not like a henpecked husband. More like somebody she might be doing business with ..."

Amanda rattled on, speculating over every tiny detail of the encounter she had seen. Most of it sounded meaningless to Kelly, but she listened anyway, feeling a little guilty about listening to gossip but desperate for anything to help her in the inevitable battle she would have to face when she and Midge finally confronted Mrs. Coldiron for the lies she had spread about Jason and Brad.

"Of course none of us believe a word she says about your boys, Ladies," Amanda now said to Kelly and Midge, as if she had read Kelly's mind. More likely she had read Kelly's face. Amanda could read volumes from an eyebrow twitch.

"Oh God," Kelly groaned. "How bad is it?"

"Word of what she's saying has spread around," said Moe Jefferson, "but don't nobody believe a word of it."

"Well, that's a relief," Kelly said. "I know I shouldn't worry, but you hear all these stories of kindergarteners accused of sexual harassment for kissing their classmates ..."

"Oh honey," said Ruth Walton, "we have more sense than that here!" All the Peculiar Ladies tittered.

"By the way, Kelly," said Virginia Moore after the laughter died down. "Are you perhaps aware of what is going on in the Brooks woods near your home?"

At this, silence spread around the quilting circle and the eyes of all the Ladies settled upon Kelly as she sat with her needle in hand.

"I know *something* is going on," Kelly said at last, "but I'm not sure what. I heard gunfire out there last night, sometime around midnight."

"I heard that too," Midge said. "I've forbidden Bradley to play there for the time being."

"Was it loud enough to wake you, Kelly?" Dorothy Sprinkles asked in her timid little voice. With her good nature, Dorothy always thought about the well-being of others before any sordid nighttime antics.

"No," Kelly replied. "I was already up. I have too much on my mind right now to get much sleep." She laughed without humor.

"It's probably just those Schmidt boys again," said Ruth Walton. "Out there getting drunk and firing off their shotguns. Someday one of those fools will get his head blown off."

"I don't think it is," said Mrs. Moore. "I bumped into Emily Greuf this morning and she said she saw some strange vehicles driving down the dirt road there on the north side of the Brooks woods."

"She saw that this morning?" Kelly asked. "*After* all that gunfire last night?"

"That's what she said," Mrs. Moore replied. "It seems something is moving around out there in those woods."

"You don't suppose it's drug runners, do you?" Joyce asked. "I mean you hear all the time of them running drugs up from Mexico through here on their way to Kansas City and Chicago …"

Moe Jefferson snorted. "I swear Joyce, you're dumber than a rock."

"I'm serious!"

"Those drug runners are a myth," said Mrs. Moore. "What I'm talking about is real. Drug runners don't leave digital recorders and camouflage tarps behind them."

All the Ladies dropped their needles and threads, and stared at Virginia Moore in shock.

"*What?*" Kelly finally said, breaking the silence.

"You didn't think I wouldn't tell Ned about some strange activity going on out there, did you?" said Mrs. Moore. She rarely brought up her husband, knowing as she did that no one would like it if she set herself up all fancy just because she was the mayor's wife, so her mentioning him now brought some extra weight to the subject.

"Ned sent Officer Randy out there early this morning," she continued, "and that's when he found the recorder and the tarp. He left this morning around seven, through the north side, around where you live, Joyce. I guess he found the recorder sitting on a camouflage tarp on the edge of a gully. I know they didn't tell me everything, police business and all that. I swear Ruth, that grandson of yours has gotten too big for his britches since he started on with the force—"

"Who is doing this?" Kelly interrupted.

"We don't know, my dear," said Mrs. Moore. "Or if the police do know they're not telling me. However, Ned did let something slip when I spoke to him about it. Apparently, the recorder had this dish-shaped attachment on it, and Ned said they use that sort of thing in the military when they want to hear sounds from a long distance away. He said they can listen to people talking inside their houses from fifty yards off.

"And Kelly," she added, "it was pointed at *your* house."

At first Kelly could only sit there, stunned and feeling the eyes of the other Ladies move over her, gauging her response. As the words sank in, a gnawing sensation of formless horror overtook her as she realized the implications of what the mayor's wife had said. Her everyday problems seemed big enough, but this was so far beyond her experience, so far beyond her control, that she felt utterly helpless before it, as if Virginia Moore had told her a natural disaster like a tornado or a swarm of locusts was bearing down on her.

"Someone is *watching* me?" Kelly said.

"*Listening* would be more accurate," said Mrs. Moore. "From what I understand, the recorder only receives sound, it isn't a camera."

Kelly started to say *That's hardly any comfort*, but then she remembered that strange Mr. Gordon and what he had said to her this morning at the Dollar General.

"Now honey this is probably just some survivalist spying on people with a gadget he bought at an army surplus store," said Moe Jefferson while Kelly sat in thought. "You give Officer Randy a couple of days and I'm sure he'll catch the little bugger—"

"It isn't that," Kelly said. "Or if it is it's an awfully big coincidence. Let me tell you what happened to me this morning at the store ..."

She told them everything Gordon had said, leaving out his little aside on the history of tree worship since it didn't seem to bear on the subject.

"An Army convoy?" Moe Jefferson asked. "One so big they'll have to shut down the highway? I haven't heard a thing about it on the news."

"Neither have I," said Midge. "Did he tell you what kind of equipment they're supposed to be moving?"

"No," Kelly said, "and I didn't think to ask. The way he put it seemed so reasonable. The guy just had something about him, something I couldn't quite grasp. It was like somebody trying to tell you something without just coming out and saying it, you know what I mean?"

"Do you think he's trying to warn you?" Ruth Walton asked.

"It did come across like that," Kelly said.

"It's a trick more than likely," said Amanda Beatty. "They just don't want you to know what they're up to!"

"Well, I think all this talk is treasonous," said Joyce Garrett. "In our age of terrorism, to undermine the nation's confidence in our military. You should be cooperating with them however they want you to, Kelly."

"The hell you should!" Moe Jefferson snapped. Sometimes she and Joyce really got into it. "The military's there to protect our rights, not take 'em away! Those Brooks woods are private property. They better have permission to be there, is all I got to say!"

"Well, I support our troops," said Joyce. "They're out there dying to protect our freedom." Her face brightened in manner of someone that has found the perfect thing to say. "Everybody thinks freedom means you can just do whatever you want, but it doesn't mean that at all. That's just anarchy. Freedom is *responsibility.*"

"Oh, bullshit!" Moe said. "You belong on an animal farm, Joyce."

"Now, Ladies," said Mrs. Moore. "Let's keep this civilized. We're not on television. Our little group discussing this issue won't undermine the nation's confidence in the military, Joyce. And there's no need for profanity, Ms. Jefferson."

Moe sniffed in disdain.

"The military may have a reason for acting this way," said Mrs. Moore, "and they certainly at times have to keep things quiet. We all recognize their undeniable heroism, but the military exists to protect our rights, and if they stray from that course then it's our civic duty to set things right. Who knows? This may be something that can be cleared up with a simple phone call."

"But why are they spying on *me?*" Kelly asked. "What do they think I could do?"

"No way of knowing, darling," said Mrs. Moore.

"I tell you this much," said Moe Jefferson, "whatever happens you got friends and neighbors here who know you and ain't gonna let anyone try and ruin your good name. If anyone unscrupulous, and I think you might know who I'm talking about, catches wind of this and tries to use it against you, we got your back on that."

Kelly managed to smile, hoping none of them could see the tears welling up in her eyes.

"Well look here," Midge said now. "I think once you finish up that stitch, Kelly, we'll have this quilt complete."

After blinking her eyes to clear them, Kelly looked around and saw that it was true. The rest of the Peculiar Ladies had cut their threads and set down their needles. Blushing a bit at their expectant smiles, Kelly finished up stitching the last bit of border-work in her square, then cut loose her own needle and thread. Working carefully, the Ladies detached their quilt from the frame and gathered it up between them.

"I think it's our finest work yet," Midge declared as she helped hang the quilt over a wooden bar nailed to the far wall. The quilt itself, which had begun as a mishmash of multicolored rags each of the Ladies had brought from their various homes, had come together into a pattern so coherent and well-designed one would have thought they had planned for it to come out just this way from the start.

"It will make a fine addition to the fair," said Mrs. Moore.

"You know you've played a very important part in the creation of this quilt, Kelly," said Midge, that venerable Lady Grace.

"No more so than the rest of you," said Kelly.

"Oh, we all contributed equally to the labor," said Midge. "That's not what I mean. You see, our little quilting society has quite a venerable history. It started at the state's inception, when a group of ladies came together to make a quilt as an inauguration gift for Meriwether Lewis, Missouri's first governor. We started auctioning them off for charity during the Great Depression, and haven't stopped since. We've given our quilts to presidents, patriots, and captains of industry. Our quilts have been sold to benefit veterans, the handicapped, the elderly … and now you, my dear."

For a moment, Kelly didn't realize what Midge meant. "I don't understand," she said.

"We're giving you the proceeds from the quilt auction, you silly girl!" Moe said, and burst out laughing.

Kelly did not laugh. She stared at the quilt and put her hand over her heart, feeling her evil pride unfold inside her like a dark bird spreading its wings.

"Oh no," she said. "Oh no, oh no, oh no. I absolutely refuse to accept it! That money goes to charity! *It's tradition—*"

"We're making a second quilt this year," said Midge. "Really Kelly, it's only June. Do you think we would let this lovely spread just lie about and collect dust until August finally rolls around?"

"Don't be smart, Marjory," said Moe Jefferson. Sometimes she found Midge's Joan Collins accent a bit affected.

Kelly could only stare at the group of them, a quilt of faces made from a mishmash of ages, incomes and backgrounds. Her mouth worked as she tried to speak, but she couldn't think of a thing to say.

Finally she just stammered, "Oh ... oh you guys!" And then she burst into tears.

The Ladies gathered around her in a group embrace, their voices joined in a chorus of gentle consoling laughter that made her love them even as it wounded her secret pride like a wooden spike through her heart.

14

Coldiron Comes Home

Walter Coldiron sat in his living room, enjoying the quiet and waiting for his wife to come home. He felt very good. He had a snifter of brandy in his left hand, an excellent (and highly illegal) Cuban cigar in his right, and between the two had worked up a damn fine buzz.

He had not enjoyed a moment like this in the last thirteen years of his marriage. Since the brat had come along he had hardly experienced a full five minutes of quiet, from the crying as a baby to the non-stop video games and television of today. And the wife had certainly never allowed him to smoke a cigar. Great God no, it might inflame the little fatass's delicate lungs.

As for the brandy, well, it was too good to open for anything less than a very special occasion. His father had given it to him on his wedding day. *You'll need this*, Hector Coldiron had said with a knowing, ironic smile. Walter hadn't opened it then and he had not opened it on any of his wedding anniversaries. Are you kidding? Walter had known he had made a *very* big mistake within his first week of marriage, during which his wife, the former Debra Caldwell, had refused him sex for six out of the seven nights of his honeymoon. Just the wedding night, and that was it! She had lain as still as a corpse with her eyes squeezed shut the whole time, like it was the most revolting thing she had ever endured. Big romance! After the honeymoon Walter had overheard her on the phone, gabbing with her friends about how liberated she was and how he had acted like such a pig.

Still, she had somehow managed to get pregnant. After hearing that news, Walter became convinced that God existed and he had done something to piss Him off big time.

He did not open the bottle of brandy after the birth of his son. Why bother? Debra had not allowed him to so much as listen to the baby's heartbeat or feel him kick.

"Men don't care about those kinds of things," she had said. When he had tried to tell her that he did, in fact, care about those things a great deal, she had just repeated the same thing, only louder. She became loud more and more often. By the time the baby was born he had seen how things would go with this kid. Every time he tried to hold him, Debra would find a reason to take him out of his arms. Every time the kid cried she found some way to blame it on him. If she had to go to the store or the post office or something, she would drop the kid off at a babysitter's rather than leave him alone with Walter for more than half an hour. It was like she didn't want him in the kid's life at all. Whenever he had business associates over for dinner, Debra always held up the baby and said, "This is my son, Timothy." Never "our son." The one time he had confronted her about it, she had laughed until she nearly doubled over. (And what a cruel laugh she had!)

"Oh Wally," she had said. "That's so sweet! But what difference does it make if you're around?"

He supposed he could have fought it out with her, but by that time his career had started to take off. His little realty office had grown in the year since he had opened it and had become the biggest private real estate company in Dayton. And if Hector Coldiron's son Walter liked one thing more than any other, it was success. Hours he could have spent at home fighting with his increasingly strident wife he decided to use building his business, and it paid off. He took his biggest, and most brilliant, risk by expanding into the corporate market. Working with loan agencies and independent contractors, he bought land cheap during the recession years and built office buildings on it. When the recession passed and the economy bounced back, he suddenly had dozens of companies competing to lease from him at extravagant rates. Others bought land from him at several times the price he paid for it. His secret was rural property. Farmers were going broke left and right during the recession years and had to resort to selling off plots of land to pay down their debts. Walter made it his business to snatch up that property dirt cheap, a pun he loved to use at parties. He was a ruthless negotiator; sometimes those hicks would leave his office in tears after he had talked them down to a fraction of their asking price. When the economy made its inevitable rebound, the cities always expanded, and Walter Coldiron now owned the land into which that expansion would take place.

By the time the brat turned two, Coldiron Realty had become the biggest real estate developer in Ohio, and Walter felt the time had come to go national. Such an effort would require them to move around a lot, since Walter insisted on handling all key business matters himself in every state where he established his company. Winning Debra over was the biggest obstacle, but here his negotiating skills came to his rescue. He only had to dangle the prospect of wealth in front of her, real multimillion-dollar wealth, and she came around with hardly an unpleasant word.

So he had packed them up and taken them to Atlanta in time for the urban sprawl explosion, and after he had established himself there he had heard the realty market in the Southwest had started to take off. People loved that dry desert climate. Off they went to Arizona, and after that Nevada to cash in on the swift growth of Vegas. Then the Seattle scene had ignited, so they moved to Washington until that cooled down. And then Nebraska. And Idaho. And Pennsylvania. And Texas.

And so on.

During all of this movement, he had kept his father's bottle of brandy hidden. Never once had he opened it, not for a successful business deal, not for his fortieth birthday, certainly not after his wife's unfortunate bout of breast cancer went into remission. Every time he thought about it, every time something in his career or family life seemed worth celebrating, he had remembered his father's dark ironic smile and his cryptic message, *You'll need this.*

And now, sitting in his living room and watching the dark liquid swirl within the fine crystal glass, Walter wondered just how the old bastard had known his life would come to this. How did he know that Walter would need a bit of bottled courage for this day? Or had his father made his own prophecy come true just by relating it to Walter on his wedding day?

Walter supposed he didn't much care anymore. Right now all he cared about was the marvelous sensation of perfectly aged brandy blended with fine Cuban tobacco coursing through his veins, lifting up his brain to heights above the rain.

He chuckled at this little rhyme and sipped a bit more of the brandy. And did he hear the sound of his wife's Explorer pulling into the driveway? He believed he did, and with the brat still out of the house. Things could not be going better. Yes, it was the perfect day to open the brandy.

Footsteps stomped up the sidewalk and onto the porch, and then the door swung open and Debra Coldiron marched into the room, a triumphant smile on her face.

"Well I guess I showed that snotty little twit from the land management office," she announced as she entered the room. Her allergies had bothered her ever since they had moved here, so he supposed she did not yet smell the cigar smoke. "He came up to me acting so rude, oh you never heard such rudeness in all your life, and I said to him, Look mister, you're not dealing with some nobody here, I have a bachelor's degree, do you understand? A *bachelor's degree!*"

She did this all the time. Often she would enter a room in the middle of one of her tantrums and expect Walter to know what she was screeching about, as if he could read minds or something. And if he didn't know what had put into her into this state, she accused him of selfishness, said he was a horrible husband, what kind of man was he and blah, blah, blah.

"Well you just better count yourself lucky that I was there to set that little snot straight," Mrs. Coldiron continued. "Otherwise you'll never get your writ of imminent domain and not a single one of these hicks will move off this property. Do you know that piss-ant said people would object to development out here? That they wouldn't like it? I mean, can you believe it? Oh, he can go on and on about *culture* and about *history*, but all that crap just falls down when you write them a check. I mean really, do you want a spacious home in a decent neighborhood with a Wal-mart and McDonalds on every corner or do you want to live in a rural slum?

"It's just like the time that back-country prostitute from across the road came over here with that scruffy, mouthy brat of hers, pleading her welfare case," Debra continued, though what the neighbor had to do with the real estate developer Walter had no idea. "And you know when I went out there to put a stop to that little whorehouse stand she puts out there by the highway, a couple of her 'clients'—" His wife made quotation marks out of her fingers as she spoke—"came up and started propositioning her right there while the police officer was talking to her and that cop didn't do a thing! Not a thing! Of course I wouldn't be surprised if he wasn't doing her himself, you know how these things go around here—"

"Out making friends, Debra?" Walter said. He had finally had enough.

She turned and took a good look at him for the first time since she entered the room. "Are … are you *smoking?*"

"You're damn right I am," he replied.

Walter saw the scream building up in her. Her jaw dropped, her eyes, always rather beady behind those thick glasses of hers, swelled to the size of quarters and her head started to shake a little, back and forth as the pressure built up from her lungs, reddening her face to the color of old blood as a screech came out of her like a train whistle.

"WHAT POSSESSED YOU TO SMOKE IN THIS HOUSE AROUND MY BABY—"

Walter lunged out of his chair and threw the brandy into her face, cutting off her scream as neatly a pair of scissors cutting through a strand of yarn.

"I've wanted to do that for thirteen years," he said. "How dare you involve yourself in my business affairs? How dare you presume to order me about like a servant when you would be just another frigid snaggletoothed harridan living off her rich daddy if I hadn't been stupid enough to marry you?"

Walter had often heard of people in a state of tremendous surprise described as "staggered," but didn't think he had ever seen it until now. Debra, standing there with brandy dripping off her nose and onto her white blouse, where it spread in swelling amber-colored stains, looked absolutely staggered.

"Do you think I've enjoyed listening to you all this time?" Walter said. "Why do you think I would stay with you when all you do is nag and scream, when you've let your looks go to hell and done your best alienate me from my own son, utterly ruining the little bastard, by the way. I've never seen such a fat spoiled brat. Well, I've had enough. I'm leaving you, Debra. I've met someone much better than you."

He leaned in close so he could look directly into her eyes. The alcoholic reek of the brandy rose from her in waves, but he didn't mind a bit. He had looked forward to this moment all day.

"I've been screwing my personal assistant for over a year," he said. "She can't get enough of me. In fact, I've slept with half a dozen different women over the course of our marriage and every one of them was better by far than you."

She smacked him across the face. It didn't surprise him, but it gave her a chance to interrupt him and start screeching.

"I'll take you for everything you've got," she said. "Go ahead and leave, just go! I made you. I built you from the ground up and I know every illegal trick you've ever used. When my lawyers are done with you the only sex you'll get will be in the prison showers! You would be nothing without me and *I will take every last penny you have and leave you ruined in the dirt!*"

Walter laughed. "Not quite, sweet pea. I transferred the last of our funds to banks in Antigua just this morning. You see, I'm ready to retire, and I think I'll do it in a warmer climate. My plane ticket is in my pocket, my mistress is waiting for me at the airport, and the extradition laws of Antigua are most agreeable to me. You will get nothing. And if you think you're such a business genius, then let's just see how well you do without me, hmm?"

"Well if you think you're going to get custody of Timmy—" Debra began, but Walter cut her off. This time he didn't just laugh; he threw his head back and *roared* at the ceiling.

"Oh Debra, you silly bitch. Keep the brat! It's not like you're getting any child support!"

With that, Walter turned on his heel and walked out the front door. It banged shut, and his laughter filtered through the ornate wrought-iron design on its front. (It was factory-made.) Soon Debra heard his car roar to life and race off down the dirt road towards town. It was a Mustang convertible, brand new. Debra should have recognized the symptom of a mid-life crisis when he bought it.

She stood motionless for several seconds, staring into space with brandy fumes burning her nose and making her eyes water. Yes, it was only the brandy making her eyes water, not that man, not at all. Well, she would destroy him. She'd find a way. What did he say, Antigua? A plan started to take shape in her mind. She could take Timmy down there and make him look at his father cavorting on the beach with his little slut. Tell him, *Here is the man who abandoned us.* Yes, make him hate his father. It was the perfect revenge.

Wait. Where was Timmy?

"Timmy," the soon-to-be-ex-Mrs. Coldiron called down the hallway that led to their bedrooms. "Where are you, precious?" She hoped he hadn't heard too much of their argument. If she had thought that he could hear them, she would have put up less of a fight.

No response from Timmy. His bedroom looked dark. Where could he be? She wanted him to see her like this, all soaking wet and reeking of alcohol. He had to know what his father had done; she had to bind him more strongly to her side. Where did he get that brandy anyway? She couldn't remember the last time she had bought some.

"Timmy, Mommy needs you!" Mrs. Coldiron cried out to the empty house. Still no response. Mid-afternoon sun slanted in through the windows. The clock over the mantle said two-seventeen. Timmy never left the house during the hot-test part of the day. What had that bastard done to him? Now she began to feel a little worried.

A drop of brandy slid out of her hair and into her left eye, making it sting. She couldn't walk around the house like this any longer. She needed to clean up. Turning around, she went into the kitchen for a towel.

She walked through the open doorway and took a few steps inside the kitchen, rubbing her stinging eyes as she went. She lowered her hands to look around for a towel and had time to wonder why it was so cold in there before she saw the thing waiting for her on the other side of the room.

The kitchen was on the north side of the house, shaded and dark. It was always cooler than the rest of the house, but now it felt much too cool, almost cold. Soft indirect light glowed through the white drapes on the window over the sink and through the French doors that led out to the patio.

A dark hunched shape stood in front of those doors.

"Timmy?" Mrs. Coldiron whispered.

She stood rooted to the spot. She couldn't move. She was paralyzed, frozen. The unnatural cold in the room sank into her flesh, but it was not the reason she began to tremble.

"Timmy, is that you?"

The cold shape did not respond.

For several seconds she stood and stared at it, and the longer she looked the more disturbed Mrs. Coldiron became.

For all her anger and selfishness, Debra Coldiron was still a mother, and she knew her son. The thing standing before the doors looked like Timmy, even though it was bloody and mutilated, but she knew it wasn't him. Somehow she knew. The thought came to her with such forcefulness and clarity that she could not deny the truth of it.

My son is dead.

No, she could not deny it any more than she could deny that the thing now standing before her had killed him.

Thorns bristled from the thing's flesh, as if the creature had slipped on Timmy's skin like fabric over a seamstress's mannequin and affixed it with hundreds of wooden needles. Bloody, filthy shreds of clothing hung from Timmy's body in ragged tatters. Backlit by the light of doors, the face remained hidden in shadow, but she could see an unnatural glint in the eyes. And suddenly she realized she could not bear it if she saw the whole face. If she saw her son's features twisted and distorted like a mask of skin stretched over the face of a monster she would simply die. If her body could not flee from this thing then her soul would do it without her.

She couldn't scream; she couldn't summon enough breath to do it, but she did manage to turn around and try to run.

It seemed like she moved with nightmarish, underwater slowness. She turned, swinging her body around like a swimmer pivoting in the water. God it felt so slow! The room rotated in her view until she saw the kitchen doorway in front of her. It seemed like she had crossed that threshold ages ago. She staggered towards it, thinking *Oh please let me get away! Oh please let me escape!*

A refrigerator stood to the right of the doorway, an enormous stainless steel affair big enough to house a frozen ox. Just before she reached the door, the refrigerator moved. It slid across the floor of its own accord and blocked off the doorway. Mrs. Coldiron didn't have enough time to stop and she collided with it, spraying stars across her vision. Her upper teeth mashed into her lip, filling her mouth with the taste of blood.

She turned again so that her back pressed against the refrigerator. She hated to look at the thing that had been her son, but she couldn't bear *not* to look at it either, knowing it could sneak up behind her while her back was turned.

It stood where it had before, in front of the French doors. It hadn't moved, not so much as an inch. The breakfast table stood between them. The salt and pepper shakers stood on their little circle of lace in the center of it. The morning paper Walter had left on top of the table still sat at its head. Nothing had changed that she could see; nevertheless she sensed something different in the air. A kind of vibration, low, deep, rhythmic. A sound so low she could barely hear it, but she could feel its deep throbbing power.

And then she saw the cats.

Cats sprawled on the countertops, on top of the cabinets, poised daintily on the shelves among the knickknacks. Cats in her breadbox, cats on her cold unused stove, cats lying on the dishtowels folded on top of the microwave. Cats lounging in the dark corners of the room in the still, unobtrusive way that all cats assumed when they did not want to be seen. The vibration she sensed in the air was the sound of all of them purring at once, a sound of very deep pleasure.

"Please ..." Mrs. Coldiron whimpered. "Please!"

"The circle breaks."

A voice, low and hissing. It came from the creature wearing her son's skin, and after it spoke weird echoes of what it had said rippled through the room. The echoes rose from the sounds made by the cats.

"circle breaks ... circle breaks"

"Please," she repeated. "Please no ..." *("... circle breaks ...")*

"The transformation draws near," whispered the awful thing.

"... transformation ..."   *"... bastard ..."*
"... circle draws break ..."   *"... knocked up ..."*
"PLEASE DON'T HURT ME!"   *"... don't go ..."*

"We have slept a long while," said the thing, *"and dreamed great dreams. But now, at last, we have awakened."*

"... dreaming great darkness ..."

It raised its dark bloody hand.

"Give us what you know," it said.

A terrible pressure built up inside Debra Coldiron's skull. She had just taken another breath to scream again when the pain struck her in searing tendrils behind her eyes and nose and ears. With it came an awful *pulling* sensation, like something was trying to turn her head inside out. She didn't understand what was happening, but it felt like an invisible hand had reached into her skull and grabbed a hold of her brain. She tried to run, but the pain had blinded her. She tried to fall to her knees and drag herself away, but the invisible force coming from this hideous child-killing thing had clamped onto her head and wouldn't let her go. It had a grip on her now and even though her legs went limp she didn't fall.

Now she felt something pull her forward by her face. She staggered a few paces towards the creature, but managed to reach back and grab the edges of the refrigerator before she went any further. Still that force kept pulling at the inside of her skull, tighter and tighter like a fist squeezing an exotic fruit, until finally something above and behind her sinus cavity ruptured with an agonizing pop. Blood spurted from her mouth and nose.

The blood flew out of her ... but did not fall. It flew through the air towards the being disguised as her son. She could see bits and flecks of greenish-gray matter in the blood.

She thought, *It can't it CAN'T OH NO!*

But then she found it hard to think at all. The force inside her head kept squeezing and pulling, drawing more blood and tissue out of her, and all of it flew across the room following the line of force that led to the thing before the doors. The bloody bits of brain tissue struck the creature in the face, and rolled up its cheeks like dark red tears moving in reverse until it was absorbed into the creature's unnaturally shining eyes.

Faster the blood came from her, and faster still, flowing out of her face, which was fixed in a rictus of pain. Blood began to spray from her eyes and ears. Dark swirls of vaporized brain matter flew across the room mixed in with the blood. Now a twisting red umbilicus connected the faces of Mrs. Coldiron and her son. The alien mind within Timothy Coldiron's body used its force to draw out every last bit of brain matter and absorb it into itself. The extraction ended quite suddenly. With a final, brutal pulse, the force disintegrated the last bit of tissue inside Mrs. Coldiron's skull and drew it out through her cranial orifices. The twisted umbilicus of blood and brain thinned, slowed, and finally disappeared. The force disengaged, and Mrs. Coldiron's now-lifeless body fell to the floor. Her head made a hollow *thonk* when it hit the tiles.

The creature swayed on its feet, reeling, as fresh memories flooded its mind. With furious heat its mutated brain collected them, processed them, and changed them to its purposes. For with the memories came power.

Such ... vast ... power.

The psychic talent that had lain dormant inside the boy was not doubled by absorbing the mother's mind. It was *squared.* The power coursed through the creature's stolen body like a vibration through a tuning fork, and before it could rein the power into check a great pulse of energy escaped, sending a shudder through the house, cracking the foundation and shattering the glass of the French doors.

The cats rose to their feet. The time had come.

The creature reached out with its mind to summon its mates.

... comecomecomecomecomecome ...

Then it left the house through the shattered doors, to return to its sacred clearing and await the coming of its destiny.

15

A Highly Anticipated Moment

Earlier that morning, Officer Randy stopped by Spencer's little farmhouse and woke him by knocking on the door. Spencer opened it wearing only a pair of jeans, which he had pulled on in a hurry after stumbling out of bed. A glance at the clock disturbed him. It said ten-thirteen, and Spencer had not slept in past eight o'clock on a Saturday since Lorna divorced him.

Nightmares had kept him up last night, or rather a nightmare, the same one that had plagued him for the past several weeks. In his dreams he would go back to that awful dying place, that place where doom hovered over him like a vulture, and when the dream progressed to the point where it reached the screeching terror of falling, he would wake, struggling not to scream, and run to the window convinced that this time he would see the thing trying to reach him waiting outside his door.

The nightmare faded a bit when morning came. Not completely, but enough so that Spencer could slip into a thin, uneasy sleep. Even in this light doze, just close enough to sleep to keep him from dying of exhaustion, he could sense the nightmare prowling beyond the dark veil of unconsciousness. It disturbed him enough to make him flinch when Officer Randy knocked, and maybe he ran to the door and flung it open a little too quickly.

"Spencer!" Officer Randy said. "Everything okay?"

Spencer thought he must look pretty bad, because Randy took a step back when he saw him, and his right hand came to rest in a not-quite-casual way on top of the butt of his gun.

"Everything's fine," Spencer lied. "I just woke up is all." His long brown hair hung in crazy tangles around his face, and Spencer ran his hand back through it to get it out of his eyes. He wondered how tired his face looked, and if those dark bags he had seen under his eyes last night were still there. Looking down, Spencer saw that his fly was undone and his plaid boxers showed. His unbuckled belt dangled on both sides of his zipper like a strange double tongue hanging from his waist.

"What's the matter?" Spencer asked as he zipped his pants and buckled his belt as casually as possible, considering the circumstances.

"I wanted to ask you a few questions about Delbert Cullim," Officer Randy said. He was wearing his reflective sunglasses again. A beautiful bright morning was in full bloom outside; the grass and the leaves of the trees glowed greenish-gold in the sunshine. Spencer could see in his reflection in each of Officer Randy's silvery lenses.

"Why do you want to talk about Delbert?" Spencer asked. Delbert Cullim lived about half a mile down the road from Spencer near the old Brown place, not nearly far enough away in Spencer's opinion.

"Because we found him dead at about seven o'clock this morning," Officer Randy said. His voice had a heavy bluntness to it that Spencer didn't much like.

"Oh," Spencer said. It was all he could think of to say so soon after waking up.

"Mind if I come in?" Officer Randy said, and took a step forward before Spencer could respond. Spencer moved aside to let him in. Normally he would take offense to a cop letting himself in like that, but Spencer was still overwhelmed by fatigue and the stress of his nightmare, and his reflexes had gotten slow.

"How did he die?" Spencer asked. It seemed like a reasonable question.

Randy opened his mouth to respond, hesitated, and then said, "We're not entirely sure. A passerby saw his door standing open for two days in a row. They looked inside to see if everything was all right and well, that was how we found out. Apparently some animals had gotten inside and … disturbed the body."

That was a pretty tactful of putting it, Spencer thought. It didn't sound like something he would say to a suspect, and Spencer relaxed a bit.

"We had to identify him by a tattoo on his knee," Randy said. "We had it on file from his police records. Good thing there was still some skin left on his legs."

Spencer swallowed in distaste. He had started to get his bearings now.

"Do you think he was murdered?" Spencer asked.

"Who knows?" Randy said. "Maybe it was just a heart attack. Or alcohol poisoning. Everybody knows Delbert drank. Have you seen any strange activity near his place? Any recent visitors?"

"To be honest, Randy, I try to avoid Delbert's place," Spencer said. "He used to come by here a lot, always asking to borrow something, usually money or booze. I finally had to put my foot down and tell him he wasn't welcome anymore. These days, I don't even drive by his trailer, since he sometimes waves me down to tell me some sob story and ask to borrow twenty bucks or something."

"Do you know if he was involved in any illegal activity? Drugs? Theft?"

"I've heard rumors, but that's it," Spencer replied. "I don't want to know, quite frankly. I have enough problems of my own."

"I understand," Randy said. He took his wallet out of the back pocket of his pants, pulled a business card out of it and handed it to Spencer. "If you think of anything, will you give me a call? We've sent the body to the state medical examiner's office, but there may not be enough left of it to determine how he died. Any tips you might have would help a lot."

"Sure," Spencer said, putting the card down on the counter that divided his living room from his kitchen. "I'll let you know if I hear anything."

"I appreciate it," Randy said. He turned to go, but stopped just before the door.

"Do you know if Delbert had any pets?" Randy asked.

"Pets?" Spencer said. "Sure. He had that big Rottweiler of his. Buford, I think his name was."

"Just the dog?"

"Yeah, I think so. Why?"

Randy paused in thought before he spoke again. "Well, we found cats all over his house. Biggest, fattest cats you ever saw. But we didn't find any cat food or litter boxes."

"You mean the cats were the animals that …?" Spencer didn't feel the need to finish that sentence.

"Yeah," Randy said. "They were. It might mean nothing. Maybe Delbert was just a man who really loved cats. I mean, a killer using cats to get rid of evidence is a pretty strange M.O."

"But that doesn't make any sense," Spencer said. "With that dog of his, no cat would come within fifty yards of Delbert's house. You sure Buford didn't go after Delbert's body when his dog food ran out?"

"That's just it," Randy said. "We found the dog in the living room with Delbert. Something had ripped open its neck."

Spencer didn't know what to say. He couldn't believe something like this had happened in Peculiar.

"You think the cats did that?" Spencer asked.

"They couldn't have," Randy said. "Because the dog was killed out in the yard, dragged up the front porch stairs and left in the living room. There was a trail of blood. Now how could a cat do that?"

Spencer shrugged, feeling dazed. "I don't know. I guess a group of them could."

"But have you ever heard of a group of cats doing something like that?"

"No," Spencer said. "Never have. I guess a pack of coyotes could have done it." He pronounced the word in the local fashion: *kye-oats.*

"Maybe," Officer Randy said. "I was going to tell you to start locking your doors, but I notice you've already started doing that."

"Yes," Spencer said, staring at his reflection in the policeman's sunglasses. "My house was broken into when I lived in Blue Springs, and since then I've never felt comfortable unless the doors were locked. Just a habit, I guess."

That wasn't true at all, but he couldn't very well say that he had started locking the doors because of the nightmares, as if a deadbolt could keep them out.

"All right," Randy said. "That's a good habit to get into. Be sure to call me if you hear anything."

"I will," Spencer said. "Thanks for stopping by."

Officer Randy nodded as he turned to go. Spencer shut the front door behind him and turned the deadbolt. Walking back to the kitchen counter, he looked down at the card Randy had left.

Cats, the policeman had said. Now why did the mention of cats disturb him so? He shuddered. Goosebumps rose up on the skin of his bare chest.

Spencer was surprised and a little saddened, but not shocked by Delbert's death. He had always known Delbert would not come to a happy end; he just didn't think it would come so soon. And the values his upbringing had instilled in him had taught him to treat the loss of any human life as a tragedy.

He looked at the clock on the panel over the stove. Officer Randy had not kept him long. It was now just past ten-thirty, but Spencer remembered today was the day he was supposed to work on Kelly Ross's truck. It made him feel a little guilty to be excited to see her after hearing the news about poor Delbert, and more than a little disturbed that a killer might be on the loose in Peculiar, but in the end was not life for the living and the fearless?

Suddenly as self-conscious as a boy before his first dance, Spencer rushed to the shower.

He jumped out of his pants, already wondering which of his overalls he should wear, if any. The idea of wearing the ratty, oil-stained clothes he wore to work in front of Kelly made him self-conscious. He wanted to make a good impression, of course, but he couldn't very well change her distributor wires in a three-piece suit, could he?

He cranked on the shower, waited a bit for the water to warm up, and then stepped under the flow. Warm hissing water surrounded him as steam filled the bathroom.

What about just a pair of jeans and a simple gray t-shirt? Nothing fancy, but he didn't wear them to work, so they were clean. Lorna had once said he sure could fill out the seat of his pants. He laughed, remembering. She had said that a few months before she said get out, out my house.

He paused for a moment, feeling disturbed and not sure why. But the warm water felt nice, and he had the prospect of a good day ahead of him, so he brushed it off.

He picked up the soap, thinking of how happy he had felt when Lorna had told him she was pregnant, had said she was knocked up, honeybunch. She—

Spencer froze. The soap slipped from his hand and fell with a clatter to the floor of the shower. Water rose from the dark depths of the earth and passed through the modern electric systems of his home, which filtered and heated it without changing the secret it held. It passed from the shower head looking innocently transparent and pure, ran down Spencer's body in streams to the drain and returned to the earth. Spencer stood, paralyzed. His long wet hair clung to his face, droplets hung from his eyelashes, and his lower lip trembled so that he looked like a terrified boy with streams of tears running down his cheeks. The water flowed over his skin like a shimmering liquid chrysalis.

He said: "We are one mind." But he did not hear himself speak.

A thought shuddered through him, as quick and jolting as an electric current. *Something has awakened in the forest.*

On the heels of that came something that was less a thought than a chilling realization.

I am so cold!

He jerked awake, nearly falling on the slick floor of the shower. Gasping in surprise, he inhaled water and choked. He put out his hand on the shower door and managed to catch himself. He was grateful the glass door didn't break. A friend of his from Grandview had once slipped in the shower and put his hand through the lower half of it. The top half had then slid down like a guillotine and severed his arm. The guy had survived by luck and the quick thinking of his wife, who had rushed into the bathroom and put pressure on his severed stump with her hands to keep him from bleeding to death. The two of them had then sat there, trapped, until the neighbors heard his wife's screams and called the police.

Coughing, Spencer stood with icy water pelting his skin. He flailed at the shower's handle, slapped it off, and then stood shivering for a few moments as he tried to recover and figure out what had happened.

He had drifted off in the shower. How long had he stood there? It seemed like a long time, and he had just felt the proof of it. All the hot water had run out. That never happened in less than twenty minutes.

He opened the shower door, stepped out and grabbed a towel from the bar on the wall. Cold seemed to have penetrated him down to his very core. He looked into the mirror, which had not fogged up, and saw that his lips had turned blue.

He couldn't stop trembling. Wrapping the towel around his shoulders, he stumbled out of the bathroom. The clock on his dresser said twelve-oh-four. Past noon. He had stood in his shower for almost an hour and a half. No wonder the mirror hadn't been fogged up. More than enough time had passed since the hot water ran out for it to clear.

You can't go, he thought. How could he see Kelly now? What if he drifted off when he was in the middle of a conversation with her? Or around her boy? What if ... something worse happened?

He looked at his phone by the bed, and had almost reached out to pick it up and call her when something in him rose up in rebellion.

The grief had to end. He had fought with every last bit of strength he possessed as a man and a human being to get his life back on track after Lorna's miscarriage and the divorce, and now when a bare, slim chance of happiness had come his way, he would not, *would not,* let it pass him by.

Moving with careful deliberation, Spencer stood, dried himself off and ran the towel through his hair. Then he walked over to the dresser and focused on choosing the clothes he would wear that day. He didn't feel any dreams trying to creep into his mind, but he had not felt this last one coming on either. Didn't matter. He would at least try. Even if things went badly, he had to know he had tried his best.

He decided on a clean new pair of overalls and a white t-shirt. A little grease might show up on the white shirt but they were the best clothes he had. He took his time dressing and now it was almost twelve-thirty, so he got a bite to eat and washed it down with a bottle of orange juice from the fridge. Then he did the dishes and straightened up the house a bit before he left. (*Neat freak,* he heard his brother saying in his mind. This made him pause, but after a few moments he decided it was probably just a memory and not another episode.)

He finished with just enough time left to drive over to Kelly's in time for their two o'clock rendezvous. He tied his hair back into a ponytail, then took his wide-brimmed hat off the hook on the wall and placed it on his head. Just as he turned to head out the front door, he saw his reflection in the mirror over his dresser, visible through his open bedroom door. He saw a handsome young man staring back at him, clean, healthy and strong. He had big brown eyes, wide and deep over his strong cheekbones. A well-shaped jaw line framed his rather prominent chin. The tired old stranger he had seen in the mirror after his nightmares had disappeared for now, although Spencer could sense him waiting below the surface, like a skull below the skin. But for now he felt like himself again; he felt like he had a future. He felt hope. Closing his eyes, he silently mouthed two words: *Please God.*

Then he turned and walked out the door, remembering to lock it behind him. The bright beautiful morning he had seen outside the door earlier had evolved into a blustery June day. Normally he would like the heat, but he wondered if sweating too much would turn Kelly off. This concern he didn't bother him much. Trying to look your best was one thing, but he would still be himself no matter how much he wanted to make a good impression. He liked to work outside in the heat. Anyone who wanted him would just have to accept him as his sweaty old self.

He reached Kelly's house at two o'clock, right on the button. Her little pickup sat out front in the gravel driveway. As he stepped out of his own truck, he happened to catch a glint of something moving across the edge of his peripheral vision. Looking over his shoulder, he saw a red Ford Explorer pulling into the driveway of the house across the road.

Don't tell me that Coldiron woman lives there, Spencer thought. *What must it be like for Kelly to have her as a neighbor?* He dreaded to think about it.

The Coldiron house sat close to the road. Too close, really, since whoever built it apparently failed to realize that gravel roads put out a lot of dust. Kelly's schoolhouse sat further back, maybe a hundred yards from the road. Spencer saw the squat form of Mrs. Coldiron, fuzzy with distance and the pall of dust, hop out of the Explorer and march into the house. He supposed if she saw his truck sitting there she would spread some more nasty rumors about Kelly around town, but he couldn't do anything about that, other than trust in the respective goodwill he and Kelly had built up in Peculiar.

As he walked up to the porch, Spencer couldn't help but notice the way the old red paint on the sides of the schoolhouse had started to peel, and the sag that had developed in the middle of the wooden porch. Looked like the central support of it had gone out. Rain and sun had long since turned the old wood gray and made it split. The yard was mowed though, and some patches of wildflowers and herbs stretched their leaves to the sun in flowerbeds set out of the shadow of the schoolhouse. Someone who didn't know better might mistake those plants for weeds, but Spencer's mother had enjoyed wildflowers herself and had kept some beds of them for her own. Now Spencer rather wished he had taken the time to learn about those plants, since it seemed Kelly enjoyed them too.

The porch creaked under his weight as he walked up the steps. As he approached the doorway he saw that the wooden inner door was open, probably for the fresh air, with the outer screen door shut to keep out the bugs. Spencer raised his fist to knock, but paused when he happened to look inside.

The interior was clean, simple and charming. A little TV sat on a metal stand in the corner to Spencer's right, and a couch stood about six feet back from the television, marking off that part of the room as the living area. Just past the living area sat a small table of polished wood with three chairs around it. The table sat in front of a window with three potted plants sitting in its sill, soaking up the afternoon sun. Across from the table and on the other side of the room was the kitchen area, just a stove, a sink, and a little refrigerator lined up against the eastern wall, surrounded by a hive of cabinets. The refrigerator looked like a relic from the nineteen-fifties, all rounded-off corners with a big chrome handle. On the far side of the room he saw three doors all in a row, presumably leading to the bedrooms and bathroom.

Looking in, he saw Kelly sitting on the couch in the living area, her head tilted onto her shoulder, fast asleep.

Spencer couldn't help but smile. He remembered how tired she had looked the last time he had seen her, and thought of how hard she must have to work to stay afloat, living on what she made at the Dollar General and all.

He couldn't see her face, just the back of her head and her legs stretched out in front of the couch. Sitting on her lap was an enormous, beautiful quilt. Spencer had visited the state fair up in Sedalia on more than one occasion and recognized a real handmade quilt when he saw one. It wasn't spread over her like a blanket, but sat neatly folded, as if she had drifted off while sitting on the couch and admiring it. One of her hands lay in the center of an embroidered star.

He hated to disturb her by knocking. This seemed like such a peaceful moment, beautiful in its way. For the first time in a long while he felt the perfect quiet of the country, miles of somnolent fields dreaming under the summer sky, untroubled by the sounds of traffic or business, and here in the peace of the afternoon lay a woman sleeping alone in an unlocked house, a stranger to fear.

Spencer felt such an overpowering sense of rightness in this moment, and an aching desire to be a part of it.

Please, he thought as he lifted his hand to knock, *let me in.*

Let me in.

The words echoed through his mind. He halted with his fist raised. A low painful moan, barely audible, escaped from him as he felt the dream rise up.

... *comecomecomecomecomecome* ...

The doorway flew from him, a threshold retreating as if on wheels. Darkness spread like ink over the bright face of the sun. He saw before his eyes a clear universe of unblinking stars. The schoolhouse, the fields, the summer afternoon, the entire idyllic day dissolved into mist, and as the mist cleared a silver river became visible, flowing through an alien landscape with topography never seen on the surface of the earth. A land with none of the present peace of Spencer's moment at Kelly's door; the sight was like the memory of a doomed place in the distant past.

I don't want to die!

And there, rising above the horizon, beckoning them with its gravitational voice, was the blue third world, drawing them to their doom, to the fires of its atmospheric embrace. No, he did not want to die and so *the child must live!*

An eruption of heat propelled them upwards. He had seen this dream many times before and knew the geyser was coming; he felt the great tension of its pressure building until it burst out in a jet. He and his mates flew into space and plunged into the sea of air surrounding the blue planet. They fell so quickly that the air became fire, which ripped their molecular bodies to pieces. The three of them surrounded the circular molecule that was their only child and protected it from the flames. They had to hold on long enough for it to reach the surface. And when it did ...

... *comecomecomecomecomecome* ...

Suddenly the fires cleared, and he saw ...

... *he sees a great tree covered in thorns emerge from the midst of the flames. Though the clearing in which it stands is burnt, the tree is unconsumed. Within its branches move a pair of creatures with glowing eyes, and about its base pace hundreds of worker cats. It is they who sustain the tree, yet they are its servants.*

Standing before the tree is a dark figure. Like the tree, it is covered in thorns. Its face is hidden in shadow, but its eyes gleam in the light of the Lifesong like the silvery river of home.

The figure speaks, and he recognizes its voice. It is the voice of one of his resurrected mates, and it resonates with the air of command. She calls to him, beckons him, saying come Come COME-!

NO!

The rebellious anger rose up in Spencer once more.

No I won't do it! I won't come to you!

He fought the dream. The fear was there, like always, but now, standing outside the schoolhouse door, he fought it. He clenched his teeth until his head threatened to burst open and expel the dream by force. His long ponytail, that hippie hair his father had so ragged him over, swung back and forth as he shook his head in negation.

I won't do it, I won't come now leave me alone!

And he awoke.

Just like that, it ended.

He let out his breath, not realizing until just then that he had been holding it. He panted like a wrestler after a match, and trembled all over, sweating in the afternoon heat. The implications of the dream should have terrified him; it had come without warning in the middle of the day, while he was still awake, but right now he felt too exhilarated to worry about it. He had fought the dream ... and won!

He laughed in triumph. God, it felt so good to laugh again!

"Hello? Is someone outside my door?" Kelly's voice, slurred with sleep, drifted through the screen door to his ears.

His laughter had woken her. How long had he stood there? What did he look like? Feeling more self-conscious than ever, Spencer did a quick check. He was sweaty, but not too bad considering the heat of the day. His wristwatch said two-twenty-one, so he hadn't lost too much time. Okay, he could do this.

"It's me, Kelly," he said. "Spencer. I came by to work on your car, remember?"

"Yes," Kelly said. "I was expecting you. Sorry, I must have drifted off. Working too hard, I guess."

Footsteps echoed inside the house like the ticking of a giant clock counting down his anticipation, and then her face appeared at the door, a little red from sleep but radiant with a smile. Spencer smiled back, and the expression felt strange and new on his face, like his smiling muscles had gotten out of shape.

"Come on in," Kelly said. "It's good to see you. How has your week gone?"

"Oh, pretty good," Spencer replied. Not true at all. But still, exchanging these little social niceties had a comforting feel about it, known and predictable, easy baby steps back into life.

As he stepped across Kelly's threshold, a gust of cool air came out to meet him. It felt refreshing after the humidity outside, and he remarked on it to Kelly.

"Wow, it's nice and cool in here. I guess you've had the air conditioning on."

"No, actually it's the walls," Kelly said. "They're two feet thick, mortared fieldstone. Great at keeping the heat out."

"Really?" Spencer said. "Two feet thick? This place is really built to last."

"Through a hundred tornado seasons so far," Kelly said. "Knock on wood. Can I get you something to drink? I can only offer some ice water right now ..."

"Water sounds great," Spencer said. "Actually, I should take it outside. I picked up some new distributor cables from work, and it occurred to me that you might need a new cap. I seem to recall that one of your cylinders wasn't firing, and a corroded contact in your distributor cap could cause that."

"I guess I'll have to take your word on that for now," Kelly said. "Will you teach me some more about those things? I really need to learn more about cars. That last breakdown just showed me how little I know, and how much I'll probably need it."

"Happy to," Spencer said.

She became serious. "You know you don't have to do this, Spencer, not at all. Don't feel like you have to work for me. I can get by on my own."

"I know," he said. "I want to. It's all right. Let's get started, okay?"

They went outside and Spencer spent the next hour working on her truck and outlining the basics of automotive repair. Kelly brought out a Tupperware pitcher of ice water, which they split between them. They managed to empty and refill it twice in the next hour as they worked in the hot summer sun. Spencer realized that he shouldn't have worried about his sweating turning Kelly off, since both of them were pretty grungy by the time they finished.

They replaced her distributor wires and cap, Spencer checked her spark plugs and Kelly changed the oil herself, with some oil she had bought at the Dollar General. Although Spencer would never put such cheap stuff in his own truck, he figured it wouldn't hurt Kelly's vehicle since she didn't drive very much in the course of a day. Also, she looked so proud at having bought the correct oil weight for her vehicle's engine that Spencer didn't have the heart to criticize her. So he talked her through the steps involved in changing her oil and recommended she get an oil additive to boost the performance.

They spent an hour at it, and when they were done Kelly suggested they take the truck for a test drive to see how it ran. Very well, as it turned out. Getting that bad cylinder to fire again made a big difference in truck's performance.

"My pickup has a lot more pickup," Kelly said, and they spent ten minutes zipping along the gravel roads, kicking up dust behind them and laughing like idiots. They got back to the schoolhouse around four, sweaty, oily, and covered in road dust, yet filled with a sense of accomplishment and satisfaction.

"The bathroom is behind door number two if you want to wash up," Kelly said as they walked inside.

"Don't you want to go first?" Spencer asked.

"I have a half-bath off my bedroom," she replied. "I'll use the sink in there, don't worry about it. I'm not going to shower or anything yet. I still plan to pick some mulberries later on, so I can finally get some jam made before the season is over. I did ask Jason and Brad to pick me some, but you heard how that turned out. I ended up losing a good pot."

Spencer smiled. "Okay. Mind if I stick around and help out?"

"I'd love it! Oh, and don't let me forget, I owe you a couple baskets of tomatoes. I'll throw in a jar of mulberry jam too for free."

"At this rate I'll fill up my pantry by the end of the day," Spencer said, and stepped laughing through the center door at the far end of the house.

The bathroom was as simple, clean, and charming as the rest of Kelly's home. A clawfoot tub stood against the far wall, with a metal frame mounted above it for a shower curtain. The showerhead itself hung directly over the tub from a pipe coming out of the wall. It was a big old-fashioned thing that probably used a lot of water but made for a great shower. Spencer, used to well water, could tell right away that Kelly got her water from the city from the ice water she had brought out for them to drink as they worked on her truck. It didn't taste bad; on a hot day like this it tasted great, but it made him wonder about her water bills. Spencer had seen his share of tough times, but he didn't have a kid to support. Not by choice.

He went to the sink to wash up, and had to soap his arms up to the elbows to get all the grease smudges. He had what he liked to call "mechanic hands," where his fingers were permanently stained dark. No amount of soap or scrubbing would get the oil stains out of his skin. He felt rather proud of it, like wearing a badge of his profession for all the world to see.

Looking into the mirror over the sink, he examined his reflection for the second time that day. This time he felt much better about what he saw. He looked like an adult, mature and at peace with himself. He wondered if simple loneliness had caused his recent mental troubles, but for some reason that didn't seem quite right. However it did seem right that most of the loneliness had retreated today.

He rinsed his face and combed back his hair with his fingers as best as he could. When he looked decent again, he stepped out of the bathroom and saw Kelly standing in the center of the open space that made up the front three-quarters of the house. She was talking in soft tones to two young boys. He only caught, "... don't want you to feel uncomfortable, so if anything bothers you—" before they heard him come out of the bathroom and turned to look at him.

Kelly looked a little nervous, which seemed strange on her face. He hadn't taken her for the nervous type. Then the thought that Spencer was probably the first man her son had seen in the house since his father died finally worked its way through his thick head.

"Spencer," Kelly said, "this is my son, Jason."

"Hello Jason," Spencer said, and stepped forward with his hand out. "It's nice to meet you."

The boy looked at him with naked suspicion in his big brown eyes. His black hair came down almost to his shoulders. Unusual to see long hair on a boy so young, but it brought out his strong cheekbones. With the cast of his features, Spencer saw that Jason had Indian blood running through him with all the power of a herd of buffalo stampeding across the Great Plains. He had not heard that Jack Ross was Native American. The Peculiar citizens had praised his character and his hard work and that had been enough for them.

Jason took his hand and shook it once. "Hi," he said. He did not smile, and Spencer thought he seemed a little stunned from the way he leaned close to his mother's leg.

"I'm Brad," the other boy announced, stepping forward. He had buzz-cut blond hair and a face full of freckles. Spencer recognized him from a trip his mother had made to Fred's garage, and recalled that Kelly had mentioned him the last time they met.

"I'm Jason's best friend," Brad said. His tone seemed to say *You got a problem with that?* Spencer couldn't resist smiling.

"Well, I imagine that's a pretty good thing to be," Spencer said.

"Yep," Brad replied, just as pert as you please.

While Brad introduced himself, Spencer happened to see Jason look back and forth between Kelly and himself. Jason seemed to draw himself up, and then spoke again.

"It's, uh, it's nice to meet you too," he said.

It was only a moment, but Spencer got the unmistakable impression that Jason had read something on his mother's face and forced himself to speak. More than that though. Had Jason read something on Spencer's face too?

It seemed too amazing to be real, that a kid so young could have the empathy to understand the feelings of two adults. If so, then Jason was just as remarkable as his mother.

"Where have you been all day, Jason?" Spencer said. "Your mom told me about you earlier and I was looking forward to meeting you."

"Me and Brad went-"

"'Brad and I,'" Kelly interrupted softly.

"Brad and I," Jason amended, "went out to look at Mr. Snow's new baby goats."

"Baby goats are called kids," Brad announced. "And one of them had little horns on its head already and Mr. Snow let me hold one but then the momma goat, she's called a nanny even though she's really the momma, got real mad and started head-butting her pen so I had to put her kid down and Jason said his mom wanted us to come back here and-"

"I thought we could go mulberry picking, sport," Kelly said, putting her hands on Brad's shoulders and looking down into his face. Spencer smiled, guessing Brad could have gone on all day if Kelly hadn't intervened.

"I never got any berries for cobbler the last time," she continued, "and I finally have a little time to make jam, so I thought it would be fun for us all to go out and pick some. Sound good?"

"Okay!" Brad chirped. Jason only nodded. Spencer wondered how a quiet kid like Jason had become friends with a little chatterbox like Brad, but he supposed they had their reasons. Children often worked in mysterious ways.

"Okay," Kelly said. "Are we all ready then?"

They all agreed, so Kelly passed out a pair of wooden bowls to the kids ("No more of my good pots," she said), handed Spencer a Tupperware pitcher of ice water, and they stepped outside into the late afternoon sunshine, headed to the mulberry grove.

The sun still hovered on the western side of the sky. The long summer days afforded them plenty of sunshine, and they took their time trotting through the fields. The kids scampered around them, chattering and laughing. Kelly described some of the history of her house and land, pointing out landmarks as they went. Sunlit cottonwood fibers drifted in the breeze over the wild hay, which came up to their waists in spots, and somnolent insects buzzed through the dreaming day.

"Let's go the field route to the mulberry grove," Kelly said. "It's a little longer, but I'm not dressed for hiking through the woods."

"Lead on," Spencer replied.

The field route involved walking over some uneven terrain, but it did avoid all the briar patches in the woods. They headed south, almost to the Grace home, until they reached a small depression in the earth that would narrow and deepen into a gulley the closer it got to the old Brooks farm. The depression acted as a natural border between the Ross and Grace properties, and looked rather like a scoop taken out of the broad shallow valley. So far they had followed almost exactly the same path that Brad and Jason had taken when they had gone out berry picking and found Rachel, except that now they walked closer to the tree-line to enjoy the shade. When they reached the depression they startled a flock of wild turkeys pecking at the hickory nuts scattered over the ground. The sleek black birds half-ran, half-flew into the shelter of the woods, the toms trailing their long chest plumage behind them.

They turned right when they reached the depression and followed it for a few hundred yards. If they had kept going, they would have ended up at the Brooks farm, but before they reached that point Kelly directed them off to the left, up layers of limestone that formed a natural staircase out of the depression. From there they picked up a convenient game trail, a branch of the same one Jason and Brad had followed earlier until they had strayed from the path. This trail led them to the meadow where the mulberry trees grew at the edge of the forest.

As soon as the trees came into sight, the boys ran across the meadow straight for the branches grown heavy with dark purple berries.

"Hey, leave some for the rest of us, okay guys?" Kelly called, but she may as well have told those wild toms to stick around for tea and sandwiches. Soon the boys had purple mouths and purple fingers from eating the plump, wrinkled berries. Kelly rolled her eyes and Spencer laughed.

Kelly saw something in Spencer's face as he watched the boys, a soft wistful expression that she recognized. She had last seen it on her late husband's face during her seventh month of pregnancy with Jason, when both of them had finally overcome the shock and accepted that they were about to become parents. It had surfaced one day while he was stroking her stomach and felt Jason kick. It was the expression of a man who wanted kids, a man who wanted to be a dad.

Hold on, girl, said a voice in her mind that sounded an awful lot like her mother, *make sure the hook is set before you try to reel him in.*

Kelly promptly told this inner voice to shut up and mind its own business, and unlike her mother it did.

After standing in one place and picking berries for a while, the boys became bored and fidgety, so Kelly told them they could go play, since their bowls were about half-full. They ran over to the other side of the meadow, where they would turn up rocks and look at grubs, climb trees, and God knew what.

"Pick me some lambsquarter or poke if you see any," Kelly called after them, "I want some greens to go with dinner."

Turning back to Spencer, she said, "Stay for dinner if you want. It's just fried chicken and mashed potatoes with some wild greens, nothing special, but we'd love to have you."

"That sounds nice," Spencer said.

"Of course Brad will have to go home," Kelly said as she picked mulberries. "Don't get me wrong, he's a great kid and has stood by Jason during some really tough times, but sometimes it's like I have two sons, you know? Besides, I think Midge would appreciate me sending her son home once in a while."

She smiled and turned to look at Spencer as she spoke, but when she did she saw that Spencer was not smiling back. His eyes had focused on something beyond her, an expression of surprise and concern filling his face.

Kelly turned back just in time to see Rachel emerge from the woods like a ghost.

Rachel froze when she saw them, looking like a deer caught in the headlights of an oncoming car. Kelly, rather surprised herself, could only stare back at her for a few seconds. Rachel looked terribly ill. Her black hair clung to her cheeks in lank, sweaty tangles. Dark circles had formed under her eyes, looking deep and prominent against her pale skin. Her feet were bare and her clothes looked old and rather dirty. Sticktites clung to her cut-off jeans and black blouse. Rachel clutched her arms and shivered despite the heat of the afternoon, looking feverish and thin. Kelly wondered why on the earth the girl was out wandering through the woods when she was sick. Where was her mother?

Rachel tensed when she saw them, and Kelly feared the girl would bolt like a wild animal.

"Rachel, honey," she said, trying to keep her voice low and soothing. "It's good to see you again. Do you remember me? I'm Ms. Ross. I'm Jason's mother."

Her dark eyes ... how wide and suspicious of kindness they seemed, like a kicked dog's. Kelly sensed Spencer's presence just over her shoulder, watching, and she hoped Rachel would not run off at the sight of a stranger.

"This is my friend, Spencer," Kelly said, hoping Spencer remembered what she had told him about the girl.

"Hello, Rachel," Spencer said. "What brings you out here today?"

She stared at him with those dark eyes of hers, so wide you could almost fall into them if you weren't careful. Spencer began to think this poor strange girl wouldn't respond when she finally spoke.

"The dream made me come," she said.

Coldness sank through Spencer's spine at these words, from the back of his neck to his heels, and he hoped Kelly didn't see him shiver.

"Well, we were just picking some mulberries," Kelly said. If she thought Rachel's words sounded strange, she didn't let it show. "Would you like some?" She held out one of the wooden bowls full of the dark fruit.

Rachel looked into the bowl for a moment, then turned and picked a berry off a branch beside her. She ate it in two dainty bites, and Kelly felt rather foolish for offering Rachel something she could get for herself, which she now realized was what the girl had meant to show her.

Just then a shout came from across the meadow. Jason and Brad came running up to them with their fists full of wild greens. They halted at exactly the same time when they saw Rachel, their faces dropping into almost comical expressions of surprise. At that moment, they looked so much alike that it explained why so many people thought they were brothers. Then they cried out with their voices full of excitement.

"RACHEL!"

"Boys!" Kelly shouted, but Jason and Brad were too full of spirit to realize she wanted them to stop. She fully expected Rachel to disappear into the woods at the sight of a pair of rambunctious boys, but the girl didn't seem bothered by them at all. She even smiled a little bit as the boys crowded around her, Jason patting her on the shoulder and Brad chattering like an auctioneer. Of course, they had saved her life; no wonder she didn't fear them.

"She's afraid of adults," Spencer murmured.

"What's that?" Kelly said.

"The boys don't bother her," he replied, "but she was suspicious of us. She must be afraid of adults."

They spent a moment in sad silence as they wondered why.

Jason and Brad did a better job of keeping Rachel around than Kelly and Spencer, so the adults went back to picking berries while the kids talked and played in the high summer grass. While she picked berries Kelly kept trying to think of a way to get Rachel to trust her. She had to figure out a way to help her, since Rachel clearly didn't have a proper home life, but she couldn't do that with the girl ready to bolt if she made so much as a sudden movement. She kept glancing back at her through the corner of her eye, looking for something in the children's play that would give her a hint.

Rachel only sat in the grass while the boys scampered around her, probably because she didn't feel well. The sunshine would do her good, Kelly figured. Might help her sweat out the bug she had caught. At the very least it would ease her chills, and the girl seemed to enjoy it. She kept closing her eyes and turning her face up to the sky, following the sun like a flower.

But soon Brad became impatient, as was his nature. "Rachel, play with us," he said. "We can play hide-and-seek with three, come on!"

"No, thank you," Rachel said. She had such a soft voice. Every other kid in her situation would have whined, but Rachel was no whiner.

"I don't think she feels like playing right now, Brad," Kelly said. "I still don't have enough greens for dinner. Why don't you and Jason go find me some more poke, okay? If you can't find any then some milkweed will do, but I'll have to cook it twice. Oh, and some Queen Anne's Lace too. Now Jason, you know how to tell if it's Queen Anne's Lace, don't you?"

"Wait," Rachel said.

"Yeah, look for the purple flower," Jason said. "I know."

"Wait," Rachel said again, a little more insistent this time. "Wait, don't eat Queen Anne's Lace!"

"What's that, honey?" Kelly said.

"Don't eat Queen Anne's Lace," Rachel said. "It's poisonous!" She pulled herself to her feet. Both Kelly and Spencer noticed the amount of effort it took her to do it. They exchanged a worried glance.

"What makes you say that, darlin'?" Kelly said. She dropped to one knee so she could look Rachel in the eye.

"Because I tried it once," Rachel said. "I heard on TV that you could eat Queen Anne's Lace, so I tried it and I got really, really sick."

"Is that why you don't feel well now?" Kelly asked. "Did you eat a plant that made you feel bad?"

"No," Rachel said, her voice tinged with impatience. "I ate Queen Anne's Lace last year. I'm okay now. I just have a little cold, that's all."

"Oh, all right," Kelly said. "I misunderstood you, I'm sorry. Tell me about the plant you ate last year. Did it have a tall thin stalk with frilly leaves, and kind of a flat blossom on top made up of a bunch of tiny flowers?"

Rachel nodded. "Yes, that's Queen Anne's Lace. The man said you could eat the roots, so I tried some. Just a little, to be careful you know, and just that little bit made me really sick. You shouldn't eat it."

"Well honey, I think the plant that made you sick was probably hemlock," Kelly said. "Queen Anne's Lace is a mimic of hemlock."

"A what?" Rachel's eyebrows picked up, just a little bit.

Go carefully, girl, said the voice in Kelly's mind. *You just might have her attention.*

"A mimic," Kelly repeated. "That's something that looks like something else. Sometimes a plant or an animal looks like something poisonous so predators won't eat it."

"It does?" Rachel said. "How does a plant know how to look like something poisonous?"

"Well, it doesn't *choose* how it looks," Kelly said. "That's just a way Nature gave it to protect itself. Insects often do the same thing. A viceroy butterfly looks like a monarch butterfly because monarchs are very distasteful. So if a bird sees a viceroy then it won't eat it because it thinks the viceroy is a nasty-tasting monarch. It's a similar thing with Queen Anne's Lace and hemlock. Most animals that eat plants know by instinct that hemlock is poisonous, and Queen Anne's Lace looks enough like it that animals will avoid it even though Queen Anne's Lace is perfectly good to eat."

"It could still go the other way," Rachel said. "You could mistake hemlock for Queen Anne's Lace. How do you tell the difference?"

Kelly smiled. "I'll show you."

She stood up again and walked a few paces into the meadow, scanning through the grass for the distinctive white flower. She waded through wild wheat and crabgrass and stepped carefully around tall thistles with their sharp pink crowns. Grasshoppers bounded all around her. Finally she found the plant she was looking for. She stooped down, pulled it out of the ground with a firm yank and brought it back to Rachel.

"This is Queen's Anne Lace," she said, going down on one knee again. "It looks just like hemlock, except for one thing. One tiny purple flower. See?"

Kelly ran her thumb through the flower cap on the tip of the narrow plant, sending up a spray of golden pollen. The plant looked like a very drab, unattractive weed ... until you looked closer. Then you saw the flower cap was made of hundreds of tiny white flowers growing in clusters, very much like an intricate pattern of lace. In the very center of this lovely snow-white circle was a single purple flower the size of a pencil dot, like a lady's lacework stained with a single drop of wine.

"You see?" Kelly said.

"That one little flower means it's okay?" Rachel asked. She reached out to touch the flower, but pulled her hand back at the last moment, as if she didn't quite dare.

"That's right," Kelly said. "Also, Queen's Anne's Lace has a taproot, while hemlock has branching roots." She turned the plant over so they could look at its roots. Her Midwest accent came out when she said the word, so it sounded like *ruts.*

"See how the root looks like a little white carrot?" Kelly asked. "That's a tap-root. Hemlock isn't like that. It only has a bunch of stringy roots that branch off in all directions. Queen Anne's Lace is closely related to carrots. Here, smell."

She broke the taproot in half with a firm snap. Although the tough fibrous root didn't break all the way in two, its skin did tear open and exposed the stringy white insides. Kelly held the root under Rachel's nose, and the girl's eyes widened in surprise.

"It smells like carrots!" Rachel exclaimed. A smile of pure delight filled her face, for an instant replacing her ill expression with a wild, radiant beauty.

Kelly smiled herself. She had achieved her goal.

"They're too tough to eat raw," she said, tossing the plant aside. "But they're good to season a stew or a pot roast with. Sometimes I'll send Jason out for a couple if the bugs get the carrots in my garden."

Kelly stood up, wiping her hands on her cutoffs, and happened to see Spencer smiling at her in admiration. She lowered her eyes, blushing.

Rachel sat back down in the grass, seeming to digest what Kelly had just told her. After a while, she said "Just that one flower. It's hard to tell the good one from the bad one."

"Well, it's hard to tell the poisonous plant from the nonpoisonous one," Kelly said. "They're not really good or bad. Everything has its place in nature, even if we don't see it right away."

Watching this exchange brought back a lot of memories for Spencer. He remembered his own dad teaching him how to hunt and fish and camp. Only now as an adult could he appreciate how many dangerous things his parents had let him handle, guns and knives, in addition to teaching him which berries were safe to eat and which were poisonous. But they felt there was no safety in keeping children ignorant about the dangerous facts in life. They believed they could best protect their children by teaching them to protect themselves, and how to stay away from things that would harm them.

The boys, who had become distracted during all this talk, had run off somewhere and now returned with their hands full of dandelions.

"We couldn't find any poke, Mom," Jason said, "but we can have dandelions greens too, right?"

"That'll do," Kelly said. "Just put them in one of the bowls with the mulber-ries. I'll sort them out when we get home."

"Here," Jason said, handing her a dandelion flower as bright as a smile.

Kelly took it and tucked it behind her ear. "Thank you, sweetie," she said.

The mention of dandelions seemed to have made Rachel notice one growing near her. The flower had gone to seed, and turned into a lacy globe. She picked it and sent the seeds floating through the air with a puff of her breath. Looking up, she watched them drift off into the world, where they would spread their species.

"Oh! Oh!" Brad exclaimed. "I heard of a cool game you can play with dandelions. Jason, hold out your arm with your palm facing up."

Jason looked suspicious. "Why?"

"Just do it!"

Jason warily extended his arm, but looked ready to yank it back on a moment's notice.

Brad took a dandelion flower and placed it facedown in the crook of Jason's elbow.

"Okay," he said. "Now pretend this flower is a little boy out playing in his field. All of a sudden, he has to go the bathroom. So he runs home as fast as he can."

Brad ran the dandelion down Jason's arm in a series of light taps to his wrist.

"But when he gets home," Brad said, "he doesn't have to go anymore, so goes back out to play in the field."

He ran the flower back up Jason's arm to the crook of his elbow again.

"But he when gets back to the field," Brad continued, "now he has to go again, so he runs all the way back home." He moved the flower back down to Jason's wrist.

"But then when he gets back home, he doesn't have to go anymore, so he goes back out to play in the field." The flower bounced back to Jason's elbow again. Jason began to look a trifle uneasy.

"But, for a third time," Brad said, "when he reaches the field, he has to pee, really, really bad. So he runs back home as fast as he can."

Brad moved the flower again, but instead of running it down Jason's arm in a series of light taps like before, he pressed it down hard, so that it left a long yellow smear down Jason's arm.

"He didn't make it!" Brad bawled, and burst out laughing.

"Oh gross!" Jason said, wiping at the smear on his arm, but soon he started laughing as well.

"I have one," Rachel said. The boys immediately took interest. Kelly thought they would have become bored with her, since she couldn't roughhouse, but they seemed to think the world of her.

Rachel picked another dandelion flower, stood, and walked over to Jason and Brad. She held the flower in her fist with her thumb under the blossom.

Smiling, she said, "Momma had a baby and its head popped off!"

With a flick of her thumb, she popped the blossom off its stem and sent it spinning through the air. The boys roared with laughter.

"Oh, let me try!" Brad almost screamed. He picked another dandelion and put his thumb under the blossom as Rachel had done.

"Momma had a baby and its head popped off!" Brad cried, and sent the blossom flying. Soon all three of them had started in on it, picking dandelions like mad and popping the flowers off their stems.

"I'm going to be hearing that for the next three days," Kelly said, shaking her head in dismay. Spencer thought his cheeks would soon grow sore from smiling.

"Momma had a baby and its head popped off!" Rachel cried. Being sick, she couldn't move as fast as the boys, but she did seem to be having fun playing this rather weird game.

"Momma had a baby and its head popped off! Momma had a baby and—"

Her words cut off in mid-sentence. The way she suddenly stopped made Kelly and Spencer look up from berry-picking in surprise.

Rachel stood frozen, staring into the trees. A flower tumbled from her hand to the grass below. Her eyes grew wide and then, just barely audible, she spoke.

"The man," she whispered.

"Rachel," Kelly said. "Rachel, what's wrong?"

The girl began to tremble. Her eyes never left the woods. A low moan escaped her throat, soft and filled with pain.

Kelly walked over and kneeled in front of her once more. After a moment's hesitation, she put her hands on the girl's arms. Rachel shuddered beneath her grip like a violin string on the verge of the note that snaps it. The boys sensed something was wrong and stopped their strange chant. They stared at Kelly staring at Rachel, who in turn stared at the woods.

"Rachel," Kelly said, "what's the matter?"

"The *man*," Rachel repeated, the words escaping her in a tight little stream.

Confused, Kelly turned her head in the direction Rachel was looking. Her breath caught when she saw the thing standing in the woods, watching them. Spencer followed their gaze, and after a moment he saw it too.

It was a deer.

A lone doe, standing beneath the shelter of the tree limbs at the border between the forest and the meadow. None of them had heard it approach. It stood in a stiff, motionless pose like a statue and kept its eyes focused on Rachel.

Spencer often went deer hunting when the season rolled around in November, and over the years he had shot his fair share of them for some meat to fill his freezer. But he would never shoot this doe for meat. If he had a gun now, he would shoot it out of pity, just to put the poor thing out of its misery.

It had an enormous tumor growing out of the side of its neck. Dozens of oozing sores covered its body and most of its fur had fallen out. And its eyes, those soft beautiful doe-eyes, were filled with so much pain! It didn't move at the sight of all these humans, or show even a trace of fear. Spencer couldn't help but wonder if it was too far gone now to fear anything.

"The man!" Rachel whispered again.

"Rachel," Kelly said, "Rachel honey, there is no man there. It's just a deer. A poor sick deer, but a deer is all it is."

Within her shell of terror, Rachel heard this nice Ms. Ross lady, but she knew better. Oh, they might see a deer standing there, but Rachel saw a man. *The* man, the one who had visited her window in the night. Somehow his bones had reassembled themselves, scrambled out of the well, and come leaping and prancing across the nighttime fields to find her. But now it was done playing games. Now it had come for her. Beneath the shadow of the branches she saw the gleam of a skull, its permanent grin. Bones without the cover of flesh moved beneath its old-fashioned top coat and trousers. Extending its skeletal hand, it curved its finger bones back towards itself in a gesture of beckoning.

No, Rachel thought. *No please!*

She couldn't let it get her. She had to escape somehow. Somehow …

Spencer had been staring at the deer in horrified surprise when he heard Kelly cry out.

"Spencer!"

Turning, he saw Rachel lying in the grass, her entire body twisting in convulsions.

"Oh Spencer, she's collapsed!" Kelly cried.

He ran over to where the girl lay shuddering in the summer grass with dandelions in her hair. Her eyes had rolled up to the whites. Bubbles of saliva formed at the corners of her lips.

Without wasting a second, Spencer bent and scooped her into his arms.

"Come on, we'll get help!"

He ran back towards the game trail with Kelly and the boys in close pursuit.

"Take her to Midge's house," Kelly cried. "It's closer and we can—"

She never got to finish her sentence. They never even got out of the meadow. No sooner had one great shock fell on them than another one came. As they ran alongside the tree-line towards the game trail that would lead them back to the depression, a loud male voice boomed from the trees.

"FREEZE! DOWN ON THE GROUND!"

The bushes to each side of the game trail suddenly rose up. Briars and brambles rustled and lurched upwards like trees sprouting up full-grown with unnatural speed. It looked bizarre, surreal, as if the forest was rising up and attacking them.

But then they saw the guns. This was even stranger, a grove of trees jumping up holding pistols and rifles, but when the figures rushed forward and emerged from the shadows under the branches everything became clear. They weren't trees; they were men wearing camouflage fatigues with brown and green masks covering their entire faces. They had branches and twigs attached to their helmets and tied to their clothing, so that they blended in with the forest. Had they been there, waiting, all this time?

"DOWN ON THE GROUND!" The man in front roared the command at them, waving a shotgun in their faces.

"What the hell is going on—!" Spencer started to say, and then the soldier swung the butt of his gun around and smashed it against the side of his head. Shooting stars exploded across his vision, white and blinding. Spencer fell over backwards; Rachel's unconscious body tumbled to the ground.

"Boys run!" Kelly screamed. They bolted for the trees, but the soldiers had them surrounded. They seemed to have sprouted up from the ground itself; they must have been slowly and carefully maneuvering around them while they had picked berries in perfect innocence. As Jason and Brad took off in different directions, a pair of soldiers moved to chase after them, and Kelly saw she only had a fraction of a second, no time think or the soldiers would get too far apart for her to stop them both, so she threw herself to the ground in front of them. Both soldiers tripped over her. One of their boots caught her in the jaw, chipping a tooth. Their feet struck her chest, her ribs, and her stomach, and then they both fell on top of her.

In an instant, one of the soldiers rolled over and slammed his forearm into her back, pinning her against the ground. She felt the cold metal tip of a gun barrel pressed against the back of her head.

"Don't move," the soldier growled, his voice muffled by the mask. "Don't you dare."

With her face mashed against the ground, Kelly could only see out of one eye, but she caught a glimpse of Brad and Jason dashing into the woods.

Oh please see him to safety, God, she prayed. *Whatever is happening, watch over my son. Please, he is my only child.*

And as she realized she had not prayed for Brad, also the only child of a widow, a hot flood of selfish guilt washed over her, and she watered the soft meadow grass beneath her eyes with her tears.

Not far away, Spencer felt hands roughly turn him onto his stomach, and then a knee pressed into the middle of his back. His face throbbed where the soldier had hit it and he struggled to remain conscious. The voices around him were deadened, indistinct. He felt like a man who was underwater, or underground, or both, listening to people talk in the free air. Only one voice came clearly to him. It was distant, but coming closer. It was calling out his name, but not in a language of words.

The soldier on top of him bound his hands with a tough strip of plastic and hauled him to his feet. The blood ran out of his head and he nearly fainted. The distant voice grew loud and insistent. It nearly overwhelmed him, but he managed to fight it off again by biting his tongue until he tasted blood. The pain forced him awake and gave him a measure of clarity. Kelly and Rachel and the boys needed him now; he didn't have the luxury of unconsciousness.

The soldier holding him shouted an order through his mask.

"Move!"

He stumbled forward. As he did, his vision cleared and he saw another masked soldier lifting Kelly to her feet, her hands bound behind her and her face red with tears. A third soldier was wrapping Rachel's body in black plastic while another fixed some kind of air-mask to her face. Armed and masked soldiers surrounded them on all sides; the soldier holding Kelly kept a pistol aimed at the back of her head and Spencer could only assume he had a gun pointed at himself in much the same way.

"Who the hell are you people?" Spencer demanded. "What do you think you're doing here?"

"Move it," the soldier behind him repeated. "Don't make me tell you again."

Spencer stumbled forward. This had all happened so quickly. Less than five minutes ago everything had been all right, or on its way to being all right, and now his world had been blown to pieces.

"We have a sick child!" Kelly cried. "Please, she needs a doctor!"

Spencer didn't see the boys. Had they gotten away? They must have; he didn't remember hearing any gunshots. A soldier had picked up Rachel, now wrapped in plastic, and was carrying her in the same direction the other soldiers were herding Spencer and Kelly. They led them away from the game trail and made them walk through the undergrowth into the woods on the opposite side of the meadow.

As Spencer stumbled through the briars under the relentless push of the soldiers, he happened to look down and to his right. What he saw there chilled him more than he would have thought possible under the circumstances, for reasons that still seemed vague and malformed. It was the deer Rachel had seen before collapsing. It was lying on its side in the green grass with a shaft of sunlight warming the flies crawling over its skin.

Dead.

16

The Matter Grows

When she was a little girl Kelly read of a legend, which said that if the teeth of a dragon were planted in the ground, they would spring up as armed warriors overnight. She recalled this legend as the soldiers propelled them through the woods.

Kelly stumbled onwards under the force of their relentless advance. With her hands tied behind her, she could not catch herself if she fell, nor could she shield herself from the brambles, which were everywhere. She could only stagger forward as best as she could and try to keep from falling. Soon a hundred scratches and scrapes covered her skin, until it seemed like her entire body had been scraped raw. With her bare legs she suffered the worst of the forest's hardships. Spencer's overalls protected his chest and legs, although without his arms to protect his face he soon developed scratches all over his forehead, cheeks, and neck. Red spots dotted his white t-shirt. Branches snagged in his hair and yanked it loose of the hair tie holding it in a ponytail, so that it stuck out at crazy angles.

As concerned as she was for Spencer, she couldn't spare much thought for him right now. Someone else dominated her mind.

Jason.

Did he get away? Was he out of danger? Would they let him go or send other soldiers after him? What-?

Stop! She forced her mind away from her son. As much as she worried about him, down that path lay hysteria. If she kept thinking of all the things that could happen to him she would begin to scream and beg until she couldn't think at all anymore, and then what would the soldiers do to her? What would happen to Jason if he lost his mother a year after losing his father?

Her foot snagged on something and she fell to the ground. With her hands bound she couldn't catch herself and she landed with a tooth-rattling thump. Sticks and twigs jabbed her in a hundred places. When she opened her eyes she saw that she had landed in a patch of poison oak, just what she needed on top of everything else.

"Kelly!" Spencer cried. "Are you okay? God, someone help her up! She hasn't done anything to anyone! She doesn't deserve to be treated like this—"

A dull thud and Spencer cried out in pain.

"Shut up, you," said one of the soldiers.

Rough hands pulled Kelly to her feet. As they lifted her up, Kelly saw that she had tripped on an old barbed-wire fence half buried in the grass. Looking at it, she reasoned they must be near the Brooks farm.

"Look," Kelly said. "I don't know where you're taking us, but there's a gully near here. It's always dry in the summer. If you'll just let us walk down there it will take us out of these woods a lot faster."

But for some reason the soldiers wouldn't even consider that idea. Kelly couldn't imagine why. She could tell this hike was rough on them, even though they all had thick camouflage uniforms protecting them from the thorns. They were all breathing heavily through their facemasks. The soldier carrying Rachel had a particularly difficult time. The plastic he had wrapped her in kept snagging on branches and briars. The edges of the plastic had grown tattered before they had gone a hundred yards.

But protection from thorns did not explain the soldiers' facemasks or their thick black gloves.

"Forget it," said the one in the lead. "Start walking and quit asking questions."

They pressed onwards. One of the soldiers held Kelly by her upper arm as they walked to keep her from tripping. This seemed oddly courteous, although she supposed it was in the soldiers' best interest to keep them moving quickly. Still, she had to suppress an urge to ask the soldier his name. She had a habit of wanting to acquaint herself with people who showed her some courtesy. She glanced at the front of the soldier's uniform, looking for a name badge or something, but of course she found nothing that would identify the man. These weren't the kind of soldiers who wore their names out for everyone to see.

She had to wonder at her naiveté. Even now part of her thought, *Surely they don't mean kidnap us! They can't possibly arrest us and hold us without a reason and without a trial, can they?* She knew logically they intended to do exactly that. Of all the hardships she had faced over the course of her life, she had never encountered a situation like this, or ever dreamed she would.

Onwards they went, leaving little bits of their hair, clothes, skin and blood snagged on the branches and thorns in their path. With all the pieces of themselves they were leaving behind, Spencer thought, even the most inexperienced of hunters could track their path through these woods. But no hunter could track the false sense of security they had left behind. The shock of this encounter had ripped that away like a scab, leaving them raw and bloody.

With all the ruckus the soldiers were making as they hiked, Kelly wondered if anyone could hear them. Their boots made a terrific noise as they stomped over all the leaves and twigs scattered over the ground. At this point it was the only the hope she had left.

The woods ended quite suddenly, like they had crossed a divider line. It felt so good to be free of them that for a moment Kelly and Spencer didn't notice their surroundings. But when they finally looked up, surprise drove away their relief.

They had emerged at the road that marked the northern edge of the Brooks woods. They recognized it at once. Spencer had driven through the area once or twice; Kelly had traveled these roads her entire life. But neither of them had ever seen it like this before.

Two big tractor-trailers had parked perpendicular to the road, blocking off each end of it. Half a dozen smaller trucks had parked between them, half on and half off of the road itself. Small was a relative term. The trucks were far bigger than any of the monsters driven by some of the good ol' boys around Peculiar. They looked like big military vehicles used for transporting troops into a combat zone, all painted camouflage with their beds enclosed by tall curving frames with green and brown tarps hung over them. A couple of smaller trucks, also painted camouflage, stood near the tractor-trailers. Both of the trucks had wooden crates loaded into the backs of them. Large red stickers on the sides of the crates said, "CAUTION: FLAMMABLE MATERIAL."

Kelly took one look and remembered the strange man from that morning.

The convoy, she thought.

The gravel road was scored with tire tracks and deep ruts, which the tractor-trailers must have dug up when they were moving to block off both ends of the road. Spencer and Kelly could see a few dozen footprints scattered around, but not many. The air above the hoods of the tractor-trailer engines shimmered with heat, and the area enclosed between the two of them still smelled of exhaust. It looked like this little convoy had just recently arrived.

At about the same time Spencer arrived at Kelly's door and Debra Coldiron became acquainted with the creature in her kitchen, a convoy passed through Peculiar. It came just as Agent Gordon said it would, down 71 highway until it reached the Peculiar exit. It came remarkably close to town before anyone noticed it. The townspeople saw convoys on 71 all the time. Military personal were always moving something down the highway, so the sight of trucks and cargo vans with camouflage paint jobs didn't raise any eyebrows, at least until they took the Peculiar exit.

The convoy took to the back roads before it reached the town proper; nevertheless plenty of people took notice. Kids out playing in their treehouses or riding around on their four-wheelers stopped to watch it pass. All of the big vehicles kicked up an enormous cloud of dust, which hung in the still hot air of the afternoon for several minutes after the convoy passed.

The convoy itself barreled forward with all the momentum of a freight train, stopping for nothing in its way. Clint Hipsher, that estimable drinking buddy of the late Delbert Cullim, happened to meet it coming over the rise of a hill, and had to swerve his decrepit Chevy pickup into the ditch to avoid a collision. After the convoy had passed but before the dust had settled, Clint had scrabbled out of his truck, run into the middle of the road and shouted curses at the departing convoy, daring those government sonsabitches to just try to take *him* away like they did his buddy Delbert. When the convoy did not change its course, Clint swore, "Damn right," and sauntered back to his truck like a Chihuahua trotting back to its doghouse after chasing off the mailman for another successful day.

The convoy followed the same route Hicks's team had taken during the night mission. They arrived at the north side of the Brooks woods around three. Working in silent efficiency, soldiers put up roadblocks on all routes leading to their position within a mile radius. Fortunately, due to the position's remoteness that amounted to only three roads. Guards, camouflaged or disguised as electric company line workers, took up positions at all of the roadblocks. The ones dressed as line workers made a show of inspecting the transformers at the tops of the electric poles. Hiding in the thick summer foliage, the camouflaged guards watched the roads through the telescopic sights on their rifles.

Once they were safely concealed, the vehicles of the convoy arranged themselves along the gravel road that ran parallel to the north side of the Brooks woods. This was the same road where Ames had dropped off the night mission team. The two tractor trailers parked perpendicular to the road at each end of the convoy, blocking off the area that would become the convoy's base camp. The other vehicles in the convoy took up positions along the road between them. The soldiers within those vehicles spent the next couple of hours setting up their mission site and arming for the secret slaughter to come.

Now the soldiers led Spencer and Kelly to the big truck parked at the western end of the road. A door opened into the side of the trailer, and a small set of wooden steps had been placed on the ground in front of it. They went up the steps and inside the back of the trailer.

They found themselves in a narrow chamber with a bench along one wall and a small table in the center of the room. Fluorescent lights shined down on them from above. Everything was white, the walls, the bench, the table, and the floor. Kelly didn't see so much as a bottle of water in the barren room.

"Take a seat," said one of the soldiers, and something in his tone seemed to threaten dire consequences if they didn't do as he said, so Spencer and Kelly sat. Then the soldier turned to the other members of his group.

"Take her to the lab," he said to the man carrying Rachel. "The rest of you go to decontamination"

Decontamination. The word reverberated in Kelly's mind, calling up thoughts of chemicals, disease and radioactivity.

"Who are you people?" Kelly shouted again, conscious of the ragged, fearful tone of her voice. "Where do you think you're taking her? That girl needs a doctor! We're—"

The soldiers ignored her and walked out of the trailer. The heavy steel door slammed shut behind them with a boom that cut her off in mid-sentence. A metallic click rang through the trailer as the door locked behind them. Now she could only sit there, her hands tied behind her back, with Spencer beside her.

That poor girl, she thought. *Why did they take her too? She's sick near to death. How could she harm anyone?*

She stood up and walked to the door. Standing before a locked door with her hands tied behind her back, she looked like a study in futility. She became aware of a mild tingling on her face. The poison oak must be starting to work there. An itch she couldn't scratch. God, what were they doing to Rachel? What had happened to Jason? To Brad?

A thousand thoughts, a thousand worries, rampaged through her mind. She jumped when she sensed a shadow near her, but when she looked up she saw that it was Spencer. He had risen as well and walked over to her.

"Are you all right?" he asked. "You took a tumble back there in the woods."

"I'll be okay," Kelly said. "I'm worried about Rachel. Why don't they get her some medical attention, Spencer? She's just a little girl." She felt tears coming on and fought them back. If she started crying now she didn't think she would be able to stop.

"Oh God, Spencer, what *is* this?"

Spencer leaned forward and rested his cheek against Kelly's. At first she didn't understand what he was doing, and then she remembered that he couldn't hug her. Given their circumstances, he was comforting her as well as he could. For a moment she stood there, feeling the pulse in his temple against the side of her head. She did not know how to convey to him how much this meant to her. She could only stand there and accept the comfort.

And then she realized someone could see them.

No one had entered the room, and the trailer didn't have any windows, but she had that almost clichéd sense of being watched. She didn't see any cameras in the corners, but she knew they were there just the same. It didn't have anything to do with intuition, although Kelly did trust her intuition. It came from a combination of sharp hearing, natural skepticism, and common sense. People like this wouldn't lock them up unobserved. Kelly had never received the privilege of a higher education but that didn't mean she was stupid. The people holding them would want to keep an eye on them and make sure they didn't try to start any trouble. Without windows that meant cameras.

The next clue came from her sharp hearing. A low electric hum had started somewhere in the room, the kind of sound that came from a speaker that was turned on but not broadcasting any speech or music. Microphones didn't make that sound; only speakers. That meant someone was about to announce something to them through a speaker hidden somewhere in the back of this trailer. This person had turned on a speaker to talk to them ... and then paused. Maybe that pause had to do with the tender moment she and Spencer had just shared. The only way this hypothetical person could know that was if he could see them.

She pulled away from Spencer. He sensed it too; she could tell by the way his eyes slowly scanned the corners of the room. As soon as they separated, a gravelly male voice spoke to them from above.

"Hello, Mrs. Ross. Mr. Dale. I'd like to have your attention now."

Their eyes instantly went upwards. The speakers must have been hidden in the ceiling.

"Who is speaking to us?" Spencer said.

"I'm Sergeant William Rollins, U.S. Army, and you're wondering just why the hell you've been locked up in the back of a tractor-trailer."

That was true, of course, but not what they had expected to hear. The effect of it startled them, which this Sergeant Rollins had probably intended it to do.

"I can tell you why," Sergeant William Rollins, U.S. Army, said before either of them could respond. They still didn't know if he could hear them if they responded. "You've been taken into custody because you may have been exposed to certain biological agents a hostile foreign power is trying to introduce into our country. This is the age of terrorism, folks, and you live in the heartland of America. Where else does a killer strike when he wants the blow to be fatal, if not the heart?"

The voice paused, and to Kelly it seemed like a troubled pause. The undertones made her wonder why it seemed troubled, but Spencer took advantage of the gap.

"Can you hear me?" Spencer asked.

"Right now, your country needs you—" the voice continued, but Spencer barreled on.

"I asked you a question!" The strength in his voice amazed Kelly, who had felt her stomach sink when Rollins said they may have been exposed to a biological weapon. Rollins did stop speaking when Spencer interrupted him, though, and that answered Spencer's question. He could not have interrupted a man who couldn't hear them.

"Mr. Dale, you had better just settle—" Rollins said, but Spencer interrupted him again.

"I'll do nothing!" Spencer roared. "I'll tell you what I think of you, Sergeant Rollins. I think you're a damned liar. If what you're saying was true you could have come to us and explained things decently and we could have gone with you of our own free will. Instead we have been assaulted and locked up like criminals, your men have threatened Kelly's children and kidnapped a girl who just might be dying, so don't bother trying to feed us some line of bull about a terrorist attack while you hide behind your microphone like a coward because *we are not buying it for a second!"*

"And just what do you think is killing that girl?" Rollins's voice filtered down to them in a low growl. "Right now we don't have the time or resources to deal with your bruised ego, Mr. Dale. Do you want her to die? We are here for your own good, that is why we exist, and if we have to exercise our authority arbitrarily sometimes then that is what we will do."

"You can't do this to us!" Spencer shouted. "We're American citizens! We have rights—"

"Don't trot that old horse out," Rollins said. "I'm trying to tell you that we are dealing with a threat here. Do you hear me? A *threat.* I would rather step on a few civil liberties than see people die. That's what we do, Mr. Dale, or had you forgotten that? We die protecting liberty so you don't have to. All we ask in return is for you to do what you're told when we need you to do it."

"You never had to—" Spencer began, but this time Rollins interrupted him.

"What is that girl's name?"

"I'll have my say!" Spencer shouted.

"What is her name?"

"We don't know!" Kelly said. "We were trying to find that out when your men took us! My son and his friend found her, she's sick and we don't know why and we don't know who she is!"

Silence.

"How long has she been sick?" Rollins asked after a few seconds had passed.

"I don't know," Kelly said. "When I last saw her a few days ago she seemed okay, but today she's sick and we don't know why."

"What are her symptoms?" Rollins asked.

"You're the ones holding her," Spencer said. "You can see for yourself."

"She's feverish," Kelly said. "She was flushed, that's how I could tell. I noticed she flinched when she tried to turn her head, and I saw a mild rash forming at the base of her neck. If that means anything to you."

Another thoughtful silence, and again something in the way Rollins let the silence draw out gave Kelly the impression that the man was frustrated, annoyed, even angry.

"Now listen," Rollins said after a few moments. "This is how things are going to be. We are going to secure the area where we think the threat is concentrated, and then we are going to remove it. Securing the area means just that; nothing gets in, nothing gets out. It's our best way to contain it. While this is going on, you will be detained for your own safety. And I want you to remember that my people are out there risking their lives for your protection. Once the threat is gone, we'll release you on your own recognizance."

"You don't really expect us to believe that, do you?" Spencer said, but Kelly overrode him.

"What about my son?"

Again, silence.

"What about my son?" Kelly repeated. Her voice had gained a shrill, fearful tone. "You said nothing gets out! What are you going to do about my son?"

But Rollins did not respond. She realized she no longer heard the subaudible sound of his presence; he had turned off the speakers transmitting his voice into the trailer. Apparently this Sergeant Rollins considered their conversation over. But he had left them with her greatest question still unanswered, and so she could not stop asking it.

"What about my son? Answer me! *What are going to do with my son?*"

She kept shouting it, until her fear obliterated the words and she skirted to the edge of hysteria for the first time in her life. Her cries became screams, the words lost clarity and her voice hitched with sobs.

And then Spencer was next to her, saying her name. He put his chin over her shoulder and pressed his cheek next to hers. She tried to push away from him, but he sidestepped her until she backed herself into a corner and couldn't escape. Once more she had no choice but to accept comfort, which was the only thing he wanted from her.

"Kelly, stop," he said. "He can't hear you anymore. He's gone. Jason will be okay. We can get through this. Everything will be all right."

She didn't believe it, not one word. Life had taught her that things very rarely turned out all right. And for saying that, she hated him. The bitter intensity of it shocked her. How dare he tell such a horrible lie to her? The hatred was born of her awful pride, and the instant she realized that she saw how fear for her son's safety had caused her hatred, as fear caused all hatred. Realizing this was the first step in transforming that hatred into love.

With her face pressed against Spencer's broad shoulder, she wept for the fate of her only child.

17

A Deal Is Made

Sergeant Rollins stormed out of the cab of the tractor trailer, fuming. His detainees could not tell from the way they were brought inside the trailer, but the cab had a small chamber in the back, a place where truck drivers would sleep in ordinary big wheelers. In this smaller room was a set of monitors that displayed the interior of the detention chamber, and a microphone for communicating with the detainees. It was from this smaller room that Rollins had spoken to Kelly and Spencer.

That conversation had not gone as he had planned, not at all. The sheer livid rebelliousness that Dale had displayed, he had not counted on that. Rollins had expected a little outrage, but figured they would to defer to his authority once he put a little fear into them. But that seemed to have made things worse, which didn't make any sense. In times of danger people naturally deferred to authority. He had not counted on these small-town types wanting to handle things themselves.

Didn't matter. Those two would never handle anything for themselves ever again. After all this was over, Kelly Ross, Spencer Dale and anyone else who might have been exposed to the contagion were going to disappear.

His boots crunched over the gravel road. He wondered how long they could remain stationed here before some of the locals came out to see what they were doing. Not long. Impatience ground at him. He wanted this mission completed before nightfall, and judging by the lengthening shadows under the trees that would come sooner than he would like.

Another problem: when Dale and Ross had said they didn't know the girl's name, had he gotten a faint impression that they weren't telling him the whole truth?

As he approached the other big rig, which pulled the mobile lab unit, he saw Private Benton standing in front of it with his chest all puffed up with pride. The dimwit was actually expecting praise.

"Three days to find a little girl," Rollins said as he drew near. "And even then she had to practically fall right into your arms. So why do you look like you expect a freaking medal?"

Benton's face fell. "Sir ... I didn't—I mean ... I ..."

"I! I! I!" Rollins mocked him. "Quit stammering and listen. Two other members of the group escaped when you took the girl into custody, correct?"

"Yes, sir!" Benton said. "Two boys, I believe one was Mrs. Ross's son and the other—"

"I know who they are!" Rollins said. "What I want to know is why you let them get away."

"Sir, they escaped while we were securing the rest of the group, sir," Benton said, slipping into boot-camp formality. He had started beginning and ending his sentences with "sir." Rollins must have made him nervous. This pleased him.

"I don't want excuses, soldier," Rollins said. "Those two boys pulled that girl from the well. They were exposed to her before anyone else. Now they're going to run off and tell everyone they can find how we took Ross and her boyfriend into custody. Which means more people exposed and more potential for this contagion to spread, not to mention the security breach. I need to know that you can find those boys and get them detained within the hour. Can you do that, soldier?"

"Sir yes sir!" Benton snapped back.

"Then go do it," Rollins said.

Benton turned to go, shouting at the other members of his team to follow him, but Rollins stopped him before he could run off.

"And Private?"

"Yes, sir?" Benton replied, turning back.

"Take out anyone who gets in your way."

"Yes, sir."

Rollins nodded his dismissal, and Benton ran back into the woods followed by the rest of his team. They disappeared almost instantly, as their camouflage fatigues blended in with their surroundings. Rollins didn't want to think about the consequences if they failed. If those boys blew their cover he might have to come up with a bogus criminal charge against Kelly Ross and Spencer Dale, like domestic terrorism or something. Such a thing could be done, he could run their names through a public-relations sewer if need be, but all the same he would rather avoid the attention.

He turned to enter the trailer with mobile lab unit inside. He wanted to observe the techs stabilizing the girl. They would fingerprint her, of course, and take dental impressions, DNA samples, and anything else they could use to iden-tify her. Something might have to be done about the girl's parents, if they could find them.

If only they could have detained her while she was still conscious, they could have questioned her and got all the information they needed. The matter of the girl's health had now become imperative. If the girl didn't make it, well, she would just become one of the thousands of children who disappear every year, but the loss to this mission would be irreparable. They would never know how many people she had come into contact with and how far she might have spread this thing. Gordon could spout all the polysyllabic nonsense he wanted, none of it made a bit of difference to Rollins. It was one thing to *say* the contagion could not spread by casual contact, it was another thing to prove it. And until he saw concrete evidence indicating otherwise Rollins would assume the worst … and take the appropriate measures. Rollins cursed Benton for not finding the girl sooner. He cursed Gordon for spreading his confusing technobabble. He cursed them all, although he didn't yet know all the people "them" encompassed.

He entered the second trailer. The door opened into a narrow decontamina-tion chamber. Nothing fancy, just a room with plastic lining on the walls and a nozzle in the ceiling. The room was big enough to hold a couple of men, who stripped naked and disposed of their contaminated clothing in a haz-mat con-tainer in the corner. The nozzle sprayed disinfectant, which then drained through a hole in the floor. An extra pair of haz-mat suits hung on a hook from the wall. A door leading into the laboratory section of the trailer stood in the wall adjacent to the entryway, and next to that was a transparent panel that looked into the lab. Rollins didn't bother stripping and disinfecting himself, since he had no plans to enter the lab. He had only come to watch the techs working on the girl.

The two techs inside both wore white haz-mat suits. They bustled around the lab, apparently in a hurry. They had placed the girl on a stretcher in the middle of the narrow room. Rollins watched as they hooked the girl up to monitoring equipment, put an IV in her arm, an oxygen monitor on her finger, and attached some kind of breathing apparatus to her face. The techs moved in an efficient rush. The girl needed to be stabilized, and soon. The mission had passed its half-way point and they still had a lot to do before they could leave.

Too much potential here for things to go wrong. Rollins looked forward to the final stage of the mission, when he and his soldiers would descend on the clearing in the Brooks woods where the infected animals paced and muttered. Burning the clearing, slaughtering the cats, and sowing alkali salts into the Earth so that nothing could ever grow there again, those were definitive goals on which he could set his mind and give himself a sense of purpose. Destruction as an act of cleansing.

His radio beeped, making him jump a little. He always got nervous whenever his thoughts waxed poetic. Taking the slim black radio from the holster on his belt, he flipped it on and held it to his ear.

"Rollins," he said.

"I know what you're doing," said a voice from the radio, a low, familiar, and maddeningly knowing voice.

"Neglecting your duty again, Agent Gordon?" Rollins said, a little too quickly. He hadn't counted on Gordon discovering him this soon. "You were sleeping while we were organizing the pre-emptive strike. Bad form for you. I'll be sure to note it in the report."

"The girl is dying, isn't she?" Gordon asked.

"I don't know what you're talking about."

"I know why," Gordon said, as if Rollins had said yes. "You remember those tissue samples from the mutated animals I sent to Quantico to have the genes sequenced? I got the results back today."

"It's a shame you won't be here, Gordon," Rollins said. "You might have redeemed yourself for that farce you put on in Africa. Instead, once again it's my men putting their asses on the line for your incompetence. I wonder how your superiors will react when they hear you fumbled it again."

"I wonder why you're not asking me where I am," Gordon said.

Rollins froze. He glanced nervously left and right, as if he expected Gordon to jump out of the shadows in the corners. Then logic made the meaning of Gordon's words click into place.

Gordon had called him on the radio. No need to worry about anyone hearing them, the signal was well encrypted, but the range of their radios was limited. With all these trees and hills around it couldn't be more than a couple of hundred yards. Which meant Gordon was nearby, somewhere within the perimeter. Had he slipped past the guards, or did he come out here before they arrived? Rollins suspected it was the latter. Gordon had probably hidden in the woods where he could watch them. Somehow he had known this convoy was coming. And there was only one way he could know that.

"You read the log notes," Rollins said. Anger tinged his words, but a certain satisfaction was mixed in with it. Gordon had finally broken a rule. "That information is classified to my department, Agent Gordon. You have just violated the privacy of my rank, and I will make sure—"

"You're outraged," Gordon said. "I'm sure Kelly Ross feels the same way. Think of the respect you showed for her privacy."

Rollins gripped the radio until he heard the plastic creak, on the verge of breaking. He fought his anger, knowing Gordon wanted to enrage and confuse him. But still, to throw that back in his face and make him see his own hypocrisy. It galled him.

"You might not like it," Gordon said, "but the fact is I'm here and I'm not going anywhere. You're going to have to get used to it. You had better believe that the information I have could save that girl's life, if I can get her treated in time. If you try to play any more games with me and she dies, I will never stop hounding every single one of your superiors until all of them know I offered you a chance to save her life and you refused it."

"So what do you want?" Rollins said. "Trying to blackmail me now, are you? So what is it?"

"I shouldn't have to do this," Gordon said. "We were sent here together because our superiors felt we both had something to contribute to this mission, but your pride keeps getting in the way. So I'm proposing a deal. You give me access to that girl and your full cooperation to the completion of this mission. I'll do my best to save her. I don't imagine that mobile lab unit will have all the tools I'll need, no matter how advanced it is, and those lab techs you have working on her certainly won't do her any good. If she doesn't make it, at least I'll be there to share the responsibility."

And I'm sure you'd do just that, Rollins thought. He had no reason to suspect Gordon would turn on him if things went bad, but in his experience people almost always turned on you if given the opportunity.

"You've got nothing to offer, Gordon," Rollins said. "My technicians already have the girl stabilized-"

"Do they now?" Gordon breathed in a knowing tone.

"... and we don't need you to complete this mission. I have all the soldiers I need for that."

"Do you remember Africa, Rollins?" Gordon asked, his voice taking on a slightly urgent tone. It was the most disturbed Rollins had ever heard him become. "Remember those hyenas I told you about? The ones we infected intentionally in the lab? We had them stabilized too. Right up until they died. Those techies of yours know less than nothing about this contagion, and might even make things worse in their ignorance. Everything about this organism is classified, remember? Every second you waste arguing with me is time this thing has to grow inside that girl."

Gordon did not bother to reiterate his threat to report Rollins to their superiors, like a little boy threatening to tell on his brother to their parents. It hung over his last sentence like a predatory bird. Rollins might have to relent ... a bit. But he would keep his mind open to any mental traps that Gordon might fall into along the way.

"Tell me your location," Rollins said. "I'll send someone out to escort you—"

"You don't need to," Gordon said. "I'm already here."

Gordon had timed his phrase perfectly. No sooner had he said it than Rollins heard an uproar outside. Stepping out of the lab trailer he saw Gordon strolling onto the gravel road. In seconds armed soldiers swarmed around him, waving their rifles and shouting for him to get down on the ground. Gordon ignored them and watched Rollins approach, unperturbed.

"Stand down," Rollins said.

The soldiers stopped shouting, staring at Rollins as if they expected him to repeat his order, something he did not do. A power play had begun, and Rollins had lived too long through too much to make such a mistake. He kept his eyes focused on Gordon and strolled towards him with a casual gait, although inside he was howling in rage.

Gordon stared back at him with those unremarkable no-color eyes, seeing right through to the war in Rollins's mind, and when he spoke his voice was as mild as milk.

"Take me to her," he said.

18

The Wolves and the Buffalo

As every American child knows, vast herds of buffalo once roamed the Great Plains, before white men came with death all around them. Native Americans husbanded the buffalo with scrupulous care, using a seasonal pattern of controlled burns to clear out the thick prairie grass. This encouraged the growth of the tender grass shoots upon which the buffalo fed. With a rich food supply the buffalo grew healthy and reproduced, until uncountable numbers of them stretched across the landscape and the dust of their passage darkened the sky. The first white pioneers wrote of a single herd that covered almost as much land area as the state of Nebraska encloses today. The Native Americans encouraged these enormous herds to support their way of life, since they depended upon the buffalo for food, clothing, and the materials to make their shelters and tools. But they were not the only predators on the Plains.

Other hunters had evolved in the unique Great Plains ecosystem, not the least of which were the North American wolves. They were as shadows in the prairie grass, circling always at the edges of the herds. A shadow into which the occasional straggler would fall, and never again emerge. As predators, the wolves were second only to humans, and the race was close. So close, in fact, that some Native Americans took to wearing wolf skins as they hunted, in the hope of imitating their success.

In the manner of all organisms living under a threat, the buffalo adapted. This adaptation took a form similar to one taken by the elephants of Africa, as a defense against lions and hyenas. It took the form of a circle.

At the first whiff of a predator, the buffalo arranged themselves into a circle, with their heads facing outwards. Any predators trying to attack them would face a wall of sharp horns, while the vulnerable calves huddled safely within the center of the circle. This defense was a natural formation for a herd animal. Fear drove it to face its enemy while pressing close to the other members of the herd to protect

215

its flanks. When the predators came from all sides, a circular formation resulted from these two protective instincts.

As Private Benton raced through the woods with the shadows of evening pooling under the trees, he could not help but feel rather lupine. Something about the secret nature of their mission, running through the trees to track down their prey, and knowing that they were almost invisible between the camouflage and the coming night thrilled him, made him feel swift, elemental, predatory. The other members of his team raced alongside him. The feeling was one of a pack with one mind and one purpose. He had never felt so exhilarated.

They had spent the past few days in these woods hunting down the girl. Benton had realized quite early on that searching for her through the usual channels would yield no fruit. Hicks had shown him that during the meeting at sunset three days ago. No accessible school records, no fingerprints ... all that indicated backwoods country folk to Benton. At that point he knew that the best way to find the girl would be to hunt her down like a wild animal, unlike Hicks, who wanted to spend hours thumbing through file cabinets in the public records.

How Benton had envied Hicks during the first stages of this operation! Hicks had first surveyed the impact site, Hicks had discovered the exposed children, Hicks had led the night mission. Hicks's military career had started with a fire; it seemed a foregone conclusion that he would make it into special operations. Meanwhile Benton's career had languished. Benton couldn't understand it. They were the same age; they had joined the Army at almost exactly the same time. All through training Benton had smugly flaunted his superior performance in PT and his higher grades. Yet out here in the field Hicks had flourished while Benton had stagnated.

Well, that was all about to change. Now Benton's opportunity had come around at last, and he didn't plan on wasting it. Obviously Sergeant Rollins had realized that they didn't need a bookworm on this mission. They needed a predator.

He grinned as he raced through the woods.

Per their orders they stuck to a path that steered away from the burned-out clearing. This was a bit of an inconvenience, since the most direct route to their destination took them past it, but Benton didn't plan on screwing this up through disobedience.

He had heard rumors that the night mission had encountered something terrifying in that clearing, something that had to do with a pack of infected cats. It made him very curious and he wished he could accompany the team assigned to sterilize the clearing. But again, his orders came first. That was how one got ahead in the military.

Benton sped up. The other members of his team increased their pace to match him, and his grin spread wider. He set the pace; he was the leader. This was how it was meant to be.

They had surveyed these woods well over the past few days, and they knew exactly where to go. Their path stretched on beneath their feet, their boots stomped over the earth, and Benton could not suppress the grin on his face. He knew he would succeed in capturing the children. He was running to meet his destiny.

His destination, in fact, was a house built into the side of a hill. The Grace home. Life had continued in Peculiar while Rollins set up his operation outside the Brooks woods, and the house of Grace was no exception.

Around the same time Kelly and Spencer arrived at the convoy camp, Midge Grace had just set down a tray of tea and cookies for the Peculiar Ladies Quilting Society. The group had come by Midge's house for a break after planning a charity auction for the March of Dimes all afternoon. While talk during the meeting had been all business, here in the comfort of Midge's parlor the discussion turned to distinctly *un*-businesslike matters.

"Well, spill it, Midge," Dorothy Sprinkles said. "We're all just dying of curiosity!"

"Darling Dorothy, dear," Midge said. She had a habit of slipping into alliteration when being coy. "I'm sure I have no idea what you're talking about."

"Oh you know darn good and well, you heifer!" Moe Jefferson snapped. "What's all this we're hearing about Kelly and that Dale boy from down at Fred Dillon's garage?"

"Really now," Midge replied. "That is Kelly's personal business and I for one have no interest in spreading gossip."

Eyes rolled all around the room.

"Well, I say good for her!" Ruth Walton announced. "Jack passed more than a year ago. It's about time the girl moved on."

In the pause between sentences, a very brief one at that, a thin distant cry came from outside the house. It must have come from the eastern side, the only side of the house aboveground. For a moment the group paused in their discussion, troubled by the sound of the cry, but then they dismissed it. It was probably just some kids at play. The silent moment passed through them unmentioned, like a shadow moving across the Sun giving them a momentary chill.

"They were supposed to get together today, weren't they Midge?" Dorothy pressed.

"I'm sure I don't know," Midge replied.

"And you sending Brad over there to play had absolutely nothing to do with that?" Amanda Beatty said. The old gossip queen was practically salivating.

"Amanda dear, if you weren't a friend I would take offense," Midge said, still as cool as a spring rain. She sat back on her divan and sipped her tea. "The very idea that I would have my son spy on my neighbor."

"Then why did Kelly drive off with Brad after the Society meeting?" Amanda asked, with a can't-fool-me tone to her voice.

"Bradley and Jason wanted to go over to Lance Snow's to see his nanny goat's new kids, and I asked Kelly to drop them off on her way home. It's within walking distance of the house, but I didn't know if I would make it back in time for the boys to see the goats before dark. Nothing more to it at all."

"I don't know how Lance finds the energy to speak at those 4-H clubs, at his age," said Virginia Moore. "The man must be getting into his eighties."

"What's that, Virginia?" Midge asked. "Brad isn't in 4-H."

"Then how did he know Lance had some new baby goats?" Mrs. Moore asked.

"Well … I …" Midge trailed off. Finally she smiled sheepishly, and blushed. She knew she'd been caught.

"You often give Lance's grandkids singing lessons, don't you, Midge?" Mrs. Moore offered casually.

The Ladies burst out laughing.

"Oh you!" Midge said, flapping her napkin in Virginia's direction.

They laughed so hard that at first they didn't hear the pounding at the front door. But when the sound of screaming came from the other side, the laughter died away.

"What is all that commotion?" Moe Jefferson asked.

They were on their feet in an instant, but the Ladies did not move to answer the door. This was Midge's home, and that was her prerogative. They waited, silent and apprehensive, as Lady Grace set aside her cup and rose from her seat. But in the few seconds it took her to cross the room the pounding stopped, and the screaming faded away. Midge's hand paused over the doorknob as she wondered what might be waiting for her on the other side. Then she pulled open the door.

To an empty porch.

She turned back to the Ladies to remark on it when the screaming came again, this time from her left, beyond the sliding glass doors that opened onto her deck.

Brad and Jason scrambled up the deck's wooden staircase and into view. They must have sprinted around the house after Midge did not open the door right away.

She always kept her doors locked, a habit she had picked up while living in the city.

Brad flung himself at the patio door and pounded on the glass with both his fists. Even with it shut against the summer heat she heard him screaming.

"Momma!"

"Bradley what on earth?" Midge cried. She dashed to the door, slid down the lock and pulled it back. Brad ran inside and buried his face in her stomach, nearly bowling her over. Jason came right behind him, clutching the back of Brad's shirt. Both boys were sobbing, hysterical. They kept trying to say something, but they were crying so hard and talking so fast that Midge couldn't understand them. Beneath a layer of tears and snot, the boys' faces were covered in scratches and welts, like they had been running full tilt through the woods in a panic. Their clothes were torn in dozens of places, and Jason had a leaf caught in his long hair.

The other ladies crowded around them, chattering questions. Midge knew they meant well, but with everyone talking at once she couldn't understand anyone.

She drew back from Brad just enough for her to get down on one knee. It was like trying to pry a cocklebur from the coat of a dog, but she managed to do it. After she was down she let Brad throw his arms around her neck and clutch her once again.

Now at least she had her lips next to his ear. "Bradley darling," she said, stroking his hair, "what happened?"

"There was men in the woods!" Brad sobbed.

Jason spoke up an instant later, like an echo. "There was men in the woods and they took my mom!"

All the women in the room went silent at once.

"They had guns!" Brad said, pulling back from his mother. He had forced himself to calm down so that she could understand him. "They were waiting for us in the woods and all of them had guns! And Mr. Dale yelled at them and they hit him really hard, and Rachel was there and she was really sick-"

"They took my mom!" Jason cried again. "They all had guns and they took her away! *They took her away!*"

"It's all right, Jason—," Dorothy Sprinkles began, but Jason interrupted her.

"It's not all right!" Jason cried. "They took her! I lost her too! I'm all alone!"

"You have *not* lost your mother," Mrs. Moore said. The finality in her voice seemed to leave no room for argument. The memory of Jason's dead father rose in all of their thoughts. No wonder the poor kid was so afraid. "We'll call the police, first. Boys, can either of you tell me what the men looked like?"

Jason and Brad shook their heads. "We couldn't see their faces very well," Brad said. "They had all this green and brown makeup on, and they were all wearing camouflage so we couldn't see them coming. It's just like when we found Rachel. She said she saw a man like that hiding in the grass, but we didn't believe her." He shook his head sadly. "We *should* have believed her."

"Camouflage?" Mrs. Moore said. "Like military, you mean?"

"The convoy," said Ruth Walton. She clutched the little cross she kept on a chain around her neck. "The one Kelly told us about, the people watching her house ..."

"It doesn't mean that," said Joyce Garrett. She sounded a little desperate. "Our own military wouldn't do a thing like that!"

"Where you been livin', Joyce?" Moe Jefferson snapped.

"It doesn't matter!" Midge said, her voice rising. "Whoever they are, they're clearly a threat."

"What has Kelly been doing to bring all this down on us?" Amanda Beatty wondered aloud. Her voice held a kind of confused awe. This was clearly the biggest gossip she had ever heard in her life.

"Amanda Beatty, shut your mouth!" Mrs. Moore snapped. She nodded her head in a pointed way towards Jason, who was still in tears.

"Well, I didn't mean it that way!" Amanda said.

"Just watch what you say, will you?" Mrs. Moore replied. "Now Midge, I need to call Ned and tell him about this. Maybe he can—"

Ruth Walton interrupted her with a gasp of shock. She pointed her finger towards the open door and cried, "Look! Look!"

They all looked. Outside the threshold of Midge's front door, a dark figure in military fatigues came running towards the house with a black semi-automatic in his hands. A low-hanging masked helmet hid his eyes from their view, but they could see the sharp line of his chin and jaw, painted green and brown. If Midge had not left the front door open they would not have seen him coming.

Midge rose to her feet with Brad still in her arms. In her shock she did not even notice his weight, which would have tipped her over normally. She began to back away from the door, and all the other Ladies followed her. Jason tagged along still clutching the tail of Brad's shirt. For an instant the Ladies could only huddle together in shock and confusion, for they had nowhere to go. Now they could see more soldiers racing towards them through the trees, moving with swift, predatory exactness. The natural shock of seeing armed soldiers charging down on them had paralyzed them, living as they did in the heart of a free society. They had accepted the children's stories well enough, but it was one thing to have a child tearfully insist the boogeyman was in the closet; it was another to open the door and see him leering out at you.

"The phone!" Virginia Moore suddenly cried. "Everyone who has a cell phone, grab it now, in case I can't do it! Hurry!"

They all scrambled through their purses, except for Midge, who whirled around and set Brad down on the floor behind her, sweeping Jason along with him as she did. Then she turned back to face the soldiers as they pounded through the open front door.

"DOWN ON THE GROUND!" The first soldier through roared the command. More of them poured in through the open patio door. Six, then eight, and then ten of them piled inside. Midge's parlor suddenly became very crowded. A mass of roaring green and brown faces surrounded them. Bedlam broke loose, furniture was overturned, glass shattered. Midge couldn't tell what parts of her home were being destroyed, she couldn't see anything through the crush of people, but she heard the damage being done. She saw the barrels of the guns waving inches from her face and black gloved hands reaching out to grab her.

"STEP AWAY FROM THOSE KIDS RIGHT NOW! MOVE IT!"

Midge did the first thing that came naturally: she reached out to her friends for support. The rest of Ladies had thought the same thing, because in an instant all of them had interlocked their arms. It happened by reflex, without so much as a plan or a word of order. The Ladies formed a solid line encircling Brad and Jason. The kids crouched on the floor and peered out from between their legs.

The lead soldier roared his command again, his voice filled with anger and authority, and as he did he cocked his gun in preparation to fire.

"FINAL WARNING! MOVE AWAY FROM THOSE KIDS OR I'LL—"

As he spoke, Midge saw the black barrel of his gun come to bear on her, and she knew that if he shot her she would fall backwards onto Brad and Jason, showering them with her blood. That would be their final memory of her, a memory of death that would haunt them all their lives. The sheer horror of branding such a memory into the minds of these children, who had endured so much, overwhelmed her, and to match it rose an equally powerful drive to prevent that from happening.

And that was when she felt her voice return to her.

It was not just a voice that came to her, but a Voice, a Voice that began somewhere far, far below her feet, down near the spinning molten dynamo at the center of the Earth. The Voice rose up through the hot mantle of magma and stratified layers of living rock, an ancient and powerful force born at the beginning of the world. It burst through the Earth's crust just below her feet; it rose burning and tingling through her body, filled her lungs and erupted from her like lava, and she the volcano. What came from her throat was the voice that had thrilled audiences in opera houses around the country and brought them to their feet shouting *"Brava!"* and *"Encore!"* A ringing contralto filled with elemental fire and the unquestioning air of command.

"YOU WILL TAKE NOT ONE STEP CLOSER!" The Lady Grace declared, and then like a miracle came a blinding flash of light.

The soldiers froze where they stood.

Midge stared down at them, trembling all over but not with fear. She trembled with excitement and hot righteous anger. She wondered with queer detached calmness if the flash of light had come from one of the soldier's guns. Perhaps she had startled one into firing, and right now it did not seem impossible that her voice had simply drowned out the sound of the gunshot. But then she saw a metal gleam to her left, a gleam that was not dull like the metal of a gun barrel, but shiny, almost gaudy. The gleam had come from Mrs. Moore's cell phone, one of those thin sleek models with a pink case and a digital camera installed.

"Smile boys," said Mrs. Moore, "you're live on the World Wide Web."

The soldiers stiffened; their backs got a little bit straighter, like kids whose mothers have just caught them misbehaving.

"I told you to get down on the ground," said one of the soldiers. He had shouted all of the earlier commands, and acted like the leader of this bunch. "You're all under arrest, every one of you. You'll—"

"GET OUT OF MY HOUSE!" Midge roared. She had not lost one bit of her fury. "Not one of you has proven that you have the authority to be here! Not one of you has so much as identified yourself and I order you out of my house this instant!"

"You heard the lady!" Moe Jefferson shouted. "Either show us some warrants or get the hell out!"

"We don't need warrants—" the lead soldier began.

"Keep talking, just keep right on talking!" Amanda Beatty cried out. The old gossip queen's voice was high and reedy with fear, but she spoke up anyway. "We'll make sure everyone knows every word you say!"

Amanda stood at the back of the circle, facing the rear wall of Midge's living room. On the other side of that wall was the rock and earth of the hillside into which the house was built. Amanda looked to her left, her right and over her shoulder as she spoke so that she could look the soldiers in the eye, even though she was trembling the whole time.

"We all know you people have been skulking around in those woods," Ruth Walton said. "Spying on people! Firing off guns in the middle of the night! We know everything so don't think for a minute that you have us fooled!"

One of the soldiers turned to the leader of the pack. "Benton," he asked, "are we really going to …?"

"Shut up," Benton snapped. He never took his eyes off the children hiding inside the circle of women. "I don't know what kind of monsters you take us for, ladies, but those kids have been exposed to a potentially deadly disease. We have to take them in to start treatment now if we're going to save their lives. We're here to help you, but we can't afford to waste time like this—"

"*Liar!*" Midge shouted. "Invading my home, is that helping us? Waving guns in our faces? Abducting this boy's mother? Is all that to protect us? These boys aren't sick. We can see that for ourselves! The only disease here is you!"

"It's contagious, you know," Benton said. A wolfish grin spread over his face. "Highly contagious. You could all be exposed. Is that worth it? Small town or not, I bet most of you aren't related those kids. Are you going to catch something that could kill you for the sake of some child that isn't even your own?"

"Not buying it, boy," said Moe Jefferson, "so go sell it somewhere else."

Another flash of light. Mrs. Moore had taken another picture.

"I have pictures of all of your faces!" Mrs. Moore shouted, pressing buttons on her cell phone. "As we speak I am emailing them to half a dozen friends of mine at the *Star-Herald*, who will send them on to the *Kansas City Star*, and I can only imagine where things will go from there. The gist, gentlemen, is that if anyone in this room is harmed then everyone will know that you, you personally, are responsible. They will know your guilt by your faces! They will identify you, they will find you, and you will be answerable for everything! *Everyone will know what you have done!*"

"I don't think you realize who you're dealing with," Benton said. This was slipping out of his control. He couldn't allow that to happen, not when it meant so much for his career. "It doesn't matter how many pictures you take or who you send them to. Everything that happens here can be denied. You think you have contacts? You're standing there talking about email and small time newspapers to people who can put the screws to multimedia conglomerates. Who's going to believe you? People will believe what the authorities tell them to believe, not a bunch of random nobodies. Go ahead and take your pictures. It's not going to matter when CNN announces they're fakes."

It was a desperate grab on his part, and the Ladies knew it.

"*We* know what is true," Midge said as a smile slowly spread over her face. "And we know what is right. I'm going to tell you again. Get out of my house."

Benton smiled back, but it looked nothing like Midge's smile. "Then you can't say I didn't give you a chance," he said, raising his gun. "Take them out!"

No one fired, not even Benton himself. The soldiers had all begun to look nervous. They had been exchanging glances during Benton's exchange with Midge and Virginia Moore.

If Benton himself had fired first, the others may have followed his lead, since a shot from their leader would have committed them, but Benton was not the man to take the first shot. He did lift his gun and settle the sight directly between Midge's eyes, but Midge only stared back at him over the barrel of the gun. Her face did not show a trace of fear. His finger settled on the trigger, but hesitated.

"Benton," said one of the soldiers. It was Ames, the man who had driven the night mission out to the Brooks woods. "These people are Americans."

"Obey your orders, Private!" Benton barked.

"It doesn't have to be like this," Ames said.

Benton turned away from Ames and shouted to the rest of the soldiers. "Don't listen to him! I told you to fire!"

But this just seemed to make things worse. The other soldiers had lowered their guns. They weren't listening to him.

"Every one of you took an oath!" Benton said. "Disobey my orders now and it's insubordination! Every one of you will go to prison for treason!"

"Benton, we joined up to *defend* Americans," said one soldier. It was Private Turner.

"Oh, this is stupid!" Benton snarled, whirling around. He marched straight over to Midge, grabbed her arm, and started to pull her away from the circle. The other ladies cried out, their circle almost broke, and another flash of light went through the room as Mrs. Moore took another picture.

Then Ames stepped in. He probably had twenty pounds on Benton and stood a good four inches taller. Moving with uncanny fluidity, he put his arm between Benton and Midge and clamped his hand onto Benton's shoulder. His big hand squeezed Benton's clavicle, and Benton had to struggle to keep from crying out in pain. His grip on Midge's arm loosened and she pulled herself free.

"I said that's enough," Ames said. "You have let this whole thing spiral out of control, Benton. You should have never been put in command, and I'm hereby relieving you of it."

"Oh now it all becomes clear!" Benton shouted. "I bet you had this planned all along, didn't you? You were just waiting for your chance to step in and take over! What, did Gordon put you up to this? Or was it your good buddy Hicks?"

"Get him out of here," Ames said, and three soldiers stepped forward to comply. Ames hadn't even picked them out. No one had ever responded like that to any of Benton's orders.

"Come on, Benton," said Turner. He had been the first to step forward. "Don't make this difficult."

"Oh, don't you worry about that," Benton said, smiling bitterly. "I'll make sure Rollins knows about this, and he will be the one to make things difficult for you."

Benton jerked his arm out of Turner's grasp and marched out the front door, stopping to knock over a lamp out of spite. With a nod from Ames, Turner and the two other soldiers followed him out to make sure he didn't cause any more trouble.

"As for you all," Ames said, turning back to the Peculiar Ladies, "we need to have a talk. There really is a potential threat to the health and safety of those kids. We got off to a real bad start here, but we can't let that put them at risk. We'll all just take a minute to settle down, and then we can discuss it."

"At last, a man with sense!" Midge declared.

"Well, I'm notifying my husband," Mrs. Moore said. "He's the mayor, and if there is something threatening the citizens of this town then he needs to know about it."

Ames exchanged a glance with his fellow soldiers, then nodded. "All right. That's going to cause a bit of trouble, because this is a very sensitive issue. We'll call our superiors and they can hash it out too."

"Fine," Mrs. Moore said. "Midge, I'll need to borrow your phone."

"Why don't you just use your cell phone?" Ames said. "You were using it to email all those pictures."

"Oh darling," said Mrs. Moore. "I don't get service out here in the sticks. Don't be ridiculous."

19

The Evolving Circle

Gordon did not wait.

The second Rollins ordered his men back to their posts Gordon marched past him to the mobile lab unit where they had detained the girl. He did not need anyone to tell him where to go, Rollins noticed.

"I assume you've been spying on us all this time," Rollins said. "So you're CIA, that's obvious." Actually, it was not obvious. Gordon knowing how to spy on people didn't mean he was CIA, NSA, or Boy Scouts of America, but he hoped this casual dismissal would set Gordon off his guard. Rollins trailed after him, nipping at his heels like a small yapping dog.

"The fact of the matter is you're the one who has violated protocol by reading my log notes," Rollins went on. "It's entirely within my rights to organize a task force and conclude this mission. I suppose I could report you, but I'm above making threats to get my way, like you did. I don't have to. Real men don't need to make threats. People like you don't understand that."

Gordon stepped up to the trailer, typed the security code into the keypad by the door, and entered, letting the door slam shut behind him. Rollins was surprised that he knew the security code. Sneaky bastard was more resourceful than he thought.

Gordon strode into the decontamination chamber like a man with a purpose. He had a small leather pack strapped to his back and now he stripped it off. Rollins thought he must be disrobing to start the decontamination process, but then he took a small plastic card from the pack and inserted into the access panel beside the door.

"What are you doing?" Rollins asked.

Gordon ignored him and typed the security code into the pad by the lab door. This was even more surprising. The outside door and the lab door had different access codes, as an extra security measure. Gordon had somehow learned both.

226

Air hissed around the doorframe as the seal opened. Rollins watched in horror as he realized what Gordon was doing.

He was entering the lab without a haz-mat suit.

"What the hell are you ... stop!" Rollins stammered. He lurched away from the door, thoughts of contagion and infection swirling through his brain.

They all died, Rollins remembered. *Gordon said all the people they infected died!*

His hand flew to the pistol he kept in a shoulder holster underneath his camouflage jacket. *Maybe I can take him out before he gets the door open!* But it was too late. Making haste, Gordon had already swung the laboratory door wide, and it took every last ounce of Rollins's will not to shoot him in the back. At this point, he had to think logically. Whether or not Gordon had really discovered the secret of this contagion, he was clearly willing to risk exposure to it himself. Gordon had always believed the plasmid could not spread by casual contact, and by walking inside the lab's medical chamber, he had extended a kind of non-verbal dare for Rollins to follow him. If Rollins shot him in the back he might have difficulty justifying it to a board of inquiry afterwards, even with the lab techs as witnesses.

These same techs were now staring in shock as Gordon entered the lab unprotected. Rollins had flown them in from Fort Leavenworth just this morning and they knew nothing about Agent Gordon. Rollins wondered if they would respond to Gordon's intrusion with lethal force, but it didn't come to that, unfortunately. Gordon produced a badge from his back pocket. It was his mission I.D., which identified him as a field operative with security clearance granting him access to almost anything he wanted. Rollins couldn't hear what they were saying and that put him at an unacceptable disadvantage. So Rollins set his jaw, steeled himself, and marched into the lab.

"... no concerns about it becoming airborne," Gordon was saying. "So infection precautions don't need to be taken beyond your standard blood borne pathogens. As it stands we have very little time before the girl's condition becomes serious so I'll need you to assist me in stabilizing procedures."

"We understand, Agent Gordon," said one of the techs through the speaker on his haz-mat suit. "Just tell us what you need and we'll—"

"I'm afraid both of you are going to have to leave," Rollins announced as he entered.

The tech he had interrupted looked confused. "I'm sorry, sir?"

"Neither of you have the clearance for any epidemiological knowledge of this contagion," Rollins said. "That's classified to Red Level. You were brought here to stabilize the girl's condition, nothing more. Since Agent Gordon is insisting upon treating the girl himself right now, I'm afraid you'll have to go outside."

"Do not listen to a word of this," Gordon growled. "This girl needs the benefit of a team treating her—"

"I'm sorry, Agent Gordon," said the lab tech, "but Sergeant Rollins is the commanding officer here. We have our own protocol to follow."

With that, he and his lab mate marched out of the lab. Rollins smirked.

Without responding, Gordon took his leather pack and set it on the countertop. Zipping it open, he removed a large sealed envelope, some loose papers, a small black case, some glass vials, and a few small electronic instruments that Rollins couldn't immediately identify.

"I could be persuaded to let them to assist you," Rollins said. "Of course you couldn't tell them anything that would violate security. That means you say what I tell you to say and do only the medical procedures necessary to save the girl. And I will personally supervise every single thing you do." Rollins suddenly raised his voice to a roar, magnified by the enclosed space of the chamber. *"Do you hear me soldier?"*

Gordon suddenly whirled and flung something at him.

Rollins lurched back, his hand flying to the butt of his gun. He had it drawn before the object hit the floor.

It was the sealed envelope Gordon had taken from his pack.

"Read it!" Gordon said.

Rollins didn't move. "You really think—"

"Shut up," Gordon snapped. "Everything you need to complete this mission successfully in is that envelope. Quantico faxed it in this morning."

Glancing down, Rollins saw a red label on the side on the envelope. Red level information. Of course fax machines don't print envelopes and red stickers. Gordon must have done that part himself. Could be a trick.

"If you had not chosen to go behind my back," Gordon said, "you would have had access to this data before you ever assembled this convoy and we would have been prepared to deal with this thing. As it stands we'll have to do the best we can with what we have."

"What does it say?" Rollins said. He did not move to pick up the envelope.

"They sequenced the plasmid," Gordon said.

Rollins struggled to grasp the implications as he tried to remember their discussion during the meeting at sunset three days ago. "You said they couldn't sequence the plasmid's genes because they couldn't get the bacteria it infected to reproduce."

"That's still true," Gordon said. "The plasmid samples we had in storage from Alpha Site still produce the same results."

"Are you saying something has changed?" Rollins asked. Now he could not resist bending to pick up the envelope. He holstered his pistol as did so, but did not take his eyes off Gordon.

Rollins expected Gordon to use his knowledge as a wedge to get what he wanted, a play Rollins would have made himself if their positions were reversed, but Gordon didn't. He answered him without a trace of guile.

"The cellular samples we took from Beta Site successfully reproduced in the lab," Gordon said. "They were finally able to analyze the plasmid's genes. That's a paper copy of the sequencing autoradiograph."

Rollins broke the seal on the envelope and pulled out a sheaf of papers. Flipping through them, he scanned the contents, but he couldn't understand any of the scientific jargon or complicated graphs. A paper at the back caught his eye. Vertical rows of short, thick black bars covered it from top to bottom. The header of the page said "Sequencing Autoradiograph (Beta Site Specimen #3)." Beside one vertical row of bars, someone had drawn a bracket, and written in the margin "Probable 90% sample content."

Rollins turned the page and pointed to the bracketed section. "Is this the plasmid's genes? These black bars?"

"Part of them," Gordon said. "They got that DNA from the cat we took from Beta Site. It's the area where we think the plasmid inserted itself into the cat's genome. That's not a very good copy. Real autoradiographs are a sheet of film, rather like X-ray film, but they scanned me a copy and marked the affected sections of the gene so they could get it to me sooner."

"Well, it's all moot now," Rollins said, although he tucked the papers back in the envelope and put it under his arm for safekeeping. Very stupid of Gordon to give that to him.

"We're here to kill the infected animals and take the carcasses back to base for storage and shipment, so all this fuss you've made is for nothing," Rollins said, affecting a dismissive tone. "I'll be sure to note that in the report."

"It is *not* moot," Gordon said. "It makes our situation far more serious than before!"

"Why?" Rollins snapped, trying his best to sound impatient. "What does all this say?"

"It's not what it says," Gordon replied. "It's what it shows. We didn't use the cat's cells to sequence the plasmid. We found another sample."

"Another sample?" Rollins asked. "You mean the rabbit?"

Gordon shook his head. "No. We used a third sample."

"A third sample? What third sample?"

"The one taken directly from the well," Gordon replied. "Those samples did reproduce in the lab."

If Gordon had any kind of a point, Rollins didn't see it, and he was beginning to suspect that Gordon didn't really have anything here at all. He could have torn the pages out of an old issue of *Scientific American* and tried to pass it off as a report from Quantico, for all Rollins knew. But still, it might pay to be sure.

"What is all this supposed to mean?" Rollins finally asked.

"They can sequence the plasmid now because we know how it reproduces," Gordon said. "It was so obvious I don't know why we didn't think of it before."

"And this would be?"

"The plasmid doesn't reproduce in animal cells," Gordon said. "It reproduces in plant cells."

"Plant cells?" Rollins repeated.

"Hicks found a root fragment in the well water sample," Gordon said. "The root cells were swarming with the plasmid. Apparently, by sheer bad luck, the plasmid encountered a species of plant life compatible with it. Remember what I told you about *Pseudomonas Aeruginosa?*"

"The transport bacterium," Rollins said.

"Right," Gordon said. "It can infect both plants and animals. *Pseudomonas* would naturally grow in that well. Once the *Pseudomonas* got into that compatible plant, bacteriophages carried the plasmid into the plant's cells. There it altered the plant cell's life cycle to manufacture more plasmids. *That* is how it's been spreading to all the animals in this area. A species of plant life at Beta Site is manufacturing new copies of the plasmid and releasing them into the ecosystem, infecting the local wildlife."

Rollins suddenly understood. "The sapling Hicks' team found on the night mission. The ones the cats were trying to protect."

"The one that grew up in a matter of days," Gordon said. "It must be the infected plant species. Those plant cells have no problem making more copies of the plasmid. In fact they're doing it at rates no one has ever observed in terrestrial plasmids."

"Wait," Rollins said. "You said this was the DNA sequence of the plasmid in the *cat's* cells."

"It is," Gordon said. "In plant cells, the plasmid stays whole and independent of the plant cell's nucleus. But it acts differently in animal cells. In animal cells, it acts like an episome. That's a plasmid that can integrate itself into the chromosomal DNA of the host organism. After the Quantico lab techs sequenced its structure from the plant cells, they knew what to look for in the cat's genes. They identified which gene incorporated the plasmid and they now have a pretty good idea of where the plasmid inserts itself on that gene. Fortunately it landed on a part of the genome that's fairly well mapped. They think they have about ninety percent of it sequenced now."

"And what does it show?"

"Look at the next autoradiograph," Gordon replied.

Rollins flipped through the pages again and found another sheet covered in vertical rows of narrow black bars. Like the previous graph, this page also had a handwritten bracket marking off a section of the page. The note here read "Probable 87% Sample Content."

"I suppose this section here is the plasmid?" Rollins asked.

Gordon nodded.

"The two graphs are different," Rollins said. "The percentages changed."

"The one you're holding came from the rabbit I found at Beta Site," Gordon said. "The first one came from the cat."

"I guess they're comparing them to the plasmid taken from the tree cells then?" Rollins asked.

Gordon nodded again.

"So why are they different?" Rollins asked. "If they were both infected by the same plasmid it should be the same percentage, right?"

"Right," Gordon said. "But they're not the same."

Rollins realized that when he was feeling confused, he self-consciously blinked his eyes, which he found himself doing now. Was Gordon trying to confuse him? It would do to adopt a more aggressive tone.

"So why are they different? That was my original question."

"Because the plasmid mutated," Gordon replied. "That's why they're different."

"It mutated?" Rollins said.

"Think about it, Rollins," Gordon said. "That rabbit had been dead for quite some time before I found it, but I had just killed the cat that same night. That means the plasmid mutated sometime after the rabbit died but before the cat was infected. Now do you realize what that change means?"

Gordon too had adopted a more aggressive tone, but he seemed more concerned about something in all this scientific data. Rollins still couldn't see what that something was, but now he remembered when Gordon had dissected those animals in the lab after the night mission.

"The tumors," Rollins said. "The rabbit was covered in them."

"That's right," Gordon said. "The cat was probably predisposed to the plasmid's mutation anyway, but that still doesn't explain how the plasmid itself changed. The clue is in the infected animals, why some develop carcinoma and others do not."

"What about the animals you took from Africa, from Alpha Site?" Rollins asked. "Surely after all those tests—"

"It still behaves like cancer!" Gordon snapped. "The plasmid mutates the brains of the animals it infects. The tissues of the hippocampus start to grow with speed only seen in cancerous cells."

He looked down at the unconscious girl lying on the table with tubes running in and out of her, breathing for her, monitoring her pulse and heartbeat. Gordon clenched his fist and a look of hopeless frustration passed over his face with such intensity that for a moment Rollins couldn't recognize him. Now Rollins understood why Gordon had gone to such lengths to involve himself in this mission. He had done it all out of concern for this girl. Not for career advancement, not for scientific research, not for any kind of self-interest whatsoever. Having lived so long in a cut-throat environment geared towards victory at all costs, Rollins found he could barely comprehend why anyone would go to such lengths with no hope of personal gain. The only time in his life he could ever remember doing such a thing was when he first enlisted in the military, simply because he had wanted to serve his country. What had happened to him over the course of his long career that had mutated his motives?

"The neural cells," Gordon suddenly whispered, a look of sudden realization passing over his face. "The cats were eating brain tissue ... and the plasmid changed."

Again, Rollins blinked in confusion. "What?"

"Remember, back in the lab, I found a shred of brain tissue in the cat's teeth," Gordon said. "That might explain it."

"Explain what?" Rollins said.

"When we infected the hyenas in the lab, we fed them dried meal, rather like dog food," Gordon said, "and the mutated tissue grew out of control until the hyenas died of brain tumors. But in the wild they could kill other animals and get brain tissue they were craving. The mutation might need those neural proteins to function."

"They needed to ingest brain tissue or they would die?"

"This is all conjecture," Gordon said. "I'm remembering mice running through a maze. I think it has something to do with why the plasmid mutates the hippocampus. That part of the brain is the gateway of our memories, and if plasmid is changing it then it might need ..."

He trailed off. Suddenly he pressed his hand to his forehead and cried out in pain.

"What's the matter with you?" Rollins asked, and then he felt it too.

... comecomecomecomecomecome ...

The papers tumbled out of its hands.

"No," Rollins whispered. He wanted to run, just as fast as he could, but the ice of fear had frozen him.

A *presence* was gathering around them. He felt something drawing near, something old and powerful. Never in his life had he felt anything like it. It was, in effect, something completely alien to his experience. His reaction was mindless, instinctual: fear.

Gordon stumbled back against the counter, knocking metal instruments to the floor with a crash. His face had gone red with effort, and Rollins realized Gordon was forcing himself to speak. Rollins could only stand there frozen in terror as he felt the presence gathering around them. Its cold gaze had focused on this very spot, and all of their human conceits fell before its ancient desires.

"It's not mutating," Gordon said, forcing the words through his clenched teeth. "It's adapting! It's evolving! It's—"

Finally he collapsed, blood streaming from his nose.

On the examining table, Rachel opened her eyes.

From outside the trailer there came the sound of screams.

20

Movement and Retrieval

Jacques and Rodriguez felt it coming first.

As they carried a tank of napalm over to the equipment checkpoint, Jacques said, "Man, they gotta let me use one of these babies! I'm ready! I'm *on* it!"

"You need training to operate a flamethrower, Jacques," Rodriguez said. She had taken one end of the tank and Jacques had taken the other.

"Training nothin'!" Jacques exclaimed. "Point and shoot, baby! Point and shoot!"

Rodriguez rolled her eyes. Jacques had been keyed up and defensive ever since the night mission, after that *mariposa* Gordon saved his ass. He taken a lot of ribbing from the guys about other things Gordon would like to do to his ass, and now Jacques thought he had something to prove. This *pandejo* actually thought Sergeant Rollins would let him operate a flamethrower? He'd crisp them all in ten seconds flat.

"You don't even know if Rollins will let you go to the—" Her sentence cut off as they jerked to a halt. Jacques had stopped walking without warning her. She glared at him, ready to unload a stream of Spanish curses. This tank was heavy and dangerous to move. She didn't want Jacques dragging his heels and making her drop it. But when she saw his face, the curses froze in her throat.

Jacques was crying.

At first she thought she must be mistaken, like it was allergies or something. Jacques always acted like such a tough guy. But now she realized she wasn't mistaken. Jacques had stopped in his tracks, still clutching the tank of napalm. His thick lower lip trembled. His entire body shivered, as if he was cold, and tears had started to run out of his eyes. Why on earth was he crying?

"Man, what's the matter with you?" Rodriguez snapped. Men who cried always disgusted her.

Jacques moved his jaw, trying to speak. A dry-sounding croak came from his throat. Rodriguez was getting ready to snap at him again when she heard a dull metallic thud. Looking up, she saw a big gray cat standing on the roof of a truck to her left. A branch swung up and down over its head. The cat must have jumped out of the tree. It hissed at her, pacing anxiously.

Again, Jacques tried to speak. This time he managed to release a strangled moan. Rodriguez glanced back at him. The tank of napalm felt heavy and ominous in her hands. A cold breeze had sprung up, making gooseflesh break out on her arms and shoulders. The cross she wore on a gold chain around her neck suddenly felt hot and chafing against the skin between her breasts. She had a sudden and unnerving sense of being watched. Looking around, she saw the branches of the trees surrounding the camp start to rustle and sway. At first she thought it was the wind, but the breeze wasn't strong enough to move the branches so much. Then she saw the dark bodies of cats moving in the trees, and she realized the branches were swaying with the weight of their bodies. *Dios*, there must be hundreds of them! Now she understood why she had felt like she was being watched. The branches were all a-glitter with their eyes.

The wind grew stronger. Voices seemed to call out to her from the forest.

Jacques once more tried to speak, and this time he succeeded.

"Something is coming," he whispered.

Rodriguez jumped at the sound of his voice and almost dropped the tank. Jacques didn't move. He just stood there, still holding up his end, staring directly into Rodriguez's face. A disturbing thought came to her. Wondering if Jacques had seen something behind her, she glanced back over her shoulder.

She saw nothing but more trucks and the big trailer where they had detained the Ross woman and her boyfriend. Cats skittered between its tires. Nothing else, but she didn't feel relieved. Of course nothing was there, because it was coming from the other direction. It couldn't wait any longer, their time drew closer every second, it-

"It can't wait any longer," Jacques hissed. "It has to come now!"

Now Rodriguez felt it too, a vast and terrifying intelligence drawing closer, its mind focused on this very spot. The being's psychic presence thrummed through the air. It felt like they were standing inside a giant ringing bell. The very idea of this inhuman thing seeing her made mindless, overpowering terror course through her veins.

An acrid, ammoniacal stench came to her on the cold breeze. Looking down, she saw Jacques had wet himself.

Something creaked below her. Lowering her gaze, she watched in disbelief as a valve on the tank of napalm started to turn of its own accord.

All the hair stood up on the back of her neck, the way it sometimes did before a storm.

A voice so low it was almost instinct echoed through her mind.

... *comecomecomecomecomecomecome* ...

Then, as if in response, a second voice. It seemed to burn into her skin from the cross around her neck until it reached her heart, and then it shot straight into her brain.

Run! The disembodied voice screamed the word. It sounded almost like her mother, the voice of her conscience. *Run, chica! Run, Run, RUN!*

Opposing commands, stay or flee, fight or flight. In a few more seconds she would have made the choice on her own, but as it was terror decided for her.

She whirled, dropping the tank, her legs tensing as they prepared to drive her away.

The tank had not yet hit the ground when she felt the explosion, hot and insistent, launch her into the air. Searing pain went through her back. She flew several feet before she hit the ground, and when she did she immediately started to roll. The napalm had stuck to her and she could feel it burning all down her spine and between her shoulder blades. It hissed and whistled as it burned; her nose filled with the nauseating smell of her own cooking flesh. It felt like a rabid animal had landed on her back and was now ripping into her with its claws. Rolling only seemed to spread it around. She flopped onto her back and stayed there, hoping she could smother it, but it still felt hot and painful. She could feel the fire waiting to burst back to life the second it came into contact with air.

And then she felt again the presence of that alien mind, and the pain became secondary to her fear.

Turning her head, she saw it coming. It had walked into their base camp while she had been trying to put out the fire on her back, and now it was coming down the center of the road with slow measured strides. Directly towards *her.*

She screamed and started dragging herself backwards. The fire on her back did leap back to life as soon she got up, but she didn't care. Nothing else mattered but getting out of the path of the monster walking towards her.

It looked like a bloody mutilated boy, hardly more than a child. Torn rags hung from its scarecrow body and hundreds of thorns protruded from its skin. It was thin beyond the point of starvation. Its arms looked like sticks. Its head was little more than a skull with thin wisps of hair clinging to it. And its eyes ... it had no eyes. Only two gleaming metal orbs sitting in the sockets above its cheekbones.

Men and women ran everywhere, panicking. It was unbelievable. These were highly trained, combat-tested soldiers but at the sight of this thing all their reason left them. Rodriguez felt it too, just as bad as any of them and even though she knew logically that panicking was the worst thing to do she couldn't help it. The force of this being's mind rang through her skull, stirring up fear and confusion.

Jacques stumbled past, engulfed in flames, writhing on his feet. Some of the soldiers had pulled their guns and started firing on the creature. The sound of gunfire thundered through the air, but none of the bullets reached their target. Sparks flickered all around the mutilated being as the bullets ricocheted off some kind of invisible wall around it. The being continued walking, unperturbed, relentless, unstoppable.

One of the trucks exploded.

Fire came up from the rear of the vehicle, around the gas tank. The force of its explosion sent a shudder through the ground. People and debris flew everywhere.

Rodriguez's burnt shoulder struck something, sending a bolt of pain through her entire mid-section. Turning her head, she saw she had backed into one of the trailer's tires. She crawled around it and ducked underneath the trailer to hide, praying the mutilated being wouldn't see her and focus its awful metal gaze upon her. Peeking out from behind the tire, she watched it come.

Fire had engulfed the camp. The cats had jumped down from the trees and were scampering around, yowling in strange, humanlike voices. A soldier ran by, screaming as cats crawled all over him, eating his face. Clouds of black oily smoke filled the air, making the evening prematurely dark. Through the midst of all this the being walked, moving directly towards the trailer beneath which Rodriguez was hiding.

The engine of one of the unburned trucks suddenly roared to life. Someone was behind the wheel, and now it leaped forward with its gears grinding.

The thing didn't even glance in the truck's direction. The truck was knocked away before it even got close to it. The side of the truck imploded like a huge invisible fist had punched it aside. The vehicle exploded as it rolled, moving directly towards the other trailer where they had detained the girl.

Agent Gordon and Sergeant Rollins stumbled out of the trailer just as the truck came rolling towards them. Gordon tackled Rollins, knocking them both out of the way as the truck crashed against the side of the trailer.

The being had reached the opposite side of the camp, and now stood before the trailer where they had detained Kelly Ross and Spencer Dale. Rodriguez heard a metal clang as the lock disengaged, which was impossible since those doors had electronic locks protected with codes. But the door unlocked anyway, and the mutilated being flaunted its impossibility like a bright new set of clothes.

Something behind Rodriguez growled.

Turning, she saw a pride of cats advancing on her. Not wanting to set them off with any sudden movements, she slowly moved her hand to the pistol in her belt. She had to clench her teeth to keep from crying out in pain as the burnt skin on her back crinkled and sloughed away.

She saw a flicker of movement out of the corner of her eye. Turning her head to the right, she saw another group of cats approaching her from that side as well. More of them crawled under the trailer from the front, moving towards her face.

She should have never crawled under the trailer. She had trapped herself under here.

She pulled the pistol from its holster but it was too late. The cats leaped forward, bared their teeth and claws, and were upon her.

Her screams filtered up through the bottom of the trailer, to the room where Kelly and Spencer were detained. They were the last ones to see the mutilated being, and feel the awful force of its mind.

Before the carnage started, they had been sitting on one of the benches inside the trailer, leaning against each other for support. Kelly had started to doze off. It seemed incredible, but after all the stress of their kidnapping, she had come down off her adrenaline rush. Now she could barely keep her eyes open. Being locked inside this glorified holding pen didn't help. Of all the high-tech gadgets they had on this trailer, air conditioning apparently wasn't one of them. The summer heat had made the trailer stuffy and uncomfortable. She felt she like was suffocating. She and Spencer both became soaked with sweat after a few minutes. The lack of air conditioning was probably intentional. Their hosts obviously wanted to sweat information out of them.

Crying didn't help her fatigue. It seemed like the body's natural defense against emotional stress was to shut down and escape into sleep. Kelly and Jason had cried themselves to sleep many times after Jack had died. Now she was crying for her son. Her own mother had once told her that having children was an invitation to sorrow that you gladly accept. Today Kelly understood what she meant.

She tried to stay hopeful. After all, Jason had escaped, and he knew his way around those woods. But not knowing what had happened to him was agonizing, like turning on a spit. Losing Jack had done this to her. If she wasn't careful, she could easily become one of those overprotective mothers that suffocated their children with their own needs. The effort of keeping her love in check had exhausted her.

Now, sitting in the warm trailer with her head resting against Spencer's good strong shoulder, it seemed like the only thing keeping her awake was a nuisance. The poison oak. Her face had started to tingle and itch. She knew she wasn't supposed to scratch it, that would only spread it around, but it was a moot point with her hands tied behind her back. For some reason, knowing she couldn't scratch it even if she wanted to seemed to make it worse.

The sound of an explosion startled her awake.

"What was that?" Kelly said.

Spencer woke more slowly. "Wha ... What?"

"I heard something," she said. "A boom. Didn't you hear it?"

"I don't know, I ..." Spencer trailed off again. Kelly looked up at him, wondering if he was okay. Those soldiers had hit him pretty hard. A big purple bruise had formed around his jaw. His eyes had gone all bloodshot, and the lids had started to turn red as well. She wondered if he might have a concussion, but his pupils didn't seem too dilated. Seemed she had read somewhere that dilated pupils meant a concussion.

Another muffled roar came from outside the trailer. The sound of gunfire seeped through the walls, along with the fainter, higher-pitched sound of screams.

"What is going on out there?" Kelly said, standing.

Spencer tried to stand as well, but he stopped short and winced, like he was in pain.

"No," he whispered. Kelly could just barely hear him. He mumbled something else but she couldn't make it out.

"Are you all right, Spencer?"

"Yeah," he replied, a little too quickly. "My head just hurts a little. That guy really socked me. I'll be okay."

The trailer shuddered. It felt the like the earth beneath it had moved, just a little bit. Kelly had never experienced an earthquake, but she imagined a very small one would feel similar to the little shudder that now passed up through the floor.

Spencer staggered to his feet. For a second it looked like he might fall, and with his hands tied behind his back that could be trouble, but he managed to turn himself against the wall and keep his feet by leaning on it.

He gasped suddenly. "God it's so hot in here! I can't breathe!"

Concerned now, Kelly went to him and looked closely at his face. Gooseflesh had broken out all over his skin, but he was sweating at the same time. His long brown hair stuck to his face in tangles. His breath came in gasps, his chest hitching with effort as he inhaled.

"Sit back down, Spencer," Kelly said, trying to stay calm. "You must have picked something up." Thoughts of poison passed through her mind. Their captors hadn't given them anything to eat or drink. Were they releasing something into the air? If so, then why wasn't she getting sick too?

A thud came from above them, like something had just dropped onto the top of the trailer. Then another one came, and another. The commotion outside grew louder. Gunshots. Screaming. The sounds started to pile up on one another. Kelly felt a sudden, overpowering sense of claustrophobia, of being trapped in an increasingly dangerous situation. Now a high-pitched scratching sound came from above them, like something was clawing at the metal roof of their prison as it tried to get inside. Above that, very faint, was it *growling?* Not a dog's growl. It was a cat, several of them, she was certain of it. Kelly had heard growling like that dozens of times over the course of her life. It was the sound of a frustrated cat, growling as it tried to reach its prey.

Spencer started to hyperventilate.

"Hey, come on now," Kelly said to him. "Stay with me, Spence. Don't faint. This couldn't be a worse time to—"

A thunderous impact shuddered through the trailer, like a heavy fist pounding on the door. The trailer swayed with the impact. When the boom of it faded, all the sounds outside somehow faded with it. An eerie silence descended, as if the whole trailer had fallen into a vacuum. Spencer's breath rasped harshly in the new silence.

Suddenly his breath caught short. He jerked upright.

"It's coming," he whispered. "It's trying to get in."

Kelly began to speak, but he interrupted her.

"Oh no," he said. "Oh no, no, no! Not now!"

Kelly had been standing close to him out of concern, so she saw what happened next in nightmarish clarity. Spencer's bloodshot eyes had gone wide, and as she watched all the little red capillaries in the whites of his eyes started to turn silver. They went from the outside in, like liquid mercury had started flowing into his eyes; thousands of thin shining threads displaced all the red.

When it reached his pupils, it flooded into them and turned them completely silver, iris and pupil both, erasing all the color in his eyes and leaving them flat, blank and metallic.

Spencer's face, which had been contorted with fear, went slack. Every bit of human emotion drained out of it until it was as expressionless as a poorly carved statue.

Kelly, stunned beyond all reason, could only whisper his name in shock.

"Oh Spencer …"

And then she felt the *presence.*

Some kind of psychic presence entered the room and cast its gaze upon her. The disembodied awareness moved over her like a spotlight. The growling and scratching outside the trailer took up again, metallic and inhuman-sounding, but this time she thought she heard words forming from out of all that noise. But that didn't frighten her. Spencer's sudden, bizarre transformation didn't frighten her. Any fear she might have felt at those things paled in comparison to the sheer terror she felt when the presence found her.

Like most people, she had an occasional psychic experience. Sometimes Jason would walk into the room when she happened to be thinking of him, or a song she liked would come on the radio a few seconds after she had started humming it to herself. Nothing fancy; she could never use it to win the lottery or predict a plane crash or anything, but it was amusing every now and then.

If she had a spark of psychic talent, then the presence that was now surrounding them had a nuclear explosion of it, and it was sending out pulses of its awareness in all directions. At the touch of that awareness, all rational thought in her mind shorted out.

The fluorescent lights in the ceiling suddenly turned off. Perfect darkness enclosed them. The only sound that disturbed the unnatural silence was the sound of her own breath. She couldn't hear Spencer breathing anymore. What had happened outside? What had caused all that screaming and gunfire, and worse yet, what had made them all suddenly stop? She didn't know and she didn't have time to figure it out, because now something had happened to Spencer and she was on her own, trapped in the dark with her hands bound, alone with the alien presence.

jack

A whisper, harsh but familiar. She whirled, but could see nothing in the darkness. Her hip banged painfully against something and she cried out—

jack no

The presence was here. She could feel it all around her. The air vibrated with it. It crawled over her skin like worms, seeking a way inside her, looking for something it could use.

oh no not jack please god don't take my jack

The presence sighed. She felt its pleasure like sweaty moans in the darkness. It had found her greatest pain, and now it swarmed into her mind, down the pathways to her past, sparking her memories to life. Against her will, Kelly's mind went sixteen months back in time as the presence within her gave a command: *remember.*

An echoing metal boom went through the chamber as the door unlocked. The hinges screamed as it swung open. Orange firelight filled the room, and silhouetted against it stood a bloody mutilated youth scourged with thorns. Behind it human figures writhed and screamed in pain. Cats skittered among them, hissing like demons with their eyes all aglow. But the wind that came inside the chamber was not a gust of heat from all that fire, but a gust of cold. As the memories rose up against her will, she felt ...

... a gust of icy cold wind as the door swings wide, and standing outside on her front porch is Officer Randy. The spinning lights on his cruiser cast blood red shadows into the night. Ice falls from the sky and coats the house, the ground, the branches of the trees and every stone in her gravel driveway, filling the night with glittering ethereal beauty. Icicles hang like fangs from her gutters. Ice rubies gleam on Randy's uniform and his broad-rimmed hat, glowing red in the light from his cruiser.

"I'm so sorry, Kelly," Randy says. The words sound hollow and pathetic to her ears. "The paramedics tried everything they could. Those downed power lines, all this ice ... nobody could reach him. He was so brave, Kelly. Jack saw that pole start to fall. He must have shoved three guys out of the way before it hit. I ... I just ..."

He stammers, words fail him. "I can't begin to tell you how sorry I am," he finishes.

She can't bear any more and turns from him, her hands covering her mouth. But when she turns her eyes fall on Jason, huddling by the woodstove, for the storm has killed the power. He stares at her, uncomprehending, and as she looks at him she thinks of doing something for which she will never forgive herself as long as she lives. She looks at her son and sees only a mouth that needs food, a body that needs clothes, a mind that needs education, a growing malignant organism steadily eating her life, and in that moment all she wants to do is turn and run away into the ice storm, shoving Randy aside if he tries to stop her. Just run and run until the ice coats her body and steals away her life. Better to die that way than to drag it out over years of struggle. Better to let the storm coat her body in a layer of ice so thick no one will find her until the spring thaw, and by then Jason will have—

"Oh no," she moans. "Oh no, not Jack. Oh please God not my Jack ..."

"Kelly!" Randy shouts as her legs fail her, and she falls ...

She fell to the floor, moaning in pain and terror. Kicking her legs, she backed herself into a corner with her arms wedged painfully behind her. Ahead of her she saw Spencer's back; somehow she had wandered behind him in the dark. Beyond him she saw the open door and the thing standing in its threshold.

She heard a snap, and the tie binding Spencer's hands fell to the floor, broken to pieces.

Spencer walked forward to the thing in door, moving in stiff, robotic strides. For a moment she saw him in the threshold, outlined in fire, and then he passed beyond it and was gone.

Kelly remained crouched in her corner with her knees drawn up to her chest, hoping that if she stayed very quiet and still that terrible being would not return, and force her to relive the cold winter of the previous year, the darkest hour of her soul.

21

Gordon's Run

Gordon looked up after the wrecked truck crashed into the trailer. Debris clattered all around him. Smoke swirled in the air, stinging his eyes. The wreckage seethed like a furnace, baking the skin of his face. The air above it shimmered with heat. He had to get away from it or the smoke would asphyxiate him.

"Are you all right?" He shouted the question to Rollins over the deafening roar of the fire.

"Get off me!" Rollins shouted, shoving him back. The shove felt weak; Rollins still looked dazed. Gordon grabbed him by the shoulder and hauled him up. Together the two men stumbled away from the wreckage.

Once they got across the road and over to the treeline, Gordon looked back. The flames over the truck had grown. Great clouds of black oily smoke rose up from it.

"We have to go back!" Gordon shouted.

In between bouts of coughing, Rollins looked at him like he was crazy.

"The girl is still in there!" Gordon said. "Those trailers have fuel tanks in them for the generators! We have to get her out of there before the fire reaches it!"

Still coughing, Rollins shook his head. "That's the only door," he managed to say. "The fire's blocked it off. There's no other way in."

Gordon stood. Shaking his head to clear it, he scanned the trailer. There had to be another way in. They had left the trailer to confront the threat they had sensed approaching and left the girl inside thinking she would be safe. Now this.

In addition to the fire, they had to worry about the smoke. When they dove out of the path of the truck, they didn't have time to shut the door behind them. The smoke could fill the trailer in minutes. It would not take long for the girl to suffocate.

For a moment he had thought she had regained consciousness. But after opening her eyes, she had lain motionless and unresponsive on the examining table. Just lying there staring at the ceiling, as still as the dead. Gordon wondered if she had sensed the alien consciousness as well. The feel of it inside his own mind had been almost more than Gordon could bear, the sheer malevolent *focus* of it! The experience was so at odds with everything he had thought was possible, so alien and strange, that he could not blame the soldiers for panicking. The feeling had even paralyzed Rollins, whom Gordon thought had inured himself to fear.

The moment he had felt that alien presence, he had known it was the plasmid. Nothing like that mind had ever existed on this earth. He didn't need to study it and quantify it to know it was true. When he had felt it inside his mind, he had sensed the sheer scale of its cold alien difference and known. *Not one of us.* His response was as old as instinct: fear. It was the same kind of animal fear that lay behind all bigotry and racism, homophobia, nationalism, and even the fear of the dark. It was the fear of something unfamiliar and strange, magnified now because the source was not even of this earth. What else could cause it other than the alien plasmid? It had taken all of Gordon's mental strength to recover, and only then after the presence had taken its focus away. If it was like this for them, what must it have been like for the girl, after being infected? What did that alien presence find inside her mutated mind?

No time to think about it. He ran back to the trailer, but the heat from the fire hit him like a wall and forced him back. He could still feel the alien presence nearby but it wasn't so bad anymore. It seemed to have taken its focus elsewhere and he could think more clearly without it filling his mind and obliterating his concentration. Rollins was right. The trailer only had one entrance. The lab had an air filtration system, which would help thin the smoke. That would buy him a few seconds. The next major problem was the fuel. The tanks were at the back of the trailer; the fire was at the front, but spreading. It was much too big to put out with a fire extinguisher. So if he couldn't keep the fire away from the fuel ... maybe he could get the fuel away from the fire.

He ran to the back of the trailer, going around the other side of it to get past the fire. The orange firelight flickered around his feet, disturbingly close. A locked metal door in the back of the trailer sealed the compartment with the fuel tank inside, but the locks were no obstacle for someone with Gordon's skills. Using the curved hunting knife and the file that he kept in a pouch on his belt, he jimmied the first lock open and had started on the second when he felt a sharp pain on the back of his neck, like a wasp sting. He slapped at it and felt something hot. Looking up, he saw the lower branches of the trees had started to burn. Sparks drifted down all around him, gleaming like fireflies. One of them had landed on the back of his neck.

The firelight seemed brighter now, closer, and taking a breath made his lungs burn as the air filled up with smoke.

Wasting no time, Gordon flung open the fuel compartment door and assessed the situation. The large cylindrical tank sat in a metal frame bolted to the floor of the compartment. A fuel pump with an array of tubes and wires came out of the top of it. The fuel line came out of this tangle and ran into a big red generator mounted beside the fuel tank. He had no time to be careful, but he couldn't afford any spills with all these sparks around.

He found the outflow valve for the fuel pump and twisted it shut. Now no more fuel could come out of the tank. A little bit would be left in the fuel line, but not enough to worry about. Using his hunting knife again, he cut the fuel line, as well as the wiring for the pump. Then he undid the clamps securing the tank to the metal frame, grabbed the handles on top of the tank and pulled.

It was heavy, almost full. Had to weigh two hundred pounds at least. The pungent reek of gasoline shot straight up his nose, mixing with the smoke. Gritting his teeth, Gordon hauled the tank out of the compartment. Once he got his leverage he could carry it a little easier. He took it around to the back side of the trailer, staggering under the weight. The road sloped down a little here. With no time to lose, Gordon dropped the tank and shoved it down the hill. It rolled about a hundred feet, bouncing and grinding on the uneven gravel road, until it fell into the ditch. Not the safest place for it, but it was the best he could do. Turning back to the trailer, he began to look for another way inside.

He walked around it, searching. Nothing on the sides of the trailer other than the door blocked off by the burning truck. No access panels, no windows. Nothing underneath it either. That left the roof. Looking up, he thought he saw a way.

He cursed himself for not thinking of it earlier. He had known the trailer had an air filtration system. A vent was installed on the trailer's roof to expel the waste gases. It would be blocked off by a grate, a fan, and an air filter, but he might be able to remove them before it got too hot inside the trailer.

He ran back into the base camp. Fire was everywhere; smoke filled the air, soldiers ran past screaming. The noise was deafening. Rollins stood in the center of the chaos, screaming orders at the soldiers running past. At a glance, Gordon saw at least a dozen people that needed help; soldiers with charred skin crawled among the overturned trucks. Not all of them were burned. Some looked like they had been mauled by wild animals. God, what had done all this?

No time to think about it. The fire had spread to the surrounding trees, and once the sparks hit the dry grass and deadwood on the forest floor, there would be a real burning in these woods.

He climbed onto the hood of an unburned truck parked close to the lab trailer. From here he had enough height to jump over to the trailer and grab the top edge of it. If he didn't fall, he could haul himself up to the roof.

He tensed his legs in preparation to jump ... but then he felt the alien presence return.

Before this mission, he had never in his life felt another consciousness enter his mind, so he had no point of reference to define what was happening to him. But still, in defiance of all logic, it seemed like he remembered feeling this way, a kind of déjà vu. He felt cold and afraid; he couldn't breathe. The strength ran out of his legs as the alien presence stirred up fear and confusion in his mind.

... comecomecomecomecomecomecomecomecome ...

He felt suddenly sure a monster was hiding underneath the truck, and it would grab him if he let his legs slip over the side. He gasped for breath, drew in a lungful of smoke, and fell, choking, to his knees, still crouched on the hood of the truck.

The wind rose up, clearing out the smoke a little, and through the tears in his eyes he saw the thing come walking through the fire.

It was once human, and it was clearly infected by the plasmid. He realized that immediately. The body was wasted, ruined, a walking skeleton, bloody and bristling with thorns. The eyes were two metal spheres set in the sockets of its skull.

Beside it walked a man with long hair. Gordon had never seen him before, but he could see a metallic glint in the man's eyes, like a lesser version of the being walking beside him.

Wherever they walked, destruction followed. Trucks turned over and exploded. People who ran into their path were knocked aside. The ground itself shook and cracked as they walked over it. All around them scampered dozens of cats, somehow unharmed by the force that emanated from that pair like a magnet. The sight of the cats confirmed for Gordon that this was the plasmid at work. Ripping his gun from its holster, he unleashed a volley of shots at the mutilated being. He screamed as he pulled the trigger, thinking only *Kill it! Kill it! Kill it!* The feel of the being's mind inside his own stirred up an atavistic fear and hatred so powerful he could not suppress it. At the touch of that alien mind all the walls built up by education and enlightenment came tumbling down, and all he wanted to do was kill the awful thing that had invaded his territory.

None of the bullets reached their target. Sparked flashed around the man and the mutilated being. For a second a faint sphere of light surrounding them became visible. The bullets couldn't penetrate this force field, whatever it was, and ricocheted off of it in all directions. The being ignored him, but the man walking beside it turned and looked in his direction, unmolested by the bullets. Gordon felt chilled when that cold metal gaze fell on him; the man's face was as expressionless as the face of a corpse. Gordon kept firing until he emptied the clip.

They approached the lab trailer as Gordon fumbled in his belt for his spare clip. He had just reloaded and was aiming the gun at the mutilated being's head as they reached the burning wreckage of the truck in front of the trailer's door. The being turned its head slightly, and the wreckage flew out of its way. The burning truck rolled like a boulder directly towards Gordon.

He jumped off the truck a second before the wreckage hit it. The shock wave knocked him into the woods. Branches snapped across his back. Shrapnel from the wreckage flew all around him. He rolled when he hit the ground until he came to rest against the trunk of a big oak. He lay there dazed for a moment, before forcing himself to rise again. A sharp pain in his back, just above his left shoulder blade, stopped him short. Reaching back, he pulled out a chunk of metal that had gotten imbedded there. It took him a second to realize it was a burnt piece of a truck's door handle.

I guess I'm lucky that didn't go through my head, he thought as he threw the broken handle away. Stooping once to retrieve his pistol, Gordon stumbled back to the base camp.

He had to go around the back of the trailer again, as the other way was now blocked by the burning wreckage of the trucks. As he came around, he saw the alien pair walking off into the woods. The man was carrying Rachel in his arms.

At the sight of all three of them together, Gordon realized what they meant to do.

He raised his gun to fire, but stopped himself this time. The presence of the alien being's mind had left the camp and Gordon could think again. Shooting at them would be pointless now. Even if the force field surrounding them had dropped, he might hit Rachel by mistake. The man might still be saved as well. Gordon realized he would need some help.

Turning around, Gordon raced into the ruins of the base camp to look for survivors.

The smoke made it as dark as night. Gordon stumbled through it, holding the tail of his shirt over his mouth and nose. It didn't help much. His lungs burned and tears streamed from his eyes.

"Is anyone out there?" he shouted, but no one answered. All the screams had stopped. Everyone seemed to have fled or died. His foot struck something. Looking down, he saw a severed human arm, charred black, lying on the ground.

He turned left, following the thin strip of grass growing down the center of the old gravel road. That grass was now burned black. A red glow came through the smoke to his right. He assumed the woods had caught on fire. He heard the sound of burning everywhere, crackling, sizzling, hissing. The nauseating smell of burning meat and spent napalm.

"Hello!" Gordon shouted. "Can anyone hear me? Does anyone need help?"

The wind changed, clearing out the smoke a little. From out of it rose the dark box shape of the second trailer, the one where they had detained Kelly Ross. The heavy metal door hung open. He ran towards it. Kelly Ross was an innocent bystander. If anything had happened to her ...

Gordon had watched Benton's team bring the man into the base camp with Kelly when he was hiding in the woods. That was how he had known the time had come to call Rollins on the radio. The man hadn't been displaying any obvious symptoms then. Benton's team must not have known the man was infected when they took him, whoever he was. Gordon himself hadn't known anyone else was exposed besides the girl and maybe Jason Ross or Brad Grace.

Then came the question of the thing that invaded the camp in the first place. That had once been a human being, a teenaged boy from the looks of it. How had the plasmid done that to him? Obviously it had given the boy great power but was killing his body. The man still seemed physically healthy, even if the mutation had taken over his mind. But Rachel was dying, and may yet die if she wasn't rescued. Gordon saw a progression, and a theory took shape in his mind.

He raced up the steps and into the second trailer. It was almost completely dark inside, and the air was thick with smoke. From the back of the trailer came a faint sobbing.

Gordon moved in, edging along the wall in the darkness. His eyes slowly adjusted, so that by the time he reached the back of the trailer he could just make out the pale form of Kelly Ross huddling in the corner. He moved over and crouched next to her. The smoke wasn't so bad down here near the floor. Kelly had her face pressed to the wall and was quietly crying. Her chest hitched as she sobbed.

"Oh Jack," she whispered. "Oh God, Jack."

"Ms. Ross," Gordon said.

Kelly gasped in surprise, inhaling smoke, and started to cough. She shrank away from him, but since she was in a corner she had nowhere to go. The whites of her eyes floated through the dimness inside the trailer.

"I wish you had listened to my warning, Ms. Ross," Gordon said.

Her eyes narrowed in concentration, and then widened again as recognition dawned in them.

"You," she said. She did not sound shocked; rather she sounded like she suddenly understood.

"Me," Gordon confirmed. "Come on, these trailers have fuel tanks in them and the fire is spreading. We have to get out of here."

"Who are you?" Kelly hissed, not moving. "What is going on? What was that thing?

"I'll tell you everything," Gordon said, "but not here."

Taking her by the arm, Gordon pulled Kelly to her feet. Then he took out his hunting knife and cut the plastic tie around her wrists. As her arms flopped to her sides, Kelly cried out in pain.

"I know it hurts," Gordon said. "That's the blood flowing back into your arms. I'm sorry, but right now I need you to come with me."

"Do I really have a choice?" Kelly said, bitterness giving a sharp edge to her words.

"I'm afraid not," Gordon replied, and taking her around the waist he led her out of the trailer and through the destruction beyond.

22

The Substance of Memory

Rollins slowly recovered from the nightmare. He staggered away from the ruins of the base camp, blood streaming down his face from a cut on his scalp. He didn't remember how that happened, nor did he remember how he came to be here, stumbling through the woods while behind him the fire crackled and the black smoke billowed into the sky like the rising souls of his murdered soldiers.

Shut up! he thought at this unprofitable comparison. *No more of that queer crap! Shut up!*

The last thing he remembered was shouting orders to some of his less hysterical men while the whole camp went to hell all around them. If they had just kept together, kept organized! Obviously the thing could ignite the gas in their trucks; they didn't need to know what the thing was or where it came from to realize that. He had kept shouting at them to get away from the vehicles, but not one of them had listened to his orders. They had all gone mad with fear. Of course he knew why they were panicking. He had felt the alien presence as well. It had exerted a kind of mental push to make them afraid and confused. But Rollins had spent the vast majority of his life suppressing his emotions, so he had been able to resist it to an extent. For all the good it had done.

He had been standing in the middle of the road, shouting orders no one was listening to, when he encountered the alien being. It had come from behind him, from the direction of the trailer where they had detained Kelly Ross and Spencer Dale. He hadn't been able to see it coming through the smoke, but he had felt its psychic presence drawing closer. He had turned and caught a brief glimpse of it, some kind of walking corpse with thorns sticking out all over it. Dale had been walking beside it, his eyes all silver. So Dale was infected after all. Rollins had felt a moment of righteous vindication as he realized he had been right to take Dale into custody, then the being's mind had lashed out and hit him with an invisible wave of force. He had flown through the air, the world spinning all around him, and then impact and darkness.

He had awakened choking on smoke, his face sticky with blood. He was lying in the ditch by the side of the road. Pain throbbed across his head and back. It looked like the entire world had caught on fire. The trucks were burning, the trees were burning, and if he did not move soon he would be burning too. A wall of fire had started to spread through the grass by the side of the road, and it was headed right towards him. He had crawled to his feet, struggling to conquer the pain in his head, fighting to stay conscious with each step. He must have been seeing things at that point, because he could have sworn he saw a big group of cats bounding off into the woods, like they were following something. He was hearing things too, voices chattering far off among the trees, muttering something about children and circles and darkness. He had ignored it, and focused on putting one foot ahead of the other. The only thing that had mattered was getting away from the fire.

And off he had went, and now here he was, stumbling through the woods with no idea where he was going, lost and without a clue. His entire mission had been destroyed in seconds, but he was still alive. And in the great tradition of military men, he vowed he would return.

Something came crashing through the underbrush and he whirled around, nearly falling. But he had his pistol drawn and the safety off, ready to fire, with the same speed that had been drilled into him at boot camp more than thirty years before. Some things never left you, no matter how bad it got. A rush of adrenaline shot through his veins and he was ready to show anything hunting him that William Rollins was nobody's prey.

At first it looked, bizarrely, like the forest had come to life and was attacking him; he almost fired. But at the last second one of the trees lifted a pair of human hands and shouted, "Don't shoot, Sergeant! It's me! It's Private Turner!"

Rollins froze, his finger putting just enough pressure on his pistol's trigger to keep the hammer back. Sure enough, the eyes on either side on his pistol's sight belonged to Private Turner. The face was all black and green with camouflage makeup, but that didn't startle Rollins. He had been on so many covert missions that camouflage makeup didn't look strange to him at all anymore. He lowered the gun, and Turner gave a visible sigh of relief. Now three more men came out of the woods behind him. The middle one was Benton, who had his arms tied behind his back. The moment he laid eyes on Rollins, Benton rushed forward, tripping and nearly falling on his face. But he recovered in time and scrambled forward, babbling.

"Sir, the men mutinied!" Benton cried. "I was doing everything I could to take those boys into custody, per your orders sir, and they refused to do it! They mutinied and they tied me up like this—"

"We had to restrain him, sir," Turner interjected. "He kept trying to take a swing at us and run off."

"Benton made some serious errors in judgment, sir," one of the other soldiers said. Rollins didn't recognize him offhand.

"Ames led them on, sir!" Benton continued. "I was doing everything humanly possible, all of it per orders, sir, and I wasn't doing anything wrong and they refused to back me up! Right now Ames is back there letting those women—"

Rollins had enough. He lifted his gun and fired a shot over their heads. The thunder of its report shut them all up quite nicely.

"Do any of you worthless maggots have eyes?" Rollins said. "You useless incompetent babbling idiots! Where were you when *this* happened?" He jabbed his finger at the blood on his face. "Or that? Did any of you happen to notice there is a giant cloud of smoke where our base camp used to be?"

He pointed at the tower of black smoke rising into the evening sky.

"Sir, we were in the woods, it wasn't visible," Turner said. "We heard the gunfire but we thought that was the team clearing out the infected cats. We didn't know—"

"I don't want to hear your worthless excuses!" Rollins screamed. "The rest of our team is dead, do you hear me? Dead or scattered! Now get your asses over to the guards on the roads and tell them to radio in backup! There's going to be a wildfire raging through this area! That means local fire departments, police, civilians! That smoke is going to draw in everybody for miles around and they cannot be allowed to reach us! They cannot be exposed to this contagion! It is absolutely imperative that no civilians witness this mission and if anyone tries to slip through the perimeter you tell those guards to shoot to kill! Tell them to bring in helicopters, blockade the roads, do whatever it takes but bring in some backup before this thing kills us all!"

They turned and scrambled away. Benton ran with his hands still tied behind his back, his outrage at his team's mutiny apparently forgotten. Rollins made a mental note of it, however. He would have to look into this mutiny when all this was over, and he would have to send out a special team to apprehend the Ross and Grace boys. Something to worry about another day. For now, he needed to get out of these woods.

He considered following Benton and Turner and the rest, but then dismissed it. He had nothing to gain by doing that. Encountering that bumbling group had served one purpose; it had cleared his head. Now he could think again, instead of wandering through the woods in a daze. He didn't think he had to fear the being that had visited the camp. He would feel it coming long before it got to him, from the way its consciousness shined out of its mind. Another interesting point was that it hadn't killed him outright back at the base camp. He hadn't posed a threat to it, so it had simply knocked him out of the way. It seemed to have an agenda of its own, one that involved Spencer Dale and the infected girl. It had only harmed the ones who stood in the way of it reaching those people. Logically then, he didn't need to worry about it coming after him in the woods.

But he did need to worry about one thing, something that posed a direct threat to him.

Gordon.

Unlike Benton and his crowd, Gordon could be clever and persuasive. He had turned Hicks, once his most trusted soldier, against him. Rollins did not have any evidence that Hicks had decided to follow Gordon, but nothing else explained the amount of time those two had spent together since the night mission. (God knew what *else* Gordon had turned Hicks over to.) Gordon could also be skillful and elusive. Look at how easily he had discovered this operation and infiltrated the base camp. Was Rollins to believe that Gordon had perished in the alien being's attack? He didn't think so.

No, Gordon would look out for his own interests, just as Rollins would himself.

The fact remained that this mission had become a disaster. God knew how many people had been killed. Clearly the plasmid had somehow adapted to this environment and started working a different mutation in the people it infected. One only had to look at the different reactions in its victims. The girl was dying, as Gordon had said the people who had been infected with the plasmid samples from Alpha Site had died. Spencer Dale, with those silver eyes of his, had clearly mutated, but was passive and apparently harmless, judging from the ease with which that imbecile Benton had apprehended him. It was the creature with the thorns that was the real threat. Obviously it was once a person, a teenaged male judging from the height and the clothes, and nothing else explained it but the plasmid. The mutation seemed to have given it psychic abilities, something Rollins had never believed in before today, but the being's attack had eradicated that skepticism in all the time it took for it to burn his base camp to the ground. Rollins had none of Gordon's high-brow scientific training, but it didn't take a Ph.D. to realize this thing was evolving.

But into what?

He didn't know, but while he may not understand exobiology, he did understand politics, and one thing always happened in political circles when things went wrong: finger-pointing. Congressional sub-committees and boards of inquiry always chose a scapegoat they could crucify before the public, and Rollins would be damned if they laid the blame for this farce on him. It had been Gordon who had withheld information from him, Gordon with his swishy limp-wristed arrogance, Gordon and all his snotty lab-rat kind. But if Gordon managed to position himself just right, he would come out of this looking like a hero and the politicians would throw Rollins to the wolves. He couldn't allow that to happen. He had to find Gordon and figure out his plans before any more outside forces came into the picture.

Turning back to the cloud of smoke rising from the fire at base camp, Rollins took a bearing on his position. The road on which they had set up the camp ran east and west, and the sun was now sinking low in the sky to Rollins's left. That meant he had wandered south after regaining consciousness. He could easily backtrack to the road.

Something told him Gordon would stay close to base camp at this point. He would need time to recover and plan his strategy, just as Rollins had. It wouldn't be difficult for someone with Rollins's training and experience to find him. And who knew? Maybe the opportunity would arise to get rid of Gordon permanently. He could always blame it on the thing that had attacked them and let the fire destroy any evidence to the contrary.

Crouching low to the ground, Rollins raced back to the road. The adrenaline rush had come fully upon him now. His heart virtually sang with it. He had a mission and a purpose again, and everything in his life was at stake. Failure was not an option. He hadn't felt so alive in years.

The woods rushed past, and he hadn't gone a hundred yards before he saw the pale gravel road through the trees ahead of him. The pillar of smoke was still to his right, so he was west of the base camp. As he approached the road, he slowed his pace and took extra care with his footsteps so he wouldn't make too much noise as he moved. Always a careful soldier, Rollins would make sure the coast was clear before proceeding into the open.

He stopped at the treeline, listening, and in the distance he heard the sound of voices. It was to his right, closer to base camp. He moved in that direction, watching every step. He jumped over fallen branches and detoured around piles of deadwood, taking care not to step on anything that would snap and reveal his presence. Gradually, as he moved closer, the voices became clearer.

Soon enough he recognized Gordon's dry, neutral tone. He couldn't believe his luck! It seemed like a stroke of divine intervention until he heard the other voice with him. That was Kelly Ross's husky Midwestern twang. Now it made sense. With her in tow, Gordon couldn't sneak past the guards on the road or disappear into the woods, so he taken her just far enough from base camp to get away from the fire. The only thing Rollins didn't understand was why Gordon had rescued her in the first place. The fire would have conveniently eliminated her, and surely a civilian would only slow Gordon down. He must have his reasons, which further compelled Rollins to get close enough to hear what they were saying.

Now he could see them walking down the thin strip of grass that ran down the middle of the road. Gordon had his arm around Kelly's waist, apparently to hold her up, but as Rollins watched she pulled away from him and started walking on her own, rubbing her arms as she did. Gordon had removed her plastic handcuffs, so he didn't plan to keep her as a prisoner. What was his angle? He crouched lower to the ground and moved closer.

Now their voices became audible over the whisper of the wind through the leaves.

"... promised me you'd tell me what this was all about," Kelly said.

"I will," Gordon said. "At this point I think it's important you understand. But first I need you to tell me something. Was a man taken prisoner with you?"

"Maybe," Kelly replied.

"Was a man taken prisoner with you?" Gordon repeated. "Yes or no!"

"Yes!" Kelly said. "Why do you want to know? He hasn't done anything. He isn't a threat to anyone!"

"That's yet to be determined," Gordon said.

Now Rollins was close enough to see them. He hid behind a tangle of briars and watched them as they walked together.

"What's his name?" Gordon asked Kelly.

"You can't possibly expect me to trust you," Kelly replied. "Do you really think I'm that stupid?"

"I know you're not stupid," Gordon said. "And I know you are intelligent enough to recognize when someone is trying to help you. I need to know who that man is because he may be infected with something very dangerous, more dangerous you can imagine. Now what is his name?"

A long pause, and then Kelly said, "You know his name."

"I'm sorry," Gordon said, "but I don't."

"Sure you do. That Sergeant Rollins knew both of our names."

"Sergeant Rollins and I have not had an opportunity to share much information recently," Gordon said. "But if we're going to save your friend, I need you to open up a little. I promise I'll do the same for you."

Well, aren't you the little diplomat, Rollins thought. *I bet you could charm that sweet thing right out of her panties, if you were into that.*

Kelly sighed, a rather hopeless sound. Rollins judged it was a sound she made quite often. "His name is Spencer Dale," she said. "He's a mechanic over in town."

"Do you know why we're interested in him?" Gordon said.

"Well, you just said he was infected with something."

"But do you believe me?"

Kelly said nothing, but she nodded.

"What have you seen?"

Again, silence from Kelly, but it was not mistrustful. It was a thoughtful silence, and Gordon waited it out. Rollins felt disgusted with him. If he were down there alone with that woman, he would have smacked the information he needed out of her, especially with the stakes so high.

Finally Kelly spoke. "Something attacked you while I was locked up in that trailer. Is that right?"

"Yes," Gordon said.

"What was it?"

"I honestly don't know for sure," Gordon said. "But it's related to the thing that has infected your friend. That's why I need to know what you saw while you were locked up with him."

Another pause. Once more Gordon waited it out while the flames from their base camp rose higher into the sky.

"His eyes," Kelly said finally. "They ... they changed."

"How did they change?"

"They turned silver," Kelly said. "All the little capillaries changed first, then his pupils. Does that mean anything to you?"

"I think so. I can't explain the color change, but I've seen silver fluid form in cells infected by this organism."

"There was more though," Kelly said.

"What?"

"*He* changed," she said. "Does that make sense? Everything about him changed. It was like I was locked in that room with ... a thing. Something that wasn't even human."

"That I do understand," Gordon said. "I saw him walking away. What about the girl? What's her name?"

Again, Kelly paused. This seemed like a moment of truth to Rollins. He had not been able to get the girl's name out of Ross or her boyfriend. Now he would see if Gordon could do it.

"I don't know her name," Kelly said. "Her first name is Rachel, but I haven't had a chance to learn her last name."

Rollins exhaled a low breath to still his anger.

"Do you know how long she's been sick?" Gordon asked.

Kelly shook her head. "Not for sure, but I just saw her a few days back and she wasn't sick then. I guess she and Spencer have the same thing?"

"I think so, yes," said Gordon.

"I've told you what I know," Kelly said. "Now you do your part. What's wrong with Rachel and Spencer? What is all this about?"

Gordon paused to collect his thoughts, a habit which had always irritated Rollins. Gordon sighed, then seemed to make a decision. Sometimes people make certain gestures when they do that in silence; they nod their heads a bit and square their shoulders. Gordon did this now, and then he raised his eyes to Kelly.

"What I'm about to tell you is extremely classified information," he said. "Things some of the more shadowy branches of our government would kill to keep secret. I wouldn't draw you into this if it wasn't absolutely necessary, but everyone else on my team is missing or dead. If we're going to save Spencer and Rachel, I need you to help me. So for their sake and our own, I need to know if I can trust you with this, because if this goes beyond the two of us it will mean both our lives. Can you keep this secret?"

Hidden among the trees and listening, Rollins tensed. *He can't possibly mean to tell her! That's treason!* Surprisingly he felt no outrage at all. Rather he felt a kind of liberating, soaring happiness. This was his chance! He could storm out of the woods right now and put a stop to this, but if he waited he could catch Gordon in the act of leaking classified information. At Red Level, that meant he could administer field discipline right then and there. The kind of discipline that consisted of a bullet to the brain. Then he would be free of Gordon forever, and praised as a hero for it. He decided to wait.

"I won't tell," Kelly Ross said. "If it'll help Spencer and Rachel, then I swear I won't tell anyone."

Gordon nodded, and then began to commit treason.

"About a year ago, a meteor fell to earth," he said. "It landed in east Africa, near the border of Kenya and Tanzania. It didn't get much media attention at the time and only attracted a few meteorite hunters and astronomy buffs. The whole thing was forgotten after a few weeks. Not long after that, about a month to be exact, the local hospitals started getting large numbers of patients coming in suffering from sudden onsets of brain cancer."

"We had a meteor land here just last month," Kelly interjected. "It started the forest fire that burned down the Brooks farm. You think this was similar thing?"

Gordon nodded.

"And something was in the meteorite that caused cancer?" Kelly asked.

"In a way, yes," Gordon said. "I was stationed at a military base in the area and doing some volunteer work at the local hospital. While all these patients were coming down with cancer, we started hearing an unusually large number of reports of animal attacks coming out of the same area. Specifically attacks by hyenas. Local hunters tried to kill them off, but the hyenas turned out to be extremely difficult to kill. They no longer behaved like animals. They acted like they understood what the hunters were trying to do and were figuring out ways to avoid them, to circumvent their traps, or even the turn the tables and kill the hunters themselves.

"In every attack," Gordon went on, "the hyenas broke open their victims' skulls and consumed the brain tissue."

Kelly flinched in revulsion.

"Finally some local officials asked the U.S. embassy for help, and a team of American soldiers stationed in Kenya was sent out to do the job. I was with them. It was supposed to be a simple operation, just go out and hunt down some wild animals that had turned into man-eaters, but it turned out to be so much more."

Kelly listened in silence, letting the tale unfold. Rollins listened as well, the memory of Africa softening his anger a bit, as Gordon's words took him back.

"We hunted the hyenas at night, as they're nocturnal animals, and we found them at the exact spot where the meteor landed, in the middle of the Kenyan bush veldt. They were circling the impact crater and making these strange vocalizations. A hyena's laugh is already an eerie sound, but the laughter of these hyenas sounded almost like words. Strange random words that didn't make any logical sense. While they paced around the crater they would shake their heads constantly, like their heads were hurting them. It's hard to describe their behavior, but it was like they were looking for something that should have been inside the crater, but wasn't.

"Anyway, our team went in and slaughtered them. The hyenas put up almost no resistance, which was strange considering that they had been so cunning in avoiding the local hunters, but I think by this time the mutation had reached its limit with them. An essential component that they needed for things to go further was missing in their environment."

Now Kelly interrupted. "The mutation?"

"Right, you're not familiar," Gordon said. "Sorry, I forgot. A mutation caused the hyenas' unusual behavior. We discovered it after we took some of the carcasses back to our lab to study them."

"The thing that was in the meteor," Kelly said, "that caused cancer in people, was that what made the hyenas mutate?"

"Yes," Gordon said. "We dissected the brains of the hyenas and found some unusual growth in the areas associated with memory."

"Was it like the tumors you found in the people?"

"Similar, but not as disorganized as a tumor," Gordon said. "We decided to take a look at the hyena's DNA, but when we tried to sequence it, we found some gaps in our results. These kinds of gaps are always associated with a microscopic life form inside the cell, called a plasmid."

Gordon then explained what a plasmid was, and how this particular specimen traveled into the brains cells of the animals it infected through a chain of transport bacteria and viruses. He went on to explain how they were never able to sequence the plasmid itself because of the unique mutation it caused in the bacteria it infected that prevented them from dividing, so they could never make enough copies of the plasmid to run through the machine that would have sequenced its DNA.

"So this is what you think has infected Spencer and Rachel?" Kelly asked. "This plasmid thing?"

"Yes," Gordon said, "It was only recently that we were able to sequence it, because the plasmid itself has now undergone a dramatic mutation."

"You said the people who got it in Africa all died of brain cancer. Does that mean Spencer and Rachel …?"

"Have cancer? No. Remember, the plasmid has mutated, and I don't think it has only done it once. Those infected hyenas were looking for something, and now I think I know what it was."

"What?" Kelly asked.

"The plasmid lives in animal cells," Gordon said. "But it requires a plant host to make copies of itself. We don't yet know why, but the plasmid can only undergo division inside plant cells. I don't think a species of plantlife compatible with the plasmid was available in Africa, but I know it has found that species here. We've obtained some cell samples from the infected tree, but they're so altered now we can't figure out which species it is."

"The mutated animals were looking for an infected tree," Kelly said, working through all this as best as she could. "Why? If they're already infected, why do they need to go back to something that is making more copies of the plasmid?"

"Think of ants and bees," Gordon said. "They have workers tending to the well-being of their queen. I think the infected animals are like that for the tree. They're tending it, keeping it safe, and providing optimal conditions for it to grow. Those hyenas were looking for something to protect, but couldn't find it."

"But how does that explain why it caused cancer in the Africans and not in Spencer and Rachel?"

"Because the plasmid itself is mutating," Gordon said. "It doesn't benefit the plasmid for its hosts to die. I think this is another reason why the infected animals consume brain tissue. A few nights back we sent a team out to the Brooks farm, where the infected tree is growing, and we witnessed the birth of a pair of highly mutated cats that are living on the tree itself. They also consume brain tissue. I think they may be part of a food chain that delivers proteins from the brain tissue to the tree. The tree then adapts the plasmids it's manufacturing to be more compatible with terrestrial organisms."

Kelly rubbed her forehead in confusion. Too much had happened all at once for her to take in. "I'm sorry. I just don't understand this."

"This of it this way," Gordon said. "Rachel was infected first, and she's sick, nearly dying. Spencer became infected next, and he seems to be doing much better than Rachel. A third person was infected as well, and we have just witnessed what that person is now capable of."

Turning, Gordon drew Kelly's gaze to the massive column smoke rising into the evening sky.

"Did you see it?" Gordon asked.

Kelly covered her mouth with her hand and closed her eyes, but she nodded.

"And did you feel it as well?" Gordon continued. "The force of its mind? You did, didn't you?"

Kelly didn't respond.

"Who is Jack, Kelly?" Gordon said. "You were saying his name in the trailer. Who's Jack?"

"I saw it!" Kelly snapped. Audible pain was in her voice. "I saw it and I felt it! That's all you need to know!"

Gordon nodded. "All right. I think that third person represents the ultimate evolution of the plasmid, a kind of goal it's trying to reach using the genetic tools available in this environment."

"How could it do this?" Kelly said. "It's just a germ! A little loop of DNA. How is that possible?"

"We don't fully understand it yet," Gordon said. "But I think the key lies in the part of the brain the plasmid infects. A part called the hippocampus, where memories are processed."

"Memories?" Kelly said.

"Do you know how we make memories?" Gordon asked.

"You mean other than just by living?" Kelly replied. "No. I didn't think anybody knew."

"We don't, not really," Gordon said. "But we do know what goes on in our brains cells as our minds accumulate memories. Have you ever heard of a synapse?"

"Yes I know what a synapse is!" Kelly snapped. "I don't have much schooling, but I do own a T.V. I watch those documentaries on public television. A synapse is like a gap between two brain cells, where an electric spark jumps across."

"Right," Gordon said. "More or less. Each of our brain cells have hundreds of these synaptic connections on them. And somehow, for some reason we don't fully understand, each of those synapses corresponds to a memory."

"A synapse *is* a memory?" Kelly repeated.

"In a way, yes," Gordon said. "Experiments have shown that new synapses form in our brains every time we have an experience that leaves a lasting memory. Now, our brain cells are supported by a network of supportive glial cells, and the whole thing is swimming in a bath of calcium ions, all of this in the brain pan of our skulls. When the synapse fires and that electric current hits the neuron, the surface of the neuron depolarizes, sending calcium ions flooding into the cell. Those calcium ions set off a chain of chemical reactions like a row of dominos that goes all the way down to the DNA at the center of the cell. When the DNA gets hit by the enzyme made from those reactions, it releases proteins that travel back to the surface of the cell and strengthen the synapse, making it permanent and creating a lasting memory."

"The DNA makes the memory last?" Kelly said.

"The proteins it creates makes them last, yes. This was an incredible discovery. It was a direct link between DNA and memories. People have debated for years whether it's nature or nurture that creates our personalities. Now we know it is a measure of both. Memories come in from the outside, and those experiences define who we are, but they are processed and strengthened through our DNA, which is a kind of lens through which we see those memories. Through this balancing act, the people we are emerge."

"The plasmid," Kelly said, her voice low and thoughtful. "It's made of DNA. Is it … hijacking this process?"

"Exactly. When the synapse kicks off that chemical chain reaction that leads to the DNA, the plasmid catches those enzymes first, and releases its own proteins. These proteins cause the growth of new synapses in the brain cells, which creates memories the infected individual has never personally experienced."

"But you said this plasmid fell to earth on a meteor," Kelly said. "So the memories it's creating, they …" She trailed off, but Gordon finished the sentence for her.

"They are not of this Earth," Gordon said. "Think where this leads, Kelly. The hippocampus processes those memories and moves them to the cerebral cortex for storage, which is connected to every other part of the brain, parts that control consciousness, personality, identity. Our memories define who we are. Take them away and replace them, and the result is an entirely different person. This plasmid does not simply create new memories. It creates a new consciousness in the people it infects, a consciousness completely alien to this world. This isn't just an infection. This is possession. It's not an epidemic. It's an *invasion*."

Concealed within the cover of the woods, Rollins silently took the safety off his pistol and prepared to move in.

Kelly couldn't respond. It was much too much, too stunning, too shocking for her to immediately accept. This thing had Spencer. It had Rachel. This unearthly thing was loose in her hometown, a place where the most exciting thing to happen in the last ten years was the opening of the boat dealership off the main drag.

Finally she said the first thing that came to mind. "What do they want?"

"What do you mean?" Gordon asked.

"You said this is an invasion," Kelly said. "They must have a purpose to it. What do they want?"

He looked at her as if she had just asked something incredibly obvious.

"They want what every organism wants," he replied. "To reproduce."

"What does that—?" She was interrupted by Rollins stumbling into the road. Crashing through the brush and stepping on sticks, he staggered towards them with his head down, the bloody side facing out for them to see. He clutched himself around his middle as if he was hurt, keeping the pistol concealed under his arm.

"Help me!" Rollins cried. "Oh god, it hurts! You have to help me!"

Gordon and the Ross woman came right up to him, looking all concerned, just as he'd planned. They reached out to catch him when he made it look like he might fall. When they got close enough, Rollins whipped out the gun.

"Your last mistake, Gordon!" Rollins said. "You just leaked classified information. Consider yourself plugged." He grinned like a wolf at this *bon mot*. All this time Gordon had flaunted his higher security clearance, his far greater knowledge of the contagion, and now Rollins had caught him throwing it all away. This could not have worked out in a better, more *poetic*, way.

He squeezed the trigger.

Gordon spun.

It happened so quickly that neither Kelly nor Rollins registered it until after it was over. Suddenly Gordon had Rollins's gun in his left hand. He had snatched it when he spun around. Rollins's hands hovered in the air for a moment, still in the same position they had been in when Gordon had taken the gun, and then they slowly fell to his sides. All three of them stood in silence for a moment as they tried to understand what had just happened. They stood in a roughly triangular formation, with Gordon and Rollins facing each other and Kelly standing off to the side, looking rather confused. Rollins stared at Gordon, blinking in surprise.

Finally Kelly could no longer remain silent. This situation was so awkward that she didn't know what to say. Finally she just said the first thing that came to mind.

"Are you all right?"

"What?" Rollins said. As he turned his head to look at her, a cut across his throat gaped open. Blood sprayed onto the dry gravel road.

Without taking his eyes off Rollins, Gordon put the curved hunting knife in his right hand back into the sheath on his belt.

Kelly screamed in shock, stumbling backwards with her hands over her mouth. Gordon didn't move at all. He only watched as Rollins raised his hands to his neck. Blood covered both of his palms in seconds. Rollins looked at them with eyes so wide that the whites showed all the way around the pupils.

The sides of the cut were so perfect and smooth that it wasn't visible until Rollins opened it up by turning his head. An amazing flow of blood came out of it. He began to choke and sputter, sending blood spraying out of his mouth as well as his neck, and Gordon had to step back to keep from getting hit by it.

Rollins fell to his knees as the blood poured down the front of his shirt, onto his pants and then onto the ground. The sheer quantity of it was shocking. Kelly couldn't remember how much blood a human body could hold, but it seemed like Rollins had an endless supply. A slowly growing pool started to form around him.

Rollins reached out to Gordon with one blood-soaked hand as he tried in vain to cover the cut on his neck with his other hand. Blood streamed out from between his fingers. Gordon watched Rollins reach out to him, but made no move to help. His expression, as always, remained unreadable.

Finally Rollins pitched forward into the bloody dust and gravel. He tried to crawl, but couldn't quite manage it. A final gasp escaped him, and he became still.

Gordon turned to Kelly. She tried to bolt like a deer, but he overcame her with his unearthly quickness. He took her by the arms gently, but firmly. She could not escape his grasp.

"Kelly!" Gordon said. "Kelly, listen to me! Don't run!"

He might as well have told an eagle not to fly. Kelly strained with all her might against his grip, the wings of panic battering against the walls of her mind.

"I'm sorry you had to see that, Kelly," Gordon said. "I wouldn't have done it if it wasn't absolutely necessary. Rollins would have never let you go back to your normal life. He would never let a civilian that had witnessed our mission go free. Do you understand what I'm telling you, Kelly? *He would have made you disappear.* You, Rachel, Spencer, all of you, so no one would ever know what happened here today."

Kelly could only stare back at him. His grip on her arms did not yet loosen.

"I'm going to let you go now," Gordon said, "and you can walk away if that is what you feel you need to do. I won't stop you. You can find your son and pick up your lives again as if none of this had happened. But I will tell you that I can't save Spencer and Rachel alone. Right now they are under the control of the thing that destroyed our base camp. We may still be able to rescue them, but it's too much for one person. So I'm asking you to help me."

"My son needs me," Kelly managed to say. "I can't put myself at risk. I'm the only one he's got."

Gordon nodded. "I understand. I'll do what I have to do then."

He let her go. She nearly fell to the ground, so much of the strength had gone out of her legs, but she managed to keep standing somehow, as she had done throughout her entire life.

"What will you have to do?" she asked.

"This organism has to be destroyed," he replied. "Look at what it has done so far. It has enslaved three human beings to an alien will. Imagine what could happen if it spreads. I can't allow that. If that means I have to sacrifice Rachel and Spencer in order to save millions of others, then that is what I will do."

The cold, unbending logic of his mind chilled her right down to her heart's blood.

"But if I help you, then you could save them?" Kelly asked.

"If they can be subdued," Gordon said. "And if it's possible to treat them, then yes."

"How can you treat them for an infection of memories?"

"I don't have any idea," Gordon replied. "I'm only choosing to believe there is a way."

Kelly stared into Gordon's slate-colored eyes. All the values she had been taught her entire life battled inside of her. If she went with Gordon and died, she would make her son an orphan. If she turned her back on Rachel and Spencer, she would have to live with it for the rest of her life.

She remembered all the hope she had felt with Spencer. She remembered her concern for Rachel, alone and adrift in the forest, and how she had wondered, *Where is her mother?*

She couldn't work out all the possible consequences in her mind, so she followed the advice of her heart.

"I'll go with you," Kelly said.

Gordon nodded. "All right. We'd better hurry then. We don't have much time."

23

The Breeding Tree

Through the woods, over the gulley, past the vine-draped maple and the old locust tree, the trio walked.

The male took careful steps. A lifetime of human memories told him how to use this body, but he was not infallible. Too much depended on the three of them reaching their sacred clearing. He had not yet perfectly adapted to this world; the tree had not had enough time to work its changes in them before its life cycle neared its peak, and so the operation of this organism's mind and body still felt strange to him, a situation ripe for mistakes. But his was not the most difficult task.

He looked down at the child in his arms, the dark-haired human girl. She had received the least evolved form of their plasmid, and so the Motherworld's third avatar had not been able to fully form in her. This was a weakness that could be their undoing.

The male looked to the female walking beside him, though she wore the body of an adolescent human male. She had grown from the most evolved form of the plasmid; she even wore the tree's blessed thorns, but even she had developed problems with her host body. The massive energies she wielded were wasting away the host, for the human body could not channel such power without damaging itself. Now she had reined in that power, but some of it still seeped out of her and shook the branches of the trees around them, sending down showers of leaves.

The male called out to the female in the strange radio voice they had developed to communicate, an offshoot of their power to hear the stars. It still felt awkward and uncomfortable to him, and he missed the familiar chemical language of home.

The third sex is dying, said the male, indicating the child host body in his arms. *Its memories are tainted by some long-ago sin.*

We must attempt the joining regardless, replied the female. *There is no time left to find another host that will grow the third sex.*

And if it cannot catalyze the memories? asked the male.

Then we will find another way, said the female. *At every step in this process we have encountered obstacles, and at every step we have overcome them. This will be no different.*

Silence descended between them. They walked on, and all around them the worker cats scampered, circled, and muttered.

Soon they reached the sacred clearing. Here the remainder of the worker cats had stayed to protect the tree. The great swarm of them covered the burnt ground in a living sea of writhing feline bodies.

In center of them stood the tree. It had now grown to prodigious height and girth. The male could not embrace it within the span of his host body's arms, even without the clusters of foot-long thorns bristling from all sides of it. The tree's long limbs stretched over the clearing, dangling its tassels of leaves. The tree itself shuddered and groaned. Its rate of growth had increased, and now it was so large that it was becoming cumbersome. Soon gravity would pull it down, but before that happened they would fulfill the tree's great purpose: to spread their kind through this world.

The breeder drones crawled down from the upper branches and perched on the thick lower limbs to watch the three of them approach. The drones could now move nimbly among the thorns, and when they laid eyes on the trio, their jaws spread into an expression almost like a smile.

The sea of cats parted as they entered the clearing. The female did not need to use her great power to make them move. Their communal consciousness knew they must not hinder the trio's progress. This was the fruit of all their labors.

The trio approached the tree. With a hiss, the two breeder drones separated, and moved to opposite sides of the tree to wait for the process to begin.

Integrating themselves into the organisms of this world had been a difficult and painful process. They had changed their fundamental structure and still disparities existed. Lethal complications had arisen in both the terrestrial organisms and the children of the Motherworld. Now they must attempt something that had never been done, something that in terms of complexity made all the other adaptations they had devised so far pale in comparison.

They had to come together within the bodies of their hosts, and create their child of memory once more. This time it would have the combined strength of all three of its parents, with none of the weaknesses. It would become perfect. It would be able to grow their memories with none of the complications its parents had faced, and before it the creatures of this world could offer no resistance.

The female turned to the left side of the tree, while the male went to the right. As the third sex was immature and stunted, it could not compel its host body to walk. Therefore the female used her power to levitate it out of the male's arms and hold it in its place by the tree. When they were all in position, they joined hands. The female compelled the third sex's arms to rise. For a moment the human girl hung there, suspended in the air with her arms outstretched and her eyes closed. As the female took the girl's hand, she felt the life within the host body beginning to fade. It may not survive the joining, but this did not concern her. It did not matter how many terrestrial organisms died, as long as their own children lived.

The male took the hands of the third sex and the female, completing their circle. They needed to hurry. Time was running out, and their enemies were gathering. The breeder drones crouched in their positions, staring into the eyes of the male and female, the radiance of their gaze reflected in their silvery eyes.

Slowly now, carefully, the female summoned her power.

Their communal mind had devoted much thought as to how the joining could be done. The tree had originally created the breeder drones to harvest the genetic material, which would destroy the host bodies. They would gladly sacrifice themselves for the sake of their children, but with their enemies drawing close that would leave only the worker cats to protect their offspring.

Then, after the female emerged in all her strength, they had devised a new plan.

As she summoned the power, the female felt her body's heart begin to pound. The lungs labored to draw in air, and the bodily tissues withered a little more as the power coursed through the nervous system. With every dying cell in her body singing, the female called out to her mates with her mind's voice.

The third sex opened its eyes.

It was here! She felt it, the old consciousness they had known on the Motherworld. It had not failed them at this crucial moment. Encouraged, the female sent her power pulsing through her left hand, into the male.

The veins on the male's face bulged. The skin on his face rippled a bit, and then a red mist began to emanate from his eyes.

Just as the female had taken the substance of memory from her host body's human mother, so she now took it from the male. With exquisite precision and care, the female took out only the proteins from the male they needed to start the process of joining. She could not afford to harm the male or its host body, in case this first attempt failed.

Now a red cloud twined about the male's head, vaporized particles of his mutated brain, taken so carefully as to do minimal harm to the host body or to the mutation that created the male's consciousness. Using all the focus at her disposal, the female kept the cloud together and protected it from airborne contaminants. When she was done removing the brain matter, the veins in the male's face relaxed and the rhythms of his host body grew steady again. She had not harmed the male in removing the memories she needed. Now the next step could begin.

When she felt she had the cloud fully under her control, she made it descend to the face of the third sex.

The cloud flowed through the air like a mist in motion, and condensed on the third sex's skin in droplets like dark red tears. These tears flowed upwards into the eyes of the third sex. The amount of control it took for the female to manipulate the cloud required all the concentration at her command. If she slipped even the tiniest bit, the cloud could become contaminated, or irreparable harm could be done to the third sex, without which the joining could never be completed.

Finally the cloud was completely absorbed into the third sex. The female could at last relax her concentration. Now the waiting began. If the third sex was too weak to catalyze the reaction, the female would not be able to create their plasmid child. They would lose everything.

The third sex hung its head, the long hair of its host obscuring its face. Its sleepy appearance belied the intense chemical reactions taking place within the host body's mind. Its two mates waited, still clasping hands, for a sign. The seconds dragged out. Their cold silver eyes did not show a hint of emotion, but they knew their lives depended on the third sex changing those memories.

They were beings made entirely of memory. Their bodies were the molecules that created memories in the brain. Their entire existence consisted of the remembered experiences of other beings.

But despite this, they had their own memories as well. They retained a sense of the communal consciousness that had existed on the comet they called the Motherworld, from which they had been separated so long ago. If the genes that created these memories were damaged or destroyed, they would cease to exist. This was the crucial role of the third sex in their reproductive cycle. The male provided neural cells from his host body, the raw material of memories. The third sex would then take those neural cells and insert the genes that created the Original

Memory of the Motherworld into their DNA. This DNA was then transferred to the female, who would create the plasmid that would go on to infect another host, and the process would begin again.

But there was a wider range to their life cycle. The female could pass the plasmid on to the breeder drones that cared for the tree. The tree would then absorb the plasmid through their droppings and start manufacturing billions of copies of it, to spread them into the environment.

But even this was not the end.

The tree grew with breathtaking speed, and would soon collapse under its own weight. What would spread their plasmid after it was gone? It was not enough to make just one more tree. The reproductive drive of all life forms pushed them to increase their numbers. No, they needed dozens, hundreds, thousands …

For the third and last time, the third sex raised its head. Not being as evolved as its mates, it could not communicate using their new radio language, but now it wasn't necessary. As they watched, the host body's dark eyes filled with silver.

It was done.

The third sex had successfully transformed the memories. Unable to bear waiting any longer, the female again reached out with her power.

The telepathic link between her and the third sex had grown stronger. Receiving the memories had given the third sex a little more strength. As a result the female could now feel the rhythms of the third sex's host body, such as the flow of its breath and the circulation of its blood. She used this greater sensitivity to draw the substance of memory from the third sex. With exquisite delicacy and care, she guided it through the pathways of the host body, out from the brain that had catalyzed the memories through the channels and passageways of the host body's head.

The sensitivity went both ways. When the female was ready, the third sex exhaled, and a silver mist came out with its breath. The female again used her power to guide and protect the cloud of mist.

Now it was ready for her. Every second of her existence had led to this moment. With her telekinetic power, she drew the cloud of silver mist into herself.

It flowed into her through her host body's eyes, nose, mouth and ears, as fast as she could handle it. She felt it moving in a cold flood through the crevices and cavities of her skull, on its way to the brain.

And then she felt nothing at all. Nothing but the power of the ancient memories.

A bolt of clear whiteness burst through her mind. It felt so clean, so pure. All the hardships they had suffered on this hostile world were forgotten. The pain and discomfort of her host body melted away. In that moment she knew she had fulfilled the purpose of her life. An indescribable sense of relief and joy filled her mind, as she felt the memories take shape. The white light cleared, and through it she saw the Motherworld.

All this time while she and her mates had struggled back into existence, the dim memory of their Motherworld had danced, forever it seemed, just beyond their grasp. The heartbreaking doom she had felt, knowing they were forever separated from Her, had nearly destroyed her will to live. And now, by this miracle, she had returned to the one place where she had felt peace, acceptance, love.

Home.

She heard once more the beautiful Lifesong, deity of the third sex, and the distant chorus of the stars that represented the Celestial Father. Her mates were also reliving this time, transported within their memories, while the joining had connected their minds.

The memory held, trembling, like a bubble of light. Once it had always been this way, all of them joined in one communal consciousness, until forces beyond their control had smashed them apart.

They would stop at nothing to make it like this again.

They could never return to the Motherworld, but they could possess every sentient mind on this planet with Her children. Once more they would be one communal consciousness, and they would bring the paradise of the Motherworld to the Earth.

The transformation would come *now.*

Like a mist clearing, the vision faded from her mind, and she awoke with a renewed sense of purpose. The thorns in her host body's skin bristled with energy. The breeder drones paced in the branches of their tree, anxious, for they could smell that the female was ready. She gathered her power. Her enemies had drawn closer, and she would need every last reserve of strength left in her for the battle to come. She would defend her young to the death.

No longer necessary, she let the male and the third sex fall to the ground. They landed with a thud, and lay there insensate. The joining had severely drained them; indeed they may not recover at all. It was entirely possible their host bodies would not survive, but that no longer mattered. They had served their purpose, and would each live again in one third of the Earth's population after the transformation was completed.

Now she alone stood before the breeding tree. Telekinetic energy vibrated the air around her and kicked up a pall of ashy dust from the ground. She felt the plasmid forming inside her host body's cells, felt the DNA turning in upon itself to form their child of memory. She had set her own reincarnation into motion when she had last created the plasmid back on the Motherworld, and now she had truly and completely come full circle.

She spread her arms wide, as if she would embrace the breeding tree, thorns and all. The breeder drones pranced and hissed among the branches; the worker cats snarled and snapped at each other, all of them could sense it coming. Finally she felt it, the moment had come, it was ready, she had to give the plasmid to the tree now! One of the breeder drones darted forward like a snake to take it from her eyes, but she couldn't wait, and used her power to send it rushing across the air between them like an electric arc. An energized stream of particles flowed out of her eyes, directly into the mouth of the breeder drone. When the stream hit it, the drone froze, transfixed. Its glowing eyes began to flicker and blink. A scream tore through the female's mind, but with all her energy focused on releasing the plasmid she couldn't voice it. Then, far away, she heard the worker cats screaming with their lungs the way she was screaming with her mind, as they released it for her.

The arc of energy coming out of her eyes went on and on, with the breeder drone writhing at the focus of it. It grew so powerful that it lifted the drone into the air, where hung suspended, bathed in white fire. Its long, serpentine body curled and twisted. As the energy reached its peak, it released a hideous scream and exploded.

The drone burst into a red cloud of vaporized blood, flesh, and bone. The arc of energy coming out of the female's eyes snapped off, and she staggered back, reeling with shock.

What had she done?

She had tried too hard. She had only meant to send the plasmid to the breeder drone so it could pass it on to the tree, but she had used too much energy and destroyed the drone. The entire side of the tree was now red with the drone's blood and pulverized remains. The whole army of worker cats stood frozen and still, paralyzed by the shock they felt coming from her.

They would have to try again somehow. The other drone still lived. Weakened as he was, the male might still be able to grow more of the memories, but the third sex could never catalyze them in its current state. It had barely been able to do it the first time; now it was out of the question. All of their struggles, all of their hardships and pain, all for nothing …

A hissing sound reached her ears.

She lifted her eyes, and more. She sent out her mind's awareness. Her enemies had called in reinforcements, but this was not what had drawn her attention.

Looking down, she saw the blood splattered over the side of the tree begin to darken and steam. Soon it started to bubble. Tendrils of white mist rose from it.

The second breeder drone lowered its head from its branch to sniff at the rising fumes. Its long forked tongue flicked out to taste the air.

Could she dare hope ...?

The blood began to seep into the bark of the tree. She could see it spreading beneath the surface, up through the trunk and limbs, out to the branches and the tips of the thorns, a dark red stain circulating through the entire length of the tree, until it reached the leaves, and changed them from green to dark red. The stain spread like a shadow through the tree's foliage.

The tree was absorbing the blood.

The few seconds the fast-growing drone had been exposed to plasmid had been enough. The tree had accepted her blood sacrifice and begun the transformation.

The ground began to tremble. The vibration shuddered up through her feet. The tree's growth, already fast, accelerated. Cracks opened in the parched ground as the tree's roots spread with unnatural speed. The trunk creaked and groaned as its woody body expanded. The leaves rustled, though the air was still.

Then, as the female watched, a pale glow appeared inside the trunk of the tree. At first it looked like the blood stain had started to fade, but it kept growing lighter until the fading of color became a glow, which spread into the bark and the thorns. White light began to shine through the dark blood stain. It looked the same as the light that shined from the eyes of the breeder drones, and traveled the same path through the tree that the blood had traveled, starting at the base and then circulating outwards to the tips of the branches and finally to the leaves, until the entire tree was bathed in silvery white radiance. It grew brighter, filling the clearing with its shine and catching flinty reflections in the eyes of the worker cats that watched in slack-jawed wonder. Soon a corona of bright white fire surrounded the tree, but did not consume it.

It had begun. The transformation was here.

Lifting her telepathic voice, the female broadcast her declaration to the world, and her mental call echoed from the clearing as the cats repeated her words aloud:

THE CHILDREN WILL LIVE!

At the tips of the branches, radiant round buds swelled up, split open, and blossomed into fiery white flowers burning bright, which spread their glowing pistils and prepared to go to seed.

24

Metastasis

Before heading to the clearing, Agent Gordon searched Sergeant Rollins's body.

He crouched next to the dead man, carefully avoiding the pool of blood, and started going through his pockets.

"What are you looking for?" Kelly asked.

"His radio," Gordon replied. "I lost mine during the attack on the camp."

Kelly stood back a ways, clutching her arms. She kept glancing over her shoulder at the fire growing from the ruins of the base camp behind them, and wondered how long it would take for it to spread to her house. The setting sun lined the great tower of smoke with a red glow.

"Found it," Gordon said, pulling a small black radio from a holster on the side of Rollins's belt. Rollins had landed on top of it when he fell and Gordon had to pull the body up to get it out. Kelly had to look away as Gordon handled the corpse. All of this seemed so … so big. So out of her control. Right now it took all of her strength not to break down in a panic and she wondered just how this Agent Gordon expected her to help him when she could barely handle the situation.

Gordon took up the radio and flicked a switch on top of it. A small green light went on next to the switch.

"This is Agent John Gordon," he said into the radio, "Base camp Beta, priority one-alpha-tango, does anyone copy? Over."

He released the switch. For a few maddening seconds only the sound of static came out of the radio's speaker.

"Come on, come on," Gordon whispered. "There has to be somebody left …"

Static, hissing and crackling over the sound of the approaching fire.

"Agent Gordon to Beta Site mission team!" Gordon said into the radio. "Is anyone left alive out there? Over!"

The static continued for a few more seconds and then suddenly cut off. A man's voice came out of the speaker.

"This is Private Turner, Agent Gordon," he said. "I copy, over."

"What is your status and location, Private Turner?" Gordon asked.

"Myself, Private Manderly and Private Benton are in route to the eastern perimeter guards to call in backup."

"Guards must be out of range of the hand radios," Gordon muttered. He spoke into the radio again. "What is the status of Jason Ross and Brad Grace?"

Kelly's ears pricked up. Apparently Rollins had sent those soldiers to pick up her boys. Her stomach seized in anticipation.

"Private Ames took over command of the retrieval mission," Turner replied. "When we left, the boys were in the custody of Marjory Grace. They seemed all right."

A wave of relief washed through Kelly like a cool shower from head to toe. She closed her eyes and silently mouthed, *Thank you, God.*

"Did they display any symptoms?" Gordon asked. "Any signs of fever? Any strange vocalizations or muscle spasms? Did they faint at any point?"

"Nothing obvious, sir," Turner said. "Currently Private Ames is talking with Marjory Grace about setting up testing for them."

"Good," Gordon replied. "Now Private Turner, when you reach the perimeter guards, you are to tell them to relay a message to headquarters. This message has the utmost priority. Tell them to institute Operation Arc Light."

Turner paused for several seconds before replying.

"Agent Gordon, confirm message please," Turner said.

"I repeat," Gordon said, "institute Operation Arc Light, on my authority. Focus on these coordinates. Thirty eight degrees, forty-two hours, twenty-eight point seven one minutes north …"

Gordon rattled off a bunch of numbers. Kelly guessed it was something like latitude and longitude, but he went too fast for her to follow it. This Private Turner, whoever he was, must have been pretty quick to catch it.

The static came back on the speaker after Gordon had finished, and in the background they heard Turner whisper something he probably didn't intend for them to hear.

"Jesus," Turner said. "The Arc Light."

He spoke again, louder this time.

"Message confirmed, Agent Gordon," Turner said. "I will relay. Over."

"Gordon out," Gordon replied.

"Turner out."

Gordon clicked off the radio.

"Time to go," Gordon said. "We don't have much time now. Twenty minutes, maybe thirty at the most."

"What is Operation Arc Light?" Kelly asked. "Is that something I'm allowed to know?"

"Operation Arc Light is a clean-up maneuver," Gordon replied. "It's a last resort to eliminate a disastrous situation, one that could jeopardize the security of the entire nation. Basically the Air Force sends helicopters to the site of the threat and they bomb the place into oblivion."

"And this place they're about to bomb," Kelly said, "is where we're going right now?"

"Yes," Gordon said. "You know it as the Brooks farm. We now have one objective: retrieving Spencer and Rachel. The helicopters can't receive the signal from our hand radios and the perimeter guards are too far away, so we have no way to recall them after Turner gets out of range. Those helicopters will obliterate everyone and everything at those coordinates, no matter who's there, so we need to hurry."

Now the stakes of their circumstances drove home to Kelly, but she still couldn't walk away.

"All right," she said. "Let's go."

They set off together into the forest. To reach it they had to cross the ditch on the south side of the road and go over the barbed-wire fence beyond it. Gordon slipped through the top two wires with ease, and then held the wires apart while Kelly crawled through them. After she made it across, they ran through the trees in the direction of the gully that would take them to the Brooks farm. Kelly struggled to keep up with Gordon. The strange man, who was strange in his sheer ordinariness, had started to make sense to her, as well as her fear-addled mind could make sense of anything right now. He was a mimic.

Every summer day out here in the country she saw insects like walking sticks and katydids, which looked like sticks and leaves so they could blend in with the trees. The rabbits turned white in the wintertime to blend in with the snow. The striped bobcats' dappled fur made them almost impossible to see as they stalked their prey across the sun-dappled forest floor. Animals mimicked their surroundings for safety from predators or to give themselves an advantage in hunting. In their own way, people were no different. Human beings often pretended to be something they're not to give themselves an advantage or to feel safe. This strange Mr. Gordon, secret agent man, made himself look ordinary and unremarkable so he wouldn't attract attention. It was the old camouflage trick.

The woods raced past. The sun had dropped low on the horizon now, and the shadows had lengthened under the trees. The sky above them had gone red. As the smoke spread over the face of the sky, it caught the light from the sunset and held it like crimson clouds ready to rain blood down on them.

Gordon ran through the underbrush like an expert, knowing just where to step to avoid tripping or making too much noise. Again, some of Gordon's qualities reminded Kelly of the local people, this time in the way he moved through the woods. Kelly herself used to run through the woods just as well when she was a teenager, although she had gotten out of practice after she grew up and had kids and didn't have time to go running through the woods for fun anymore. Logically, she knew Gordon's ability to move well through the woods didn't mean he came from this part of the country, but combined with the speech mannerisms she had picked up on when he spoke to her at the store earlier in the day created a familiar impression.

She didn't have time to wonder about it. Right now it took all of her energy to keep up with him. The heavy lifting she did working at the Dollar General didn't help her cardio, and she started to breathe hard after a few hundred yards. She found she still had her skill at moving through the brush though, and didn't stumble or trip even once. It was good to know some things never left you.

They reached the gully. Gordon jumped down into it and took off running in the direction of the Brooks farm. With the clearer path they could move much easier. Gordon raced ahead, and Kelly had to push even harder to keep up with him now that the brush wasn't around to slow him down. Her legs muscles started to burn.

They had backtracked to find the gully, and now the column of smoke from the burning camp was directly behind them. The evening breeze blew most of it to the east, but the acrid smell of it still hung in the air, burning their throats and making their eyes sting. The tears in Kelly's eyes combined with the growing shadows of the evening made it very hard to see. Now she had to struggle to avoid any rocks or tree roots jutting out of the ground that might trip her up. As the light bled away from the land, it grew in the sky. Great cumulonimbus summer clouds floated overhead, and as the sunset progressed they caught the sunlight in a dazzling array of red, gold and orange. Combined with the smoke, the clouds created a sunset more spectacular than anyone had seen in recent years. Darkness spread through the land under this burning sky, except in the clearing where the Brooks farm had once stood.

They saw the light as they drew near the clearing, just after they had passed the old locust tree. Rays of silvery white light shined between the dark silhouettes of the trees. It made it easier to see, although everything around them looked flat and shadowless. It didn't look normal, not at all like healthy yellow sunshine. Under this unearthly white glare the woods looked eerie, unnatural. Ethereal glints of white light caught in a billion fluttering leaves.

They came to the vine-draped maple, like an old photograph fluttering towards her face. Gordon slid to a halt beside it and crouched low beneath the edge of the gulley. Kelly followed suit, being careful not to pass into the view of anything in the clearing that might look their way.

Gordon took his pistol from the holster in the side of his belt opposite the sheath for his hunting knife. He cocked it back to put a bullet in the chamber, then looked Kelly's way.

"We'll keep it quick and simple," he said. "Dash in, grab them, dash out. A swarm of cats is protecting that place, enough to bring down both of us. You'll need a weapon. Here."

He took his hunting knife from its sheath and handed it to her handle first. The small blade did not look very deadly, but Kelly had just seen proof of its sharpness. A curved notch on the flat side of the blade provided a resting spot for her thumb, and the handle fit well in the palm of her hand, so that she could hold it without shaking too much. Right now it was the only thing on her body that wasn't shaking.

"Use the trees for cover until you get to the edge of the clearing," Gordon said, "and then we'll charge into it together. You take the easiest one, probably Rachel, since you don't have a gun. I'll get Spencer and back you up as best as I can. Are you ready?"

She opened her mouth to say yes, but stopped when she heard a low rumbling coming from above them. A steady, beating *thwap thwap thwap* drawing closer by the second. Gordon heard it too, and as he lifted his eyes upwards a great wind arose and whipped through the branches of the trees. It felt like a tornado had suddenly sprung up around them. The roar grew louder, became something almost like a scream, and then a shadow passed over them across the red sky, the black angular silhouette of a helicopter with its blades chopping through the air. It was headed directly towards the clearing.

Kelly wondered how it had gotten here so fast. Gordon had said they would have twenty or thirty minutes. Had that much time already passed? More? Time seemed to be slipping away from them; events had started to accelerate, moving faster and faster towards their inevitable conclusion. She had to suck it up and learn how to cope before everything blew up around them.

She and Gordon exchanged a glance, knowing what the helicopters meant to do.

"Hurry," Gordon said, and scrambled out of the gully with Kelly following close behind.

She struggled to climb up the friable, crumbling slope. Gordon made it up in two nimble leaps. Kelly felt clumsy and awkward with only one free hand. What was she thinking, doing this? She would get her stupid self killed-

She made it out of the gulley and had just regained her feet when she looked up and saw the clearing.

She froze in wonder.

It was the most beautiful thing she had ever seen.

A burning tree stood in the middle of the clearing. Bright white fire covered it from roots to branches. The fire did not crawl over the tree like someone had doused it in gasoline and thrown a match on it. Rather the fire seemed to come out of the tree itself, like it was seething outwards through the bark and the leaves and the thousands upon thousands of glittering thorns.

Sometimes in the winter when she got the fire going nice and strong in her woodstove, the intense heat would cause the logs to go up in a similar way, all quick and hot. The wood itself glowed so brightly as the fire came out of it that you couldn't see it until the edges of the flames got a few inches away from the wood. The effect was a glowing hot coal sheathed in semi-transparent fire.

The burning tree was like that, except this fire had no heat. It glowed so brightly she could barely look at it. The light was pure white, not a trace of red or blue within it. She could make out each part of the tree in perfect detail, every glowing thorn, branch, and leaf. It looked like a tree sculpted out of fiercely glowing alabaster, surrounded by a nimbus of fire.

The fire swirled around the trunk and up into the branches, where it seethed and flared like the top of a torch. Although she was close enough to feel the heat that would naturally come from such a large fire, the wind coming out of the clearing felt cool and pleasant, an evening breeze in summer. It seemed like a miracle, this beautiful glowing thing, this fire that could not burn. Kelly felt drawn to it, like a moth. She was not the first. A dark form stood in front of the tree with its arms outstretched, silhouetted by the fire's bright light. All around the base of the tree circled hundreds of cats, flowing around the charred columns. The cats chattered in excitement, and words drifted to her on the breeze.

"... *one mind* ..."

"*darkness great* ..."

       "... *home home* ..."

"... children will children live ..."

The scene was so eerie and beautiful, almost hypnotic, that Kelly had started to walk towards the clearing before she even realized she was doing it. She might have strolled right into crowd of cats if two more helicopters hadn't roared by overhead, lashing the woods with their wind and noise, startling her out of her reverie.

She shrieked in surprise, and almost fell over when the wind hit her. The helicopters must have been flying very low. Dust, leaves, and debris pelted her skin.

Suddenly Gordon appeared beside her, holding one of her arms to keep her up.

"They're going to firebomb this entire area," he said. "That tree will make an easy target with all the light it's putting out. They'll be able to see it for miles. Hurry!"

They dashed forward, keeping low, and stopped when they reached the edge of the clearing. Taking shelter in the shadow of a good-sized heaven tree, Gordon paused to weigh their options.

"We need to take the most direct way in," he whispered. "The cats look agitated. I can tell you from experience that they are very protective of that tree. Even if we get past them, we'll have to worry about ... that."

He nodded towards dark thorn-riddled being standing in front of the tree, its arms thrown out in ecstasy.

Kelly nodded, remembering the hellish destruction it had brought down on the base camp.

"What do we do if it sees us?" she asked.

"At the base camp, it didn't harm anyone that wasn't a direct threat to it," Gordon said. "It left that to the cats. Try to stay out of its line of sight. We'll go in at an angle to it, so the tree will give us some cover."

"Are you sure it will ignore us?" Kelly said.

"No."

This did not make her feel any better.

"Do you see Spencer and Rachel?" Gordon asked.

She scanned the clearing, but couldn't see them anywhere.

Suddenly the helicopters swooped over the clearing again. At the sight of the burning tree they had fallen back to examine the scene at a greater distance. Now that they had surveyed their target, they were flying in for the kill.

As they approached, the cats in the clearing screamed and clawed at the sky, climbing on top of each other like they would try to swipe the helicopters out of the air. A gap opened in the crowd of them as they moved, and Kelly caught a glimpse of a white arm against the dark ground, lying at the base of the tree.

"There," she whispered, pointing. "I see Rachel. God, she's right at the base of the tree, right next to that thing!"

"Spencer must be close by," Gordon said. "All right, we should go in. The helicopters will start firing any second now. You follow behind me. I'll try to cut a way through for you."

They got up and moved to enter the clearing. They had to circle around a ways before they got to an angle where the tree would hide their approach. Once Gordon felt they had a safe way in, he nodded, and together they charged into the clearing.

They would never know if the helicopters set off the thorn-covered being or if they did it themselves by crossing into its territory. Regardless, as they charged into the clearing a helicopter roared in at almost exactly the same time, no more than a few hundred yards over their heads. They also never found out why the pilot of the helicopter came in so close, although more than likely he just wanted to get a closer look at the damnedest thing he had ever seen in his life. He and his fellow pilots had no idea of the danger they were in.

At that moment, the being lowered its arms, turned around … and once more sent out the terrible presence of its mind.

A sense of fierce protectiveness broadcast through the clearing like a radio signal, followed by a burst of outrage. Above it all, a roaring, screaming fury.

GO AWAY!

The message hit them as a feeling without words, a kind of emotional wave. A wave of physical force went out at the same time, driving home its point. The force of it knocked Kelly and Gordon off their feet and sent them flying out of the clearing before they had taken a second step inside. The helicopter's blades screeched, it spun a few times as its pilot struggled to get it back under control, until it finally banked upwards and moved to a higher altitude to circle the clearing with the other choppers.

Branches slapped against Kelly's back as she flew. She hit the ground at a skid, rolled a few times, and came to rest in a tangle of briars. She lay there for a few seconds, stunned, struggling to catch her breath. She heard Gordon groaning a few yards away. The brush crackled as he moved around. She tried to get up but her arms and legs were having none of it. It had felt a like freight train padded with mattresses had struck her, powerful but not sharp. For a second she wondered why it had not killed her and Gordon outright, until she realized it must have used most of its power to deflect the helicopter.

Gordon crawled over to her. "Are you all right?"

"I ... I think so," she said. Nothing felt broken, but she still couldn't quite move.

"Come on," he said. "We've got to hurry."

He grabbed her by the arm and pulled her into a sitting position. All the muscles in her back and abdomen clenched in objection. She screamed as the cramps pounded through her.

"I'm sorry, Kelly," Gordon said. "But if we don't move we'll be right in the—"

A loud boom interrupted him. Looking up, they saw one of the helicopters hovering over the clearing like a giant black insect. A puff of smoke came out of the back of it. It had just fired a missile.

"Back in the gulley!" Gordon shouted. "Move!"

Before she even realized it, Gordon had his arm around her waist and was hauling her backwards. His strength stunned her. He had lifted her right into the air. The pressure caught her tight across her middle. For a minute, it simulated the kind of cramp she had felt when she had gone into labor with Jason, and then the pain subsided as Gordon pulled her ahead of him and the new position eased the pressure. At first she thought he was pushing her forward to make her run, and then she realized he had put himself between her and the explosion that would come when the missile hit the ground.

They didn't make it to the gulley. They didn't even come close. The missile moved much faster than they did, and when it hit its target the sound of the explosion rolled through the woods like a peal of thunder.

Kelly screamed, whirling around. They had failed Spencer and Rachel; the explosion had to have blown them to pieces. But when she turned she saw that no such thing had happened. The tree still stood, burning bright, in the center of its clearing. The cats still swarmed and screamed around it. Everything was the same, except that now an enormous transparent sphere had enclosed the entire clearing, like a giant dome. A fiery explosion was spreading across the outer surface where the missile had struck it. Ripples went through the sphere of force, so that it vibrated like a bell. The force field looked much brighter on the side the missile had hit than it did on the opposite side, but as the explosion faded the dome seemed to equalize, and became the same brightness all over.

The field radiated directly from the thorn-covered being.

Gordon set Kelly down on her feet. "Can you walk?"

"Yes," she said. Her muscles, after cramping in shock initially, had started to limber up again. "I'll be okay."

He nodded and walked back to the edge of the clearing, stopping when he reached the transparent barrier. Kelly followed him. Her legs still felt a little shaky, but not as bad as before. She and Gordon stared in wonder at the transparent barrier now surrounding the clearing. Cautiously, she put out her hand to touch it.

She had expected it to feel smooth, like glass, judging from its appearance, but it didn't feel like that at all. It felt almost elastic, like pressing her hand into a plastic sheet that would stretch to a certain point, but no further. It blocked sound as well. The voices of the cats now sounded muffled and distant, as if they were underwater.

"What do we do now?" she asked. From this angle, they could see both Spencer and Rachel lying unconscious at the base of the tree. The cats had moved to the opposite side of the clearing, where the missile had hit the barrier. Bizarrely, they had gone closer to the source of danger rather than further away.

Gordon scanned the barrier, his flint-colored eyes hard and sharp. He looked down, noting how the field parted the grass at the edge of the clearing. Branches that had overhung it had burst in half when barrier came up. The broken limbs hung white, splintery and ragged.

Inside the clearing, the thorn-covered being stood with its back to them, preoccupied with the circling helicopters.

"Can you get in?" Kelly pressed. They were running out of time. Something was happening to the tree. Among the flames moving through its branches, several points of light had appeared.

"That barrier stopped a missile," Gordon said. "We can't force our way in. We—"

A pair of loud booms interrupted him. Looking up they saw two more helicopters had fired missiles. They streaked through the air, leaving trails of smoke behind them.

Kelly moved to run, but Gordon grabbed her arm.

"Wait," he said.

"What do you mean, wait?" Kelly cried. "They're coming right at us!"

"We've got the barrier in front of us, just wait!" Gordon said.

The missiles exploded against the barrier, sending waves rippling through it. At the same moment, Gordon shoved his right hand against the barrier, holding onto Kelly with his left.

At first she could still feel the barrier resisting them, pushing them back with steady implacable force. But as soon as the missiles hit, the field gave, just a little bit, and the two of them moved a little further inward than they did before.

The moment of weakness passed, and the field re-established itself, pushing Kelly and Gordon back as it did. But they had felt it give, no question about it.

"It gets weaker on the side opposite the explosion," Gordon said. "It must have to divert its force to hold back the missiles. Let's wait for the next shot."

Kelly stared at Gordon, dumbfounded. "And what if they circle around to our side for the next shot?"

"We'll just have to adapt as the situation changes," Gordon replied.

Kelly did not have time to weigh her options or consider her next move. The helicopters started to circle the clearing at a lower altitude, and much faster. They roared over their heads, stirring up the wind like a tornado. Leaves and dust flew across the forest floor, hitting Kelly and Gordon in the face like slapping hands. The dust got in Kelly's eyes and made them water. Her vision doubled; now the forest seemed twice as thick, twice as dark, twice as frightening. The sunset-reddened clouds above them swirled together, making it seem like she was standing at the bottom of an ocean of blood. She shielded her eyes and turned her head away from the wind, so that she faced the barrier. The scene inside looked twisted and magnified now, but after blinking away her tears she got a clear sight of the most visible object inside the clearing, the burning tree. The points of light in the branches had grown brighter; now she could almost make out the shapes inside the glowing starlight objects. They looked like ... like ...

"They're coming around!" Gordon shouted over the wind. "Get ready!"

"Wait!" Kelly shouted, but she couldn't even hear herself. A helicopter swooped by overheard, so low the wind nearly bowled them over. It coursed to the west and banked across the face of the sunset, a dark insectile silhouette. Two more helicopters flew in from the north and south to join it. The three of them now bore down on the clearing together.

"Get ready!" Gordon repeated. His legs tensed, and his grip on her arm did not weaken. They could hear the muffled screams of the cats inside the barrier as they faced the approaching helicopters. A kind of electric tension had developed in the air that made the hair on the backs of their necks stand up like it did during a thunderstorm before the lightning strikes. It radiated directly from the entity in the clearing as it gathered its power to defend itself.

All three helicopters fired. This time they each fired two, one from each launcher on the sides of the helicopters. The six missiles shot straight towards the clearing.

"*Now!*" Gordon shouted and yanked her forward.

As they jumped into the barrier, she felt the same resistance pushing her back, firm and resolute. But less than a second after they jumped she heard the missiles strike the barrier, six explosions in quick succession, one right after the other. They sent vibrations shuddering through the field like a hammer striking a giant church bell. Kelly felt those vibrations in the roots of her teeth, in the tips of her hair, everywhere. It felt like a magnified version of fingernails scraping down a blackboard and she squeezed her eyes shut in pain. Then the resistance suddenly dropped; the barrier yielded for only an instant, but it was enough. Kelly and Gordon dropped to the ground inside the clearing. They had made it through.

Kelly landed in the ashy ground, kicking up dust. Gordon landed beside her but managed to keep his feet.

"Come on," he said, his voice harsh and urgent. "The choppers won't stop until this place is a crater. We've got to hurry!"

He pulled her to her feet, and they ran towards burning tree in the center of the clearing. The fire swirled around it, miraculous, beautiful. Now the shining points of light in the branches became clear to her. They were flowers. Brightly glowing flowers unfurling into bloom on the branches of the burning tree. Incandescent petals unfolded showing long pistils with glowing tips. They grew unbelievably fast. Burning pollen drifted down from them in showers of sparks.

She saw something moving in branches, a long snakelike creature. It moved through the fire and thorns with impunity, unharmed by anything. As she watched, it fixed its eyes on her and hissed, showing its long fangs and forked tongue. She cringed in horror, until she saw its eyes. Beautiful glowing eyes. She felt she could stand right here and stare into those eyes forever, never mind all this noise and confusion around her. Those eyes offered peace, comfort, security. All she had to do was walk a little closer ...

Gordon grabbed her and shook her. "Don't look at it, Kelly! Don't freeze on me now! I need you!"

He turned her away from the sight of the tree and shook her again, breaking the trance. She felt overcome with horror as she realized what had almost happened, but there was no time to dwell on that. Dozens of cats had turned to look at them and were now advancing in their direction.

Another missile struck the outside of the barrier, making an unbelievably loud explosion. The force of it almost knocked Kelly off her feet. As she turned to steady herself, she saw the thorn-covered being. It had its back to them, and through its skin she could clearly see the outline of its bones, the spine, collar bones, everything. It was wasting away to nothing, but still it stood, expending all of its power to defend the burning tree.

The barrier around the clearing suddenly faded. The glowing force field moved inwards to the thorned being and focused there, vibrating and flickering around its head like a halo. Then all of that energy shot outwards from its brow in a beam of force directed at one of the helicopters.

The helicopter had been flying straight towards the clearing to make another shot, and it veered upwards as soon as the beam hit it. The windshield shattered, the spinning blades shrieked, and then snapped off. The body of the helicopter went into a roll and fell to the ground, moving roughly along the same trajectory it taken before the beam of force struck it. The chopper's body exploded as soon as it hit, spreading more fire across the forest floor, while the blades went spinning over the ground chopping down trees like a scythe through wheat until they finally broke to pieces.

The wreckage of the helicopter rolled towards the clearing, but now the barrier had reestablished itself. The chopper crashed against the side of it and came no further.

Gordon had to shout for Kelly to hear him over the noise. "There's Rachel," he said, pointing. "I'll find Spencer! Don't wait for us, just grab her and get out the second you can!"

She looked where he was pointing and saw Rachel lying unconscious where she had last seen her, at the base of the burning tree. Some of the white flames licked across Rachel's hair, but since the fire had no heat it didn't burn her.

Cats scampered and growled everywhere. All around her she heard words forming from out of the sounds they made.

"... bastard ... "

"... have what's mine ... "

Bizarre, but she had no time to worry about it. The helicopters roared around the clearing. Every five seconds a missile struck, it seemed. Kelly could only focus her attention on getting Rachel and then getting the hell out of here.

Gordon remained at Kelly's flank until they drew near the tree, then he dashed to the other side to get Spencer. The tree was so big that Kelly could not see him on the other side. On her own now, she hurried to Rachel's side.

A cat twined between her feet and she tripped. She went sprawling in the ashy ground. The hot, angry weight of a cat slammed into her back. Pain ripped through her as its claws and teeth scourged her skin. She screamed as it grabbed a mouthful of her hair and ripped it loose. Reaching behind her, she grabbed it by the scruff of its neck, a hissing, spitting monster, and threw it away from her.

No sooner had she thrown it away than another one jumped onto her face. She managed to grab it with her left hand and hold it back, but the cat held onto her shoulders with its foreclaws and snapped at her face. Two strips of cloth came away from her shirt as she tore it off her shoulders.

Somehow she managed to climb back up to her feet; dodging and fighting off the cats that were swarming around her. She remembered the knife Gordon had given her, but she had lost it when the force field pushed her into the woods.

Finally she managed to bolt through a gap in the mob of cats and dash towards the burning tree. If all of the cats in the clearing had been after her she would never have been able to escape, but most of them were mindlessly following the helicopters circling above them, crowding at the feet of the thorn-covered being, or running around in a blind panic.

Gordon hurried to the other side of the tree and saw Spencer immediately. He was lying in the ashes, apparently unconscious. Cats crawled all over him. As Gordon approached, the whole crowd of them turned his direction and hissed at him in unison. Apparently, the cats remembered the last time they saw him.

With no time to plan his next move, Gordon dove into the thick of them. He kicked one of off Spencer's chest, knocked two away from his face, and knelt to grab Spencer under his arms. As he did, a bobcat lunged towards his face, and he turned just in time to save his right eye. Instead, the bobcat tore three deep scratches across his cheek. Bringing his pistol to bear on the cat, Gordon shot it away.

No sooner had he pulled the trigger than Spencer's hand grabbed his wrist. Looking down, Gordon saw a pair of silver alien eyes boring into his own. All around him, the crowd of cats swarmed inwards.

As Kelly ran towards Rachel, she saw two things that almost stopped her in her tracks.

The burning flowers growing in the limbs of the tree were losing their petals. They fell to the ground, extinguishing as they did, in a shower of withering tongues of flame. As the petals fell, a growth appeared in the center of the flowers, a tiny swelling bud that glowed like a white coal. The bud lengthened, and drooped down under the force of gravity. As they grew, Kelly realized that the buds were developing into pods.

Seed pods.

Movement at the base of the tree caught her eye. Looking down, she saw Rachel was beginning to stir.

A missile struck the field directly to her left, and the force of it knocked Kelly off her feet. The report was deafening. It seemed like the missiles were growing stronger, but soon she realized that couldn't be the case. The field was growing weaker. Climbing to her feet, she turned and looked at the thorned being. It was still standing with its arms outstretched, like a scarecrow. It had lost most of its hair; what was left clung in wispy strands to its pale skull. Skin hung in flaps from its sticklike arms. And still waves of energy radiated out from it, causing the body to wither as she watched. The creature would die defending this tree.

Kelly turned back to Rachel. She understood enough of their situation to realize the barrier over the clearing would drop the instant that creature died, and the missiles would blow everything left inside of it to pieces.

When she turned back, she saw that Rachel had climbed to her feet as well. Her little legs shook, but she was standing. A look of utter terror and confusion burned over her face.

"Hold on, baby!" Kelly screamed. "I'm coming!"

But Rachel did not hear her, because Rachel was not awake. Another mind had awakened in the girl's brain, and it did not see what the rest of them saw. That mind did not see a terrible battle raging at the start of the twenty-first century. That mind was seeing something that took place on this very spot over eighty years earlier. The mind was Daniel's, and it was very frightened.

The outdoors is airy and disorienting. Daniel looks around, confused. He sees the house, the shed, the barn, and the well. He sees the rolling hills with trees growing in the low places like islands on a sea of grass. A classic American landscape. Everything looks the same as it always has, yet he feels like something is wrong. He feels like he has experienced this moment before, but this time something has changed. He'll have to worry about it later though, because Jeremiah is becoming very emotional.

Kelly ran up to Rachel, but the girl recoiled in terror. She remembered Rachel's fear of adults but couldn't believe it would matter to her now, considering the circumstances.

"Rachel!" Kelly cried. "Come on honey, we have to get out of here!"

"Bastard," Jeremiah says, "I mean to have what is mine."

He is wearing Daniel's wide-brimmed hat and his face is lost in shadow, for 'round his head burns the light of the Sun. He clutches the rock in his right hand. Roaring like an enraged bull, he charges.

Daniel turns and runs to the barn, where the 'still and the guns are hidden.

Rachel turned and bolted.

"Rachel wait!" Kelly screamed. Rachel was running the wrong way. She was headed directly towards the thorn-covered being with the mob of cats around it. God alone knew what would happen. Kelly scrambled after her.

Daniel hears Jeremiah's footsteps pounding after him. He runs as fast as he can, but his brother has a head start, his legs are longer, and he has the force of anger propelling him. Jeremiah slams into Daniel's back like a runaway freight train. They tumble to the dark mouth of the well. Even with death bearing down on him, Daniel senses that something has gone wrong; this train has gone off track. He feels like he has lost something very important but can't think of what it is.

Kelly had almost reached Rachel when another missile struck. Her fingers actually brushed the back of the girl's shirt, and then thunder, explosion, and a shock wave that knocked her off her feet. The helicopters were flying lower now, and circling faster. Their shadows stretched outwards from the clearing like the turning hands of a giant clock, for the sunset had faded to a blood-red glow and the light of the tree now outshined it. The missile strikes came every few seconds, but still the thorn-covered being stood its ground and the barrier remained upheld. The glowing seed pods hung bloated and full. The burning branches of the tree sagged under their weight.

Kelly struggled back to her feet. Looking up, she saw Rachel staggering backwards with her arms raised. It looked like she was struggling against an invisible attacker. Cats scampered around her feet, but none of them tripped her. When she went, it looked someone pushed her. Rachel fell towards the dark pit of the well.

"Rachel no!" Kelly screamed, and bolted after her.

The impact lifts Daniel off his feet, and he drops his handkerchief. The wind catches it before it hits the ground and sends it flying several yards through the air like a white and black bird until it snags on the barbed-wire fence.

He sees the black, stone-lined maw of the well rushing up to receive him.

Rachel stopped at the edge of the well. Dust sifted down from her heels into the pit. She held her arms out in front of her, shoulder height, palms pressed flat against the chest of her unseen enemy. Her back was bent, like something was pushing her against a low wall. But no wall was truly there, and Rachel's center of gravity tipped closer to the point that would send her tumbling into the well.

The two of them slam into the low fieldstone wall around the edge of the well. The mortar cracks, knocking up dust, and one stone falls loose. Daniel sees it in his peripheral vision tumbling down into the darkness, bouncing once off the side of well and then splashing into the water at the bottom.

"BASTARD!" *Jeremiah screams.* "YOU BASTARD!"

White dust falls from the underside of the rock as Jeremiah lifts it high. Saliva sprays from his lips as he roars like a furious ape.

"Jeremiah no!" *Daniel screams.*

The rising stone eclipses the sun, filling the sky with red fire. Daniel draws breath to scream again, and in that instant he feels that peculiar sensation he had felt earlier in Father's study. That sense of dreaming of the future, of being someone else. It feels like another mind has plunged into his own, swirling together like hot and cold water, and suddenly he remembers.

He remembers the whistle and crack of a switch across Jeremiah's back. He hears Father's righteous fury, Jeremiah's screams, and his own laughter. In that instant he understands their lifelong rivalry and the reason for the distance between Father and Jeremiah. He realizes why Jeremiah has always been the outcast while Daniel has bathed in the loving glow of the favored child. For the first time he remembers and understands.

Just before the rock comes tumbling down, Daniel throws his arms around his brother and screams …

"I am so sorry!" Rachel screamed as Kelly tackled her. The girl threw her arms around Kelly's neck and clutched her so tightly that she cut off her breath. The dirt slid under Kelly's feet as she skidded to a halt at the edge of the well; Rachel's weight tilted her forward and Kelly could feel the two of them begin to fall together, into darkness.

Jeremiah writhes in Daniel's arms like a furious snake, but Daniel will not let go, not until he has his say.

"I'm sorry, brother!" Daniel shouts. "I remember! I remember everything and I pray you will find a way to forgive me, for I shall never forgive myself!"

"NO!" Jeremiah roars. "NOOOO-!"

Kelly screamed in exertion as she struggled backwards, kicking at the dirt and leaning back with all her strength. At first it felt like they wouldn't make it, but then the balance tipped. She managed to push their center of gravity away from the well, and together they fell back into the ashes.

On the other side of the tree, Agent Gordon knelt by Spencer's side as the cats closed in.

"The new world has changed us," Spencer said, and then Gordon had to wrench his arm free of Spencer's grasp to fight off the cats. He tore one off his shoulders, shot another one in mid-air. More cats started to move in on him. He couldn't fight them all; sooner or later they would overwhelm him. Taking advantage of a pause in the cats' advance, Gordon stooped and hauled Spencer to his feet.

This was the first time Gordon had ever seen him, but the sense of strangeness and unfamiliarity went much deeper than what he felt around someone he didn't know. This was an unfamiliar *species*, and Gordon had to resist an urge to turn and leave Spencer to the mercy of the missiles.

Fortunately, Spencer did not sag limply like a dead body. He seemed pliant and cooperative, but stared at Gordon as if he didn't really see him.

"She will defend our young to the death," Spencer said, nodding towards the thorn-covered being.

Gordon had no reply, but he realized what he had to do next. Turning, Gordon fired three shots directly into the thorn-covered being's back.

The cats howled in outrage. Gordon sensed a pain-ridden scream vibrating through the air, but he did not hear it with his ears. He sensed it in his mind. Spencer's body went rigid beside him. Spencer did not scream, but now Gordon saw his left eye begin to change from silver to brown.

He had no more time to watch. With the cats in close pursuit, Gordon dragged Spencer back to the other side of the tree, towards Kelly, Rachel, and the outer edge of the clearing.

Kelly struggled to get back up, but she couldn't do it. It was too much. She had reached her limit. The helicopters circled above the clearing, firing off their missiles. Explosions thundered all around her, held back by the mental force of an undead alien being; cats ran by screaming in weird human voices around a giant thorn tree swathed in white fire.

Get up! Kelly screamed to herself in her mind. *Come on, girl, move it!*

She pushed at the ground and tried to get her legs underneath her, but Rachel was too heavy. The girl clung to her neck like a dead weight, screaming apologies. Kelly commanded her muscles to move, but they just couldn't do it.

Oh Jason, I'm sorry, she thought. *I tried, baby. I really did.*

An explosion went off nearby, louder and closer than any of the others. In the corner of her eye, Kelly saw some of the cats that were closer to the barrier go flying into the air.

The thorn-covered being raised its bony trembling arms, but the power radiating from it had started to dim. The bullet wounds on its back went all the way through to its chest, and silver blood oozed down its skeletal body. It lifted its head, and as it did half of the skin on its face slid off, thorns and all, exposing its skull and half its jawbone. A shrill, high-pitched scream rose from the cats as the being's jaws spread wide, as if the cats were screaming for it, and Kelly heard the single word they cried.

"NO!"

Kelly's ears popped as the air pressure suddenly fell. She knew immediately what it meant. The barrier had dropped. Looking around, she found she could see the world outside the clearing with perfect clarity, the sky darkening towards night, the rising glow of the forest fire, and the lights of the helicopters coming in for their final strike.

Gordon came around from the other side of the tree, dragging Spencer with him. Spencer had one arm over Gordon's shoulders, and half-ran, half-stumbled along beside him.

"Go! Go!" Gordon shouted.

Somehow Kelly found the strength to stand. Planting one arm against the ground, she shoved upwards with all her might. The muscles in her back clenched and twisted. A hundred burning knives stabbed her up and down her spine, but she managed to get her legs underneath her. Then she forced herself up and forward. With Rachel clasped in her arms, she went stumbling out of the clearing.

Soon she felt the pressure of Gordon's hand on her back, pushing her onwards. He was hauling all three of them along with him; the man must be unbelievably strong. The edge of the clearing crept closer as the roar of the helicopters grew louder. Kelly's feet kept wanting to trip up. She could feel them dragging through the ashes. Her breath seared down her throat, and the muscles in her back ached. The green shelter of the branches seemed so far away.

A high-pitched scream came to her ears. At first she thought it was cats again, until she realized the scream was coming from above. Unable to resist, she looked back.

The thorn-covered being still stood, like a scarecrow trying to climb back up to its pole. The cats clustered around it in a mob. The whole scene was lit in harsh clarity by the white glare of the tree. Among the branches, the creature with the glowing eyes hissed at the sky where the missiles blazed, trailing their tails of smoke as they streaked across the face of the evening stars. All of the helicopters had fired. Kelly saw two missiles, four, six ...

Now the cats screamed, like an echo of the missiles, and words formed from their collective voice for the last time.

"... not the children not our children NOT OUR CHILDREN!"

On the burning tree, the seed pods split open. Sizzling juices spattered to the ground. The husks spread wide, and out of them drifted hundreds of delicate fibers. Attached to the end of each fiber was a tiny glowing seed. The evening wind caught the fibers like a parachute, carrying the seeds away ...

Gordon grabbed her arm and threw her forward, so she never saw the missiles strike. The next thing she knew they were all tumbling into the gulley as the clearing exploded. A burst of orange light drowned out the white radiance of the tree, and then all of the light faded away, leaving only darkness, the retreating echoes of the explosion, and Rachel's voice in her ear, saying over and over again, "I'm sorry, I'm sorry ..."

"I'm sorry too," Kelly whispered, although for the life of her, she didn't understand why.

25

The Long Road Home

They shaved his head.

That was the first thing Spencer realized as he struggled back towards consciousness. The familiar weight of it around his face and the back of his neck was gone. His scalp felt naked and vulnerable. He tried to reach up and run his hands across it but he didn't have the strength to move his arms. Like Samson, it seemed he grew weak without his hair.

As he gradually awoke, he tried to figure out where he was. He felt a bed beneath him, but it was harder than the one he used at home. He heard machines humming and electronic devices beeping. They sounded muffled and distant, on the other side of unconsciousness. Sometimes he heard voices speaking to him; they sounded familiar, but he couldn't quite place them.

After several minutes of struggling to wake up, he would become exhausted and surrender to sleep. Then the dreams would come, and he would return to that cold doomed place. He felt certain that he would die. He could feel the female and third sex screaming in pain as the fire tore them to pieces. Their chemical screams bound themselves to him like sticktites. He heard the distant radio voice of the Celestial Father buzzing senselessly against his molecules. The blue third world loomed large in his vision.

Then pain, fire, darkness.

The sense of doom hung over him, oppressive and depressing. He would realize he was dreaming but trying to wake up just didn't seem worth the effort. Then he would hear Kelly's voice. She would talk of everyday things, nothing special, but he looked forward to hearing her during his darker moments. Having something to look forward to helped ease the sense of doom. Slowly, over time, the mists of the Motherworld grew thicker, and the life of Spencer Dale became brighter.

"They let me see Jason today," Kelly said to him once when the dreams were thin. He could not yet open his eyes or respond to her, but she spoke to him anyway. He was grateful she didn't place any demands on him.

"It's funny," Kelly said. "He seems to grow faster when I don't see him every day. He keeps asking me when I get to come home and I always tell him soon, baby, soon. Then I ask the doctors the same thing and they tell me just one more week, one more test, one more CAT scan. They don't seem to believe that I'm not infected and never have been. But people are like that, you know? They're very scared of the word infection. Agent Gordon helps a lot. I don't know who he works for, but he gets things done. He tells me he has to convince his superiors I'm not a risk, but he never says who his superiors are. The more I think about it, the more I don't want to know.

"They're telling everybody it was helicopter crash," she said. "That's how they're explaining the fire in the woods. I guess the media is all over the place. I saw Clint Hipsher on the news, can you believe it? He was spouting off a bunch of conspiracy theories about UFOs and government cover-ups. It's pretty scary when that guy is the one who's closest to the truth.

"They're asking me to sign these nondisclosure agreements, Spencer," Kelly said. "They say I'll spend the rest of my life in a federal prison if I ever tell anyone what really happened. Gordon says I should sign them. He's been fighting for our freedom all this time. I guess if it weren't for him I wouldn't even be alive right now, but part of me just can't trust him. I know he has his duties, and they aren't one hundred percent in our favor. Sometimes I feel so helpless. I wish you would wake up, Spence. I wish I had you with me right now."

He carried her voice with him like a candle when the darkness of the dreams descended on him, and the memory of her would sustain him. Each time he went down into that dark well, he tried a little harder to climb back up into the light.

Sometimes he felt needle pricks at his arms, and the mists of the Motherworld grew thick and nauseating. He would feel cold metal electrodes press against the side of his head and send an electric current through his brain. His body would shudder and dance, while the Motherworld would quake and rumble.

But after each of these trials, the memory of the Motherworld grew a little dimmer. All that sadness and doom seemed a little further away.

"How much longer is this going to go on?" Kelly said one day. This time she wasn't speaking to him.

"We don't know," an unfamiliar male voice said. "We're flying blind here. We have to come up with treatments for this as we go. We're approaching it the same way we would a brain tumor, surgery, radiation, chemo. It seems to be responding, but we don't know how far into the cerebral cortex the memories have spread. We may have to try other methods of treatment. It's going to take time."

"Mr. Gordon," Kelly said, "how will you know when the alien memories are gone, and Spencer is himself again?"

"When we wake him up," Mr. Gordon replied. "We'll speak to him and see who answers. There isn't any other way."

"And Rachel?" Kelly asked.

"The same," Gordon said. "Of course, we're still trying to figure out why the plasmid affected her differently than the others."

"I know," Kelly said. "I've spoken to her."

Rachel. He had almost forgotten about her. He hadn't known her very long, but she had made a big impression on him. The girl's haunted dark eyes loomed over his memories. She was suffering from this too?

"We found human remains in the well," Gordon said. "Bones. Private Hicks did some digging in the county records. A man named Jeremiah Brooks was hung in 1925 for the murder of his brother, Daniel Brooks. The body was never found. The date corresponds to when the Brooks dairy farm was sold, so we think it's the same family that owned it."

"And Rachel was down there with those bones?" Kelly said, horrified. "But how would she have gained his memories?"

"We have whole teams of molecular geneticists trying to figure that out," Gordon said. "But we don't even understand the full nature of memory itself. I wonder though, if the answer doesn't lie with the infected cats."

"The cats?" Kelly asked.

"They took on memories from the brain tissue they ingested," Gordon said. "Remember how they spoke? It was the same with the hyenas in Africa. If the well water preserved the neural cells of Daniel Brooks, then Rachel could have ingested them when she fell into the well, although I don't think we'll understand the physical mechanism of it in my lifetime."

"His cells survived for eighty years in that well?" Kelly asked.

"It's not unheard of," Gordon replied. "Researchers have extracted living cells from the bodies of mummies preserved in Scottish bogs for a thousand years. Bacteria frozen for three million years in the Siberian tundra have been thawed and started to divide within a few hours. Cells can be very hardy. The cold and darkness at the bottom of the well could have preserved Daniel's cells to certain extent. We're still in the process of analyzing the samples."

"How will you keep anyone else from drinking the well water?" Kelly asked.

"The U.S. Geologic Survey has mapped the local aquifer," Gordon said. "We have teams working on sterilizing and capping all the wells within a fifty-mile radius. Spencer had a working well at his home, but so far he's the only infected person we've found, besides Rachel."

"Have you spoken to her?" Kelly asked. Her voice had taken on a hushed, wondering tone.

"Yes," Gordon said. "I have."

"Do you think it's possible to get her back?"

"I don't know. I hope so."

"What I don't understand," Kelly said, "is why the Daniel personality keeps changing. One day he's asking for his brother's forgiveness, the next day he acts like Jeremiah is attacking him before he gets the chance. Which one really happened?"

"We can't rely on the Daniel personality to find out what really happened," Gordon said. "Those are only memories that have been implanted in Rachel's mind."

"But if he was there, he would know what happened to him. His memories wouldn't change."

"Wouldn't they?" Gordon said. "Memory is not a reliable source of facts. The courts rely on witnesses to describe accidents and crimes, but ten different witnesses will give ten different versions of the same event. Our memories change over time as we change, they shuffle and flow into one another. Some memories we simply block out, because they're too painful to live with every day. And sometimes we remember something the way we wish it had happened. That may have happened with Rachel. Maybe her subconscious mind changed Daniel's memories as a survival mechanism, because her body could not withstand the memory of dying. Our identities might hinge upon our memories, but neither of them ever remain the same. How does the saying go? 'Everything leaves us, all things pass, water flows and the heart forgets.' I think Rollins would have liked that phrase."

A thoughtful pause, and then Kelly asked, "How will you treat her?"

"There hasn't been much research done on eliminating memories," Gordon said. "We can use chemotherapy and surgery to reduce the size of the hippocampus, electroshock to destroy the mutated parts of her brain, and drugs to suppress the memory of the past few weeks. Beyond that, we can only hope."

"How can you know they're really gone?" Kelly asked. "Even if Rachel's personality resurfaces, how do you know she still doesn't carry some of Daniel's memories?"

"We'll just have to ask her," Gordon said. "We're already planning a series of interview sessions—"

"She wouldn't tell you," Kelly said. "Rachel isn't the type of girl that gives away all of her secrets. You'd have to know her to understand."

"That's how you can help us with this, Kelly," Gordon said. "Maybe you could tell when the girl you knew comes back."

"I didn't know her very long," Kelly replied, "but I'll do what I can."

Their voices faded away as Spencer drifted back into sleep. The cycle of dreams and treatments continued, dissolving the fog in his mind.

Once he dreamed of his ex-wife, Lorna. She was holding a baby in her arms as they stood in their old living room. Without a word, she shook her head and walked out the door. He cried and begged her to stay, but it made no difference. The sunlight swallowed her and she was gone.

Of course it hadn't happened that way at all. Lorna had miscarried; their child had never been born. That was when he knew he was dreaming, and the moment he realized that it was like a spell was broken. The dream ended, his eyes opened, and he awoke.

He knew he was in a hospital room immediately. Some things are easy to recognize. The bed he was in had a white plastic frame, and he was wearing a hospital robe. An I.V. ran into the back of his hand. Electronic devices hummed and hissed over his head.

Then he noticed the person sleeping in the chair next to his bed. It was Kelly. She snored lightly, in time to the hissing machines.

He didn't make a sound, but somehow she sensed he was awake. She opened her eyes, a startling blue shine, and smiled when she saw the recognition on his face.

"Spencer? Is it you?"

"The one and only," he replied, his voice hoarse from lack of use. Her smile made it worth the effort.

"What happened to your face?" he asked. An ugly red rash had spread across her nose and right cheek, along with about a dozen scratches and scrapes.

She smiled. "It's poison oak. I fell into a patch of it when the soldiers took us. Remember?"

"No ..." He couldn't remember much of anything.

"That's okay," Kelly replied. "They said you might have trouble remembering some things."

He looked around the room. "Where am I?"

"Belton Research-General," Kelly replied. "We have a private ward, all to ourselves, with our own special government-assigned doctors and armed security guards, courtesy of the common taxpayer."

"How …?" He meant to ask how he got here, but his strength had already run out, it seemed.

"Long story," Kelly said. He was glad she didn't elaborate, wasn't sure he even wanted to know.

"How long was I out?" Spencer asked.

"Couple of weeks. They've been keeping you sedated for the last five days while they do the treatments."

A couple of weeks. Fourteen days gone from his life. He tried to put it out of his mind but couldn't do it. It seemed like such a large chunk of his life.

"What about Rachel?" he asked.

Kelly's expression grew sad for a moment. "She's here too," she said.

"How is she?"

"She's having a pretty tough time. Agent Gordon told me the growth in her brain is causing some nervous system problems. They think they can treat it, but it's been a hard road for her. Poor girl."

"Agent Gordon?" Spencer asked.

"He's the guy who saved us," Kelly said. "He rescued you from the clearing, and pulled me out of the fire. If it weren't for him, I don't think any of us would still be alive."

Spencer paused, troubled. He had a deep and foreboding sense of having missed something of monumental importance.

"Kelly," he whispered, although they were the only ones in the room, "what happened?"

She thought for several seconds before responding, but in the end she could only shake her head in bewilderment.

"I wish I knew, Spencer," she said. "Sometimes things happen in life that we don't understand, and all you can do is try to keep going, even if you never make any sense of it. Do you know what I mean?"

"Yeah," Spencer said, thinking of Lorna. "I do."

They stayed up for another couple of hours, talking. Kelly told Spencer about the final battle in the clearing, and everything Gordon had explained to her about the alien plasmid. Since then, Gordon had overseen the installation of their treatment facility at the nearest hospital, over in Belton. From the way Kelly explained it, Spencer got the impression this Agent Gordon guy was the reason all three of them weren't locked up in a freezer in Area 51. But when Spencer said that he would like to meet him, that troubled expression passed over Kelly's face and she didn't respond.

Eventually Spencer went back to sleep, and for the first time in weeks, he did not dream.

The next morning, Spencer got his wish. Gordon came to his hospital room and Spencer was able to shake his hand, although Spencer's handshake wasn't as firm as it used to be. A couple of doctors in white coats came in with Gordon. These doctors didn't speak; they only looked at his charts, scribbled on their clipboards, and then stood silently in the corner while Gordon and Spencer talked. Their sheer creepiness made them stand apart from any doctor Spencer had ever met, and that night he had nightmares in which they were hiding under his bed with scalpels in their hands and mad, toothy grins on their faces.

His treatments continued. They pumped him full of drugs and gave him CAT scan after CAT scan. They bombarded his skull with radiation and ultrasonic waves. They even used electroshock, which was a nightmare. He would chomp down on a rubber bit while his body jerked and his muscles convulsed in spasms. Half the time he wet himself.

It was after one of these treatments that he saw Rachel for the first time since he awakened.

Lying on a cot in a puddle of sweat with drugs ringing in his skull and every muscle in his body aching, he had just discovered he had nothing left in his stomach to throw up. He asked one of the creepy doctors if he could have something for the pain, anything, but the doctor only stared at him with a detached smile and walked away. Spencer fell back into the cot. At least he didn't have to put up with the bastard getting off on watching him suffer anymore.

He dozed for a little while, and then woke when someone entered the room. It was one of the aides (no nurses here, only aides) pushing a cot. It came to rest next to him, and Spencer found himself staring into Rachel's deep brown eyes. The aide walked out, and left the two of them alone in the room.

They had shaved her head as well, but apparently it had been awhile. A dark shadow over her scalp showed where her hair had been. She had a pair of small pink marks at her temples, where they had attached the electrodes, and a freshly-healed scar on the side of her head. They must have performed surgery on her not too long ago.

Tears floated in the dark wells of her eyes as she stared at him, but she didn't make a sound.

He remembered that sickly, mistrustful girl he had met in the mulberry grove, how she had been afraid of adults. He had wondered what had happened to her to make her that way. How much of this did she understand? The adults in this hospital inflicted pain on her every day. If it truly was Rachel lying there, and not the consciousness that had possessed her, she might not understand that they were trying to help her. He had to know for sure.

"Rachel?" he whispered.

She blinked, sending out a cascade of tears. Somehow he knew she could hear him. Whether it was the strange bond the plasmid had created between them or something else entirely, he recognized her. She was here.

This was an important moment. Rachel would carry memories of this time for the rest of her life. Spencer had to make sure she had more than memories of pain.

"I know it's tough right now, sweetheart," he said. "Something hurt you really bad. But you'll come out of this all right. Those memories you have right now, they don't really belong to you. Something has put them in them your mind. I know some of them are terrible, I have them too, but they can't hurt you. They're just bad memories. You can rise above them. Remember your woods? They're still there, just waiting for you to come back to them. They've been a little burned, but they'll come back. You know how beautiful the woods are after a fire. The plants grow back, fresh and green, more alive than ever, and you can hardly tell they ever burned at all. You are like those woods, Rachel. I know you have strength within you to rise again."

She said nothing, only closed her eyes. Minutes passed as he watched her, before he realized she was falling asleep. Remembering his long sleepless nights, he knew it was a good sign. He reached out and brushed a tear from her cheek as he felt his own eyelids growing heavy. Somehow, knowing he had done something right gave him the peace of mind he needed to rest. His eyes closed before he could even withdraw his hand from Rachel's cot, and it came to rest beside her as he drifted away.

And as the darkness overtook him, he felt her fingers closing over his own …

The following week they let Kelly go home.

She had tested negative for the plasmid since her first day in the hospital. The CAT scans showed her hippocampus looked normal for a woman in her mid-twenties, and she had never had any nightmares or strange memories, so they let her go.

The creepy doctors spent all day sulking in their offices. Spencer suspected they stuck him with their syringes a little harder than normal that day. However, they did allow him to go down to the lobby to see Kelly off. Midge Grace showed up to give her a ride home, and she brought Jason with her. The second he came in through the front doors and saw her, he streaked across the room with his little legs pumping.

"Mommmieee!" he squealed.

Kelly swept him into her arms and covered his face with kisses. They hadn't seen each other in almost two weeks. The government people running their ward had strictly limited their visits, no matter how much Gordon argued on their behalf. Said government people never spoke to Kelly or Spencer directly, but they made their presence known. Figures lurking in shadowy corners trying to look unobtrusive had a way of drawing the eye, like the man currently sitting in one of the lobby chairs, casually reading a newspaper and acting like he wasn't watching them. Gordon leaned against the front desk with his arms folded, smiling as he watched Kelly and Jason.

"Momma, Momma, Momma, Momma, Momma!" Jason shouted, his arms clasped around Kelly's neck. Watching them, Spencer felt a kind of ache in his heart. Not quite jealousy, but it was close. He wasn't going to have any kids running in through the front door happy to see him. He pushed the feeling away. Seeing it as petty, he wouldn't allow himself to feel it. Nevertheless, it lurked in the shadows of his mind, making its presence known.

Must be getting pretty crowded up there, he thought.

Kelly set Jason back down on the floor and crouched beside him.

"Oh baby, am I happy to see you," she said. "Look how big you've gotten! I spent the whole time in here thinking of you. Did you get all my letters? I missed you so much!"

"I missed you too," Jason said, wiping tears from his eyes. Although Spencer had only met him once before, he knew it was unusual for a quiet kid like Jason to get so emotional, but understandable, considering the circumstances.

"How are you, Kelly?" Midge said, coming up behind them. Kelly stood to embrace her, and Jason clung to her leg.

"I'm all right," Kelly replied. "Much better now. Feels good to get out of here!"

"A helicopter carrying anthrax samples crashing in the woods, almost right on top of you!" Midge wondered aloud. "What are the odds?"

"Yeah," Kelly said. "It was ... something else."

That little double-entendre, Spencer thought, was probably the closest thing to a lie Kelly had ever said in her life.

"Thank you so much for keeping Jason while I was gone," Kelly said.

"Think nothing of it darling!" Midge said. "That's what friends are for. I certainly wasn't going to allow those gun-happy soldiers to have him! Well, I'm sure you're eager to get home. The Quilting Society put together a raffle while you were gone, for your expenses and all. Now that's supposed to be a secret, so try to look surprised."

"Oh that's not necessary," Kelly said. "The government paid for my medical bills and gave me a stipend for my troubles. Really, I think it's so I won't talk to the media."

"Money can talk," Midge replied, "or it can prevent people from talking. Amazing how that works, isn't it? Well, I have the car outside with engine running, so let's get you home. We tried to take care of things while you were gone, but I'm afraid we let your garden go to the weeds. Moe Jefferson swore a blue streak when she noticed it."

"Just a second, please," Kelly said, and then she turned and ran back to Spencer.

She hugged him, fast and tight. Spencer thought that was all to it, but then to his surprise she leaned forward and kissed him on the lips.

They had never kissed before, in all their time in the hospital together. It didn't seem right to do it in front of the creepy doctors and they had never had a chance to be alone. She must have realized they wouldn't see each other for a while now, not until they let him out of the hospital, if they ever did.

Her lips moved against his as she pulled back, and he felt the rush of her breath.

"Soon," she whispered, so low only he could hear her.

"Soon," he agreed.

She stepped back and smiled at him, then turned and took Jason's hand. Together they stepped out the glass doors of the hospital into the brightly lit world outside. Before going, Jason turned and waved at him. Spencer lifted his own hand in return, even though inside he felt like a wild animal was ripping up his guts.

He heard Agent Gordon speak from behind him.

"You'll see her again. The treatments won't last much longer."

"Not as long as it will seem," Spencer said, and walked back to his room.

The electroshock and drugs continued, along with the radiation. Spencer couldn't make much sense of the reasoning behind his treatment, other than to shrink the size of his hippocampus. He knew the doctors were flying blind, and had a sneaking suspicion they were more interested in subjecting him to weird experiments than in making him better.

Some of the procedures made no sense. Once they put a metal contraption over his face and flashed multicolored lights in his eyes. He didn't feel a bit different afterwards, but the creepy doctors hunched over their EEG readouts, fascinated by the wavy lines scratched out on the paper feed.

One day he spent three hours in a narrow room as an interrogator asked him questions about the color of the sky and the order of the planets from the Sun. Finally he had snapped, "When the Mothership comes, you'll be too busy building our giant ray gun to ask silly questions!" The interrogator had scribbled furiously in his notepad.

That night, Agent Gordon came to his room.

"Thought you might like some company besides the TV," he said.

To Spencer's shock, Gordon had then handed him a six-pack of beer.

"Are you sure I'm supposed to have this?"

"Why not?" Gordon replied. "They say beer kills brain cells. It might even help."

The beer was a six-pack of bottles, not cans, and the brew inside it was dark brown. "It's stout," Spencer said. "I always liked that better than pilsners."

"Me too," Gordon said, taking one of the bottles from the paper case. He sat down in a chair opposite Spencer's bed.

Spencer took a bottle and tried to twist the cap off the top. There was a time when taking the bottle cap off a beer required no thought or effort at all, but a month of bed-riding and weird medical treatments had sapped his strength. Gripping the bottle, he winced when he felt the folded metal pinch his fingers. He tried to turn it, but it wouldn't budge. For a second he felt like crying, and he had to use all of his willpower to keep his composure in front of Gordon. It just seemed like he had lost everything at this point. He couldn't even open a bottle of beer.

His frustration made him try harder. He twisted at the bottle cap with all the strength he had left, grimacing in effort, and finally the bottle cap gave. He heard the hiss of escaping air, and thought it had never sounded so satisfying. The cool taste of it was even better than he remembered, maybe because he had worked for it this time.

"It looks like you'll get your hair back," Gordon said.

"What's that?" Spencer asked.

"Your hair," Gordon repeated. "We've been able to keep the doses of chemo low enough that it won't kill your hair follicles. So your hair will grow back. You won't be bald."

Spencer nodded. "That's something at least."

He was grateful Gordon hadn't offered to open the beer for him. It would have only drawn attention to his weakness.

"We found Rachel's mother," Gordon now said. "Did Kelly tell you?"

Spencer looked up from his beer, stunned. "No," he said. "She didn't say anything about it." He was shocked she had kept something like that from him, especially after all the time they had spent speculating over it.

"She filed a police report about a week after you entered the hospital," Gordon said. "Rachel's mother did, I mean. We were finally able to locate her from a photo of Rachel she gave to the police when she filed the report."

"Wait," Spencer said. "She filed a missing-persons report a *week* after ... the incident in the clearing?"

Gordon nodded. "When the cops asked her why she waited so long to file a report, she just said she called it in when she noticed Rachel was gone."

"Jesus," Spencer muttered. "How do you go a week without noticing your kid is missing?"

"Apparently, she had spent a long weekend with a gentleman friend of hers," Gordon said. "After that her excuse was that Rachel often spent a lot of time wandering around outdoors and she just assumed she was around somewhere."

Spencer shook his head in dismay. "Why is it so many people who shouldn't become parents do?"

Gordon nodded. "I know what you mean. We did let her come down here to see Rachel, since the girl was so sick and she is her mother. Kelly met up with her outside Rachel's room and, well, there was a bit of a confrontation."

"Really? Kelly?" Spencer couldn't imagine Kelly starting a confrontation with anyone.

"Oh yes," Gordon said. "She was very passionate about it. Told her she didn't deserve to be Rachel's mother or anyone's mother, right to her face."

Spencer smiled. He wished he could have been there to see that.

"Finally, we had to go in and separate them," Gordon continued. "Rachel's mother started to get too loud. The sad thing was that she didn't seem to care. She cared more about shouting down Kelly than she did about her daughter's well-being."

"That must be why Kelly didn't tell me about it," Spencer said. "She wouldn't want to discuss something that would upset her so much. Or me, I guess."

"Not with you still recovering," Gordon said. "I got to know her a little, while she was here. She always thinks of other people first. Just the way she is."

A troubled silence passed between them. They both knew someone like that would have it tough in the big bad world.

"So where does Rachel go from here?" Spencer asked. "You can't possibly release her back into the custody of that woman."

Gordon shook his head. "At this point, it's beginning to look like a foster care situation."

"That what I thought," Spencer replied. It was so sad. There didn't seem to be any way for Rachel to get a happy ending out of this.

He hesitated before asking, knowing he probably would not get an answer, but he had to try anyway. "So ... can you tell me who she is?"

Gordon took a swig of his beer, an efficient way to mask his thoughtful pause.

"The local law enforcement is bringing up child neglect charges," he said. "As a law enforcement officer, I have to watch what I say. I wouldn't want her mother to get off on a technicality because I had a slip of the tongue."

"I understand," Spencer said. He thought that would be the end of it, but then to his surprise Gordon continued.

"Rachel's last name is White," he said. "She is registered as a third-grade student at Peculiar Elementary School. She has no brothers or sisters and her father is listed as unknown on her birth certificate. All of these things are part of the public record, and I see no harm in telling you that."

Something in Gordon's face made Spencer pause. Gordon looked like he wanted to go on. Spencer had long ago figured out there was a world of difference between what a man wanted to do and what he had to do. He could see those two desires battling inside Gordon now, so he waited.

"We found her house," Gordon said. "It's a little clapboard shack at the end of a unnamed dirt road, down by the southeast edge of the Brooks Woods. Most of it is a wreck. You don't think people still live in poverty like that, not in America. I guess I had forgotten how common it is."

Spencer, who had never forgotten, who had in fact lived through such poverty and managed to pull his way out of it, could only offer a sad smile.

"Still," Gordon continued. "As run down as it was, the little house was as neat and clean as anyone could want. And if Rachel's mother was gone most of the time, that means Rachel took care of it herself. An old beagle was sitting on the front porch guarding the place. It had a little ribbon on its collar that said 'Baxter.' She had stocked up jars of wildberries and greens in the refrigerator. We found a little bowl of flowers on the kitchen table, little wilted wildflowers in a plastic bowl. The way she tried to add a little beauty to her surroundings despite her circumstances, it ..."

Here Gordon paused and glanced self-consciously at the open doorway. But no one was passing by.

"... it rather affected me," he finished.

Spencer didn't how to respond. He had felt similar things when he first met Rachel, but he didn't know how to articulate them. That Gordon would tell him this surprised and impressed him.

He had to gather up the courage to ask his next question. For some reason, it seemed more daunting than the last, although he didn't quite know why.

"So ... do you think I could see her?"

"I think I can arrange a visit. It'll be tough to keep the doctors away. They'll be very curious to see what happens if you two get together again, but maybe I can set things up on their day off."

"That would be great," Spencer said. He didn't know why, and didn't think he could articulate it if he did, but since their last meeting he had felt a great and protective urge to watch over her.

"I'll see what I can do," Gordon said, getting up. "Meantime, you should probably catch some z's. You have another round of treatments tomorrow."

"Yeah, yeah, thanks Mom."

Gordon laughed, and took Spencer's empty beer bottle.

"I'll come by again tomorrow, if you don't mind," he said. "I think the Chiefs are playing Oakland, and your TV has the best reception in the place."

"That would be great," Spencer said. "I haven't seen a game in forever."

"See you then," Gordon said, and left the room.

Spencer stayed awake for a few more minutes, trying to remember the last time he had watched a game with a friend. He found that he couldn't do it. It gave him something to look forward to, now that Kelly was gone.

The days passed as the doctors scanned him and probed him, interviewed and zapped him. After a while they all began to blur together. Nothing happened on any given day that distinguished it from any other, so Spencer found it hard to remember how much time had passed. Often he forgot which day of the week it was, and he became hopelessly confused as to the day of the month. All that changed when he finally got to see Rachel again.

Gordon didn't give him any warning beforehand, probably because of the creepy doctors. Spencer had awakened one morning to find a note taped to his bedside table. MEET ME IN THE SUNROOM, it said. It was signed "G."

So Spencer had wandered down to the sunroom in his hospital robe, unshaven and unshowered. He had actually forgotten about asking to see her again, and so he was quite surprised when he walked into the sunroom and found her sitting in one of the big plush recliners.

She was sitting with her knees drawn up to her chest, her face raised to the sunbeams pouring in through the broad windows. She seemed to soak up the light like a flower. An oversized white robed pooled around her and covered the front half of the recliner. Her hair had started to grow back. Thick black fuzz now covered the top of her head. Spencer thought she looked a little too thin, her cheekbones seemed rather prominent, but better than the last time he had seen her.

Gordon and another man stood behind her, talking quietly. The other man wore gray and black combat fatigues but had a freckled baby face. His nametag said "Hicks." As Spencer entered the room, he picked up on the middle of their conversation.

"… got accepted to special operations," Hicks was saying. "I'll probably have to do a few years in the Middle East starting out, but after that, who knows?"

"You'll do fine," Gordon said. "The training is tough, but it's worth it. You'll see things you never imagined."

"I already have," Hicks said, smiling. "Look, I know we got off to a rough start, but it's been a privilege serving with you."

"Likewise," Gordon said, shaking his hand.

"Do you think it would be all right if I said goodbye?" Hicks said, inclining his head towards Rachel.

Gordon nodded, which made Spencer concerned. He wondered about Rachel's mental state, and if this guy Hicks, who Spencer didn't know from Adam, should be talking to her.

He walked over to Gordon as Hicks went around the chair and kneeled in front of Rachel.

"What's going on?" Spencer said. He sounded a little abrupt, but didn't care. He didn't like the idea of a strange man approaching Rachel.

"It's all right," Gordon said. "Hicks is okay."

"Who is he?" Spencer asked.

"Someone I worked with on this mission. He's been reassigned, and he wanted to patch some things up before he left, is all."

Spencer didn't reply. Gordon seemed all right, but Spencer didn't trust any of the other soldiers one bit, not after the way they had arrested him in the mulberry grove. He stood back and watched Hicks talk to Rachel, just to be sure.

"Hi Rachel," Hicks said gently as he kneeled in front of her. "I'm Private Hicks. Do you remember me?"

Rachel stared at him silence for a few seconds, her wide dark eyes unreadable. Sunlight glowed over her head and shoulders.

"You're the man from the woods," she said finally, her voice very soft in the bright room. "You hid in the grass."

"Yes, I did," Hicks said. "I just wanted to say that I'm sorry. I never meant to frighten you or your friends. I was just doing my duty."

"Why did you hide?" Rachel said. "I could have shown you the clearing. I went there every day. I could have told you anything you wanted to know about it."

"I don't know how to explain," Hicks said. "It's such a long story now. All I can say is that I was hiding because I wasn't supposed to let people see me. I couldn't let them know why I was there, so that nobody would get scared."

"I wouldn't have been scared," Rachel replied. "If you'd told me beforehand, I could have stayed away."

And there it was, the simple truth of it, stated bluntly by a child. A simple press release advising people to steer clear until they had investigated the area would have been enough.

"Rachel, I don't know what to say," Hicks replied. "Things went bad, but we had the best of intentions. But I guess that sounds pretty useless now, doesn't it?"

Rachel considered this, and then shook her head. "No, it's all right," she said. "You never hurt anybody yourself. You were just doing your job. It's okay."

She reached out and gripped his hand, quick and firm. "It's okay," she repeated.

"Thank you, Rachel," Hicks said. He squeezed her hand in return, gently, and then stood. "Feel better soon."

"I will," Rachel said, and smiled. It wasn't much of a smile, the corners of her lips just turned up a bit at the edges, but it was enough to let him know that what she said was true.

"I'll show you out, Hicks," Gordon said. He nodded to Spencer, and then followed Hicks out the door, leaving them alone.

Spencer knew right away what that nod had meant. *Go ahead and talk to her.* Here it was, as requested. But for some reason, Spencer felt nervous. He didn't know what Rachel was about to tell him, and her answers would have vast repercussions on his life.

He walked over and kneeled in front of her, as Hicks had done.

"Hello, Rachel," he said.

"Hello, Spencer."

She remembered his name, which was a good sign. As he recalled Kelly had only told her his name once before the soldiers had taken them.

"How are you feeling today?" The question felt rather limp, just another one of those meaningless questions people ask each other all the time, but it seemed heartless to start asking her what she knew without showing any concern for her well-being.

"A little better," she said. "Not so sick all the time now."

"Same here," Spencer said. "I guess we'll get to go home before too much longer." He winced as soon as he said those words. Rachel didn't have a home anymore. But she didn't seem bothered by what he had said.

"I hope so," she replied.

Spencer wrung his hands together nervously as he asked his next question.

"Rachel, how much do you remember?"

He didn't need to be more specific. They both knew he wasn't referring to what happened in the clearing, or to all the things since then. He meant the alien memories, the building blocks of the consciousnesses that had possessed them.

Rachel sat in silence for a long time, thinking. Sunlight glowed in an aura about her head. She was so quiet that Spencer began to keenly feel the silence of the room. No announcements over the PA system, no creaking of gurneys wheeling patients, no beeping electronics. Just quiet and light. The sunroom had a row of ferns planted below the windows. Someone had recently watered them, and the drops of moisture on their leaves caught a thousand glittering sparks in every imaginable color. All this sensory information flooded into him as he watched Rachel, lost in thought.

Finally, he couldn't bear it anymore, and he said, "I'm sorry, if it's hard for you to say—"

"No," she interrupted him. "It's all right." She paused once more; she had no time for sentiment when she was trying to remember.

"Some days," she said finally, "I can remember everything. It's like Daniel is still alive inside my mind, and he's pounding at the inside of my head, trying to get out. Other days, the good ones, he's quiet, and the only time I know he's there is when I remember something, and I think it's one of my own memories, and then I realize it's one of his. I'll remember things, like getting a wooden horse from my brother for Christmas, and then I'll realize I never had a brother. I know things too. I know how to birth a calf and how to distill spirits from barley. I can tie knots that I never could before. I know things about the town too. I know there is a crate full of whiskey bottles buried by the old railroad tracks. I know there is a lady in town, she must be very old by now, who might have had Daniel's baby. She must have been very sad when he disappeared."

"Is it like that all the time for you?" Spencer asked.

Rachel shook her head. "No. Some days I can hardly remember anything about Daniel, and I walk around feeling like I've forgotten something, but I don't know what. The doctors say I'll probably forget all about him, since I'm young. They say that over time he'll just fade away, like any other childhood memory, but I don't believe them. They're *creepy*."

Spencer smiled. He was glad he wasn't the only one who felt that way.

He also doubted their assertion that Rachel would forget everything in time. He may not know much about psychiatry or the brain, but he knew experiences in childhood shaped the rest of a person's life. Rachel's conscious mind might forget Daniel's memories, but they would linger in her subconscious forever.

At the same time though, he had felt, just by sitting here speaking to her, that she really would be okay. She'd had a tough spot, but seemed to be recovering. If she had a good home, she might even come out of this stronger than ever. Which made Spencer wonder what would happen to her when she got out the hospital.

"How is it for you?" Rachel asked him now. "What do you remember?"

Spencer thought it over. It all seemed so chaotic now. He could hardly make sense of it, but he supposed if Rachel could do it, then so could he.

"I have bad dreams sometimes," he said, "but I don't remember them after I wake up. And there are big gaps in my memory now. Sometimes I space out for a few minutes, and I'll wake up and see that I've wandered into another hospital room or something. But it's getting better."

"And the alien memories?" Rachel asked.

Of course she had cut right to the heart of the matter. Spencer discovered another change in Rachel. She was no longer the timid, suspicious girl he had met at the mulberry grove. Now she was sharp and well-spoken. She had said more words to him now than in all the times she had spoken to him previously combined.

"What do you remember?" she repeated.

"That's just it," Spencer said. "The memories are so strange, I think my mind is destroying them, or blocking them out. I think that's what is happening when I space out. The alien memories are resurfacing, and I'm lost to the world until my mind forces them back down again. It's been happening less and less. The doctors think I might suppress the memories completely, in time."

"That's good," she said, nodding and smiling a sad smile. She knew it would not be the same for her.

"All of this has changed me so much," he said. "It's hard to explain—"

"I understand," Rachel said.

"I know you do," Spencer replied, and after that there was nothing more to say. So they sat for a while in the quiet sunroom, with the burden of their memories eased now that they carried them together. They alone out of all the people in the world.

The treatments did go on for another couple of weeks, but nothing else of consequence happened to them, which was just fine by them. They wouldn't need any more excitement for a long time.

Then came the day Gordon entered his room and said they had found a foster home for Rachel.

"It's a good home," he said, "and we think it will be secure for her. She doesn't need any UFO nuts or journalists coming around, so we've put her in a place we know will be safe."

Spencer nodded. "Will I get a chance to say goodbye?"

"Of course," Gordon said. "Rachel has responded so well to her treatments that we're actually releasing her a little early. We'd like to keep you on for another week for observation, but after that we have you slated for release as well."

He could hardly believe the day would come so soon. They had been telling him for weeks that he would get to go home soon, but part of him had suspected they would find a reason to keep him locked up for years.

"I guess you're the reason I'm getting to go home at all," Spencer said.

Gordon shrugged. "It's only right. You should be able to go on with your life after this, not spend the rest of it in a laboratory being prodded by those doctors. Those guys get under my skin for some reason."

Spencer smiled. "Don't they though?"

And so the next day Spencer once again stood in the hospital's lobby saying goodbye. Rachel hugged him tight, and gave him a kiss on the cheek.

"Don't be lonely," she said.

"I won't," he lied.

The driver, some anonymous government stiff they had hired, then took Rachel by the hand and led her outside.

"Don't you be lonely either, little girl," he murmured as he watched her go.

They let him make phone calls during that last week, so that he could start making arrangements for himself. He called his old landlord, Quint Blankenship. Agent Gordon had already told him they had contacted his landlord and given him a cover story. Quint said how sorry he was to hear that Spencer had been hurt in the helicopter crash that was all over the news, and said he didn't have to worry about his old place, Quint had shut down his utilities so he wouldn't have a bunch of bills piling up on him. He was having trouble with some government folks though. They came by and told him his well wasn't safe anymore and he had to hook up to city water.

"I tell you it's an outrage," Quint said. "I mean really, did you notice anything wrong with the water?"

Spencer didn't know how to respond to that, so he just said, "Not a thing, Quint."

"Damn right," he replied. "I tell you, this day and age ..."

And off he went. Eventually Spencer got him calmed down and convinced him that switching to city water was the right thing to do.

Spencer next called his brother, Doug, and gave him the helicopter-crash story the government had instructed him to give. Like Kelly, Spencer had been forced to sign nondisclosure agreements. Doug nearly hit the roof, but Spencer assured him it was nothing serious, and that he was almost ready to get out of the hospital.

"You're coming to live with us, Spencer," Doug said. "That's just it. You're going to need time to recuperate."

"All right, Doug," Spencer said. "We can work something out. Really, I'm fine."

He felt dirty after that phone call. Being forced to lie to his brother galled him. But he did what he had to do, if he ever wanted to get back anything resembling a normal life.

Next he called Fred Dillon. Gordon had beaten him to it here as well, and given his old boss the same story he had given his landlord. Fred was glad as all get-out when he heard Spencer was doing better. The temp guy he had hired while Spencer was in the hospital barely had enough brains to drive a car, let alone fix one.

"You're just about the best mechanic I've ever had down here," Fred said. "Anytime you want to come back just say the word."

Spencer thanked him and said he would give him a call when he felt up to working again.

Finally he called Kelly. She sounded very happy over the phone, back into the rhythms of her life. Spencer was shocked at how much he missed her.

"You know your truck is still parked out here at my house," she said. "Do you need me to come pick you up?"

"No, they're providing a driver for me," Spencer said. "If they have to keep me locked up in this place like a prisoner, then I figure they can foot the bill for a drive home. A good one."

Kelly laughed. "It won't be much longer. This last week will be over before you know it."

"I wish," Spencer said. "I'll have the driver bring me back to your house first, if that's okay. I'd like to pick up my truck first thing, so I can get around on my own. Lord knows I'm going to have a lot to do when I get out."

"That's fine," Kelly said. "Come inside and say hello when you do."

And that was it. Kelly was right about that last week; it did pass a lot faster than he thought it would. He had so much to do, so much to catch up on, to get his life back in order again, but now at least he could see the other end of the tunnel.

The night before he was released, Gordon visited his room.

"Just some things we need to talk about before we let you go," he said. "First off, this doesn't mean your treatment is over. Agents will contact you every three months for the next couple of years for counseling. You'll also have to come in for tests to make sure your hippocampus is remaining normal. If they don't find anything after two years, then the contacts will decrease to twice a year for the next five years, then just once a year after that."

"Do you really think I could have a relapse?" Spencer said.

"I doubt it," Gordon replied, "but we don't have any case histories to go on here. We're doing this with Rachel too. We want to make sure there are no long-term side effects."

"And they want to study me," Spencer said. "Those creepy doctors."

"That too," Gordon said. "I won't lie to you. But you'll be free again. That counts for something, doesn't it?"

"Yeah, I guess it does," Spencer said, but he didn't feel free.

When the last day came, he walked into the hospital's lobby. The staff he passed on the way out bid him farewell politely enough, but Spencer thought they would be happy to get their hospital wing back in use and things around there back to normal. When he reached the lobby, he found a man in military uniform waiting for him.

"Mr. Dale," the man said. "My name is Private Turner. I'm here to drive you home today."

"Where is Agent Gordon?" Spencer replied. "I thought he would be here to say goodbye."

"I can't say sir," Private Turner said. "I haven't seen him."

Spencer was disappointed; he thought he and Gordon had struck up a friendship and that he would be there to send him off. Maybe something had delayed him. But still …

"Are you ready to go, Mr. Dale?" Private Turner asked.

"Yes, I am," Spencer said, not a shadow of doubt in his mind. The hospital had treated him well, but he was ready for the big bright world outside of it.

Turner led him outside, to a car idling in the hospital's throughway. It was a Jaguar, very swank. Turner got behind the wheel and Spencer took shotgun.

"I spoke to Kelly Ross earlier," Spencer said. "I'd like you to drop me off at her house instead of my own. My truck is parked there and I need to pick it up."

"That's fine," Turner said. Spencer noticed he did not ask where Kelly lived, but he supposed this Private Turner already knew.

Spencer didn't say much during the drive. He was too busy looking out the windows. After being locked up for six weeks, the outdoors seemed so big. He stared at the clouds above and the hayfields below. The highway seemed very broad and fast. For the first time in years, he felt a little carsick. He clutched the little bag they had given him to carry the few possessions of his that had made it to the hospital. He was glad when he saw the little red schoolhouse come into view.

His truck was there, right where he left it in the front driveway. Kelly's own truck was parked behind it. Turner parked the Jaguar behind Kelly's truck, and Spencer got out.

"Thanks for the ride," he said.

"Anytime," Turner replied.

"I sure hope not," Spencer muttered as he walked away.

He walked up the front porch steps. Just climbing those few stairs left him short of breath, and he paused at the top, disgusted with himself for being so weak.

He realized he had stood on this exact same spot, in front of Kelly's door, on the day the soldiers had taken them.

I'm back where I started, he thought, although he knew that wasn't accurate. The plasmid had infected him long before that day, but for some reason it felt right anyway.

Now he noticed the way the rickety old porch creaked and swayed when he stepped on it. Looking around, he saw the paint peeling in strips from the sides of the old schoolhouse. Suddenly he had an idea on how to get back into shape.

I could fix this place up, he thought. *Yeah, I bet I could really make this old school shine.* Kelly would be hesitant to take more free help, but it would give them a lot of time together and whip him back into shape. Yeah, he could do this.

He mounted the last few steps and had just raised his hand to knock when he realized why Kelly had wanted him to come here. But it was too late.

The door opened wide before he ever knocked. Beyond its threshold stood Kelly, smiling widely. The little red schoolhouse was filled with people. Over their heads hung a long white banner saying "WELCOME BACK SPENCER!"

"Surprise," Kelly said.

"Surprise yourself," Spencer replied.

They hugged, very tight. Then Kelly raised her face to his and kissed him. Apparently she had missed him as much as he had missed her.

"Good to see you, handsome," she said.

"Good to be seen."

Everyone applauded as he stepped inside, and came forward offering good wishes.

The Peculiar Ladies were there. They gathered around him, clucking and exclaiming.

"Well, look at this strong good-lookin' man!" Moe Jefferson thundered. "There's nothing wrong with this man at all. Nothing a few drinks can't fix. Ruth, don't just stand there, heifer, get the man a drink!"

"Oh, get him one yourself," Ruth Walton grumbled.

"Spencer darling," Marjory Grace drawled in her Joan Collins accent. "Welcome home! How are you, dear? Feeling better?"

"Much better, ma'am, thank you," he replied.

"Ma'am! Listen to you, so polite."

They clustered around him like over-affectionate aunts. At any moment, Spencer feared, they would start pinching his cheeks. Kelly caught his expression and grinned.

"Spence!" A familiar voice bawled over the chorus of the Ladies. "You old sonnafa-gun! How the hell are ya? Let me through, ya old bags! Let me through!"

Fred Dillon jostled his way through the Ladies, to their vocal discontent.

"Spence!" Fred exclaimed. "Where'd your hair go? Jesus boy, you look like a lawnmower ran over your head!"

"Good to see you too, Fred," Spencer replied.

A good-sized crowd had now developed around him, some of them people he didn't even know. But they all smiled and wished him well just like they were old friends. When he saw a familiar face, he was stunned.

"Doug!" Spencer said when his brother stepped into view. "How did you get here?"

"This little lady called me," Doug said, nodding towards Kelly. He raised his thick eyebrows suggestively. His waistline had grown and a few strands of gray had appeared in his black hair, but otherwise his brother looked the same as he did the last time Spencer had seen him.

"You don't know how hard it was to track him down," Kelly said. "But I remembered you mentioning him, so I managed to dig up his phone number."

"And we're unlisted," Doug said. "Smart lady." Again the eyebrows went up. Doug still had the ability to embarrass Spencer silly, just like when they were kids. They hugged, and Spencer said hello Doug's wife Irene and their twin two-year-old girls. Spencer exclaimed over how big they were getting. Doug patted him on the back and said he wanted to talk to him after the party, to make sure he was getting along okay.

He recognized other faces moving through the room. He was stunned when he saw Officer Randy, but pleased that the guy had taken time out of his day to see him and wish him well. Even the mayor was there, probably at the urging of his wife, who was one of the Peculiar Ladies.

But the one that surprised him the most was the one he didn't notice until he was right beside him. A voice called his name, and Spencer turned.

"Gordon!" Spencer exclaimed. He knew the guy's first name was John, but had gotten so used to calling him Gordon that anything else seemed weird.

"Thanks for coming!" Spencer said. "It's good to see you."

"Good to see you too," Gordon said. "Feeling better?"

"All the time. How did you know this was going on? I guess Kelly struck again."

"She did. Of course, she knew where to find me."

Spencer had always thought Kelly didn't care much for Gordon, from the way she always stiffened up whenever he came into the room. She must have seen how well he and Spencer were getting along and invited him for that reason.

Spencer was half right. Kelly had invited Gordon because Spencer liked him. Kelly herself would never like him. She tolerated him because he had saved Spencer and Rachel, but Gordon had cut a man's throat open right in front of her. He did it to save her life, and she respected him for it, but she would never like or trust him. She could never trust anyone who killed so casually and without remorse.

While Spencer and Gordon talked, Kelly moved over to the kitchen area. She had to keep an eye on some pots on the stove. She had set up the party as a pot-luck and all the Peculiar Ladies had brought dishes, but as the hostess Kelly felt she had to prove herself. And with the financial security the government stipend had given her, she had outdone herself. The long table in the middle of the room groaned under the weight of her labors. She had tried to keep a good balance of the German dishes her mother had taught her and the Native American foods Jack had liked with old-fashioned American classics like fried chicken and mashed potatoes. It made for a pretty satisfying mix. She went to see about a pot of spaetzle in chicken stock she had left on the stove when Spencer arrived. As she stirred the pot, the steam wafted the aroma of the food to her nose. Smells always evoked the most powerful memories. Jack had loved this dish, and making it now reminded her of him. On the other side of the room, she heard Spencer laugh from the middle of his crowd of well-wishers.

Don't be mad at me for Spencer, Jack, she thought. *I love you and I always will, but you're dead and gone. I'm still alive.*

She put the lid down on the pot as if to close the matter.

From behind her, she heard Fred Dillon speaking to some buddy of his, profaning her inner moment with his lewd talk.

"I'm telling you man, you should have seen this stripper!" Fred said. "She had 'em out to here!"

As he held out his hands to indicate the size of said stripper's anatomy, Kelly picked up her wooden spoon, turned around, and rapped him on the knuckles with it.

Fred jumped, yelping like a dog with his eyes all wide and startled.

"You can talk however you want outside these four walls, Fred Dillon," Kelly said. "But in my house, you'll watch your language, as a courtesy to me. Understand?"

"Yes ma'am," Fred replied, looking appropriately contrite.

Kelly grabbed a pair of hotpads and took the pot of spaetzle over to the table. It was getting hard to find an empty spot; suddenly her pantry was very full and she wasn't used to it yet. As she looked for a place to set down the spaetzle, she heard Spencer and Gordon talking.

"So where are you going from here?" Spencer said. "You heading out to the Middle East, like Hicks?"

"Actually, I'm thinking about finding a new line of work," Gordon said. "Maybe settling down somewhere in the country. I noticed the house across the road is up for sale."

"The Coldiron place?" Spencer said. "How 'bout that. Whatever happened that Coldiron woman?"

"I'll … tell you later," Gordon replied.

The afternoon wore down to evening and the party started to take off. People clapped Spencer on the back and rubbed their hands through the peach-fuzz covering his scalp. Midge's rich laughter echoed off the fieldstone walls. Agent Gordon and Officer Randy stood in a corner and talked for quite a while. Those two seemed to have taken a shine to each other.

When the front door opened and the party's final guest arrived, almost no one noticed.

Except for Spencer.

He couldn't explain it, but he happened to look up as the door opened. Later he thought it was just a coincidence, but part of him knew that wasn't true. He had felt a presence drawing near the house, moving in from the spreading shadows of evening to the island of light and life that was the little red schoolhouse. He had sensed this presence hesitating for a moment outside the door's threshold, felt it gather its courage, and he had known the right moment to turn his head and see the door open. What he saw there left him breathless with surprise, despite all his premonitions.

It was Rachel.

Fred was still yammering away, but Spencer no longer heard him. The whole party faded into the background. Nothing else existed now but him and his surrogate daughter.

She lingered in the doorway, intimidated by the crowd of people. Her hands were clutched over her chest. She looked so *healthy*. The recuperative powers of the young were famous, but this ... *this* was almost miraculous! Rachel had filled out, the hollows in her cheeks and under her eyes had vanished. Her skin glowed with a healthy tan. Her hair had grown out a little, so that it now looked fashionably short. And though the crowd of people had made her pause, she did not look afraid. She was merely examining her surroundings with a critical eye before proceeding.

Spencer felt certain this must be a dream; they had let him out of the hospital too soon, he had started hallucinating again. But he blinked his eyes and Rachel remained, as solid as life.

Somehow he forced himself to walk over to her. She saw him coming immediately. The dark mystery of her eyes betrayed nothing, but it seemed her gaze softened a bit.

He knelt so that he could look her in the face.

"Rachel," he whispered. "How ...?"

Before he could finish the question, something moved within her clasped hands. He looked down and immediately forgot everything that had been going through his mind.

Cradled against Rachel's chest was a tiny black kitten.

It gazed at him with bright, gold-coin eyes like it knew him.

Spencer froze, unthinking. A terrible certainty overcame him that he would soon plunge back into the cold doom of the Motherworld. He waited for it, terrified, but nothing happened.

"It's okay," Rachel whispered. "She's not like the others. You don't have to be afraid."

He raised his eyes to look at her. A tiny smile spread over her face, as intriguing as the Mona Lisa's. For some reason her smile calmed him, and everything seemed good again, as if by magic.

"What is her name?" Spencer asked.

"I'm calling her Shadow," Rachel replied. "Because she follows me everywhere I go."

He laughed, he couldn't help it. And Rachel laughed too, a beautiful clear sound. He had never heard it before.

Suddenly Kelly was there.

"There you are, Rachel," she said. "I was getting worried about you. Are you hungry, sweetie? There's plenty of food. What's that you've found? A kitten? Are you sure Baxter will get along with it?"

"Kelly, you?" Spencer asked before Rachel could respond. "You became Rachel's foster mother?"

She nodded. "It was the best solution for everyone. I can afford it now, the government doesn't have to worry about its secret, and Rachel doesn't have to leave her hometown."

"That's ... Kelly that's ..." He couldn't finish. "I think I have to sit down."

"Okay, over here, it's all right."

They hustled him over to the couch. He needed a few minutes to catch his breath.

As soon as he sat down, Jason and Brad ran out of the crowd with a skinny beagle dog galloping at their heels.

They clustered around Rachel, the boys acting comically similar to the dog in their happiness at seeing her. All three of them sat down on the floor at Spencer and Rachel's feet, letting the dog and kitten touch noses as they chattered away like magpies.

Kelly scratched the stubble on top of his head. "You feeling better, handsome?"

"Yes," Spencer replied. "Very much so."

They sat for a while and watched the children play. Spencer let the goodwill and fellowship of this moment wash over him with its abundance. All memories of pain and failure had faded from his mind. He had love, friends and family. Life was very full.

The End

First draft completed
August 20, 2006
1:53 am

Author's Note

Peculiar is a real place. The story of how the town got its name and its geography within the city limits as described here is accurate.

That said, however, the Brooks woods and the events that took place there, the Peculiar Ladies Quilting Society, the little red schoolhouse, and all characters and situations described in this book are fictional. Any resemblance to actual people is coincidental.

978-0-595-45761-8
0-595-45761-4

Water damage noted 6.2.15

Printed in the United States
132974LV00006B/56/A